Ending Nightmares

Désirée's Story - Part Four

D. Riesau-Moreno

Casa Moreno Publishing

Ending Nightmares

Désirée's Story ~ Part Four

Print version ISBN: 979-8-9916800-3-5

This book contains material that may be considered offensive, controversial, or triggering to some readers. This includes, but is not limited to, themes of violence, discrimination, sexual content, and strong language. The historical and cultural backdrop of the story may contain elements that conflict with present-day values or perspectives.

Reader discretion is advised. If you are sensitive to such topics, you may wish to consider this before proceeding.

Published by

CASA MORENO PUBLISHING

Original Cover art and design by Trent & Annalise Shadburne – Shadburne Creative

Ending Nightmares

Désirée's Story ~ Part Four

a novel by

D. Riesau-Moreno

Books by D. Riesau-Moreno

Désirée's Story ~ Series

A Child of War – Part One

Waiting in the Crescent City – Part Two

Hiding as just Désirée – Part Three

Ending Nightmares – Part Four

Like Ashes in the Wind – Part Five-coming soon

Dedication

for Desi

and lost girls everywhere

Contents

1. Friday the 13th 1
2. Another Picasso 8
3. The Lake House 13
4. Saturday on the lake 24
5. A Crowded House 36
6. Glen Oaks 49
7. Starting Over 62
8. An uneasy compromise 75
9. The Inquisition 85
10. Therapy with benefits 97
11. Bobby 107
12. Elijah 115
13. New additions 131
14. Confessions 144
15. Vial Choices 155
16. Dining out 163

17.	Charlottes' gift	171
18.	Outside Challenges	179
19.	Bill	187
20.	An Almost Perfect Party	195
21.	Kitchen adventures	208
22.	You have to break a few eggs	218
23.	Bridges to cross	226
24.	Making plans	236
25.	New Information	246
26.	Crescent edge of madness	255
27.	How to end a nightmare	269
28.	Mama and Decisions	281
29.	Vanquishing Doubts	290
30.	Wedding plans and other calamities	298
31.	The Kommandant	304
32.	The end and beginning	317
	Acknowledgements	327
	About the author	329

Chapter 1

Friday the 13th

New Orleans is a city that never sleeps, especially once Mardi Gras season begins. The Twelfth Night Revelers Ball a week earlier on January 6th kicked off the festivities for 1950, giving the city a fresh new license for its nocturnal activities.

The past thirty-six hours had left me so numb that Mardi Gras slipped from my mind. I thought there wouldn't be any prying eyes after three in the morning to raise the alarm on my escape. I was wrong. Cars filled with late-night party goers still roamed the streets in the wee hours looking for their next adventure, raucously celebrating their latest.

You'd think they'd be more cautious, what with all the unsolved Phantom murders, but very little impeded Mardi Gras once it started.

The good people of New Orleans didn't know it yet, but the Phantom was dead. I killed him. I knew once Uptown society discovered who he was, they wouldn't be thanking me.

Carson Bentley was one of them, shared a long history with the elite of the city. They hosted him, dined with him, considered him a friend and business associate, even offered their daughters for his consideration, yet none of them really knew the monster lurking beneath the charming Southern gentleman. His family name and familiarity blinded them. Only his victims truly knew him, and they were all dead, except me... and Evie.

My only option was to stay in the shadows and avoid detection as I headed north into the heart of the city, away from the destruction I'd wrought and toward an unknown future.

Mid-January in New Orleans is more like Spring anywhere else: mild temperatures and the occasional rain shower, but mostly clear skies and breezy. Once well on my way, the hooded winter coat I wore became unnecessary for anything but concealment. My zig-zag route through the sleepy streets of Uptown and around the Tulane campus kept me hidden from view until I reached Carrollton Avenue. By the time I made it to the corner of Carrollton and Claiborne, I didn't care about anything but reaching my destination.

I collapsed onto a bench at the last streetcar stop on the Carrollton line, where one lone streetcar stood empty and waiting for its schedule to begin, which wasn't for a few hours. I would be long gone before anyone showed up for that ride, but I needed to rest for a few minutes before heading up Carrollton toward the lake. With my bag next to me on the seat, I wrapped myself in the coat, pulled the hood over my head and closed my eyes... just for a minute.

"Excuse me, miss. Do you need a ride?"

The taxi had stopped right in front of me, idling at the corner, the driver leaning out of his window to get my attention. "You need a ride to the train station? Maybe the airport? Looks like you're headed somewhere."

He looked normal enough, an older man wearing a black beret and a friendly smile. His offer seemed sincere and accepting it would mean fewer miles to walk.

"Sure," I said, keeping my bruised face sheltered inside the hood. "Orleans Marina on Lakeshore Drive, Stella's Café."

"Climb in. I'll take you up there."

He glanced at me in the rearview mirror with concern in his eyes, as I settled into the back seat of his cab, which smelled strongly of liquor and cigarettes.

"It isn't safe for a young woman to be out this late. The police haven't caught that Phantom fella yet."

"I'm fine, sir. I appreciate the ride." Informing him why the Phantom was no longer a problem wasn't necessary. He'd find out soon enough.

The cab stopped in front of the café a couple of hours before dawn. A row of fishing boats sat tied to the adjacent dock, giving me hope I could execute my escape plan.

"You sure you're alright, miss?" the driver asked. "You meetin' someone?"

"I'm fine, thank you. Yes, I'm meeting someone." I handed the fare across the seat to him.

He knew I was lying. The bruises on my face told a different story. His wrinkled brow and squinting eyes said he was concerned, but didn't really want to know what happened, was happy to drop me there and go home. I wasn't his problem. He'd done his good deed for the day.

I stepped out of the cab and stood on the sidewalk outside the café entrance for a moment, scanning the docked boats and the men manning them. Fishermen, I presumed, and most were old, scruffy-looking creatures who inspired little trust. Except for a younger man standing on the deck of the fourth boat down. He looked in my direction as if he were expecting someone.

When I entered the café, an overhead bell announced my arrival, and a row of curious men turned to see who'd come in. My heartbeat quickened as I scurried past them, taking the farthest seat at the counter and leaving four empty stools between us.

The young fisherman followed me in a moment later, nodding to the men at the counter, then he sat on one of the vacant stools. He smiled at me, nodded, then politely looked away.

The waitress left her regulars and stood across the counter, staring at me like she'd never seen such a sight. "Are you alright, honey? You need some help?"

"I'm fine, thank you. I need to get across the lake to Mandeville. Do you know anyone who can take me?" My voice was a little shaky, and I knew I looked horrible, but I hoped this middle-aged woman with a kind face would take pity on me and recommend someone trustworthy.

Every pair of ears and eyes at that counter turned their attention to the waitress and me.

She stared at me, trying to decide if she should get involved. In my experience, most people avoid uncomfortable situations, but I was difficult to ignore, sitting at her counter with a battered face and asking for her help.

"There's a bus that goes around every day from the depot up by the airport. That'd take you," she said, apparently believing that would be the simplest solution.

"I can't wait that long. My grandmother is sick, and I need to be there as soon as possible," I whispered, turning away from the prying ears.

"Let me see what I can do, honey." She patted my clasped hands sympathetically. "Meantime, here's some coffee to warm you up."

After pouring a mug of hot coffee, she pushed it in front of me, along with a pitcher of cream, a spoon, and a bowl of sugar cubes. She did the same for the young fisherman a few stools down, giving him a questioning look and then a nod before walking away.

"I can take you across the lake," the young man said.

Every man at the counter raised his head to stare, but the waitress gave them each a scathing look. "Mind your own damn business," she said before disappearing into the kitchen.

"My name's Elijah Tillman," the young fisherman said. "I live over there, on the Bayou Liberty, by Slidell. It's no trouble to take you to Mandeville." He shifted on his stool, giving his back to the men at the counter, as he lowered his voice.

Not that it would do much good in the tiny café. It could barely seat thirty customers, with the dozen stools at the counter and four booths beneath the front windows. But it was the kind of place I dreamed of having some day; a place where locals could gather with friends for a chat and a good meal.

That will never happen now, Désirée. Not here.

"Thank you, Mr. Tillman," I said, attempting a smile. "Would it be too much trouble to go now? I can pay you for your time and gas." I was eager to keep moving, to escape the inquisitive stares and avoid unanswerable questions. The morning newspaper was lying on the counter, and I worried about what it said about Carson's death.

"I've got some business to take care of with Stella and Tom before I head back," Elijah said, shaking his head. "We can go as soon as that's done. How about you warm yourself up with that coffee? I'll be back in a minute." He rose from the stool, but waited for my response, as if unsure I would be there when he returned.

Elijah reminded me a little of my best friend Bobby Easton, only older, maybe in his early twenties. He had dark hair, blue eyes set in a handsome face that had seen a lot of sun. With his muscular arms and large hands, he looked like a man who worked hard for a living. There was something gentle about him, something in the way he looked at me, that made me feel like I could trust him to see me safely to Mandeville.

"Alright. I'll use the ladies, then I'll be ready when you are." I slipped off the stool and ducked into the restroom.

The thing about old buildings in New Orleans, especially ones like Stella's Café, is the walls and doors are flimsy, and sound flows easily through them. As I stood at the washbasin, I could hear the conversation taking place on the other side of the door.

"Ya seen this?" someone asked. "Looks like the Phantom met his end. He picked the wrong girl, and she fought him off. Killed him dead."

"Bert, it don't say nothing in there about the Phantom, and why the hell did they have to print that poor girl's name?" Stella sounded angry. "Hasn't she been through enough without the entire city knowing her business?"

I didn't want to go out there; feared the looks I would receive, feared they'd know I was the girl they were reading about. The bruises on my face and neck were fresh and unmistakable. No matter how I tried to hide them, they weren't going anywhere for a while. So, I did what I'd been doing for the past five years: put on a believable mask, pretend everything is fine, and then move on. I wouldn't see any of them again, so what did it matter?

When I sat back down at the counter, the coffee was cold. I pushed it away and lit a cigarette, avoiding the side-long glances from the old fishermen at the other end. Elijah had yet to return, and I wondered if he changed his mind about taking me across the lake, or worse, had discovered who I was and was calling someone to come get me.

A few anxious minutes went by, then Stella came out of the kitchen, followed by Elijah with a thermos in his hand.

"All set?" he asked, raising his dark eyebrows and the thermos with a question.

"You need me to call somebody, honey? To let them know you're coming?" Stella asked, walking us to the door.

Her question raised alarms. I didn't want anyone to know where I was going, at least not yet. I needed time to recover, time to think things through.

"No. Thanks for your help," I said, stepping out the door into the pre-dawn light.

Chapter 2

Another Picasso

"Elijah, you take care crossing over, ya hear? Wind's picking up. Don't be giving this poor girl a rough ride," Stella called out while we stood on the dock waiting for him to ready his boat. "And tell Ma I'll be out to see her for her birthday."

La Belle was a pretty boat, around twenty-five feet long, painted robin's egg blue with a small captain's hut about mid-way on the deck. She didn't look new but seemed well maintained, all gear stowed securely in its place. Elijah obviously took pride in her.

"Yes, ma'am. I will. You ready to come aboard, miss?" he asked, reaching for my hand.

I hesitated. I could change my mind, could still turn back, call someone to take me home. There was still time, but the only thing I'd find there would be the mess I left behind and a host of ghosts to haunt me.

It's better this way, Désirée. Better to end it now.

"Yes, I'm ready," I said, taking Elijah's hand to climb down onto his boat.

"Take a seat, and we'll be on our way," he said, releasing the ropes from their mooring posts and giving Stella a final wave goodbye.

Experience has taught me to be cautious, so I kept my distance from him, sitting on a side bench at the stern, my bag close by. He maneuvered the small craft through the narrow canal leading to the lake, then increased his speed as he cleared the jetty.

"Don't you want to sit up here, out of the wind?" he shouted over the roar of the motor.

I shook my head, turning back toward the receding city. After several minutes of staring into that muddy green water furiously rushing by, a memory flashed into my mind with full force, sending me back in time to the banks of the river Seine. I trembled with the same overwhelming feelings of despair and loneliness, the need to end it for good.

Just one step, Désirée, and it will be over. Just one more .

I stepped up onto the bench, my bag clutched in my hand, intending to drop off the boat as it sped across the lake.

Suddenly, the engine cut out, toppling me from my perch.

"Hey, you don't want to do that!" Elijah yelled, snatching my bag away and reaching for my hand.

Tears streamed down my face as I tried to grab my bag from him. "I do. I want to sink to the bottom and drown."

He pushed my bag out of reach but didn't attempt to touch me again. "I really wish you wouldn't. I'd have to go in after you then we'd both be wet and muddy, and I hate getting wet in the morning."

"I'd be on the bottom before you could find me," I countered, looking down into the water.

"Nah, I'd have you out before you needed to take a breath. It ain't over ten or twelve feet deep around here."

"Is that all?" I asked, slumping back onto the bench in defeat.

"Yeah. Lake Pontchartrain ain't nothing but a big shallow bowl fed by the delta."

"It figures," I said, huffing a breath. A watery grave was obviously not in the cards. Fate had thrown another hero in my path.

"Why don't you sit up front with me, out of the wind?" Elijah asked, a hopeful look in his eyes. "I'll pour you some of Stella's coffee."

There wasn't any point in doing otherwise, so I dried my tears with my hankie and followed him into the captain's hut, taking a seat on the corner bench.

He pulled the anchor, then stood at the wheel and started the engine. Once *La Belle* was on course, he turned to me.

"We're a little less than halfway there. You want some coffee?" He reached for the thermos tucked into the shelf in front of him, then poured a cup, handing it to me before I said anything.

"If you want to talk about it, I'm a pretty good listener. Gran always says it's good to get things off your chest. It might help."

His kind face tempted me to share my misery with him, but that was the last thing he needed, though he didn't know it. I wouldn't burden him with my problems.

"Why don't you tell me about yourself, Elijah? How did you become the captain of your own boat?" It was better to distract him from topics I wouldn't discuss.

A smile lit his face, the question obviously pleasing him, but there was something else behind his smile, some tender injury that brought a furrow to his brow when he looked at me.

"I've been fishing all my life. Grew up on the bayou fishing with my pa. When the war started, Pa enlisted in the Army, but he couldn't take the discipline, so they gave him a dishonorable discharge before he ever got overseas." He glanced at me to gauge my interest.

"Things got bad after that. Pa would drink up all the money, then pick a fight with someone, usually my ma. I worked as a hand on another boat, helping Ma with money. One night, I came home and found her and my baby sister lying dead in a pool of blood. Pa was sitting in his chair with his brains blown out, the pistol still in his hand."

"I went to live with Gran after that. Been there ever since. Stella, she's my aunt, Ma's sister. She and Uncle Tom loaned me the money for this boat. It took me three years, but I paid it off this morning."

"You didn't have to tell me all that about your parents." I wondered why he had.

"No, I didn't. Maybe I just wanted you to know you're not the only one with a tragic story." His gaze turned toward the approaching north shore.

For the rest of the trip, we limited our conversation to fishing; what he caught, where he fished, how the weather affected his catch. Once we got close to the Mandeville Marina, our conversation dwindled to nothing.

I could feel anxiety building in my stomach, that feeling of uncertainty. I'd made it across the lake, but now I would have to face what lies ahead, and I wasn't sure what that was going to be.

Elijah pulled *La Belle* up to the dock at the Mandeville Marina and cut the engine. He tied off the lines as if he intended to stay.

"Is someone meeting you?" he asked, setting my bag on the dock.

I shook my head.

"I can walk you to wherever you're going. It's no trouble." He seemed reluctant to let me leave.

"No. Thank you, Elijah. You've done enough. Thanks for the ride. Please let me pay you for your time and trouble." I didn't want him to know where I was going.

"I don't want your money. Keep it," he said, worry lines forming on his brow. "You sure you'll be alright?" He helped me off the boat, then reluctantly handed me my bag.

"Yes. I'm fine." I took a last look at this unlikely hero and smiled. "It's funny, you know. You look nothing like Picasso. Goodbye, Elijah," I said, turning to walk up the dock.

"Hey, wait! I don't even know your name."

I turned around, smiled, and shook my head. "It doesn't matter. Goodbye." I walked away without looking back.

Chapter 3

The Lake House

The moon had gone to bed, leaving a blanket of stars to fade into the morning light. Soon, the sun would show its full face, and I wanted to be inside before it arrived. I pulled up my hood and hurried along the sidewalk as quickly as my tired body would let me, trying to avoid detection by any early risers. The fewer people who knew I was there, the better.

The Marchand's lake house wasn't far, only a few blocks west on North Lakeshore Drive. I'd spent the past four summers there, making some of my happiest memories in that house by the lake. It was usually uninhabited in the off-season, so I figured I could hold up there until I recovered from my injuries. What I would do after that was uncertain.

By the time I arrived, I had no strength left. My body ached everywhere, my legs were trembling, and I could barely keep my eyes open. Forty-eight hours with little sleep and not much to eat was taking its toll on my traumatized body. I stood at the bottom of the front steps marshaling what strength remained, and with a burst of sheer will, I grabbed hold of the rail and pulled myself up one step at a time.

When I unlocked the front door and went inside, the house was quiet, but not as expected. There were no sheets covering the furniture, no musty smell of disuse. It felt like someone had been there recently. The family vacationed there during the spring and summer months, closing it up before the hurricane season set in. As far as I knew, they closed it last September.

No one was there, no lights were on, no smell of cigarettes or recent meals, just the feeling that someone had been there. It felt unsettling, but I was too tired to give it much thought.

My room was at the top of the stairs, facing the lake, and with one last herculean effort, I started up with every intention of falling into bed and, with any luck, sleeping forever.

When I noticed Shelby Terrebonne coming through the dining room, I didn't have the strength to avoid her. Shelby and her father, Mr. Philgood, had been caretakers for the lake house since Shelby was a young girl. They lived in the house behind the property and operated The Lakeside Bar and Grill a block away.

"Is that you, Désirée? I thought I heard someone come in. What are you doing here?" she asked, before getting a good look at me. "Oh, my god! What happened? Who did this to you?"

"I'm tired, Shelby. I just want to sleep." With what strength remained, I pulled myself up one more step.

"Let me help you, honey." She put my arm around her neck, then slipped hers around my waist, helping me up the remaining stairs and into my room.

"Here, let me take your coat. You just sit there." She sat me on the bed, kneeling in front of me to remove my shoes, then looked up to examine the damage done to my face and neck. "Sweet Jesus, it looks like someone tried to kill you."

"He raped me, Shelby. He was trying to kill me, but I killed him first." That was as much detail as I could offer.

"Who did this to you, Désirée? Does Bill know?"

"It was Carson Bentley, and everyone knows, or soon will. It's in the morning paper. The entire city will read all about it with their breakfast... Oh God, I've ruined everything." I dropped my face into my hands and sobbed, rocking back and forth, trying to catch my breath.

"Carson Bentley?! Oh my god! That evil bastard. Someone should have put him down a long time ago. I'm sorry, honey. I'm so sorry." She held me while I cried until I couldn't cry anymore.

"Does the family know you're here?" she asked as she gently wiped the tears from my ravaged face with her fingertips.

I shook my head and scrubbed my face with the soiled hankie I pulled from my pocket. "No. I left them a note, but it didn't say where I was going."

"They'll be worried sick. I've got to call and let them know you're here."

"Please Shelby. I don't want to talk to anyone or see anyone, especially not Bill. I can't face him."

"Oh honey, I understand, but it's going to be hard to avoid him. Bill lives here, Désirée. I expect him and Luke home sometime today."

"Oh... I didn't know, but I guess I should have." I blew out an exhausted breath.

Another choice gone wrong, Désirée. It figures.

"I just want to sleep, Shelby. Do you have something that could help? Maybe a glass of whiskey?"

"I'll get you some of Bill's Irish, honey. You sit tight. I'll be right back."

A few minutes later, I was sitting up in bed smoking and sipping on a healthy shot of Irish whiskey, trying to settle my mind. My total sensory memory needed to catalogue everything that had happened in the past thirty-six hours, and I was having a tough time sorting any of it away. Memories would flash across my mind and stay there, relentlessly making me relive them. They were the type of memories that easily became nightmares.

At home in New Orleans, I would use a candle to focus my attention and help clear my cluttered mind. I remembered there was a supply of candles in the hall closet, and when I went to retrieve one, I heard Shelby speaking to someone on the phone at the bottom of the stairs. She sounded angry.

"God damn it! How could you let this happen?"

"No! I don't want to hear your apologies, and she doesn't need your guilt."

She huffed out a breath, followed by a moment of silence.

"Alright. I'll see you when you get here." She hung up the phone, then went to the kitchen.

Was she talking to Bill?

I retreated to my room, certain that Shelby would never speak that way to Mama or Charlie.

The anger in her voice sounded personal, like the listener would, or should, understand the reason for it. It had to be Bill she was talking to, and I wondered what was behind her anger.

It took the entire shot of whiskey and half the candle for me to silence my mind enough to sleep. What sleep I got wasn't restful.

The sun had set by the time I woke. A soft breeze from the open window was rustling the lace curtains, freshening the room. I'd known this room for four years and felt more at home here than I did in the St. Charles house in the city. As I woke, the familiar peacefulness enveloped me and for half a minute, I thought the past three months had all been a horrible dream.

Then Elijah Tillman—my latest hero—and the memory of my trip across the lake flashed through my mind.

There must be something pathetic about me, something that attracts a certain type of male, the hero type, the kind who can't resist rescuing a damsel in distress. In my less than eighteen years, I've encountered several such heroes. Henri, Alex, Picasso, Bill, Bobby, and now Elijah. In their own unique ways, each had rescued me, saved me, offered me a moment of safety, a different path to choose. Unfortunately, the choices were never easy.

When I went downstairs, the house was quiet. The only available light filtered in from the kitchen but didn't reach the front room, which lay veiled in darkness.

I expected Bill or Charlie to be there, ready to scold me for running away. I knew their absence was just a temporary reprieve. They would show up soon enough. There was too much at stake.

"Did you sleep okay, darlin'?" Luke Terrebonne asked from a chair in the dark corner of the living room.

"I got some sleep. Did Charlie ask you to make sure I don't run away again?" I was a liability the Marchand's couldn't afford to lose track of.

"No, I volunteered. Besides, I live out here."

"Right. When are they coming?"

I took a seat on the sofa and turned on the lamp so I could see him clearly. It also gave him a clearer view of me, which wasn't a pretty picture.

Luke's brow furrowed as he lifted his fist to his mouth, pushing out an angry breath when he saw the damage to my face and neck.

"They'll be here tomorrow," he said, regaining his composure. "Charlie had a meeting with the DA today, and Miss Bea said it was better to let you get some rest. She wanted me to tell you that she's sorry about Glen Oaks."

Mama's plan was to send me to Glen Oaks Sanitorium, but I wouldn't let them lock me up in there, not if I could help it. Bobby's mother died there six months earlier.

"Where's Bill? Shelby said he lives here." I looked around for signs of him.

"He does, but he's still in town, taking care of a few things. He'll be here tomorrow."

The thought of facing Bill made my lower lip tremble. I bit down on the inside of it to make it stop, a terrible habit I needed to break.

Luke gave me a sympathetic smile, sensing my anxiety. He really was a sweet man, another hero type. Not as tall as Bill, he stood maybe five foot eight or nine, with brown hair and hazel eyes, and a wide mouth that was quick to smile. The few times I'd been with Luke Terrebonne were memorable in a good way.

"You hungry?" he asked. "Shelby sent over a couple of chicken dinners. I've got them warming in the oven if you're interested. It might be a good idea for you to eat something, darlin'. Keep up your strength."

"I don't feel like eating, Luke, but it's hard to say no to a piece of Mr. Philgood's fried chicken." My stomach gurgled in agreement.

We ate our meal in comfortable silence at the kitchen table under the window. The fare was simple: fried chicken, fried potatoes, and a lettuce salad. We shared a bottle of white wine, which helped numb the pain a little.

"Have you known Bill for long?" What I really wanted to know was how well Luke had known Carson Bentley, who'd been Bill's oldest friend, until I killed him.

Luke smiled, seeming to recognize my need for distraction. "I've known Bill since the war, but we grew up a few miles from each other. Him in Uptown and me across the river in Westwego. We met during training at

Camp Richie. The army was looking for guys with language skills and I'm fluent in French and German, thanks to my grandmothers. They teamed Bill and me together. I guess they figured two Louisiana boys would have each other's backs."

"What was Bill like back then?" The time Bill and I spent together during the war was brief and complicated.

"I didn't like him much at first. He was full of himself, like every other Uptown guy I'd met, but he was smart and a good leader. It just felt like he was searching for something, and that made me unsure of him."

"About a week before the push into Paris, I noticed something different about him. It seemed like he had found his reason for being there, but I didn't know what it was until a few weeks after VE Day, the day you bumped into me in Paris. When Bill came back that night, he told me about you and asked me to do something that could land us both in jail. He convinced me it was the only way, that it was the right thing to do. By then, I would have laid down my life for Bill Marchand and never questioned why. I still would."

"I'm not sure the risk you took was worth it, Luke. I've made a mess of things."

Luke's eyes darkened as he broached the subject we'd been avoiding. "You know, I would have taken care of Carson for you. I could have made him disappear with no one the wiser. All you had to do was ask."

"I couldn't, Luke. If I had, Carson's ghost would haunt you instead of me."

"Not a chance, darlin'. I would have done the deed, come home, kissed my wife and slept like a baby. The son of a bitch deserved to die, but I wish it hadn't been you to do it."

"It was fate, Luke. I don't know why, but I think I was supposed to kill him. Things happen for a reason; at least, I hope they do. I just need to figure out what this one is and how I'm going to live with what I've done."

"You don't have to do this alone, Désirée. You have people who care about you."

"It would have been better for everyone if I'd never come here. I should have stayed in France and taken my chances, accepted my punishment. It would have saved a lot of lives if I had."

"I don't believe that. You're not responsible for Bentley's actions any more than you are for what happened in France. None of this was your fault, Désirée."

"Maybe not, but it feels like it is," I said, rising from my seat. "Thanks for the meal, Luke. I'm going upstairs. Do you mind if I take the rest of the wine? It might help me sleep."

"Help yourself, darlin'. You get some rest. If you need me, I'll be here."

A long soak in a hot bath soothed my aching body, and the rest of the wine numbed my tortured mind a little, but it was a long time before I could relax enough to fall asleep.

I kept worrying about Evie. All I knew was that they found her alive, but badly hurt and unresponsive. She just had to wake up and tell the police who took her. If she didn't, they wouldn't believe me about Carson. It was my word against a dead man's reputation.

The detective who interviewed me said they wouldn't charge me for Carson's death, it was clearly self-defense, based on the scene and the statements from the responding officers and Doctor Easton. But in my written statement, I accused Carson of kidnapping Evelyn Duret and of being the Phantom who caused the deaths of at least eight women. That was a leap the police weren't willing to take without some sound evidence. So far, none had surfaced, and Evie was silent.

Wake up, Evie. Please wake up.

When I went downstairs the next morning, Shelby was in the kitchen, standing at the stove, just staring at the coffee bubbling over. She must have heard me coming because she turned away to wipe her eyes.

"How you doing, honey? Did you sleep okay?" she asked after recovering her composure and pulling the coffeepot off the burner.

"Not really, but that's nothing new. Is there any aspirin?" I asked as I reached into the cupboard for a coffee cup and held it up for her to fill. Coffee was a necessity in the morning.

"Over there, next to the refrigerator," she said, pointing to the counter across the room. "Do you want something to eat? There's not much here because Bill's been gone for a couple of weeks. I brought over some bread and a few things in case you're hungry."

I set my coffee on the table, found the aspirin, and quickly downed three pills with a glass of water at the sink.

"Maybe just a piece of toast. Thanks." I added a splash of cream and a spoonful of sugar to the coffee, then curled my hands around the cup and took a cautious sip. It was hot and strong. Just the way I liked it.

"Miss Bea called this morning. She said they'd be here around eleven. I've got to open the restaurant, so I won't be here, but Luke will. I'm sorry, honey, Saturday is a busy day." She placed a plate of buttered toast and a dish of jam in front of me.

"Do you think they'll force me to go back, Shelby? Or send me to Glen Oaks? I won't do it," Both options were unthinkable.

"No, honey. I don't think that's what they're planning. Miss Bea's real upset about what happened. She feels terrible about it. So do I."

"Who were you talking to yesterday? You sounded so angry."

Her shaking head said she didn't want to tell me, but something changed her mind.

"It was Bill. I hold him responsible for this. Of all people, Bill should've known who Carson was." She sat down across from me, her hands clenching her coffee cup as if it could give her strength. After taking a few sips, she looked up at me with tears in her eyes.

"Did Bill tell you what happened?" I wondered how many people knew about the first rape. Mama, Charlie, Bill, and Doctor Easton, maybe even Luke, but I wasn't sure if they told Shelby about it. I was certain they wouldn't have talked about why I didn't tell anyone.

"Luke told me that the other night wasn't the first time Carson attacked you and that you kept it a secret. I understand why, honey."

"You do?"

"Yeah, I do... Fourteen years ago, I told Bill what Carson did to me, but he didn't believe me. I was just the caretaker's sixteen-year-old daughter, trying to climb a social ladder I didn't belong on. After that, I was too ashamed of what had happened. I didn't tell anyone else; not Dad, not Mr. Marchand or Miss Bea. No one. Oh god... maybe if I had, this wouldn't have happened to you. I'm so sorry."

"That's why you didn't come to Bill's Christmas party with Luke, isn't it? You knew Carson would be there."

"Yeah, that's why. I haven't seen Carson since the night he raped me. Besides, those people aren't my crowd. I'm just a country girl."

"How could you ever forgive Bill for not believing you?" I wasn't sure if I could.

"When Bill came back from the army a few years ago, he and Luke stayed here. I hadn't seen Bill for years and fully expected him to be as arrogant as he'd been before, but he wasn't. The war changed everyone, and most not in a good way, but Bill Marchand came back a better person, a kinder man, more thoughtful. We've never talked about it, but I know he feels bad about how he treated me back then. I'm sure he regrets it even more now."

"I can't face him, Shelby. I'm afraid of what I'll see in his eyes." Looking Bill in the eyes, and exposing the shame I felt, seeing his disappointment wasn't something I ever wanted to do.

"You'll probably see a lot of guilt and regret, but there won't be any blame. This wasn't your fault, Désirée. Carson Bentley got what he deserved."

"I doubt New Orleans society will feel that way. They'll blame me because they won't want to believe Carson deceived them."

"Screw them, honey. Who gives a damn what those people think?"

"The Marchands do. The Uptown crowd will always question why I killed Carson. Even if the police connect him to Evie and the Phantom murders, I'll be the subject of endless speculation and gossip. Charlie hates that kind of publicity."

Shelby reached across the table and squeezed my hand. "Don't let them get you down, Désirée. You're better than all of them. I'm sorry, honey, but I need to get ready to open the restaurant. Luke is helping Dad with something, but he should be back soon. Do you need anything before I leave?"

"No, I'm okay. Thanks, Shelby." I really wasn't, and she knew it, but she gave me a worried smile anyway before going out the back door.

Chapter 4

Saturday on the lake

Mama and Charlie's imminent arrival meant my hope of finding solitude at the lake house was in serious jeopardy. There were consequences for what I'd done, not to mention a potential disaster to mitigate.

I spent my remaining hours of solitude in the living room, curled up on the sofa, staring out the window at the lake, and wallowing in self-pity and survivor's guilt.

Why had I survived when so many others didn't? Was my life worth more than theirs? Why was I still here? I should have died with my family in 1940. There had to be a reason my life turned out this way. If there wasn't, I didn't know how to go on living with myself.

You should have chosen option A, Désirée.

That would have been the easier route. Throw myself into the Mississippi and let nature have me. No one would question why a young woman would kill herself after killing her rapist. Most girls I knew would consider suicide a reasonable option to escape a lifetime of shame and gossip.

If they hadn't found Evie, or if they found her dead, I would have chosen the easier route, but during the long, torturous hours of waiting to hear,

I vowed to do whatever I could to help her if she survived. She just had to wake up.

Mama's Cadillac pulled into the driveway shortly before noon with Charlie at the wheel. Mr. Jefferies was behind him, driving the Ford Coupe that Bill had given me for graduation. They waited for Luke to open the gate, then drove the cars up the driveway to the garage.

My solitude was at an end.

A few silent minutes passed, but eventually, noises filtered in from the back door. The Jefferies were in the kitchen, bringing things into the house. Miss Laila was undoubtedly checking for supplies based on the sound of cupboards being opened and closed. Their mumbled conversation was beyond my hearing, but it sounded like directions were being given. Then came the sound of someone carrying a heavy load up the stairs.

I was staring out the front window when Mama and Charlie came in. The knot in my stomach eased a bit when I saw the relief on their faces.

"Mama, Charlie, I'm sorry... for everything." Every regret I possessed spilled down my face in a slow trail of tears.

They had given me so much, taken me in and risked their reputations to shelter me. I repaid them by creating an enormous scandal that could ruin them, could send them to jail if people started looking closely into my past, or if Carson's threat to expose me came true.

Mama rushed over to wrap me in her arms. "Sweetheart, please don't cry. I'm sorry too."

We stood there holding on to one another until I finally pulled myself together.

"You had us scared to death, darlin'," Charlie said, giving me a tender look and drawing me into his arms. "I thought we lost you. When Aunt Bea read your note, we all imagined the worst. How did you get here?"

"I got a ride across the lake from the Orleans Marina."

Charlie's brow wrinkled up, and he shook his head.

"Let's sit down, Désirée. We must talk," Mama said, leading me to the sofa as Miss Laila came into the living room, her face etched with concern at the sight of me.

"Eulaila, could you bring us something cool to drink?" Mama asked. "Some sweet tea or whatever is available?"

"There ain't much here, Miss Bea. I'm gonna need to send Jacob to go get some things if that's alright. But I'll see what I can find."

"That's fine, Eulaila. Get whatever you think you'll need and ask Luke to go with him."

"Yes, Miss Bea... I'm real glad you're safe, Miss Dezrae. We was all worried sick about you," Laila said before retreating to the kitchen.

"How are you feeling, sweetheart?" Mama stroked my bruised face with a gentle touch. She looked worn-out. The past three days had obviously taken a toll on her.

"I'm fine, Mama," I said, dismissing her concern. "I need to know about Evie. Is she okay? Has she woken up?" Everything depended on Evie.

"No, darling, she hasn't. I spoke with her mother last night to ask about Evelyn's condition. Her physical injuries aren't too serious; however, she's being kept heavily sedated because she becomes violently hysterical when anyone touches her. Mrs. Duret said they were transferring Evelyn to the hospital at Glen Oaks this morning."

"Then the police don't know it was Carson who took her. I must see her, Mama. She has to tell them." The urge to drive over there was so strong that I almost jumped up right then.

"You'll see her, Désirée," Charlie said, stopping my forward momentum with a look that made it clear the information he was about to share with me wouldn't be pleasant.

"We met with District Attorney Simmons, who is having some difficulty believing your account of what happened. He's convening a grand jury on Wednesday morning to decide if they should file charges against you. A judge has signed an order for a psychiatric evaluation. You're scheduled to have a complete exam on Monday morning with the court-approved psychiatrist at Glen Oaks. Bill signed a bond guaranteeing your compliance. Simmons has agreed to allow you to live here under Bill and Aunt Bea's supervision." Charlie leaned back in his chair and watched for the reaction he knew was coming.

"They think I'm crazy?! Why?" That was an unexpected twist.

"You're an underage female who killed a man during a sexual act with no corroborating witnesses. A mandatory psych evaluation is standard procedure in these cases."

"Let me get this straight, Charlie. I'm crazy because I'm a seventeen-year-old girl who killed the man who brutally raped and tried to kill me, and I had the audacity to do it without witnesses and survive. Do I have that right?" My blood was boiling.

"Yes, darlin'. That pretty much sums it up. Will you submit to these terms, Désirée?" he asked with a hopeful look.

My hands covered my face as I blew out an exasperated breath. What choice did I have? For half a second, I entertained the idea of making another attempt at plan A before Monday rolled around, but then quickly dismissed it. That would leave Evie alone, lost in her nightmare, and I couldn't abandon her.

I couldn't abandon the Marchand's either. Carson's threat to expose me and ruin the Marchands felt genuine, hanging over me like the blade of a guillotine. I had to do whatever I could to defuse that threat, to divert attention away from the family and me and onto Carson and his evil deeds.

"Of course, Charlie. Haven't I always done what you asked?" I said with a sigh.

"Yes, darlin', you have. You've been like a daughter, Désirée, and if I could spare you this, I would. I am so sorry that I didn't protect you as I promised."

Shelby was right. I didn't need their guilt. I had plenty of my own.

"I thought the police said it was self-defense, Charlie, so why does the DA want an inquest? Does he think I killed Carson on purpose? And what about the things Carson sent me? Have the police connected them to the Phantom victims? To Carson?"

"Simmons was Carson's friend, and he doesn't understand why Carson would attack you. All the evidence the police collected is being analyzed in their lab, and it will take time to process. So far, there's nothing directly linking Carson to the Phantom murders or the assault on Evelyn Duret. He was very good at covering his tracks."

"Evie must tell them who took her, Charlie. She just has to. I've got to see her."

"They might let you see her on Monday after your psych evaluation. I'll try to arrange it."

"What kinds of questions will they ask me? Will they know if I lie?" I'd been deceiving everyone, except the Marchands, since Bill brought me to the States, and I began lying to them last October after Carson raped me the first time. Since then, my self-confidence had slipped, and I doubted my ability to deceive a trained professional if questioned too closely, at least not in my current state of mind.

Charlie's face reflected his feelings; regret, guilt, and concern were clearly visible in his eyes, and the deepening creases on his brow.

"The psych evaluation is a standard test to determine your ability to discern right from wrong, good from bad. I don't believe a polygraph is involved. You shouldn't have any trouble giving the psychiatrist believable answers. The grand jury inquest is different. The DA will want you to tell the court exactly what happened and what your relationship with Carson was. He won't make it easy for you, Désirée, but I'll try to be there with you. People liked Carson, and they're having a hard time understanding why he would do this to you."

"I'm sorry for not telling you before, but I was ashamed and too afraid of what would happen if I did. Carson's threat felt real. It still does, but I should have been braver."

"I wish you had trusted us," Charlie said. "We could have helped you. We should have seen the signs, but you're too damn good at hiding things."

"I've had to be, Charlie," I said as Jolie Jefferies came in carrying a tray of glasses filled with sweet tea. My eyes widened at seeing her.

"Here you go, Miss Bea," Jolie said, giving me sidelong glances as she set the tray down on the coffee table. "Gran says there isn't much to make for lunch till Grandad gets back. She wants to know if she should order some food from Shelby's place to tide y'all over till supper."

Mama gave her a grateful smile. "Thank you, Jolie. Tell your grandmother to order whatever she thinks sounds good."

"Yes, ma'am. Can I get you anything else?"

"No, we're fine, dear. Thank you."

After one last look at me, Jolie walked away.

"Excuse me for a minute, Mama," I said, following Jolie out.

Before she disappeared into the kitchen, I whispered to her. "Hey, Jolie."

She put her finger to her lips, then pointed upstairs, suggesting we talk up there in private. I hurried up to my room to wait, leaving the door open.

A few minutes later, Jolie was standing in front of me, shaking her head.

"God, you're a mess, Désirée. What the hell did that man do to you?"

"He tried to kill me, but I got him first," I said, trying to hold back my tears. "What are you doing here, Jolie?"

Over the past four years, I'd begged Jolie to come to the lake house with me to spend an entire month cooking together, but she never would. She'd never come to the St. Charles house either, not once, even though her grandparents lived there most of the time.

"Miss Bea asked me to come, and I needed a place to stay. This seemed as good a place as any." She looked around my room, seeing how I lived for the first time. I'd been to her place countless times.

"Mama asked you? Why did you need a place to stay? What about your father? Does he know you're here?" I had a million questions, but was so grateful to see her.

"Weekend before last, Pa up and married that woman I told you about. He moved her in, her and her three kids. The house was getting way too crowded for me. Then this thing happened to you, so I packed my bag and called Grandad to come get me. I figured you'd need a friend. Then Miss Bea asked me to come out here and stay with you. She said she'd pay me $40 a week. I couldn't very well pass up an opportunity like that, could I?"

"You will not be my maid, Jolie. I won't let that happen. You shouldn't even be here."

"No, I won't be your maid, Désirée, but I am your friend," she said, her deep brown eyes studying my face for confirmation. "You always said I was important to you, right? Well, this is me being important. I couldn't let you go through this alone." She threw her arms around me in a big bear hug.

After holding on tight for a moment, I reluctantly pulled away. "I should go back down. They're probably not done with me yet. Thanks, Jolie. It means a lot that you're here."

That afternoon, Mama, Charlie, Luke and I dined together on Crab Cake salads with tangy remoulade sauce and warm French rolls. Shelby also sent over a pot of Seafood Gumbo, which was warming on the stove, and three Catfish Po Boys with fries consumed by the Jefferies at the kitchen table.

The mood in the dining room was somber. There were none of the light-hearted conversations that usually accompanied any meal with Charlie. It felt like another rug was about to be pulled out from under me.

I wondered where Bill was hiding. No one had spoken of him all afternoon. Not that I was eager to see him. I wasn't, but his absence felt odd, especially since the last thing he said to me—through my closed bedroom door on Thursday night—was that he wasn't giving up.

Maybe he changed his mind. Maybe the mess I created in his life is more than he can deal with.

"I've been thinking about something, Luke," I said, cutting into the silence at the table, and capturing Luke's eyes. "Mr. Reyes came to see me last Monday to tell me Bill had gone to Mexico to find the man he's been looking for. Mr. Reyes said they expected the man would be in Merida on Wednesday night to receive a package being delivered from New Orleans. Did Bill find that man?" I wondered if Luke had been with Bill on that trip.

Luke looked down at his empty plate and shook his head. "No. We didn't. At nine o'clock Wednesday night, we intercepted a message at the Merida airfield. The message said the cargo never made it to the New Orleans airport, so they canceled the flight. Our target vanished. The man's a ghost."

My hand cupped my mouth to hide my quivering lip. A familiar fear sent a chill down my back, bringing with it the instinct to run and hide, but I had to know if what I feared was the truth.

"Carson said he was taking me somewhere, that he was going to make his money back. Luke, did the man in Merida, did Anton Steigler know what he was buying and who was selling it to him?" I prayed the answer would be no, but I feared the worst. The very last thing I needed right then was the Kommandant knowing I was still alive and living in New Orleans.

Luke shut his eyes and swallowed hard before answering. "We don't know, Désirée. Steigler used layers of intermediaries to conduct business. The people we've questioned only know who hired them, but not who pays the bill. It's hard to say if Bentley knew who he was dealing with, but it's a possibility."

I looked over at Mama and Charlie, my eyes filled with tears ready to fall. "Do you see? Nothing has changed. I'm still a danger to all of you, and now I've created an epic scandal that none of you deserve. It would be better for everyone if I weren't here."

"Please don't say that, darling," Mama said, reaching over to grab my hand. "You're part of this family, Désirée. Whatever comes, we will face it together."

I spent the afternoon curled up in a fetal position on my bed, trying to process everything and having little success.

Old memories kept flashing through my mind, the ones I locked away because they were too painful to look at. The three years I spent with the Nazi Kommandant Anton Steigler played like a cruel movie, terrible years that changed my life forever. I wanted to forget them, completely erase them from my mind, but that was impossible. I never forget anything.

After a few hours of tossing and turning, I drug myself out of bed and went downstairs in search of Bill's Irish. I needed something to dull my mind, to silence the incessant chatter.

Mama and Charlie's quiet conversation in the living room thwarted my plan, so I changed directions and headed for the kitchen.

"You feelin' any better, Miss Dezrae?" Miss Laila asked, looking me over for signs of improvement as she rearranged the cupboards to her liking.

"Not much," I replied, opening the refrigerator to look for some wine or a beer, anything alcoholic. I found half a dozen bottles of Regal Beer chilling in the back, grabbed one, opened it, then headed out the back door, unwilling to share my guilt and shame with her.

A few minutes later, Jolie followed me out. I was sitting at the bottom of the stairs, sipping on the beer and smoking. She sat down next to me, close enough that our shoulders touched.

"You got another one of those?" she asked, pointing to the cigarette.

I handed her my cigarette case and lighter.

She pulled out a cigarette, lit it, handed me back the case and lighter, took a deep drag, then blew it out with a sigh of relief. "Thanks."

"Do you want to share the beer?" I asked, offering her the bottle.

"Sure." She took a drink, leaned her shoulder into mine, then passed the bottle back.

"You shouldn't have come, Jolie. This mess isn't anything you need."

"Well, I'm here, Désirée, and I'm not going anywhere, so you can stop saying that."

She took another drag from her smoke, then turned to look at me.

"I wish you'd tell me what the big secret is. I know it's more than just what happened the other night. You've been holding onto a secret ever since we met."

"Has it been that obvious?"

"Probably not to most people, but we've been close, and close friends shouldn't keep secrets. Maybe I can help."

"It isn't something anyone can fix," I said, crushing out my cigarette and handing her the bottle.

Just then, Bill's car pulled down the driveway, parking behind mine. Bill got out first, then Bobby Easton climbed out of the passenger side, grabbed his bag from the back seat and stood there, looking around. He saw me sitting on the stairs and rushed over, with Bill a few steps behind. My head dropped into my hands as I tried hard not to lose what little self-control I still had.

Bobby stood in front of me and pulled my hands away so he could see me. As he gently touched my bruised face, tears filled his eyes. "Ah, Dez, what did that son of a bitch do to my girl?"

I shook my head, looking away, trying to hide the shame I felt. When I looked up, Bill was there a few feet behind Bobby, with a look in his eyes that matched Shelby's prediction, plus something else. Guilt and regret were there, but also sadness and loss. Or maybe it was longing.

"Come here, girl," Bobby said, tears making trails down his face as he reached for me.

Too afraid to know what Bill was thinking, I looked away, falling into the arms of my best friend.

Chapter 5

A Crowded House

I had hoped the lake house would offer me some privacy and give me time to recover, but everyone's arrival dashed that hope. The house was getting crowded.

Out by the lake, the old cypress log bench was our spot, the place Bobby and I would sit and talk for hours on warm summer nights, stargazing and making plans for our future. He led me over, sat me down, then wrapped me in his arms, holding me as close as he dared. I couldn't stop crying, couldn't stop feeling like the pathetic mess I was.

"You shouldn't be here, Bobby. You should be at school in California."

"School can wait. You're more important, Dez," he said, squeezing my shoulder. "God, I've been frantic ever since Jimmy called."

"Oh god, poor Jimmy." I shivered, thinking of what Jimmy might have seen that night. The humiliation was unbearable.

"He blames himself, Dez. He said you wouldn't have even been there if he hadn't changed the plans. We've been so worried about you. No one would tell us anything, not until Bill called me yesterday morning. God, I'm so damn mad at him. I almost punched him in the nose when he came to get me today. This shouldn't have happened to you."

"Please don't be angry with Bill. This wasn't his fault or Jimmy's," I said, miserable because all the blame was mine... and Carson's. The friction between the people I cared about only added to my misery.

"Bill should have kept his promise and watched out for you, Dez. If he hadn't looked so miserable when he picked me up today, he'd have a bloody nose right now."

"Bobby, you can't stay. This scandal will only cause problems for you, and I don't want that to happen. I've caused enough trouble as it is. You should go back to Stanford."

"That's not gonna happen, Dez. I'm not going anywhere until I'm sure you're going to be alright. We're best friends forever, remember?"

A moment later, Jolie came toward us, trying hard to act casual, but clearly nervous.

"Excuse me, Désirée, Miss Bea asked me to come get you. Mr. Charles said he's going home soon, but he wants to see you before he leaves... Are you okay?" she asked after seeing my tear-stained face.

There was nothing to do but accept their presence as gracefully as my wounded soul would let me.

"I think I will be, now that my two best friends are here. Too bad it took a tragedy to bring you two together."

I hooked my elbows with Jolie and Bobby's, then leaned my head on each shoulder for a second before walking with them arm-in-arm back to the house.

Bill, Mama, and Charlie were in the living room talking. Their worried faces made me think something else was afoot, some fresh jolt threatening to make everything worse.

Charlie stood in front of me, holding my hands and looking as if he hadn't slept in days. "I've got to get home, Désirée, but I'll be here first thing Monday morning. You try to get some rest before then."

"Please tell Julianna and the twins how sorry I am. And Uncle Henri, too." I knew the full force of New Orleans gossip was about to hit them dead on.

"They send their love, darlin'. Julianna said she'll call you as soon as she can." Charlie put his hand to my cheek, gently touching the bruises, then bent to kiss my forehead. "I'll see you on Monday. Goodnight, Aunt Bea. Goodnight, Bobby. Ready, Bill?"

"I'll be back in a few hours, Mother," Bill said, stealing a look in my direction. "Bob, if you could watch over my ladies for me, I'd be in your debt. If you need anything, Luke is here. He'll know what to do." Bill gave me a sad parting look as he followed Charlie out the back door.

"Jolie, come help me in here. Let them folks talk in private. Come on now," Miss Laila called from the kitchen as Bill and Charlie were leaving. Jolie reluctantly obeyed, glancing back at me as she disappeared into the kitchen.

Mr. Jefferies walked through the living room, emptying ashtrays and retrieving dirty glasses. "Your bag is in your usual room, down the hall, Mr. Bobby. I put some fresh towels in the bathroom, and there's a clean robe in the armoire. You let me know if you need anything, sir."

"Thanks, Jacob."

"Can I get you anything, Miss Dezrae?"

"No thank you, Mr. Jefferies. I'm fine."

I could see from the troubled look in his eyes that he didn't believe me, but he accepted my response with a nod.

"Miss Bea, Laila says there's time for you to rest up before supper. She'll come get you when it's ready. It's been a long day, ma'am."

"Yes, it has, Jacob. If you'll excuse me, Bobby, I think I will lie down for a while. We'll catch up at supper. I'm very grateful you're here, very grateful," Mama said, hugging Bobby before heading upstairs.

Bobby watched her slowly climb the stairs and disappear into her room. "She doesn't look well, Dez."

"I know," I said, curling into the corner of the sofa, trying to ease my guilty conscious with little success.

He joined me on the sofa, shifting me over so I could lie against him, our standard position for watching television, which we didn't bother to turn on.

"Why didn't you ever tell me about Jolie?" he asked as he slipped a cushion under my head.

I knew he'd ask eventually, knew I'd need to make a full confession, but right then, I only had enough strength for one question.

"I wanted to tell you a million different times, but I couldn't. If I told you about Jolie, about my friendship with her, then you would have had to keep it a secret."

"Didn't you trust me?"

"Of course, I did, Bobby. I just didn't want you to have to lie for me, that's all. It was hard enough keeping it from you. If things were different here, I would have told you."

"How long have you two been friends?" He sounded a little insecure.

"Almost as long as you and me."

"Geez, Dez. You're great at keeping secrets, aren't you? What else don't I know about you?"

"I tried to tell you last summer."

He looked at me with guilt in his eyes. "Yeah, you did... and I wouldn't let you. I'm sorry, Dez. Do you want to tell me now?"

"Can we just sit here, Bobby? I'm so tired of talking. Can it wait till tomorrow?"

"It can wait forever, Dez, because there's nothing you could say that will ever change how I feel about you."

I lingered for hours in that delicious space between dreaming and waking, reluctant to abandon the comfort and security of Bobby's presence. Murmured conversations filtered through my mind, though none could completely penetrate the veil of repose surrounding me. Sounds washed over me like water flowing gently down a stream, their meaning barely making a ripple.

"Has she been asleep long?"

"About an hour, maybe two."

"She ain't had more than a couple of bites ta eat all day."

"She needs to rest, Eulaila."

"I'll take her up, Bobby."

Bill lifted me from Bobby's cozy comfort and held me close as he carried me up to my room. It felt familiar: the smell of his cologne, the strength of his arms, the feel of his heart beating close to mine. I wanted to stay in that feeling forever, didn't want him to ever leave me.

"Ne me quitte pas. Ne me quitte pas," I whimpered as he lay me down on my bed.

He covered me with the old shawl I always kept close by, then bent to place a kiss on my brow.

"Je suis là, ma chérie. Je reste ici avec toi. Je suis là."

With Bill's assurance, I let myself relax into a deep sleep, knowing this time he would stay.

... I braced myself, arms stretched above my head, hands gripping the bedframe he'd tied me to, legs spread wide and tied to the bedposts. My breath came in panting gasps, and my racing heart threatened to beat out of my chest.

He held the knife over the candle flame, sending swirls of smoke into the air that mingled with his cigarette smoke as he performed the sick ritual. He smiled as he ran the searing blade across my naked flesh, then pressed his cigarette twice along the fresh cut...

"No! Stop! No!" I screamed, writhing on the bed, unable to pull myself from the nightmare. That sickening moment kept playing in my mind over and over. I couldn't get it to stop, I couldn't stop screaming.

"Désirée, wake up. Désirée, you're here, you're safe. Wake up," Jolie said, desperately trying to get me to calm down. She pried my hands from the bedframe to pull me into her arms, but I fought her away, still lost in the memory.

"No! Please, not again. Stop, please!" I cried, twisting away from the monster in my nightmare.

"Désirée, it's Mama. Wake up, darling, I'm here now. Wake up. Open your eyes, sweetheart, look at me." Mama's gentle voice penetrated my terrors, drawing me back to the present.

I sat up straight in bed, panting like a frightened animal, and opened my eyes to Mama's distraught expression. Every worry I'd ever given her lay clearly etched on her face.

The bedside lamp lit the faces assembled behind her, each holding their own version of Mama's concern. Bill and Bobby stood in the doorway, staring at me with a pair of anguished faces. The Jefferies were hovering behind them, and Jolie was at the foot of the bed, looking alarmed and nervous.

"Oh god, I'm so sorry." I buried my face in my hands in a fresh burst of tears.

"Hush, darling, it's over now. You're safe here with us." Mama held me tight and soothed my trembling body with her gentle touch.

"Mother, what can I do?" Bill asked helplessly.

"I've got her, Beau. You all go back to bed now. Jolie, go sleep in my room, dear. I'll stay with Désirée tonight."

Mama was always clear-headed in a crisis, knowing what to say and do to bring the worst situation into clear focus. She held me close, letting me soak her dressing gown with my tears until there were none left to shed.

"This one must have been bad. Do you want to talk about it?" she asked, wiping the tears from my face with her hankie.

"I usually wake up before I scream, but this time I couldn't. That moment kept repeating over and over. I'm sorry I woke everyone up."

"It might help if you bring that memory into the light and talk about it, darling."

"It was when he... branded me. I should have told you, Mama. If I had, the police would know Carson was the killer, and he wouldn't have hurt anyone else. He wouldn't have hurt Evie... Oh god, what have I done?"

"The police know that the man who took Evelyn is the Phantom. She bears the same mark as you and the other victims. All they require is her statement to identify him, and then it will be over. You needn't say anything about his first attack on you."

"Oh, God, poor Evie, what she must have gone through. Do Bill and Charlie know... about the mark... on me?"

"No, sweetheart. I haven't told them, nor will Doctor Easton say anything about it. No one needs to know."

"But someday I'll need to tell someone, and he will see what Carson did, and then... Oh Mama, I hate what he did to me, this reminder I can never erase." I fell back onto the bed in a hopeless puddle of tears.

Mama laid down next to me, pulling me into her embrace. "Listen to me, darling. What happened to you will not matter in the slightest to any man worthy of being with you. You will survive this the same way you have survived everything else, with courage and strength."

I lay awake in her arms for an hour or more, absorbing her comfort and offering what gratitude I could. Eventually, her hums turned to soft purrs of deep slumber, and I slipped out of the bed.

Nightmares always left me restless. Despite Mama's comfort, I needed to walk off the residual effects of the dream and a drink to deaden the images in my mind. I went downstairs, poured myself a glass of whiskey, then headed back up.

The upper terrace lived at the end of the second-floor hall through a pair of French doors. It was twelve feet by twenty-five, with one end facing the lake and the other with stairs leading down to the lower terrace and backyard. I stepped out into the cool night air, the slate tile chilled my bare feet, and a soft breeze kissed my cheeks.

Alone at last, I went to the rail to look out toward the lake and up toward the star filled sky. As I sipped on the whiskey, the night sounds surrounded me, insects, frogs, the occasional chirp of a restless bird.

"Couldn't you go back to sleep?" Bill asked from the doorway.

"No. I'm sorry if I woke you." I didn't want to talk with him, but I didn't want to go in either, so I kept my back turned, hoping he would go away.

"It's alright. I don't sleep much these days, anyway."

His footsteps came towards me, then stopped a few feet away.

"I know you don't want to speak to me, Désirée, and I can't blame you, but I need to say this. I am deeply sorry for bringing all this into your life, and for not keeping my promises. God knows I've made a lot of mistakes, but the one I regret the most is leaving you. I won't make that mistake again. I would do anything to make this up to you, to convince you to trust me again."

His words washed over me like a wave, full of guilt and regret, and something else, but it was too late. Fate had another plan for me. I tossed back the whiskey to dull the ache in my heart, then turned to face him.

"Can you turn back the clock, Bill?"

"No, Chére, I can't."

"Neither can I... Time only moves forward, never back," I said as I passed him on my way inside.

Doctor Easton arrived unannounced on Sunday afternoon. Ostensibly to check on me, but his visit focused more on Mama Bea and Bobby after assuring himself of my progress toward recovery.

"The bruises are healing well, Désirée. They should fade in a week or two," he said, after examining my face, neck and back, then pulling my robe up over my shoulders.

"I hear you're not sleeping, that you're experiencing nightmares. Are you taking the medication I prescribed?"

"No. I don't like pills." Besides being hard to swallow, I was terrified of having access to such a quick end should my despair become unbearable.

"You should take it, Désirée. It's harmless and will help you get the rest you need. Now, has the vaginal bleeding stopped?"

"Yes." I prayed he wouldn't want to examine me down there again. The humiliation would be too much.

"When was your last menstrual cycle?"

"Three weeks ago."

"I'll order a test to be done tomorrow at Glen Oaks to determine if you're pregnant, though I doubt you are. The prior trauma severely scarred your uterus, which will make any future conception difficult, if not impossible."

His diagnosis was no-nonsense, just a realistic offering of information. There would be no children in my future, but it didn't matter because I would never subject a child to my nightmare. Still, it felt like Fate was exacting her divine justice on me, giving me another permanent reminder of my offenses.

It's better this way, Désirée.

"You can get dressed now. I'll see you downstairs," he said with a stoic nod as he stepped out of my room.

As I was dressing in the shared bathroom between Mama's room and mine, I overheard him talking with her, arguing in hushed voices.

"Bea, I'm going to insist you go home today. You're not doing Désirée or yourself any good by wearing yourself out."

"She needs me, Robert. I can't abandon her," Mama said, sounding anxious and exhausted.

"She'll be fine, Bea. Désirée is strong and will come through this even stronger. She doesn't need you to collapse under this pressure. Bill and Bobby are here, and they'll take care of her and give her the support she needs. You should be home resting, not out here where I can't monitor you. I insist you return home and plan on seeing me in my office first thing tomorrow. Promise me, Bea. If you don't, I'll bring your son into this conversation."

"No, Robert, please don't. I don't want Beau to know."

"Alright, but you must follow my orders, or you'll wind up in the hospital."

"I'll go home this afternoon, and I'll see you bright and early tomorrow. I promise."

Mama was sick, and hiding it from everyone, including Bill. This felt more serious than my problems, and it could hurt far worse than anything else. If I hadn't overheard them, I might have thought she was abandoning me.

I kept her secret during our tearful goodbye, accepting her reasons for leaving with silent grace. She sighted her obligations to family, to school and to her students, and her understanding of my need for quiet space. She promised to call nightly and visit on the weekends.

"Will you be alright here with Beau?"

"Of course, Mama. Bobby is here, at least for a little while, and Jolie is here. Luke, Shelby and Mr. Philgood are right next door. I'll be fine. Don't worry about me."

I didn't exactly answer her question because I wasn't sure how my new living arrangements were going to work. Bill and I had never lived in the same house before, at least not for more than a night or two, and it was difficult being around him. My feelings of shame and remorse were hard to shake. I didn't know how, but I'd do whatever I could to make it work. Easing Mama's worry was more important than my sensitivity.

As soon as Mama and I went downstairs, the house began humming with tense activity. Mama went off in one direction to break the news to Bill about her departure and assure herself that we would be alright without her. The Jefferies began packing up and giving Jolie a list of instructions on how to take care of me, which seemed ridiculous and unnecessary because I always took care of my own messes, at least until a few days ago. And Bobby was outside on the porch, pacing and arguing with his father.

As I sat in the living room waiting for things to settle down, I watched Bobby and Doctor Easton through the window and listened to their argument.

"Forget it, Dad. I'm not going back until I know Désirée is alright," Bobby said, scowling and shaking his head. "I won't let those vipers at Glen Oaks hurt Dez or Evie the way they hurt my mother. I'll shut the damn place down before I'll let that happen, and you know I can do it."

"Where would your friends go if not to Glen Oaks, son?" Doctor Easton asked, trying to stay calm. "Do you even know what the alternatives are? Central State Mental Hospital or Eastern are the only options for the mentally ill, and I wouldn't send my worst enemy to either place. Your grandfather started Glen Oaks Sanitorium to ensure his wife and daughter would have the care they required, and it continues to provide this community with a much-needed service, quality mental healthcare in a healthy environment. You may not like it, Robert, but Glen Oaks is the best place for both your friends."

"I'm going with her tomorrow to make sure they know who they're dealing with. Désirée is too important for me to leave this to chance."

"If you must go with her, son, try not to lose your temper. That would only create problems. And for your information, Glen Oaks' peer review board discharged the doctor on call at the time of your mother's death. They have established new protocols to ensure a similar tragedy never happens again."

That was a relief. Glen Oaks didn't sound as awful as I imagined, and better than the state mental hospitals Doctor Easton mentioned. Just knowing Bobby would be with me eased my nervous stomach a little. But I wondered what happens to the women who go to those other places. Do they recover? Do they ever go home?

By five o'clock, the population of the lake house had dwindled down to four: me, Bobby, Jolie, and Bill. What an odd cadre, whose only connection was me and my well-being. I felt unworthy of their attention, their concern, and the only way to deal with it was to put on a cheerful mask to disguise my depression. The trouble was, they each knew me in their own way, knew a piece of me, a truth about me, and any attempt at hiding was futile.

Chapter 6

Glen Oaks

Charlie arrived Monday morning at nine to take me to Glen Oaks. The dark circles under his eyes made him look even more tired than he had on Saturday, and his usual light-hearted smile was missing.

"What's wrong, Charlie? Is Mama alright? Is Julianna?" I asked as I poured him some coffee when he sat down at the dining table with a tired sigh.

"They're fine, darlin'. Did you get some rest? This might be a hard day for you." He looked me over for signs of fragility and once he deemed me whole, he took a drink of the coffee, then set the cup down with another sigh. "Mrs. Duret has given her permission for you to see Evelyn today. You'll see her after your examination by the psychiatrist. Detective Guardino will be there to witness your meeting with her."

"Is there any news about Charlotte?" Bill asked, a crease forming on the bridge of his nose.

I hadn't given Carson's sister much thought since I killed him, but knew she would show up eventually to hold me responsible for her brother's death. Why wouldn't she?

"Charlotte is still dealing with her husband's death, Bill," Charlie said with a sigh. "Joe's funeral is tomorrow. Guardino informed me that the Miami police have arrested Joe's killer, a man by the name of Amirault.

He's the brother of one of the Phantom victims, the one they found on our dock behind the machine shop. In his confession, Amirault said Carson Bentley convinced him that Joe Barone killed his sister after ending an affair with her."

"What? When did Charlotte's husband die?" I asked, looking from Charlie to Bill.

"Last Wednesday night around ten, outside a nightclub in Miami," Bill said, shaking his head. "Charlotte was in Atlanta visiting friends when it happened."

And Bill had been in Mexico on a wild goose chase. I wondered what he was feeling right then. There'd been a time, not that long ago, when both Carson and Charlotte Bentley were primary characters in Bill's life. My entrance into it was what changed things. I wondered if Bill had regrets about that.

"Why would Carson want Charlotte's husband dead?" I asked. Carson's motives puzzled me.

"We've got more important things to think about today, Désirée," Charlie said as he reached into the basket for one of Jolie's biscuits, slathered butter and honey on it and took a bite.

"You want something more than just a biscuit, sir?" Jolie asked, ready to jump up to make him something.

"No thanks, Jolie. The biscuit was plenty," he said, finishing the last morsel with a swallow of coffee. "Are you ready, Désirée? Your appointment is at ten and we have some papers to fill out when we get there."

"What papers, Charlie?" My stomach had been upset all morning, worrying about what I would face at Glen Oaks.

"Just a few legal documents, nothing to worry about. I'll handle it. We should go."

"I'm going with you, Charlie," Bill said as he rose from the table.

"Me too," Bobby added, already on his feet and reaching for my hand.

Charlie looked around the table and shrugged as if he half expected this response.

"Are you planning on coming too, Jolie?" he asked with a tired smile.

"No sir. Désirée's got plenty of protection. She don't need me holding her hand. I'll just wait here, but if you don't mind, sir, I'd like her back in one piece and in time for lunch." Jolie always spoke her mind regardless of her audience, and her blunt response elicited another tired smile from Charlie as he headed for the door, followed by Bill and Bobby.

"Goodbye, Jolie." I suddenly felt like I might not be coming back. My breath caught in my throat as I hugged her, afraid this would be the last time.

"This ain't goodbye, Désirée, so get yourself together and keep your chin up," she said, pulling my arms away, then lifting my chin with her finger. "We'll see each other later. Maybe I'll surprise you with something new for lunch."

With a smile and another quick hug, I went to join the men and face my fate with my chin held high.

Glen Oaks Sanitorium sat on a sprawling twenty-acre estate between US Highway 190 and the Tchefuncte River in Covington. Sheltered from view by an eight-foot-high brick wall, it offered the well-to-do of New Orleans a sanctuary for their feeble-minded, a place to send their wives when they became unruly or just needed a rest. According to Bobby, Glen Oaks could care for one hundred and fifty patients and normally operated at full capacity. They even had a waiting list for non-critical cases.

Charlie pulled the car up to the wrought-iron gate, rolled down his window, and waited for the guard to come out of the gatehouse.

"Good morning, sir," the guard said with a friendly smile. "Who are you here to see this morning?"

"Doctor Franklin Neville. Miss Désirée Gautier is here for her appointment."

The guard peered through the windows at me and Bobby in the back seat, then at Bill sitting next to Charlie.

"May I have your names, gentlemen?" he asked after writing my name on his clipboard.

"Charles and William Marchand, and the young man in the back is Robert Montgomery Easton."

"Thank you. Just one moment, please." After walking back into the gatehouse, he picked up a telephone, then half a minute later, the gate was sliding open.

"Doctor Neville is expecting you. Good day, sir."

Charlie headed down the drive leading to the entrance of Glen Oaks, then parked in the visitors' lot in front.

The main building was red brick, three stories tall sporting windows hugged by white shutters, and a large portico over the front entrance supported by six tall white columns. It looked like a grand old house from the outside with its lush gardens and welcoming entrance. But looks can be deceiving.

I remembered every detail of the place from my previous visits with Bobby when he would come to visit his mother during her summer stays. Beyond the grand façade and spacious lobby lay the administration offices and visiting solarium. Out of sight, but connected to the main building by covered walkways, were several buildings for various types of therapy, housing for patients, and a fully staffed medical wing. Glen Oaks may look like a peaceful country estate on the outside, but it was all business on the inside.

I squeezed Bobby's hand as we walked into the lobby, as much to give him support as to feel his. The last time he'd been to Glen Oaks was six months earlier, the day he found out his mother was dead.

A plain-faced, middle-aged man with wire-rimmed glasses and a dark beard covering the ball of his chin approached us with an outstretched hand. "Good morning. I'm Doctor Neville, Chief of Staff here at Glen Oaks. You must be Miss Gautier."

I politely refused to shake his hand, instead nodding a quiet acknowledgement in his direction.

"We weren't expecting so many to accompany you today, Miss Gautier. Which of you fine gentlemen is Mr. Marchand?"

"I'm Charles Marchand, Miss Gautier's attorney," Charlie said, shaking the man's hand.

"William Marchand, her guardian." Bill said, reaching out his hand.

"And I am Robert Montgomery Easton," Bobby interrupted. "Do you recognize the name, Doctor?"

"Of course. It's an honor to meet you, Mr. Easton. To what do I owe the pleasure of your visit today?"

"I'm here to make sure that Miss Gautier, my dearest friend, receives the finest care possible. Her welfare is very important to me. I'm sure you're aware, Doctor Neville, of my mother's tragic death in this facility last summer, so I want to make it clear to you that should anything bad happen to Miss Gautier, to Miss Duret, or any other patient while under your care, I will personally make sure that you and anyone else responsible never practices psychiatry or medicine ever again." Bobby stared without faltering until the man lowered his head in acknowledgement. I'd never heard Bobby speak so vehemently to anyone.

"Rest assured, Mr. Easton, your friends are in excellent hands." Apparently unruffled by the threat, Doctor Neville turned back to Charlie and Bill. "While Miss Gautier and I begin the examination, my secretary has a few documents in the administration office requiring your signature, Mr. Marchand. Please come with me, Miss Gautier."

Bobby pulled me into a hug before letting me leave. "Holler if you need me, Dez."

Doctor Neville led me through the lobby, past a broad staircase, and down a hallway lined with several doors on either side. He chose the fourth door on the left and held it open as I entered a small nursing station.

"This is Nurse Hansen, Miss Gautier. She will collect a urine sample for testing. Do you have any objections?"

I did, but what difference did it make? As far as I was concerned, they could have as much of my body fluid as they wanted, if it meant getting this farce over with. When I shook my head in response, he left.

Nurse Hansen opened the door to a small room with a sink and a toilet. "Right this way, miss."

I went in expecting to close the door for privacy, but no such luck. She followed me in and stood in the corner while I peed into the collection pan. Obviously, privacy was a rare commodity at Glen Oaks. I finished, washed my hands, then stood ready for further instructions.

"Thank you, miss. I'll take you to Doctor Neville now."

She led me farther down the hall and into a brightly lit room containing only a table and two chairs, with Doctor Neville waiting in one of them. There were no windows to offer distractions, and the walls were bare except the wall behind the doctor, which had a mirror that looked more like a window. I was pretty sure it was one of those two-way mirrors where someone on the other side could observe what was going on in the room without being seen. That didn't inspire a sense of comfort at all.

"Take a seat, Miss Gautier. Make yourself comfortable. There's no reason to be nervous," Doctor Neville said, waving me forward to the vacant chair.

That was easy for him to say because he didn't have any idea what being in this position felt like. I sat down in the chair opposite him and waited for whatever was coming next.

"Let's start with a few simple questions. Tell me your full name and date of birth."

"Désirée Marie Gautier. May fifteenth, 1932." The first of many lies. Gautier wasn't my real name.

He verified my answer with the file in front of him.

"Please tell me the date today, and where you are."

"It's Monday, January sixteenth, 1950. I'm at Glen Oaks Sanitorium in Covington, Louisiana, sitting with Doctor Franklin Neville, Chief of Staff, and Mr. Truman is still President." I added the last bit to let him feel my impatience with this line of questioning.

His eyebrows raised an inch above the rim of his glasses. "Yes, he is. Can you tell me why you're here today, Miss Gautier?"

I rolled my eyes at him. "A judge I've never met has ordered me to come here so you can determine whether or not I'm crazy."

"How does that make you feel?"

I huffed out a breath, trying to control my frustration with this whole thing, then I looked at him and wondered if it even mattered to him how I felt.

"Re-victimized," was my response.

"Well, let's get through these tests and then we'll talk about that."

The first test he gave was to test my short-term memory. He showed me lists of between three and six words or numbers, then asked me to repeat them in the correct order, which wasn't much of a challenge with my photographic memory, though he didn't know that. I got a couple wrong on purpose because most people are uncomfortable with perfection.

Then, he gave me the Thematic Apperception Test, which required me to analyze what was happening in a series of ambiguous images. This was more of a challenge because it required an emotional response, and I needed to be cautious about revealing any of my past. I got through it, but not without exposing my discomfort at being analyzed.

"For a young woman who has gone through such a serious trauma, you possess an unusual level of self-control, Miss Gautier. I wonder where this stems from, what trauma in your past taught you to hold your feelings so tightly."

I didn't know him, and I didn't want to be there, but I had no choice but to play along if it would get me to Evie.

"Isn't being raped and killing the man who did it enough, doctor? Does it need to be something else?"

"Not necessarily, but self-control is usually a learned behavior. Tell me how you're feeling right now."

"Frustrated."

"Can you explain why?"

I huffed again. "Will you answer a question for me, doctor?"

"Of course, if I can."

"Would I even be sitting here today if I were a man?"

He stared at me for a long time before responding. "Perhaps not, Miss Gautier, but why not take advantage of this opportunity to explore what's troubling you? With my help, I'm certain you can reclaim your life again."

"I'm not sure that's possible now, doctor." I wouldn't let him know the real me if I could help it.

"That will depend entirely on you, Miss Gautier. I hope you'll learn to trust me."

"A person must earn trust, doctor. May I see Evelyn now?"

"Of course. I'll take you to her."

It was worse than I expected. The haunted creature strapped to the bed looked nothing like the Evie I'd seen ten days earlier. Gone was the free-spirited girl certain that 1950 would be her lucky year, replaced by a shattered shell of a human being, lost in a terrible nightmare she couldn't escape.

"Why is she strapped to the bed?" I demanded. "She'll never find her way back if you keep her tied up."

"It's necessary to keep the restraints on for now," Doctor Neville said, shaking his head as he observed Evie through the door window. "She becomes quite agitated whenever touched, even by her mother. Mrs. Duret is hoping you can reach Evelyn and help her back into this reality."

"Your name is the only word she's spoken since we found her, Miss Gautier," said Detective Guardino, coming up to join Doctor Neville and me outside Evie's room. There was no accusation in his tone, just a simple statement of fact.

I hadn't known that, but now that I did, the path to reaching Evie felt clearer than it was a few minutes earlier.

"May I go in now?" I asked.

"Nurse Presley will accompany you, Miss Gautier. She has been nursing Miss Duret since her arrival. I'll be here, observing and listening."

I stepped into the room, followed by Nurse Presley, and walked toward the frail, pathetic creature lying in the bed, who used to be so full of life and hope. With her hands and legs strapped down, Evie could only move her head, rolling it from side to side and softly moaning with her eyes closed.

"We've given her a mild sedative, only enough to keep her calm during your visit," Nurse Presley said.

"What's your first name?" I asked.

"Johanna."

I nodded, then went to stand between the bed and the window, where I could see Doctor Neville and Detective Guardino at the door. Johanna stood on the other side of the bed, ready to assist should Evie become agitated.

"*Bonjour, Evie. C'est moi, Désirée. Bonjour, mon amie. Je suis là.*" I kept repeating it, trying to reach her mind with a familiar greeting.

I unstrapped the hand closest to me, motioning for Johanna to do the same with the other. Once loose, Evie clutched her arms around her body, rolling her torso slowly back and forth and moaning the same way I did the night I killed Carson. I knew where she was, had been there myself not that long ago.

"Evie, look at me. It's Désirée. I'm here with you. You're safe now. We're both safe." I put my hands to her face and whispered to her in English and French, urging her out of the darkness.

She stopped rocking and her eyes flew open as she struggled to focus.

"Désirée? Désirée! Oh no! He'll find you! He's coming back. Oh god, he's coming back! We have to hide. He'll find you. Oh god, oh god, oh god..." She grabbed my arms, desperate to flee.

"Who, Evie? Who is coming back? Tell me who hurt you, Evie." I cradled her face as panic filled her eyes. She clutched my arms, frantic to make me understand the danger.

"Carson! Carson Bentley!" she cried. "He said he was going to kill you, then come back, but you're here. Oh, God, we have to hide. He's going to kill us!"

I pulled her close, holding on tight, my tears falling silently on her head. "No, Evie, no. He's never coming back. Carson is dead. He's gone forever, and he won't hurt anyone, ever again."

"Ahh!" she cried, collapsing into my arms, her numbed keening changing into a conscious misery. "He hurt me, Désirée. He hurt me, he hurt me."

"I know, Evie, but it's over now. You're safe, and Johanna is here to take care of you. You're going to be alright... we both are." I let her spill all her anguish onto me. I deserved it because I had caused it.

Johanna stood at the foot of the bed, gently untying the restraints from Evie's legs, then priming a syringe. "It will help her sleep," she whispered when I questioned her with a look.

I nodded and motioned her forward.

"Evie, Johanna is here to help you." I lifted Evie's face off my shoulder so she could see Johanna's face.

"Hello, Miss Evelyn. I'm your nurse, Johanna. I'm going to help you feel better, dear." Johanna rubbed Evie's arm, quickly administered the sedative, then laid a gentle hand upon Evie's head as I lay her back onto the bed.

"You're safe now, Evie. You're not alone anymore. Sleep, *mon amie*, dream sweet dreams. I'll come to see you tomorrow." As I held her hand, Evie slowly drifted off into what I hoped would be gentler dreams.

Johanna nodded as Doctor Neville came into the room. "She's asleep now, Doctor."

He checked Evie's pulse and lifted one eyelid, but Evie lay as still as stone in her drug-induced slumber. I prayed she wasn't back in the nightmare, but her breathing was steady, and her body relaxed with only an occasional whimper passing from her lips.

"Please don't tie her up again. She needs to feel that she can break out of the nightmare. If she's tied up, she can't escape it."

"We're monitoring her closely," said Doctor Neville. "I believe you've helped her take the first step out of that darkness. Thank you, Miss Gautier. How are you?" His eyes held understanding and sympathy as he led me to the door.

My hand flew up to my mouth as I stumbled out of the room and into the hall, then pressed my face to the wall, sobbing uncontrollably. Why had I survived with my mind intact, relatively speaking, and poor Evie lay shattered and lost? It wasn't fair.

"Miss Gautier? Are you alright?" Detective Guardino asked, holding out a handkerchief to me.

With a monumental effort, I swallowed my sobs, dried my tears with his handkerchief, and straightened my shoulders before turning to face him. "Do you believe me now, Detective?"

"I never doubted you, Miss Gautier. The only problem remaining is discovering Mr. Bentley's motives."

"Only a sick mind could do that to a woman," Doctor Neville said, nodding toward Evie.

"Or an evil one," I added. "I'm coming to see her every day until she's better. If that's alright, Doctor."

"Of course. I believe that will benefit you both. I'll walk you out," he said, heading down the hall toward the staircase leading to the lobby.

"When do you think Miss Duret will be capable of speaking with me, Doctor? We need her full statement about what happened," the detective asked, obviously eager to close the case, or at least that part of it.

"Miss Duret is currently in a fragile state, Detective Guardino. I don't want to push her too hard. Let's give it a few days. I'll let you know."

Maybe Bobby's threat affected him after all, or maybe Doctor Neville was a decent man who wanted to protect his patient. Time would tell.

As we headed into the lobby, Detective Guardino slowed his pace to walk next to me. "Thank you, Miss Gautier. The city owes you an enormous debt of thanks. Without you, those murders would still be unsolved, and I believe there would have been more."

I shook my head as I handed his handkerchief back and kept walking. "I doubt the District Attorney shares your point of view, detective; otherwise, why convene a grand jury to decide if he should charge me with Carson's death?"

I had to get out of there as fast as possible, craved fresh air and desperately needed privacy to release all this misery with a good, long cry. One look at the worried faces of Bobby, Bill, and Charlie sent me straight for the front door without stopping. They could hear the news of Evie from Doctor Neville and Detective Guardino.

In the shade of an oak tree, I stood by the car, trying to light a cigarette with trembling hands and calm my racing heart. Waves of guilt and regret relentlessly washed over me. If I had been braver, if I had told someone about Carson sooner, then Evie wouldn't be there. She'd be home preparing for her next Mardi Gras party, not lying bruised and battered in a tormented nightmare. Somehow, even at the risk of losing myself, I would make it up to her, help her back into her life, or some version of it.

Chapter 7

Starting Over

Thankfully, the ride home was quiet. My three heroes had nothing to say, or if they did, they kept it to themselves while stealing sidelong glances at me. In the silence, I remained composed, holding back the flood of tears threatening to break loose, and stifling the overwhelming guilt ready to shatter me beyond repair. I managed, just barely, because I had to. Falling apart wasn't an option if I was going to be any help to Evie.

By the time Charlie finally pulled into the driveway, I felt guilty relief at being home and at knowing I'd be sleeping in my own room or at least trying to. As soon as the car stopped, I ran up the back stairs to seek whatever privacy my room would offer.

When I stepped into the kitchen, Jolie got a good look at me and her expression changed from relief at seeing me, to concern at my miserable state. "Was it as bad as all that?"

"It was worse." That was as much as I could say.

Charlie, Bill and Bobby came in wearing matching worried looks, but I turned away, heading for the stairs and the sanctuary of my room.

"Are you hungry?" Jolie asked before I could walk away. "I roasted a chicken using a recipe I found in one of your cooking journals. Stuffed the bird with lemons. I can have it on the table in a couple of minutes."

"No thanks, Jolie. I'm sorry," I said, hurrying away before I completely lost control.

"Dez?" Bobby reached for me, but I couldn't let him touch me, couldn't bear receiving the sympathy I didn't deserve.

"Let her go, Bobby. She needs some time," Bill said as I fled the kitchen. "Jolie, that chicken smells delicious. Any chance we can get some lunch?"

Hours passed before I went back downstairs. Night had fallen while I lingered in my misery.

"Did you get some rest?" Bill asked from the corner of the living room. He was deep in shadow, his expression unclear until briefly lit by the glow of his cigarette as he took a drag. That fleeting glimpse revealed the same expression he'd been wearing since Saturday; regret, worry, and sadness, and maybe a need to fix this, to fix me.

"No, not really. Have Bobby and Jolie gone to bed already?" I asked, unsure of the time.

"Yes, a while ago. Jolie didn't want to disturb you, so she's in the other bedroom. It's after midnight, Chére."

"I'm sorry, I... couldn't face anyone after seeing Evie... Were you there, Bill, when the police found her? Did you see what Carson did to her?" I asked, stepping into the dark living room and sitting on the couch with a pillow in my lap.

"Yes, I saw. The poor thing was out of her mind, completely hysterical, but I carried her out of the cabin and stayed with her until the ambulance got there. I hear she's coming out of it with your help."

"How did you know where to find her?"

I could see he didn't want to tell me, but he was unwilling to deny me the truth. With a deep sigh he began. “After I left Mama's on Wednesday night, Luke and I went to the Bentley place to search for the evidence he was holding against you. I knew come morning, the police would be swarming all over that place, and I couldn’t risk them finding anything that could put you in jeopardy.”

“Luke waited outside to keep watch while I went in to search. I found nothing in Carson's office or bedroom, then I remembered about a secret room hidden inside his closet. I hadn't thought about it in years. No bigger than six by nine, we used to play in there, out of sight of his sister and any inquiring adults. Carson and I used that tiny space as a secret playhouse until we both grew out of it, in size and interest.”

“When I stepped inside it felt like being sucker-punched. It took a minute for me to catch my breath and understand what I was looking at. What I found turned my entire relationship with Carson upside down.”

“In the middle of the room sat a swivel chair with a small table next to it holding a half empty bottle of bourbon, two crystal glasses, cigarette butts in the ashtray, and a pocketknife stuck into the table. The suit I lent to him was hanging on a valet stand next to the chair. Carson had spilled wine on himself last spring at the start of a dinner party at my place in the city, so I lent him one of my Brooks Brothers suits. There it was, suit, shirt and tie, like I was sitting there with him in his twisted version of reality. I don't know why I hadn’t seen this side of him, why I hadn't recognized the depth of his obsession with me. As sick as I felt, I could almost feel sympathy for him, holding onto feelings he could do nothing about. I had some experience with that myself.” He took a drag off his cigarette then a sip from his glass before continuing his story with a faraway look in his eyes.

"The right end of the room looked like an altar where Carson harbored his most secret desire. A low shelf held three framed photos. One of me looking off to my right, my senior photo from Harvard. A photo of Carson sat next to it, looking to the left. He'd positioned them to appear as if we were gazing at each other. Between them was a smaller photo of Charlotte, her debut portrait. Dozens of photos covered the wall behind the shelf, a few of him and Charlotte, but most were of Carson and me, spanning years of our friendship from childhood through college. There was a photo of us fishing off the dock at the Bentley fishing camp on the Little Irish Bayou."

"The closet door had swung shut, and the wall behind it gave me another punch to the gut. Photos of you covered the wall from top to bottom, all taken over the past four years. School photos, newspaper images (what few made it past Charlie's censure), and several random shots, taken without your knowledge. There were a few of Mama, Charlie, and Uncle Henri mixed in among them. Every image had cut marks through it, as if Carson used the wall for target practice. He had tacked a lock of golden blonde hair to the center photo of you and the thought of how he acquired that prize sickened me. I took it down, slipped it in my pocket, then I left, leaving the door ajar for the police to find. If they're any good at their jobs, they'll find that room. It explains Carson's attack on you better than anything."

"Whatever evidence he had on you, he didn't keep it there, but I found something I should have seen long ago. I've been a fool, Chére. My loyalty to Carson, to our friendship, blinded me to who he really was, and you paid the price."

"He wouldn't have hurt Evie if I wasn't such a coward, if I had said something to Mama or Charlie months ago."

"There's a big difference between cowardice and fear, Chére. You were afraid of hurting Mama and the family, of hurting me. You were afraid of what would happen if I killed him... and as sure as I'm sitting here, I would have. What happened to Evelyn wasn't your fault. You're not responsible for Carson's crimes."

Bill couldn't absolve me of the guilt I felt because it was my choice to remain silent, not only to protect them but also to protect myself, as I'd been doing for years.

"Maybe not," I said with a heavy sigh, "but Carson was right about one thing... none of it would have happened if you had never met me. A lot of people might still be alive if I had stayed in France, where I belonged."

"You wouldn't have survived there, Désirée. I brought you here because I couldn't bear the thought of losing you. If anyone should feel guilty about this, it's me. I led you into the lion's den and left you to fend for yourself. I'm the one responsible, not you."

There was so much guilt and regret contaminating the lake house, the one place I'd always felt good in. I couldn't help feeling responsible.

"I'm sorry I invaded your home with all this, Bill. If I'd known you were living here... It's just that this felt like the safest place to be, where I could be alone to think things through, where I could heal a little before..."

"This place is yours, Chére. It's been yours since the first time I brought you here. Remember? You said this place felt like home, so I've tried to make it that for you, to save it for you."

"It's funny I said that, because this house wasn't like any I'd ever lived in before, but it felt so good here; peaceful, the way it felt on the farm when I was little. Now I'm ruining it like I ruined Mama's place, like the Nazis ruined Papa's farm. I'm sorry, I just didn't know where else to go."

"This is your home, Chére, for as long as you want it. The rest of us are guests, here to help in any way we can. But the last thing I want is to make you uncomfortable, so if you prefer that I not be here, I can move into town."

That he should leave me was the last thing I wanted, even though I'd been avoiding him in the daylight hours. "No Bill. I don't prefer that. I just need time to figure things out."

"Take all the time you need, Chére. When you're ready, I'll be here waiting, and if it's easier to talk to me in the dark, then that's okay, too."

"Thank you, Bill. I think I'll try to get some sleep now. Goodnight."

"Goodnight, Désirée, Sweet dreams."

The dark cloud hanging over me the day before wasn't gone when I woke up, but at least it transformed. Swirling pink clouds greeted me as I opened my eyes to the rosy light streaming through my bedroom window, bathing the room with a warm glow.

A good omen, according to Papa. *"Red sky in the morning means good fishing, ma petite."*

Maybe today will be better. I hoped so.

Jolie and Bobby were at the kitchen table talking when I walked in. Ashamed of how thoughtless I'd been, I hung my head, unable to face them, as I poured my coffee and searched for the right words to apologize. They both had put their lives on hold to help me, and I'd thoughtlessly ignored them, had pulled away because I couldn't share the truth with them.

After taking a few sips of coffee for fortification, I turned to face them. "I'm sorry I've been such a terrible hostess." It was the best I could do without bursting into tears.

"Hostess? I didn't expect a party. Did you expect a party, Bobby?" Jolie asked, shaking her head like she wasn't sure she heard me right.

Bobby shook his head. "Nope, not even a picnic. You feeling any better today, Dez?"

I put my cup on the table and sat down across from him, then dropped my face into my hand. After taking a few deep breaths and rubbing my temples, I answered him.

"I'm not sure I know what better is supposed to feel like. What have you two been doing?" I asked, wanting to redirect the conversation away from me.

They gave each other a knowing look, two sets of dark eyebrows raised to equal heights, then Jolie answered after dishing up a plate of bacon and eggs and setting it in front of me.

"We've been getting to know each other, comparing notes on you. Eat up, Désirée."

"Did you find any contradictions?" I asked, ignoring the plate of food in favor of my coffee cup.

"Only that I knew about Bobby, but he didn't know about me. Doesn't matter, Désirée. I always knew you didn't tell him about us. Eat your breakfast, girl. You can't live on just coffee and cigarettes."

"I'm sorry Jolie." There was so much to be sorry for, and finding forgiveness felt like an impossible mountain to climb, so I tried changing the subject again. "Has Bill been down yet?"

"Bill's gone to town; said he had some things to do for Charlie today and that he'd be back for supper," Bobby explained. "He said he's going to stop by Miss Bea's on the way home, so if you need anything from there, you can call Laila and let her know."

I thought about all the things I'd left behind and realized none of it was essential anymore. "Bobby, will you go with me this morning to visit Evie?"

He looked worried, and I couldn't blame him. "You sure you want to go there again today, Dez? Yesterday was kinda hard on you."

"Evie needs me, and I need to be there for her. Will you go?"

"Course I will."

"Désirée, you ain't going anywhere until you eat something," Jolie said, giving me a commanding look that would accept nothing less than compliance.

I rolled my eyes and shrugged. "Yes, Miss Jolie, I'll eat, but may I have more coffee, please?"

"Miss Gautier and Mr. Easton, to see Miss Duret," Bobby informed the guard at the gate to Glen Oaks while I clenched my hands together in the front seat next to him.

The man wrote our names on his clipboard, then stared at me for an inordinately long time, like he was trying to decide if I was really who he thought I was. His scrutiny made me feel exposed, unsure of myself, as if I shouldn't be there.

The receptionist in the lobby gave me a similar look when Bobby and I walked in, but she tried to hide it behind a gracious smile. "Good morning, Miss Gautier. How *are* you today?"

"I'm fine, thank you. I'd like to visit with Miss Duret, please."

"Yes, of course. Doctor Neville said to expect you this morning. I'll let them know you're here."

Bobby and I stepped out of earshot to await my escort.

"Are you gonna be alright, Dez?" he asked.

I didn't know for sure. I certainly didn't know what to say that would make all this easier for him.

"Yes, Bobby, I will be," I said, because if I said it, then maybe I could believe it, at least I hoped so.

"Miss Gautier. I'm here to take you to Miss Duret. Follow me," said an orderly in a white lab coat, waiting in the hallway to lead me into the bowels of Glen Oaks.

I followed the man to Evie's room, and with each step I worried that she'd fallen back into the nightmare. Once we reached her room, he opened the door for me to enter, then closed it behind me.

"Good morning, Miss Gautier," Johanna greeted me with a warm smile. "Evelyn is doing better today."

Better was a matter of perspective. She wasn't strapped down—thank God—but she wasn't anywhere close to my version of better. Evie lay on the bed curled into a tight ball, trembling under the blanket, clutching it to her tear-stained face.

"*Bonjour, Evie. C'est moi, Désirée. Je suis là, mon amie.*" Would she remember? I didn't know, but I had to reach her any way I could.

"*Comment ça va, Evie? Dis-moi.*"

"Désirée ? Est-ce vraiment toi? Am I dreaming?" she asked from beneath the blanket.

"No Evie, you're not dreaming. It's really me. I'm here," I said, as I sat on the bed next to her, pulling the blanket away from her face so she could see me.

Through blurry, bloodshot eyes, she tried to focus on my face as she struggled to sit up. "You were in my dream, in that horrible place, and I couldn't escape until... you found me. Were you really there?"

"Yes, I was there, and I brought you back. You're here now, Evie. You're safe."

"Where am I? Where's my mother?"

"You're in the hospital at Glen Oaks. Your mother will be here soon." I hoped so, anyway.

"What happened, Désirée? Am I sick?"

"Don't you remember?"

Her shaking head and hollow-eyed stare said she didn't, said she blocked the details from her conscious mind, or the medication Doctor Neville prescribed had done it for her. Either way, I envied her that oblivion and was grateful she had it. Soon enough, her memories would return, and she would relive the nightmare all over again, only this time in the light of day.

"Maybe you can encourage her to eat, Miss Gautier," Johanna said, placing a tray with a cup of something hot and a packet of crackers on the table next to the bed. "Here's a cuppa warm broth for you, Miss Evelyn. You try to get some of this down now. It will make you feel better."

Evie looked up at her, unsure and confused. "Do I know you?"

"I'm Johanna, your nurse. We met yesterday. Remember?"

Evie shook her head, unable to grasp what was happening to her as tears filled her eyes, then fell down her cheeks while her trembling fingers covered her mouth.

"It's alright, Evie. Here, sip on this." I held the cup of broth to her mouth and urged her to drink a little.

It took a long time, but sip by sip the broth filled her starving body, fed her tortured mind with warm, nourishing comfort. She drank without complaint until the cup was nearly empty, then she lay back on her pillows, ready for a nap, like a child with a full belly. In the end, the effort was worth it.

I felt more confident than when I arrived. Evie would recover, with enough time and support, which meant so would I, though we both still had a long way to go.

She was almost asleep when I bent down to say goodbye.

"*À bientôt.* I'll see you soon."

When I came into the lobby to rejoin Bobby, he was talking with Doctor Neville just outside the administration office, their postures uneasy, effectively amping up my anxiety.

"Security just informed me Mrs. Duret has arrived," Doctor Neville said, with a look that held both relief and concern. "Could you stay for a moment, Miss Gautier, to let her know how Evelyn is doing today?" He looked as if he wanted my help, but I didn't understand why.

"Of course. Evie's a little better today," I said, though I felt certain he was aware of his patient's condition better than me. "At least she's talking clearer, but she doesn't remember why she's here. It's too hard to think about. She drank some broth, then fell asleep."

Just then Mrs. Duret came through the lobby door, clutching her handbag close to her body, appearing self-conscious, as if she feared being recognized. She headed straight toward us, then slowed her pace when she recognized me.

"You're here," she said with a look of disbelief.

"Evie asked for you today, madame. She's sleeping now, but she'll be relieved to see you when she wakes up."

Mrs. Duret covered her face with her gloved hand. "Oh, dear God, what am I to do?"

Doctor Neville put his arm around her shoulder to lead her out of the lobby. "Come, let's talk in my office, Mrs. Duret." He gave me a look that suggested he wanted me to join them, so I followed, with Bobby trailing behind.

"Please, make yourself comfortable, Mrs. Duret. Can I get you some water?" Doctor Neville asked, leading her to the small sofa. I sat in one of the side chairs facing her, and Bobby stood out of the way against the wall by the door, his face tense and arms crossed.

"No, thank you, doctor," Mrs. Duret said, dabbing her moist eyes with a hankie and straightening her back as if she was about to face her worst fear.

"My husband is insisting I have Evelyn transferred to another facility, as far from New Orleans as possible. I'm sorry, Doctor Neville, but this morning's paper convinced Jonathan that this scandal will ruin him. He said we can't afford a private hospital for Evelyn. Can you suggest an alternative?"

"No, madame! You can't send Evie away!" I cried, nearly jumping out of my seat. "She needs you and her family to help her recover. Please, madame, don't do this."

Doctor Neville gave her a compassionate look, but I could see his concern for Evie's future. "The alternatives in Louisiana are Central State or Eastern State Hospital, Mrs. Duret, and neither facility can offer Evelyn the type of care she requires or would receive here at Glen Oaks. However, if you wish to have your daughter transferred, you can choose to do so. All that's required is your signature."

I couldn't believe what I was hearing. How could Doctor Neville let her do this?

"Oh... I see," Mrs. Duret said, with a glimmer of hope in her eyes. "But they would take care of her there, and she would recover in time, right, doctor?"

"No, madame, she won't!" I said as forcefully as I could. My friend's survival was in serious jeopardy, and, therefore, so was mine. I couldn't let this happen if I could prevent it.

"Evie will die if you send her away. She needs your help. Please don't abandon her."

"If it's a matter of money, Mrs. Duret, you don't need to worry about it," Bobby said, stepping forward so Evie's mother could see he meant what he said. "I'll make sure you don't receive a bill for Evie's care here at Glen Oaks." He glanced over at Doctor Neville, who acknowledged Bobby's wishes with a nod.

"That's very kind of you, Mr. Easton, but I'm afraid my husband is insistent. Jonathan would never forgive me if I disobeyed him," she said, holding the hankie to her mouth with a trembling hand.

I couldn't hold back my fear and frustration any longer. "Evie is your daughter, madame. What is more important, obedience to your husband or your daughter's life?"

She looked at me for the longest time, just staring like she didn't recognize me, though she'd seen me ten days earlier at the Revelers' Ball. Her brow pinched into a sharp crease above her nose, then she sighed, consciously easing her face, dropping her shoulders, and adjusting her composure.

"Evelyn is, but my husband won't understand. Tell me, Désirée, how can you be... like this," she said, waving her hand at me, "and my Evelyn is so broken? Why aren't you?" Her accusation meant my survival was suspect.

"We are different, madame. I am stronger because I've had to be."

It was an explanation she could accept, acknowledging the pampered life she'd given Evie and measuring it against what she knew of my history, which was a fabrication of tragic half-truths.

"May I see my daughter now, Doctor Neville?" she asked, standing to effectively end the meeting.

"Of course, Mrs. Duret. I'll take you to her. Désirée, Mr. Easton, thank you for your time. You know the way out."

Chapter 8

An uneasy compromise

By silent agreement, Bobby and I didn't talk until we drove off the Glen Oaks property and were well on our way back to the lake house.

"Why would Mr. Duret want to abandon his daughter?" I asked, though I didn't expect Bobby to know. "None of this was Evie's fault. Do you think he can make Doctor Neville transfer her to the state hospital? Can he do that?"

"I don't know, Dez, but I'll call my attorney to find out. Don't worry, we won't let anything bad happen to Evie, not if we can prevent it."

"I'm afraid, Bobby. If Evie doesn't make it through this, then neither will I."

"Don't say things like that, Dez. I can't lose you, so we'll do whatever it takes to help her. Okay?"

"Thanks, Bobby."

As I sorted away the events of the past few hours, I kept wondering if Evie's mother was brave enough to stand up to her husband. Elanor Duret was a prim and proper wife, always deferential to her husband, and I feared she might change her mind once she saw Evie.

My cigarette case revealed only two cigarettes, a situation requiring immediate action. I lit one with Bill's old Zippo lighter, blowing the smoke out the window so it wouldn't bother Bobby—he didn't smoke or drink. Between the two of us, I'd always been the rebel.

"Can I ask you for a favor, Bobby? Will you stop in Mandeville on the way home? I need cigarettes, and I want to replace Bill's whiskey. Would you get them for me?" I needed his help because I was still under the legal age to purchase tobacco and alcohol, at least for the next four months. Bobby might scold me for drinking and smoking, but it was worth it under the circumstances.

"Sure. We can stop," he said, giving me a well-deserved frown.

A few minutes later, Bobby parked the car in front of Smokes & Spirits a few blocks from the house.

"Wait here, Dez. I'll be right back."

While I waited, I stared out the windshield, and something caught my attention. I grabbed a nickel out of my wallet, got out of the car, and stood in front of the newspaper stand outside the store, just staring down at the headline, *Is the Phantom's Reign of Terror Over?*

"That you, Désirée?" a voice behind me called out. I turned around to find Mr. Daniels coming across the street. He was an old friend of Uncle Henri's, and a neighbor on Lakeshore Drive, who made it his business to keep up with all the comings and goings of Mandeville. "I thought I recognized you. You're not usually 'round here till summer."

"Hello, Mr. Daniels. Summer came early this year." I looked down at the headline, trying to decide if I was brave enough to read what they wrote. I put the nickel in the slot, then lifted the door and removed the newspaper.

"Why ya wanna go reading that, girl? For my money, the police commissioner and mayor oughta be giving you a parade and the key to the city. They should thank you for doing their job for them."

"That's not likely to happen, but thank you for the support."

"Well, don't you be paying no never mind to them gossip mongers, Désirée. Folks that know you will stand by you, so you keep your chin up and you'll be alright."

"Thank you, sir. Nice seeing you," I said as Bobby came out of the store with his arms full.

"Ready, Dez? Oh, how you doing, Mr. Daniels?" Obviously self-conscious about being caught coming out of Smokes & Spirits, Bobby quickly stashed the bag in the back seat of the car.

"Right as rain, Mr. Easton. Glad to see you're here looking out for your girl. Y'all take care now."

"Yes, sir. You have a nice day," Bobby said as we got in the car.

Halfway down the block, Bobby blew out a breath. "Damn, that was bad luck."

"He means well, Bobby, but if people didn't already know I'm here, they will now."

"What's all this? Are we having a party?" Jolie asked as Bobby dropped the bag on the kitchen counter and she started unpacking it. Bobby had gone overboard at Smokes & Spirits, buying two cartons of cigarettes, two bottles of whiskey, and two bottles of red wine, a Merlot from California, which I suspected he intended to taste.

Grateful for his thoughtfulness and generosity, I gave him an unexpected hug. "No, not a party, Jolie, just fortification." A little extra wouldn't hurt.

"How was your friend today? Any better?" Jolie asked.

"A little, but then there's this." I tossed the newspaper on the table, the bold headline glaring up at us. Reading it felt impossible, but I figured knowing what it said was better than staying in the dark and worrying about it.

"Yeah, I heard about it. The telephone started ringing soon as you left this morning; people asking after you and wanting to talk about that article in the paper. I told them I'd take their messages, but you aren't talking to anybody right now. Here, this one's yours, and the other is for you, Bobby. Your father wants you to call him as soon as you can," Jolie said, retrieving a couple of pieces of paper from her pocket, handing one to Bobby and the other to me.

"Thanks, Jolie." Bobby took his messages and headed for the phone in Bill's office.

"Are you alright, Désirée?" Jolie asked with that same worried look she'd worn since Saturday.

I wished everyone would stop asking me that. All it did was remind me I wasn't alright, that if I was even going to get close to being alright, I needed to make amends to Evie. But they all needed reassurance, so I tried to ease their minds by putting on the bravest face I could, drawing on my years of practice.

I opened one of the cigarette cartons, took out a pack to refill my case, then sat down at the kitchen table to fill it. "I'm okay... I guess. How are you? This can't be much fun for you."

Jolie sat down across from me and lit the last cigarette from my case. "I didn't expect it to be. I'm keeping busy, taking messages, cleaning this big old house, and cooking for y'all, but I miss my cooking buddy, so anytime you feel like it, you can jump in and lend a hand."

That earned her a smile. "I will, Jolie, but can you give me a little time to pull myself together?"

"I got nothing but time, Désirée, and the kitchen ain't going anywhere."

"Thanks. Good to know," I said, grabbing the newspaper and my cigarette case. "I'll be upstairs... doing a little reading."

I settled into a comfortable chair on the upper terrace where I could read in private. Most of the messages were from people I expected; Mama, Charlie, Uncle Henri, and Sarah calling from New York, but there were a couple of names I didn't recognize, and I wondered who they were and how they knew where to find me. I put the list aside to deal with after reading the newspaper.

The Times-Picayune declared, according to police sources, that the Phantoms' latest victim, Evelyn Duret, had positively identified him. They also printed side-by-side photos of Carson Bentley, Evie, and me, adding as many salacious details about Carson's death as they could, while still maintaining respectability. The reference to the eminent grand jury inquest, scheduled for Wednesday morning, lent a seemingly unbiased slant to the story. But to me, it sounded like a reassurance to the public that the streets of New Orleans were now safe, and Mardi Gras will go on unhampered. It also left the reader with questions. Why would a prominent businessman, a respected member of the community, commit these horrendous crimes? How did a seventeen-year-old girl, barely half his size, bring his reign of terror to an end and survive relatively unharmed? The story left a lot of room for speculation, for the reader to draw their own conclusions, and there wasn't a damn thing I could do about that. I threw the paper aside in frustration.

What does it matter, Désirée? You're on borrowed time here, anyway.

Even if Carson's threat to expose me was an empty one, I was still a liability for Bill, for his career and reputation, for his family. Someone else could start asking questions, dig deeper into my background, and unravel the web of lies I'd woven for the past four and a half years. The sooner I left, the better it would be for all of them.

"Why'd you want to read that, Dez?" Bobby asked as he sat down next to me, moving the paper aside so he could place two glasses of sweet tea on the table between us.

I sipped the tea and stared out at the lake, wondering how I was going to get him to go back to school and away from all this scandal. My troubles weren't anything Bobby needed, and the longer he stayed, the more involved he would get. I couldn't let that happen.

"I just wanted to know what the paper was saying. Knowing is better than wondering."

He shook his head, unwilling to argue the pros and cons of knowing.

"I talked to Jimmy. He really wants to see you, Dez. I told him I'd ask."

Jimmy Wilcox was as loyal a friend as anyone could hope for, always there whenever needed. I didn't want him worrying or thinking too much about what he'd seen the night I killed Carson, and the only way to prevent that was to see him and talk with him face to face.

"Sure, Bobby," I said, scrubbing my face with my hands. "He can come by, but only Jimmy, okay? I'm not very good company right now. Did you talk with your father?"

"I'll call him later. He'll want me to go into town to have dinner with him and his new wife, but I'm not ready for that yet. Not this trip, anyway."

"He'll want you to go back to school, Bobby, and so do I. You can't stay here much longer. People are going to get the wrong impression, especially once they read today's paper. It's bad enough all this has ruined my reputation. I don't want it to ruin yours."

"Do you think I give a damn what any of those people think? I can count on one hand the number of people in that town who really know who I am, and one of them is sitting in front of me. It's what they'll say about you I care about. I want to be here to defend you," he said, as if his chivalry could wipe the events of the past week off my reputation.

"I used to care what people thought, Bobby, and I conformed to their expectations, but that was before. It's different now, I'm different. What they think or say about me doesn't matter anymore. Once this is over, I intend to live my life without compromise. End of story." It sounded easy, even though I knew it wouldn't be, but he needed to know that I would be alright if he left. I needed him to believe it.

"Okay, Dez. I'll tell Jimmy to come on Thursday, if that's alright."

"Sure, Thursday is fine." Maybe Jimmy could help me convince Bobby to go back to school.

The air was thick with tension around the dinner table that night. I'd never been comfortable being the center of attention, but the newspaper headline put me in the thick of it.

Prior to serving the meal, Jolie and I had a brief but heated discussion in the kitchen regarding her place at the table. I prevailed, insisting she eat with the rest of us and not by herself in the kitchen, like a servant.

After we served the meal—crab and avocado salad and seared tenderloin bites with roasted sweet potatoes—Jolie and I sat down at the table, joining a trio of lowered heads. Bill, Luke, and Bobby sat silently, waiting for someone to open the conversation. It was like they were sitting on eggshells, too afraid to address the elephant in the room, namely me.

"It would help if all of you would stop acting like I'm going to fall apart. I won't, no matter what the paper writes about me," I said to the entire table, avoiding direct eye contact with Bill.

"Glad to hear it, Désirée," Luke said, a smile reaching his eyes as he nodded across the table to me.

Jolie leaned against my shoulder. "Of course you are. You even helped in the kitchen tonight. Eat up, everybody, before it gets cold."

That gave them permission to keep their mouths busy and their thoughts to themselves until Bill piped up.

"How was Evelyn today?" he asked, looking at me for the answer.

It was too hard to look at him. The feeling of shame was too difficult to disguise, so I directed my gaze to his barely touched plate.

"A little better. At least they're not keeping her strapped down anymore. She has nightmares, but she can't or doesn't want to remember what happened. I just hope she's still there when I go back to see her."

"Why wouldn't she be?" Bill asked, glancing from me to Bobby.

I shook my head and let Bobby recount the Duret family drama that unfolded at Glen Oaks and explain how we tried to prevent further tragedy.

"What good is all this Montgomery money if I don't use it to help my friends?" Bobby asked, looking around the table and resting his eyes on me. "Besides, Désirée, I didn't do it just for Evie. I did it for you. You need her as much as she needs you."

"I guess we'll find out if your generosity made any difference." I hoped it did, because I wasn't sure what I would do if Evie's mother obeyed her husband and sent her away.

It was after midnight when I went downstairs, half dreading, half hoping Bill would be there, sitting in the dark, waiting for me. I walked softly, my bare feet making no sound on the oak floor as I headed for the bar cart in the dining room.

With only the kitchen light to guide my hand, I poured the whiskey. Two fingers full was enough to get me through the night.

"You didn't need to stop at Bart's today, Chére. There's half a case of whiskey and cigarettes in the closet under the stairs. If you need anything, let me know, and I'll get it for you."

When I turned to face him, he was standing in the dark, just inside the living room. I held the glass to my chest, then reached into my pocket and pulled out a piece of paper with the questionable names underlined, then handed it to him.

"Maybe you can tell me if you recognize these names: Phillip Reynolds and Harlan Kimble. They called here today, asking for me. I don't know who they are, do you?"

He held the paper up to what light there was, his expression darkening as he read it.

"The name Phillip Reynolds doesn't ring any bells, but I can trace the number and see where it leads. Harlan Kimble is a reporter for the Times-Picayune. He called me today and was told the Marchand family wasn't giving any interviews, but he's obviously a persistent fellow. I'll talk with his editor tomorrow."

"Doesn't Charlie usually handle these things?"

"Charlie has his hands full, Chére. He'll meet us at the courthouse tomorrow morning, but then he has to leave."

It wasn't like Charlie to leave in the middle of a crisis, and this situation certainly qualified.

"Where is he going? Why would he leave Julianna at a time like this?"

"He's not leaving her, Chére. He's taking Jules to her brothers' home in Boston. Her doctor has ordered complete bedrest for the remainder of her pregnancy. Charlie felt Jules would do better in Boston than here at home, at least for now. Madalyn is going with her."

"Oh, I didn't know. I guess you've got your hands full now, too. Watching over me and holding the fort for Charlie." I wondered if the added stress was more than Bill bargained for.

"I can handle it."

"Will they be alright? Julianna and the baby?" I needed some reassurance that another tragedy wasn't on the horizon.

"I think so. Are you ready for tomorrow?" He needed his own reassurance.

"Yes... I hope so. Goodnight, Bill."

Chapter 9

The Inquisition

Despite my prayers for a hurricane, Wednesday dawned bright and clear. The last thing I wanted to do was recount in vivid detail the worst night of my life to a room full of strange men, trying to convince them of my innocence, but that was what I had to do. If I succeeded, I would be free of all charges in Carson's death. If I failed, they would arrest me on the spot, and the house of cards I'd built would crumble, potentially burying the people I loved. Definitely not something to look forward to.

"Here Désirée. Let me tie this scarf around your neck to cover up those bruises," Jolie said as she finished brushing the tangles from my hair.

The bruises on my face were fading to a sickly greenish yellow, but the ones around my throat were still dark and ugly, physical evidence of what I'd been through.

I wore my favorite outfit, the one I felt the most comfortable in; slip-on shoes, pleated slacks, a white button-up blouse, left open at the collar, and a lightweight jacket. I figured there was no sense in dressing up for this sideshow.

"No, thanks, Jolie. If I must endure this farce, then I want them to see what Carson did to me."

Bill knocked on the door and poked his head in. "Are you ready, Chére? We need to get on the road. It will take about an hour to get there, and we need to speak with Charlie before they call you in. He's meeting us at the courthouse."

"I'm ready, Bill. Let's get this over with." I gave Jolie a hug before following Bill downstairs.

"Are you sure I can't go with you, Désirée?" Bobby asked as he walked us to the car.

"I'm sure, Bobby. Charlie said they won't let you in, and I don't want you involved in this. Anyway, Charlie said it's just a formality. I'll be back this afternoon." I'm not sure if I convinced him, but he gave me a fierce hug before he let me go.

Twelve massive Corinthian columns formed the portico entrance to the Orleans Parish Criminal Courthouse on Tulane Avenue. Above them, carved in granite, were the words: *The Impartial Administration of Justice is the Foundation of Liberty*. As Luke parked the car in front of the imposing building, I wondered if I would really find impartiality in there or if societal and political pressures would require a scapegoat.

"Ready, Chére?" Bill asked, opening the car door for me.

My heart was beating too fast, my mind racing through all the potential outcomes.

"As ready as I'll ever be," I said, reaching for his hand as I stepped out of the car.

Charlie was waiting for us in the lobby when we entered the courthouse. Still looking tired but confident—which calmed my racing heart a bit—he scanned me for signs of distress, gently touched my cheek, then led us up a flight of stairs and down a long hallway into a private waiting room.

"They'll call you in when they're ready for you, darlin'. Just try to relax. This should be over soon," Charlie said as I sat down in one of the uncomfortable wooden chairs.

"Will you be there with me, Charlie?"

He shook his head, regret filling his eyes. "I petitioned the judge to allow me to accompany you because of your age, but he denied my request. This is a closed hearing with only the DA, the grand jury, a judge, and the testifying witness present. It's not like a regular trial, Désirée. The purpose is to determine if they should file criminal charges. The DA will ask the questions, and he'll be thorough, but all you have to do is tell them exactly what happened last week."

"Why are they doing this? They have my written statement and the reports from the detectives and Doctor Easton. Why are they putting me through this?"

It was Bill who answered, his anger and frustration pouring out in waves as he paced around the small room.

"Simmons is planning to run for mayor and needs a feather in his cap," Bill snarled. "The unsolved Phantom murders have been a stumbling block to his ambitions until now. He needs to make sure he's dotted all his I's and crossed all his T's in the matter of Carson's death before he can claim success in ultimately closing the high-profile Phantom case."

"So, I'm his tool, and my humiliation is of little concern. How chivalrous of him." Once again, I felt the weight of being a pawn in someone else's game.

Then someone knocked and opened the door. A well-dressed man in his thirties stepped into the room.

"They're ready for you, Miss Gautier. Please follow me. Gentlemen, you can wait here," he said with a nod to Charlie and Bill.

After taking a deep breath, I stood up to face Fate once more. Bill caught my hand before I walked away.

"We'll be here waiting, Désirée." He touched my cheek and placed a tender kiss on my forehead before letting me go. That gesture felt better than anything I could have hoped for.

Be brave. Be strong. Be clever. I kept repeating that to myself as I followed the man down a short hallway and through a door leading to a courtroom filled with unfamiliar men.

He showed me to a singular chair on a small dais in the middle of the room, a microphone standing by. The judges' bench sat to the left, where a silver-haired gentleman in a black robe acknowledged me with a nod as I came in. The district attorney, joined by my escort, occupied a table on my right. Directly in front of me, lining the wall in two long rows, sat nearly two dozen men of varying ages—I suspected none were under forty. A lone female stenographer sat at a small table in front of the judges' bench with her stenotype machine.

They were an intimidating bunch, scrutinizing and judging me, but I would not let them break me. Fiercer foes than this assembly had tried before and failed. *You can do this, Désirée.*

"Thank you for coming today, Miss Gautier. The court clerk will swear you in," the judge said as a man came forward with a bible in hand.

"Place your left hand on the Bible, raise your right hand and repeat after me," the clerk instructed.

"I do solemnly, sincerely, and truly declare and affirm that the evidence I give shall be the truth, the whole truth and nothing but the truth."

I said the words, and they believed them, but I knew I'd have to break that oath if asked questions that delved too deeply into my past.

The DA stood up to address me. "Please state your full name, date of birth, and place of residence for the record."

"Désirée Marie Gautier. May 15, 1932. Marchand House, St. Charles Avenue, New Orleans." It was the first lie; my name wasn't Gautier.

"Thank you for coming, Miss Gautier," he said, giving me what I'm sure he thought was a pleasant smile. "Do you know why we've asked you to speak with us today?"

His condescending attitude made my blood instantly boil as I quickly formed a response.

"Of course, Mr. Simmons. The written statement of a seventeen-year-old girl wasn't good enough for you. You need to hear the details of what happened directly from my mouth before you'll decide whether to charge me with Carson Bentley's death."

My response seemed to take him by surprise, his eyes widening and brows raising above the rim of his glasses as he re-evaluated his opinion of me. "Yes, Miss Gautier, that's correct. I'll try to make this as brief as possible," he said, coming out from behind the table to stand in front of me.

For the next half hour, he questioned me about my relationship with Carson Bentley, how I knew him, my recent encounters with him, then he took a deep dive into the events leading up to the Revelers Ball, including details of the knife that Nico Garcia gave me for Christmas. His questions mimicked those the detectives asked the morning after I killed Carson. I responded with the same answers I'd given them.

"Tell us what happened between you and Mr. Bentley at the Reveler's Ball, Miss Gautier."

"It was late in the evening when Carson called me out for a dance," I said as the memory of that night flooded my mind. "I couldn't gracefully refuse without making a scene, so I accepted the dance. He held me too close, purposely making me uncomfortable. While we were dancing, he bent close to my ear and said he wondered if I tasted as good as I looked... then he said he would ask Bill for his opinion. When the dance ended, I refused his gift and walked out of the room."

"Did you tell anyone what he said to you?" the DA asked.

"No. I had already made a scene that night by not being dressed as a debutante. I didn't want to make it worse."

"Alright, Miss Gautier. This brings us to the night of January eleventh, five days later. Please walk us through the events of that evening."

Even though I'd detailed all of it in the written statement, they wanted to hear it from my lips. This was the moment I had to expose myself, make them see in lurid detail what Carson did to me and why I killed him. I wasn't sure I could do it.

My face fell into my hands and my eyes filled with tears as the memory of that night assaulted my mind. My nightmare was about to be laid bare in broad daylight to a room full of strangers.

"Are you alright, Miss Gautier? Do you need a moment to compose yourself?" the judge asked sympathetically.

Glancing up, I caught the eye of the stenographer, whose brow pinched above her glasses in an expression of horror and sympathy. Her fingers hovered over the keys of her machine, waiting to record my response.

I pressed my fingers to my mouth and took a breath to calm myself. By then, my hankie was damp and of little use, but I dried my tears as best I could and straightened my back, unwilling to concede defeat.

"I'm fine, sir. I can do this," I said with a nod to the judge.

"Alright. Whenever you're ready, Miss Gautier."

For an event that seemed to last forever while it was happening, the telling of it took less than ten minutes. I was trembling when I finished, fighting back the physical memory with every remaining ounce of courage I possessed as tears rolled down my cheeks, captured by the useless hankie. But for my haggard breath, an eerie silence filled the room for an interminable time.

"I have one more question, Miss Gautier," the DA said, breaking the silence of the spellbound room, his brow furrowed as he stood in front of me. "Did you intend to kill Carson Bentley that night?"

I looked him in the eye and told him the truth, but not the whole truth.

"There was a moment while he was raping me, while his hands were squeezing my throat till I couldn't catch a breath, that I knew he was going to kill me. In those last seconds, I thought I could let it happen, and it would be over, but a voice was yelling inside my head, 'Reach Up! Find It!'... When I did, I felt the little statue in my hand, and I chose to survive. My only intention, Mr. Simmons, was to survive."

"Do you have any more questions, Mr. Simmons, or have you heard enough?" the judge asked with a tone of annoyance.

"I have no more questions for this witness regarding the death of Carson Bentley. Thank you for your cooperation, Miss Gautier." He nodded to me with a satisfied look, like he'd won the preliminary heat and was ready for the main event.

"Bailiff, please escort Miss Gautier to my chambers," the judge instructed. "Have Mr. Marchand join her there. Miss Gautier, I will be in to speak with you and your guardian in a few moments."

The chambers of the Honorable Ronald D. Putman, Chief Judge, were beautiful; paneled in dark oak, the floor covered in lush beige carpet, heavy drapes bordered several tall windows topped with deep blue damask valances. The large mahogany desk faced a seating area with a loveseat upholstered in sky blue velvet, two mahogany side chairs, their seats covered in pale blue damask, and another side chair fully upholstered in the same fabric. An oval glass-topped mahogany coffee table sat between them, holding a brass cigarette box and matching lighter, a crystal ashtray, and an ornate brass pot containing a blooming white orchid. Judge Putnam obviously appreciated luxury.

I sat on the loveseat with my legs crossed to await whatever was coming next, certain there was going to be something that would either end or perpetuate this nightmare. To calm my nerves, and because I didn't care what anyone thought, I lit a cigarette from the box on the table, exhaling the smoke across the room toward the judge's desk.

"Désirée? Are you alright?" Charlie asked as he and Bill came into the office to join me a moment later.

"How'd it go, Chére?" Bill asked, sitting by me on the loveseat while Charlie took the upholstered chair next to me, reaching over to pat my knee.

"I'm fine," I lied, "and I don't know how it went. I told them exactly what happened, and then the judge sent me in here to wait. He said he wants to speak with us."

I leaned forward to flick the ash of my cigarette into the ashtray, then took a couple more drags before smashing the butt out, frustrated and angry about the humiliating experience the halls of justice had just put me through.

"I'm sure it's just a formality and nothing to worry about," Charlie offered, trying to ease my overly active mind.

"I'm sorry about all this, Charlie. How is Julianna?" I was concerned about the trouble I'd caused in his life and hoped to divert the attention off me.

"Jules is going to be fine, darlin', don't you worry. We talked about her going to Boston as soon as we knew we were expecting. Jules gets too excited during Mardi Gras season, and we don't want to take any chances on losing this baby. She'll be fine once she settles in with Jenny and her kids."

That was good to hear. At least Julianna would be well away from all the publicity and gossip.

Then Judge Putnam came in, and my heart stopped beating for a few seconds while he removed his black robe, hung it on the rack in the corner, and sat down behind his desk with a heavy sigh.

"Thank you for your patience, gentlemen. Miss Gautier, the Grand Jury unanimously agreed you acted in self-defense in Carson Bentley's death. The district attorney will not be filing charges."

I huffed out a breath, expressing my frustration at being used by them. "Apparently, it required my complete exposure and humiliation for them to come to that conclusion," I said with a measure of unmistakable sarcasm. Bill took my hand and held it tight, letting me know he was there to support me.

"Unfortunately, Miss Gautier, your testimony was necessary to remove all doubt regarding the circumstances of Mr. Bentley's death. We understand how difficult this was for you."

"I seriously doubt any of you know what this feels like, Judge Putnam. May we go now?"

"You've gone through a terrible experience, Miss Gautier. It is the opinion of this court and that of Doctor Neville, the court-appointed psychiatrist, that you undergo psychiatric treatment twice weekly for a minimum of three months to assist you in recovering from this trauma and to help you reclaim your place in society."

If I thought it would do me any good, I might have made a fuss, but I was an underaged girl with few options. At least seeing Doctor Neville would also give me access to Evie, and that was all that mattered.

"Yes, sir," I replied, curbing my displeasure.

"Good. I also require you to remain within this jurisdiction under the supervision of the Marchand family until your eighteenth birthday. Don't leave town, Miss Gautier. The district attorney may have additional questions for you regarding the ongoing investigation into the Phantom murders."

"She is staying at our lake house in Mandeville, under my supervision, Judge," Bill said, giving my hand another squeeze.

"Excellent. Thank you all for coming," Judge Putnam said, rising from behind his desk to walk us to the door. "Good luck to you, Miss Gautier. I hope the next time we meet will be under more pleasant circumstances. Good day."

Inquisition complete, sentence passed, and pleasantries offered. He was done with me... for now.

As we approached the front entrance, we could see Luke standing by the car parked in front, but we'd have to get past the crowd of reporters on the front steps to reach him.

Bill tensed as we approached the door. "Shit. Simmons didn't waste any time. He's out there talking to the press. We're going to have to make a dash for it, Charlie. Stay close, Chére. Say nothing and keep your head down."

With Bill on one side and Charlie on the other, both holding onto my elbows, I kept pace with them, my hands in my pockets and my head down as we exited the halls of justice.

Seconds later, not even halfway down the front steps, there were people calling out my name, photographers trying to get close enough to get a photo of me. Bill and Charlie pushed them all aside to get me safely to the car, where Luke waited with the door open.

"Désirée! Over here. Look here."

"Désirée! Do you have a statement for the press?"

"Désirée! When did you suspect Bentley of being the Phantom?"

"Get in, Chére," Bill said as we finally reached the sidewalk and the waiting car.

I climbed into the backseat, shaking like a leaf and expecting Bill and Charlie to get in after me, but Bill stood in the door, sheltering me from view as Charlie made a brief statement to the press.

"The Marchand family is grateful this tragic event is over. We ask you all to respect Miss Gautier's privacy and direct all inquiries to the Marchand family attorney. Good day, gentlemen."

As Charlie was speaking, a lone photographer came around the car and took several photos of me through the passenger window. Luke pushed him back as Charlie got in the front seat, and Bill got in the back beside me. Then Luke climbed into the driver's seat, and we sped away.

I knew I'd be seeing my face in the papers again, proving that this tragic event was far from over.

"Take me home, Bill. Please," I said, unable to control the feeling of hopelessness overwhelming me. He put his arm around me and held me close as I buried my face in his chest, ruining his jacket with my tears.

"*Je suis là, ma chérie*. We'll be home soon."

Chapter 10

Therapy with benefits

Thursday morning, Bobby and I drove to Glen Oaks for my first therapy session with Doctor Neville and to get an update on Evie. Bill left for an early meeting in town before I got up, but I was relieved it was just me and Bobby. We wouldn't have much more time together.

As I walked into Doctor Neville's office, I hid my surly mood behind a pleasant smile. It was his recommendation that convinced the judge to make me go through this.

"Good morning, Désirée. It's nice to see you again. Please, have a seat and make yourself comfortable."

He offered me the couch, then took the chair across from me, leaning back with his legs crossed as he lit his pipe.

"How are you feeling today?" There was concern in his eyes, as if he expected me to be upset.

I felt like life had stripped me naked and paraded me down Canal Street, but I wouldn't give him the satisfaction of knowing that.

"I'm fine, doctor. How are you?" I asked politely, while holding my feelings as far out of his range as I could.

"Very well, thank you." He took a puff from his pipe, watching me through the smoke.

"May I ask you a question, doctor?"

"Of course."

"What do you expect to accomplish with all this?" He couldn't erase the trauma from my mind, so what was the point of rehashing it?

He stared at me for a long time before responding. "It's what *you* will accomplish, Miss Gautier. By court order, you and I will meet twice weekly for the next twelve weeks. Why don't we take this time to get to know one another and explore what's really troubling you? I'm certain I can help."

I stared at him for a moment, angry he'd forced this farce on me. "It will be interesting to see how well you think you know me at the end of our... twenty-four hours together." I would not let him know the real me if I could help it.

"That will depend entirely on you, Désirée. I hope I'll earn your trust."

He picked up a small hand-held mirror from the table between us and handed it to me. "I'd like to start at the beginning, with your earliest childhood memories. What was your childhood like?"

I turned the mirror face down on the couch beside me, resisting any temptation to check my composure, the fit of my mask. "What has my childhood got to do with this?"

"In early childhood we learn how to navigate the world, how to behave, communicate, how to trust. Childhood experiences teach us lessons which we carry into adulthood, affecting our relationships, our successes or failures in society." He let me sit with his explanation, watching me through the smoke swirling up from his pipe.

I couldn't deny the truth of his statement. My childhood experiences certainly colored everything that happened after it ended. The tricky part was going to be giving him a believable history without revealing any details.

"My childhood was normal, I guess. I was happy, loved, and secure. Then the war happened, and everything changed."

"Tell me about the last time you were with your parents. How old were you when they passed away?"

"My parents were killed by the Nazis. They didn't just pass away like some dream."

"Of course not. Your feelings about your parent's death are understandable. What is your last memory of them?"

It was all I could do to stifle the overwhelming sadness welling up inside me, to push down the memory of that horrible day. But I had to give him something, some half-truth he could latch on to.

"I was disobedient and defiant the last time I saw them. They told me to stay there and be a good girl, but I didn't. I hid from them. When they were leaving, I ran after them, but it was too late. They were gone, and I never saw them again. I never said goodbye."

"Do you think the outcome would have been different if you had been obedient that day?"

I didn't know what would have happened if I'd stayed hidden under the porch the day the Nazis came. Maybe if I'd not gone looking for Papa, it might have ended differently. It could have.

"I'll never know, will I?" I said, clinging to what control I had but feeling it slip away.

"How did you feel once they were gone?"

"Angry, sad, abandoned. Everything I'd ever known was suddenly gone. My entire life changed. I felt like an orphan."

"You were with your grandmother. How did she help you get through it?"

I thought about the old woman, Madame Elise, and what she said and how kind she was to me. "The day she told me my parents were dead, she said I must be brave, strong and clever. That was how I would get through the loss. So, that's what I did, because an eight-year-old girl has no other choice."

"Children are often the silent victims of war. I'm very sorry for your loss, Désirée."

"Are we done, doctor? May I see Evie now?"

"No, we're not quite finished. Please take that mirror and gaze into it for a moment, then tell the girl in the mirror why you feel responsible for what happened to Evelyn."

It was an odd request, an obvious ploy to get me to reveal myself. If I looked, I risked letting my mask fall, risked revealing the truth in an emotional slip-up. If I refused, I risked losing access to Evie.

I lifted the mirror to face the girl I'd become, the 1950 version of Désirée.

The face looking back at me wasn't the eight-year-old girl who lost her family, not the orphan, nor any of the other incarnations of Désirée. This was a young woman's face, still showing signs of a beating with bruising around her neck, but there was a fierce determination in her clear blue eyes. She knew the price of survival, so I spoke to her.

"I should have tried harder to convince Evie that Carson wasn't what he seemed to be. I knew there was something wrong with him, but I said nothing to Mama or to Bill. Maybe if I had, things would be different for Evie." That was as close to a confession as I was prepared to get.

I dropped the mirror to my lap, swallowed hard, and looked up.

"When did you become suspicious of Mr. Bentley? Did you suspect he was the one who sent you those gifts?"

This was sounding like an interrogation, like the questions the DA asked me the day before.

Be careful, Désirée. You don't know this man yet, or what he wants.

"I was never comfortable around him, not from the beginning. And no, I didn't know who sent those things until the last one came, the night Carson came to the house... the night I killed him." My hand drew up to my mouth, stifling the sob that threatened to escape.

"Alright. That's enough for now. How do you feel?" he asked, as if I'd made some progress toward mental health.

"I'm fine, doctor. Will you answer another question?" I asked, mentally adjusting my mask back into place.

"Of course, if I can." He leaned back in his chair, eyes slightly squinting, as if unsure and cautious.

"Will you tell anyone what you and I talk about? Will you report to the DA about me, about what I say in here?" I wondered if he would be honest, or if I could even know the difference. His face showed little emotion, his body language gave nothing away. Maybe that's why I didn't trust him. I couldn't read him very well.

He shook his head and sighed. "No, Désirée. What we talk about is strictly confidential between you and me. Every employee of Glen Oaks is required to sign a non-disclosure confidentiality agreement, which protects the privacy of our patients. However, I am required to file monthly reports with the court on your progress, but they will only reflect my clinical analysis and nothing more. You can trust that nothing you say here will ever leave this room."

I wasn't sure I believed him or could trust him, but I had no choice. So, as hard as it would be, I had to stick to my plan of lying, giving him believable half-truths for the duration of this sentence.

"Okay. May I see Evie now?"

The sudden shift in his posture sent a familiar flutter through my stomach, telling me something had changed, instantly triggering my suspicions.

"Did something happen, doctor? Is Evie alright? Is she still here?" I could feel panic building, my breath speeding up, my heart pounding hard in my chest.

Please let her still be here.

"Yes, she's still here. We moved her out of the hospital wing yesterday and into a private room in the women's residence hall. While we were successful in convincing Mrs. Duret to let Evelyn remain at Glen Oaks, she asked that I limit your visits with her daughter."

"Why? Doesn't she realize Evie needs me? She needs to know she's not alone. I must see her." This was unexpected, and I felt blind-sided, unable to fully express my disappointment.

"Perhaps it is *you* who needs her, Désirée, but we can explore that in our next session together. At my suggestion, Mrs. Duret gave her approval for you to see Evelyn, but only on Mondays and Thursdays after you meet with me. This will be better for both of you, at least for now. I hope you understand."

I didn't. All I could do was accept their decision and hope the time I get with Evie would make a difference.

Bill was waiting for me when I came into the lobby after my visit with Evie. Bobby was nowhere in sight.

"Hello, Chère," Bill said, setting aside a newspaper and rising from his seat when he saw me coming.

"Where is Bobby?" I asked. His absence felt odd, and Bill's presence in his place felt suspicious. Bobby said nothing about this change in plans.

Bill shrugged, giving me a slightly crooked, easy-going smile, with a mischievous glint in his eyes. "I had a meeting with Doctor Neville while you were with Evelyn and figured you didn't need both of us to take you home, so I sent him back to the house. Are you ready?" he asked, offering his arm to lead me to the front door.

After a moment's hesitation and with nerves fluttering in my stomach, I took his arm. Spending time alone with Bill during the day was something I avoided—the day before was an exception—and not because I didn't want to be with him, but because I was ashamed of what I let Carson do to me. Talking to Bill late at night was easier, with shadows obscuring features, hiding feelings under the veil of darkness. The thought of being alone with him in the daylight sent shivers down my spine.

Once he drove out of the Glen Oaks gate, he headed toward home but then failed to turn south to Mandeville, instead continuing east on Highway 36 for several miles.

"Where are we going?"

"I thought we could have lunch together. There's a little place in Abita Springs I think you'll like. The food's pretty good. Are you game?" he asked, glancing over at me with a hopeful look in his eyes.

"Sure, I guess." I kept my gaze straight ahead and wondered what was on his mind.

An uneasy silence filled the space between us as he drove down the two-lane road and into the small farming town of Abita Springs. He parked in front of a café with an adjacent patio area for outside dining, where a few hearty souls were enjoying their lunch in the breezy sunshine.

Inside, the modest café offered an unpretentious environment. The cozy dining area held eight tables and three booths along the wall, and a six-stool counter. It had enough room to serve fifty-four customers comfortably.

"Afternoon, y'all. Find a seat, and I'll bring over some menus," a cheerful waitress said as we came in.

We took the vacant booth at the end, closest to the kitchen and away from the other diners. Within seconds, the waitress brought us menus and water, then stood by waiting for our order, tapping her foot impatiently.

"Mind if I order for us, Chère?" Bill asked.

I shrugged, thinking it was his party, and he knew what to serve.

Bill smiled up at the waitress, which brought a blush to her cheeks and silenced her foot. "We'll both have the Bayou omelet, grits for me, fresh fruit for the lady, both with biscuits."

"What to drink?" she asked, smacking her gum.

"Two coffees with cream and sugar. Thanks." Bill knew what I liked.

The waitress left, then quickly returned with two mugs of coffee, a small pitcher of cream and a jar of sugar with a pour top. She placed them on the table along with two sets of tableware wrapped in paper napkins, while stealing looks at Bill and me.

A feeling of *déjà vu* washed over me as I sat across from him, waiting for the food to arrive. We'd done this six months earlier in a different café, when things were equally difficult between us, and he needed to clear the air. It felt the same; the air still needed clearing.

Once the food arrived—fluffy omelets filled with a Cajun mix of shrimp, crawfish, peppers, onions and mushrooms, topped with cheese and parsley—the tension at the table eased, and Bill opened the conversation.

"How was Evelyn today?"

"Still there, thank God. But she just sits there, drifting in and out of consciousness. It's like something kept pulling her back into the nightmare every time she responded to me. I don't know if it's the medication they're giving her or something else, but I could see her struggling to stay with me. And now they're only letting me see her twice a week after I see Doctor Neville."

"I heard about that." The look on Bill's face had a lot more behind it than what he said.

"Why were you meeting with Doctor Neville?" If what the doctor said was true about patient privacy, there shouldn't be any reason to speak with Bill or anyone else about me.

"We were both fishing for information," Bill replied. "Neville wanted to assure himself that your living situation is... healthy was the word he used. And I wanted to assess the man who is handling your therapy, to make sure he has your best interests in mind."

"Were you both satisfied with what you learned?"

"Doctor Neville seems like a decent fellow, dedicated to his profession and the recovery of his patients. I gave him a description of the lake house and our group of current residents. I told him you have nightly calls with Mama, which seemed to relieve him."

"He wants to know who I am, Bill. He wants me to talk about my life, my childhood, because he thinks I'm suffering from a childhood trauma, besides the current one."

"What did you tell him?"

"I told him what he expects to hear, based on what he already believes about me, but he's persistent and perceptive, so I need to stay on guard. This whole thing is a waste of his time and mine. I don't see the benefit of talking about something I can't change."

"Maybe he's right about your childhood trauma, Chère. You went through some terrible experiences that you've never dealt with. It's not a bad idea to talk about them, maybe look at them from a different perspective. I've heard it helps."

"But you know I can't tell him the truth, so what would be the point?"

"No, you can't tell him, but you can talk to me. You can tell me anything, Chère. I know I've been distant, but it's because I wanted to give you time and... Well, it won't be long before it will be just us at the house, and I want you to be comfortable talking to me."

"Is this why you wanted me to go to lunch today? To test if I would talk to you in the daylight?" He shrugged, understanding I'd seen through his ploy.

"I'm the one who's been distant, Bill. I know you want to help, and I'm grateful for your patience, but this is so..."

"I know this is hard, Désirée, but I'm here. We used to have the best talks, tease each other, and share our thoughts. I miss that. I miss *you*. So, whenever you need to sort through your feelings, I want to be the one you come to, day or night." His eyes revealed his sincerity, filled with the longing I'd been shying away from.

If I was going to make it through the next few months, I would need help, and he was offering a way to make it through this crisis. There was no way to know how it all would end, but one thing was certain: I wasn't alone.

"Okay, Bill, I'll try to be better." I gave him a shy smile, attempting to lighten the mood with a change of subject. "Are there any other good restaurants on this side of the lake?"

"Several, and I'll take you to them if you'll let me," he said as the worry lines slowly faded from his brow.

We had finally rediscovered an old alliance, albeit an uneasy one.

Chapter 11

Bobby

When Bill and I returned to the house that afternoon, Bobby and Jimmy Wilcox were in the backyard building a group of raised planting beds around the patio.

"Surprise!" Bobby said as I got out of the car and went over to inspect their work.

"Do you like it, Dez? Bill and I thought you might be missing your garden, and since Jimmy was coming over, I thought he could bring us what we needed to build you another one."

"Bobby, you know how I hate surprises, but this is... exactly what I needed. Thanks."

Tears filled my eyes, and my throat tightened as I looked up at Jimmy. Speaking felt impossible. The words got stuck behind the flood of emotion I tried to stifle.

"Hi, Désirée. How are you?" Jimmy asked, struggling to control his feelings behind a brave face.

I swallowed the lump in my throat and croaked out a response. "I'm fine, Jimmy. Really, I am. Please don't worry about me. I'm a survivor."

"Yeah, you are," he said, stroking my cheek. "I just wish I'd never changed our plans that night. You wouldn't have been there. This wouldn't have happened to you. God, I'm so sorry."

"Don't Jimmy. This wasn't your fault. Please don't feel responsible. I couldn't stand it if you did."

"Olivia is here too, Dez. She begged me to bring her with me. I figured it would be okay. I hope you don't mind. She's inside," he said, pointing up to the house.

"No, I don't mind, Jimmy. Thanks for bringing her, and thanks for doing all this. It's lovely."

"Ah, it's nothing. I'm just happy to see you, Dez. Go up and see Liv while we finish up here."

Olivia Harcourt became a dear friend during my freshman year at Isidore Newman High School after I gave her my spot in the Delta Sorority at my first 'New Friends' party, an event I held each year after Rush Week. That single gesture endeared me to her and to several others who became my close companions throughout high school. Olivia was the gentlest, sweetest girl I knew.

She was sitting at the kitchen table with Jolie, two glasses of sweet tea and one of my cookbooks lying open between them. As they flipped through the pages, they looked like two old friends having a pleasant chat while they planned their next meal. It made me wonder why I'd never brought them together before this. Then I remembered why. In 1945, whites didn't socialize with negro people. It was unheard of in Southern Louisiana polite society. It still was in 1950.

"Oh, Désirée," Liv cried, jumping out of her seat the moment she saw me come in. She threw her arms around me, holding on tight as if afraid I'd disappear.

"It's good to see you, Liv. I'm glad you came," I said, hugging her tightly in return. I hadn't realized how much I missed my friends until then.

Olivia, Jolie and I sat on the porch outside the kitchen, sipping chilled wine and watching the men work. There was something wonderful about the way they glided through the tasks as if they'd worked together dozens of times. It gave me a warm feeling inside, like I used to feel when life was normal.

Around five o'clock, Nico Garcia's truck and trailer backed into the driveway carrying a load of fresh soil, a few sacks of gravel, and a truckload of potted plants. Nico climbed out of the truck and looked around for a familiar face.

"*Hola*, Nico," Bill called out, going over to greet the new arrival. "Thanks for bringing this out here. We're ready to fill them up." He pointed to the four large planters waiting to be filled.

"*Hola*, Mr. William. Where do you want the soil? In the driveway or next to the garage?"

"Let's dump it next to the garage. It looks like you brought more than we'll need for now. Can you angle the trailer over?"

"Sure, Mr. William. Piece of cake," Nico replied, climbing back into the truck to reposition the trailer to the right spot.

"Great. The boys and I will help unload the rest. Bobby. Jimmy. Breaks over, fellas."

That evening, we sat down to dinner together: Bill and me, Jolie and Bobby, Jimmy and Olivia, and Nico. Bill pulled out a couple of bottles of wine from the hall closet to share with the group, toasting their joint accomplishment and thanking them for their contributions. Jolie and Olivia made us a delicious Jambalaya paired with honeyed cornbread, and I contributed a tossed salad with a fresh vinegarette. Another round of toasts from the men to the chefs brought blushes to Olivia's cheeks and nods from Jolie and me. I felt normal, for a change, allowing myself to have the best time with my friends I'd had in a long time.

By silent mutual agreement, no one mentioned my unfortunate event, which was fine by me. I preferred to forget it entirely, but there was no chance of that ever happening. Instead, we reminisced about high school, shared old stories, and laughed till our sides ached.

The best part of the whole evening was their acceptance of Jolie. Neither Jimmy, Olivia, nor Nico seemed uncomfortable with her, even engaged her in every conversation. Jolie entertained them with her quick wit and unbridled opinions. It was what I loved most about her, and it felt good that my friends could see it too. Every time I looked at her, she was smiling.

When the party ended at half past ten, Bobby and Jimmy went out on the porch to talk while I walked Nico to his truck to say goodnight.

"Thanks for coming out, Nico. It was good to see you. I'm sorry if giving me that knife got you into trouble."

"It wasn't so bad. They just asked me why I gave it to you, and that was all. Pa wasn't too pleased with me, but I'm happy you're okay, Désirée. I just wish I'd given you a few more lessons with that knife. Maybe things would have turned out differently."

"Things happen the way they're supposed to, Nico. If I'd killed him with that knife, I would probably be in jail for murder right now."

"Well, I'm glad you're not. Would it be okay if I came back on Saturday morning to help you get the garden planted? I can get this yard in shape for you. Doesn't look like anyone's touched it for a while."

"Of course. But isn't this too far out of your way?"

"No, it's not that far, and I want to do it if it's okay with you."

"Alright. I'll see you on Saturday. We'll have a gardening day like we used to. Thanks for coming, Nico. Drive home safe," I said, giving him a hug before he climbed into his truck.

"Goodnight, Désirée. See you Saturday."

As I headed back to the house, I heard Bobby and Jimmy talking, and I stopped to listen—an old habit and terribly rude, but I wanted to hear if Jimmy could convince Bobby to go back to school.

"You're not doing her any good by staying here, Bob. You should go back to school."

"She needs me. I can't leave her to deal with this alone."

"She's got Bill and Jolie with her. She's not alone, and the longer you stay, the harder it's going to be for her. People are already talking. Imagine what they'll say if they find out you're staying out here with her. Unless you marry her, people will gossip about her more than they already do."

"I asked her to marry me, but she said she can't and won't, because she doesn't want to ruin our friendship."

"She's right, Bob. You and I both know that's not what either of you really wants. Go back to school and let Désirée get through these next few months with Bill's help. She'll be okay. I'll come out to see her as much as she'll let me."

"I guess you're right, Jimmy. She seemed better tonight, not so sad as she's been. I'll tell her later."

Hearing this eased the ache in my heart. Jimmy had accomplished what I couldn't, but now I had to deal with letting Bobby go and knew that was going to be difficult for both of us.

A short time later, Bobby and I walked Jimmy and Olivia out to Jimmy's truck while Jolie stood on the porch watching.

"I'm so ga-glad I insisted Jimmy bring me," Olivia said, hugging me tightly. "This was so much fun. Just like old times, right, Désirée? We sh-should do it again soon. And it was great meeting Jolie. She's so fa-funny and nice. I never knew a colored girl could be just like us."

"I'm glad you came, Liv, and that you liked Jolie. She's special."

"Thanks for supper, kiddo," Jimmy said, pulling me into a hug. "I'll call you next week. Take care, Bob. We'll talk soon."

Amid waves and endless goodbyes, Bobby and I watched them drive away. Then we climbed the stairs to join Jolie who was waiting on the porch.

"Nice party, Désirée," she said as we joined her. "Thanks for planning it, Bobby. Who knew I could fit in with a bunch of Uptown kids?"

"*I* did, Jolie," Bobby said, giving her one of his brilliant smiles. "I've got to go talk to Bill about something, but do either of you want to meet me out on the upper terrace for a little stargazing before bed? There's a clear sky tonight."

"I'll meet you up there," I said as we all walked inside, and Bobby headed for Bill's office.

I looked around the house where, not that long ago, the tables needed clearing, ashtrays needed emptying, and floors needed sweeping.

Miraculously, it was neat as a pin, with little trace of a party remaining, except for the empty wine bottles sitting on the kitchen counter.

"Jolie, didn't you leave anything for me to do?"

She shrugged as if it were nothing, but I could tell she was glad I mentioned it. "Olivia insisted on helping me clean up while you were saying goodbye to Nico. She's a handy helper to have around."

"You're the best, Jolie. Thanks for everything. I'm lucky to have a friend like you."

"I don't know about that, Désirée, but for an Uptown girl with a ruined reputation, you sure do have lots of people ready to defend your honor." She laughed and bumped my shoulder with hers.

"What little there's left of it," I said as we headed upstairs.

Bobby and I spent our remaining time together taking walks along the lake and making plans for my summer visit with him in California. We talked and laughed and cried in each other's arms until there was nothing left to say but goodbye.

"Are you sure you don't want me to stay, Dez? Another week won't make any difference for school. I can make it up." His packed bags sat waiting for his departure on Saturday morning after breakfast.

"Yes, Bobby, I'm sure. I want you to go back to Stanford and study hard, so you can build me a rocket that will go to the moon and back. And I want you to find out what those UFOs were. Okay?"

"Alright, I will, but will you promise me something?"

"Of course."

"Don't shut yourself off from Bill. He needs you as much as you need him. Promise, okay?"

"I promise, but you must promise to talk with your father and that you'll be nice to his new wife. He deserves to be happy too, you know."

"Alright, I'll talk to Dad, but I can't make any promises about her."

"Just try, okay? You might find she's nicer than you imagine."

"Are you ready, Bob? We need to hit the road," Bill said after loading Bobby's suitcase into his car.

"Yeah, I guess." Bobby pulled me into a fierce embrace, holding on tight like he was afraid he'd lose me forever if he let go. "I love you, Dez. Take care of yourself, ya hear?"

"I love you too, Bobby. Call me when you get there." I bit my bottom lip to keep my tears at bay.

"Every Sunday night, like we used to," he said, hugging me again.

"Will you ladies be alright on your own for a while?" Bill asked. "If you need anything, Luke should be here later this afternoon. I won't be back until late, maybe around midnight, so I'll see y'all in the morning."

"We'll be fine, Mr. William," Jolie said, standing next to me in the driveway. I was having a hard time keeping myself together in the face of Bobby's eminent departure.

Then Bill and Bobby drove away. They disappeared down the street as a stream of tears fell from my eyes.

"Come on, Désirée," Jolie said, grabbing my arm. "Let's go inside. The old folks are coming tomorrow, so we've got to show them that everything is going okay out here. We need to plan a meal, something special from one of your cookbooks."

Chapter 12

Elijah

The following Tuesday, Jolie and I had just pulled a batch of bread from the oven and were relaxing with a glass of sweet tea on the porch, enjoying the afternoon sunshine, when an unexpected visitor came to call.

Elijah Tillman was the last person I expected to see again, but there he was, standing at the bottom of my front steps, his cap in his hands and a hopeful look in his eyes.

"Who's that?" Jolie asked as I rose to greet him.

"Another hero."

I stood at the top of the steps, smiling down at him. "Hello, Elijah."

"May I come up?" he asked, putting one foot on the bottom step.

"Of course. Would you like something to drink?" Regardless of the warning look Jolie gave me, it would be rude not to offer something.

Jolie frowned at me, then retreated inside, but I knew she wouldn't go too far out of earshot.

"Nah. I'm alright," Elijah said, joining me on the porch and taking the seat Jolie vacated.

I resumed my seat, leaning back to better assess him and try to determine his reasons for coming.

“How did you find me, and why are you here?” I wanted to get to the point as quickly as possible.

“Captain Terry, down at the marina, told me where you live. He knows me. Turns out, the morning I brought you over here, he saw us pull in and watched you walk up the street.”

Elijah leaned forward, peering through the windows, and saw Jolie standing there staring at him. “How’s your grandmother?” he asked with a suspicious look on his face.

Unless the swamp had engulfed Elijah during the past twelve days, without benefit of a newspaper or radio, he knew exactly who I was. I never told him my name or anything about myself, except the lie about helping my grandmother, yet here he was. I wondered why.

“She’s been dead for quite a while, but I guess you already know I lied about that. Why did you come here, Elijah?” I asked, lighting a cigarette to occupy my nervous hands.

“For a couple of reasons. First, because I couldn’t stop thinking about you, wondering how you’re doing. You were the saddest and bravest girl I’d ever met. You look better, now that the bruises are fading, and you have normal color in your cheeks.” He waited for my response which didn’t come.

“Anyway, when I went home that day, I told Gran about you. She’d been listening to the news on the radio and got all worked up about something, said she needed to talk with you, and I should ask you to come see her. I told her we shouldn’t bother you, but she wouldn’t let it go. She just kept nagging me about it, saying it’s important she talk to you.”

“What does she want to talk about? Did she come with you??”

“No. Gran don’t leave the bayou much, not unless she needs to. I asked her what it was about, but she wouldn’t tell me. She said it was women’s business, and she needs to see you face to face. So, here I am. Will you come with me to see her? It's only about thirty minutes away, just this side of Slidell. I could have you back before supper."

It was a curious request, especially considering that I barely knew Elijah and certainly shouldn't leave with him. But I was feeling like a prisoner in my life and decided it was about time I took control of it. Besides, I owed him a favor.

"Alright, Elijah, I'll go talk to her. Let me clean up and I'll be right with you."

After putting out the cigarette, I went inside to wash the residual flour off my hands and face, and make sure I was presentable enough to go calling. Jolie was waiting for me with crossed arms and a face pinched up with worry.

"You ain't really going with that man, are you, Désirée?" she asked, following me into the bathroom behind the kitchen, watching me clean up and fuss with my hair.

"Yes, I am. There is no reason not to."

"Bill ain't gonna like it. You runnin' off with some strange man to God knows where."

"Elijah Tillman is not some strange man, Jolie. He's a friend who asked me for a favor. He did one for me and now I'm returning it. Simple as that. You don't need to worry. I'll probably be back before Bill gets home, anyway." He rarely got back till after six.

She followed me out to the porch, frowning at Elijah. "If anybody asks, where should I tell them you went?"

I looked up at Elijah, shrugging my ignorance. "Where are we going?"

"The Gatlin place at the end of Kettle Road on the Bayou Liberty," he explained, nodding to Jolie, which she returned with a warning look.

"I'll see you in a few hours, Jolie. Don't worry, I'll be fine." I gave her a hug before following Elijah down the front steps.

"She sure is protective for a maid. Is she always like that?" he asked as we walked to his Ford pickup truck parked in front.

His comment struck a nerve, but I held my tongue while he opened the passenger door for me. I waited until he climbed in behind the wheel before I spoke up, wanting to correct his misperception.

"Jolie is not a maid. She's my friend, and she worries about me," I said, a little too sharply.

Surprise and maybe shock marked his expression. "Didn't mean no offense. I just thought since you live in that big house and all. Don't rich people have servants to do for them?"

"Yes, but I don't. She's my friend, not a servant."

"It don't make no difference to me. Lots of coloreds live out on the bayou. They're just regular folks, like everybody else. I just thought since... well, my mistake."

Silence filled the cab of his truck as he drove through town, then turned right onto Highway 190, going east, a road I was intimately familiar with, having traveled it many times on my trips to the lake house.

The two-lane road cut across the countryside, servicing the local farm communities between Madisonville in the west and Slidell in the east. Straight as an arrow, tree-lined and well-traveled, the road's familiarity soothed my anxious mind, allowing me to relax and enjoy the ride. I knew where I was and how to get home in case something happened.

"How have you been, Elijah?" I asked, trying to break the uneasy silence between us.

He seemed to want to talk but kept holding back, biting his lip to stop himself, apparently unsure of my response. I couldn't blame him. I'd practically bit his head off about Jolie, a reaction he didn't deserve.

"I'm sorry I snapped at you back there, Elijah. It's just that I care a lot about Jolie and don't like it when people treat her less than she deserves. I know you weren't doing that, so I'm sorry if I offended you."

He glanced over, smiled and shook his head as he downshifted into low gear to drive through Lacombe. "Gran's gonna like you, that's for sure."

A couple of miles east of Lacombe, he turned right onto a long, narrow road heading straight for the lake. I didn't know the area, but it still felt recognizable: a slightly untamed countryside, with only a few farms visible through the dense brush lining the road. At the end, Elijah turned left onto Bayou Pacquet Road, an even less populated stretch than the last.

My stomach fluttered nervously as we traveled deeper into the desolate landscape. There were no farms, no side roads, nothing but wilderness, and I realized I might have made a serious judgement error by coming out there alone with someone I barely knew.

"You nervous?" he asked.

"A little. There's nothing out here. It feels so isolated, so uninhabited."

"Looks that way, I guess. Around here, everything between Pacquet Road and the lake is marshland, nothing but wilderness, but Pacquet Road will take you all the way into Slidell. Up here a ways is Kettle Road, where a few families live. Grans' place sits at the end, on Bayou Liberty. We'll be there soon."

Five minutes later, Elijah parked the truck behind an old cabin at the end of a half-mile-long gravel road bordering the marsh on the right.

I didn't expect Elijah's home to be in such a dilapidated condition. Severely weathered siding, with patches of chipping paint still clinging to it, surrounded the small structure. The roof showed signs of haphazard repair, and the shutters hung askew next to window frames holding dirty, cracked panes. The yard behind the cabin was littered with discarded items: tools, broken clay pots, old tin wash tubs, piles of wood stacked along the edge of the brush, and an old wheelbarrow with a hole rusted through the bottom, leaning up against the cabin.

"Is this where you live?"

"Nah. This is the old homestead. It's been here for a few generations. My grandfather was born in this cabin. Gran uses it for storage now and for making her medicines. Come on, I'll take you to the house."

I followed him down the path through a row of pawpaw trees and then into an open area gently sloping down to the water, where a covered dock housed Elijah's boat, *La Belle*, and another smaller craft.

Everything was so vibrantly green it was difficult to notice anything else. I became distracted by the mesmerizing beauty, the peaceful tranquility of the place. The sounds of nature surrounded me; birds, insects, wind rustling through the trees. It felt like an emerald paradise, and completely unexpected.

"It's back this way. Gran's got the door open, so she must know we're here," Elijah said, pulling me from my momentary sensory intoxication.

The house sat on high ground about a hundred feet from the water. Built on stone footings in the low-roof style of tropical homes, its expansive front porch commanded a southern view of the bayou. As we approached the house, a lush garden came into view: an herb garden, a vegetable patch, a bed of roses and azaleas, and a row of potted plants I couldn't identify. Further back, a wide-open area held a fire pit made of stone, with remnants of recent burnings, and surrounded by a few scattered chairs.

We entered through the side door into the kitchen and dining area, obviously the hub of the house. The woman standing at the stove, stirring and tasting a pot of something smelling savory, didn't look up when we came in, but continued to attend the pot until it satisfied her. Then she lowered the flame, resting the wooden spoon along the top of it, and turned to face us.

"Thank you for coming, Miss Désirée," she said with a broad smile. "I'm Louisa Ann Whitlock Gatlin. Everyone around here calls me Miss LouAnn. It's a pleasure to meet you. I wasn't sure Elijah could convince you to come. Please, make yourself comfortable. May I offer you some tea?"

"Thank you. That would be nice," I replied, taking a seat at the table and wondering what this woman wanted from me. Elijah remained standing.

"Elijah, those deer have been at my roses again. You need to spread some of your water around the yard, make them think twice before coming for my roses." The no-nonsense look on her face made Elijah turn several shades of crimson. "You go finish up your chores while I visit with Miss Désirée. I'll call you when we need you. Go on now."

"Yes ma'am," Elijah said with a respectful nod, clearly happy to escape his grandmother's blunt tongue. The anxious look he gave me as he left did nothing to ease my nervous stomach.

"You're wondering why I wanted to see you, and questioning your decision to come," she said while she set the table with a fine China tea set, just like the delicately painted China my friends would use for their Saturday afternoon tea parties. She added a spoonful of what looked like tea into the teapot, filled it with hot water from the kettle simmering on the stove, then left it to steep.

She took the seat across from me, studying me with eyes as green as the landscape she lived in. A bandana, tied with a twist around her head, held her loose braid of silver and black hair away from her sun-kissed face. She wore a man's shirt, buttoned to her bosom with the sleeves rolled up to her elbows, and a floral skirt and petticoat falling to her ankles. A pair of leather moccasins adorned her feet.

I'm not sure what I expected to find when I embarked on this adventure, but it certainly wasn't the woman sitting across from me. She had the manners of a typical southern lady, like the women in Mama's Bridge Club, but she had a quality they lacked, an uncompromising directness, which made her an enigma. It felt like she was out of place in this isolated environment, yet totally at home in it.

"Elijah said you needed to speak with me, madame." I gave her an equal amount of scrutiny, deciding I needed more information.

"Yes, I do. I wanted to look on the face of the woman who ended the Bentley curse. At least I hope you did." She poured me some tea without taking her eyes from mine, then she waited for my response.

"You obviously have read the papers and heard the news reports. The entire city knows Carson is dead. Why are you questioning it?"

"I'm not talking about Carson. Good riddance to him. From all accounts, he was the worst of them. No, I'm talking about the demon who controlled him, and every other Bentley heir since the slave times. Did you destroy it, or did my nephew plant his seed in you? If he did, the demon isn't gone."

"Carson was your nephew?" This encounter was getting stranger by the minute.

"He was my younger sister's son and the last of the Bentleys, unless there's another one growing in your belly. Is there?"

"No. I made sure of that."

Her brow pinched as she studied my face, then relaxed after accepting my answer as truthful. "Good, but what about that other girl, the one recovering at Glen Oaks? Does she have Carson's seed growing in her? The papers said you two are friends."

That was a consequence I hadn't considered for Evie, and the thought of it ripped a hole in my heart. "I don't know. Maybe. Evie is recovering, but it's slow. She has nightmares and drifts in and out of reality. Oh my god! If she's pregnant, I don't know how she'll ever recover." Panic began to set in as my stomach turned sour.

"Drink that tea before it gets cold, Miss Désirée. It will calm your nerves and your stomach."

"What's in it?" I asked, becoming suspicious of her motives.

"Just herbs. Chamomile and Valerian. Drink up. It will help you feel better."

I sipped the tea cautiously, discovering it tasted like the tea Miss Laila gave me on the night I killed Carson. My frayed nerves relaxed a little as I let the soothing brew glide down my throat.

"If your friend is pregnant, the only way she will recover is to kill what's growing inside her. Unless she does, she'll fall prey to that demon, if she hasn't already. The creature will dominate her life—what's left of it—until it doesn't need her anymore. The only way to end this, the only way to save her, is to end the pregnancy before it takes root." The look in her eyes said she was deadly serious.

"I don't understand any of this, all this talk of demons. What are you talking about?"

"Have you heard of the Mayfair family? Their house isn't too far from where you lived in Uptown."

I had heard about the Mayfairs, a strange family of mostly women that people only talked about in whispers, too afraid of being overheard by the spirit believed to be inhabiting the family. I never really believed the stories about them, but I would hasten my pace every time I passed by their house. My nodding head confirmed my knowledge.

"The Bentleys are like the Mayfairs, cursed by a demon who refuses let go. Over two hundred years ago, a demon was called to place a curse on the Bentley name. It started with a love triangle between Alton Bentley, Carlotta Madison, and a man called Antoine Dupris. Bentley won her hand, but Dupris challenged Bentley to a duel. He lost, but on his deathbed, Dupris cursed them both for eternity, them and all their heirs. Since then, every woman who married the Bentley heir died by the age of thirty-five after producing the next heir. For generations, the demon tormented every Bentley wife, including my younger sister, Beth, who died two weeks before her thirty-fifth birthday. And no female born into the Bentley family has ever produced a living child. They were all barren. The demon saw to that." Miss LouAnn took a sip of her tea, gauging my interest in her story before she continued.

It intrigued me, but I was cautious, unsure of where all this was leading.

"Clayton Bentley called my sister's death an accidental overdose, but I knew different. As sure as I'm sitting here, I knew the demon killed her, like it had all the others." She took another sip of her tea, watching me over the rim of her cup.

"When I was seventeen, my father arranged my marriage to Clayton Bentley as a business deal between two gentlemen. I had very little say in the matter. Clayton was twenty years my senior and twice widowed, with no heir to show for it. The colored women who worked for us told me stories about the Bentleys, and I believed them. Then, a few days before the wedding, the demon revealed himself to me disguised as Clayton. He tried to seduce me, possess me. It frightened me so much I ran off with René Gatlin the next day and never went back. I believe you saw the demon in Carson. You must have. That's how you defeated him. If you hadn't, you wouldn't be here."

The vivid memory of the night I killed Carson overwhelmed me, bringing back the same terror and the paralyzing fear of death unless I fought to survive. Shivers rippled down my back. She was right. I had seen it. I still saw it in my dreams, tormenting me, taunting me.

"Will you excuse me for a moment?" I quickly headed for the door, stepping out onto the porch. I needed a moment of fresh air to clear the memory, to put it back in its box, however temporary that would be.

Once outside, the vibrant colors and perfumes filled my senses, and with a sheer force of will, I pushed the memory back until I could shut the lid on its box. I took a deep breath, inhaling in the scents of nature, letting the raw and pungent smells clear my mind.

"Are you alright, Miss Désirée? I'm sure this must be difficult for you, hearing all this from a perfect stranger."

"I don't know what you want from me, Miss LouAnn. If everything you said is true—and I'm not sure it is—what do you expect me to do?"

"Help me end it, break the curse, and send the demon back where it came from."

"How? If Evie is pregnant, then there's nothing that can be done. Abortion is illegal, and the church says it's a sin."

"The church doesn't have to carry a monster in their belly for nine months, then spend the rest of their miserable lives trying to care for it." Her disdain for that institution was obvious in her tone.

"It's still illegal. The doctors at Glen Oaks would never do it."

"There's another way. Come inside, and I'll show you."

I followed her back inside, resuming my seat at the table while she rummaged in a pantry closet for something.

"Do you mind if I smoke?" I asked, reaching into my purse for my cigarette case and lighter.

"Be my guest," she replied over her shoulder. "There's an ashtray on the windowsill."

I lit the cigarette with trembling hands, then took a deep drag to calm myself down. Of all the things I imagined Elijah's grandmother would want from me, defeating a demon and breaking a curse was the very last, not to mention helping abort Evie's baby, if there was one.

When Miss LouAnn returned, she placed a vial full of a muddy-looking liquid in front of me, along with a small finely woven lidded basket. "What is this?" I asked, running my free hand over the basket.

"Do you know anything about the local Indian tribes who have lived in this area longer than the white man?" she asked, giving me a penetrating gaze.

I shook my head and took another drag from the cigarette, wondering where this was leading.

"Neither did I when I came out here. My mother-in-law was a Choctaw woman, a healer. She taught me their customs, their medicine, the sacred knowledge passed down from mother to daughter for countless generations. In that culture—unlike where you and I come from—women have as much power as men. They choose their mates, their lovers, when to breed and with whom. That vial in front of you is a native medicine that will regulate a woman's moon cycle when there are problems. It can also eliminate an unwanted pregnancy."

"What's in it?" I put out my cigarette and picked up the vial to examine it more closely.

"It's a tincture of raspberry and blue cohosh, nothing harmful if taken correctly. It's strong and unpleasant tasting, but it works. You must get your friend to drink this, all of it, and soon. It will purge her womb and make her blood flow, dislodging whatever is trying to take root."

"Will it hurt her? I'm not doing anything that will hurt Evie. She's been through enough."

"It won't harm her. After a day or two, she'll feel hard cramping and her blood will flow heavily, but that's all. There are no long-term effects. But if she waits too long to drink this, the effects are harsher and there's a chance it won't work. It's been over two weeks, and time is of the essence, Miss Désirée. The sooner she drinks this, the sooner she will recover."

"I doubt Evie's capable of making this decision right now, and even if she is, she'll believe it's a sin."

"Then you must decide for her. Would she really want this child after what Carson did to her, if she knew what you know? You said she's having nightmares, then convince her this medicine will end them. Tell her whatever you must but get her to drink it. It's the only way to save her."

"I'm not sure I can do it, even if I believed everything you said. You're asking me to kill a baby. Dear god, this is a nightmare." I shook my head unsure and worried for my friend.

"Are you willing to risk your friends' life and the lives of the women who will come next if this evil continues, all because you doubt the ramblings of an old bayou woman? And if you are, ask yourself this—knowing what you do about Carson and the evil he inflicted on you—would you drink that potion if *you* were carrying his seed?"

Another horrible memory assaulted me. "Yes, I would. I burned it out of me after the first time he raped me," I confessed, dropping my face into my hands in anguish.

"Then you know what to do," she said, slipping something over my head when I looked up. "This is to ward against evil. Quartz crystal has the power to protect you from that demon. Wear it when you are with your friend."

"Do you really believe all this stuff? Evil spirits and curses?"

"If I didn't, I wouldn't have troubled you, Miss Désirée." She reached into her pocket to retrieve a gauze bag tied with a string, then handed it to me. "Here is something I think will relax your body and mind, and help you sleep. It's a plant, like all my medicines, and useful in a variety of ways. These are the dried flower buds. You crush them and roll them into a cigarette or smoke it in a pipe. It's potent, so you won't need but a couple puffs, but I believe it will help you get through this."

"Thank you, Miss LouAnn. This has been quite an interesting afternoon." It would take a lot of sorting later to figure it all out.

"Yes, it has. It was brave of you to come out here. You're more than I expected."

"I can say the same about you."

"Elijah?" she called out through the open door. "It's time to take Miss Désirée home now."

"I'm right here Gran," he said, brushing his hands down his pant legs before he stepped inside.

She gathered the vial and gauze bag, nesting them inside the small basket, before securing the lid and handing the basket to me with a nod. I stored it in my purse, then stood to take my leave.

She walked me to the door, where Elijah was waiting. "Miss Désirée, it has been a pleasure meeting you. Thank you for coming to visit and I hope to see you again. I believe we have more to talk about. You're welcome here, anytime. Elijah, you get Miss Désirée home safe now. Supper will be ready by the time you get back."

"Goodbye Miss LouAnn," I said, but she had already disappeared into the house.

"How'd it go with Gran?" Elijah asked after he turned onto Pacquet Road, heading back to Mandeville.

"Your grandmother is an unusual woman." I might have said more, but couldn't speak about what she said, what she asked me to do. I needed time to think about it, figure out what I believed and what choice I would make.

"Yeah, she is. People around here look up to Gran. They come to her for help when they need it, respect her as a healer and wise woman. But I guess that sounds kinda strange to someone like you."

"No. It doesn't sound strange at all, now that I've met her."

"I knew she'd like you. She invited you back, which is always a good sign with Gran. Hey, we're having a party a week from Saturday, a kinda bayou Mardi Gras party for Gran's birthday. Would you like to come? You could bring your friend, Jolie. I'm sure you both would have a good time. There'll be lots of people and food and music. Gran would enjoy seeing you again."

"I don't know, Elijah. I'll have to let you know next week. Thanks for the invitation."

"Would it be alright if I came by to visit with you sometime?" he asked with a nervous look.

"Sure, but not on Mondays or Thursdays. I'm busy on those days, and you should call first to make sure I'm home." I wrote my phone number on an empty page in the small notepad I always carried in my purse, then tore it from the pad and handed it to him.

"Swell. I'll call you." He smiled, then stuffed the paper into his shirt pocket.

The sun was setting as we drove into Mandeville, crimson skies casting a glow over everything. By the time we pulled up in front of the house, my nerves were on edge again. Bill's car was in the driveway, which meant I would have some explaining to do.

"Here we are, safe and sound," Elijah said, cutting the engine. "I'll walk you to the door."

"No, don't bother. It's better if you don't. Thanks Elijah. Good night." I got out of the car and stood on the sidewalk, gathering my courage to face the consequences of my choice.

"Good night, Désirée. I'll just wait till you get inside. By the way, I like your name. It suits you," he said, giving me a shy smile before starting the engine.

Elijah really was the hero type, and I wondered if I would find another inside, or if my streak of independence had created more problems. Steeling my resolve, I headed for the door, knowing the price for my adventure was about to come due.

Chapter 13

New additions

As soon as I reached for the handle, the front door opened with a jerk.

"Where the hell have you been!?" Bill snarled when he saw me.

I stepped inside, past his glaring frown, and immediately noticed we weren't alone. Jolie, Luke and a negro man I didn't recognize stood together in the dining room, witnessing the scene Bill was making.

"Good evening to you too, Bill. I've been out. Thank you for asking," I said with as much sarcasm as I could muster.

"Damn it, Désirée, you can't go running off without telling me where you're going or who you're with. I won't have it!" He was practically foaming at the mouth. I'd never seen Bill that angry before.

But I wasn't having it either, not after the day I just had. "Excuse me? I wasn't aware I was under house arrest. And for your information, I told someone where I would be and with who." I spoke as calmly as I could, glancing over at Jolie, who just shrugged with an "I told you so" expression.

"Informing Jolie isn't good enough, Désirée. And... you're not under house arrest, but damn it, you can't be doing this again." He was having difficulty getting his anger under control.

I stared at him, unwilling to concede or keep my own anger from seeping to the surface. "Unless you're prepared to lock me in my room before you leave in the morning, you better learn to trust my judgement, otherwise this arrangement will not work. If you'll excuse me, I'm going upstairs to freshen up." I pushed past him, heading for the stairs.

"I guess she told you, partner," Luke said with a chuckle in his voice.

"Is she always this spirited?" This from the tall negro man. I wondered who he was and why he was there.

"Shit," Bill said, letting out a loud, frustrated groan. Then he followed me up the stairs, taking them two at a time.

I tried closing my bedroom door before he got there, but his out-stretched hand prevented it.

"We need to talk," he said, charging into my room uninvited and shutting the door, though not completely.

I placed my purse on the dressing table, then sat down facing the mirror and turned on the lamp. "I've already said what I had to say, Bill."

"Damn it, Désirée, I'm trying my best to keep you safe, and until I find the man who brokered that deal between Carson and Steigler, I must know where you are at all times. You need to understand the danger."

I couldn't believe he said that. As if I were oblivious to the threats against me, and those I posed to him and his family. I turned around so he could read my face and mood, so there would be no doubt about how I felt.

"For the last nine years, eight months and ten days, I have lived with that danger, Bill. I lost my family, my home, my country, and my identity because of it. I have been manipulated and controlled, tortured and nearly killed, and you think I don't understand the danger? Well, I do, probably better than you, but I will not let it, or anyone, control my life anymore. From now on, what I do, where I go, and who I go with is my choice and mine alone. So, you either trust me and my judgement, or you can try locking me up right now... if you think that will work."

He sat down at the end of the bed, dropping his hands in his lap, huffing out his frustration in heavy breaths. "It's not you I distrust, Chére. It's everyone else. Please try to see this from my point of view. If I don't know where you are, I can't protect you. I need to know you're safe, because if anything happened to you... I don't know what I'd do." He looked miserable, and I realized he wasn't angry. He was frightened.

"I'm sorry I scared you, Bill. I thought I'd be home before you got here."

"Where were you, and who is Elijah Tillman, if you don't mind my asking?"

I wasn't sure I wanted to explain, or even if I could. The whole day was still swirling around in my head, waiting to be sorted. None of it made logical sense, but then there had been no logic to the things Carson did. Maybe there really *was* a curse on the Bentley family.

"Elijah is the fisherman who gave me a ride across the lake. I went to his home on Bayou Liberty to visit with his grandmother." That's all I would say, even though his eyes were asking for more detail. I wouldn't tell him the rest.

"Alright. I'm sorry for yelling at you. Can we come to a compromise, Chére?"

"And what would that look like? Are you going to tell me where *you* go and who you're with?" I asked, challenging him to be honest when I already knew the answer. Bill never discussed what he did for Charlie or the government. That subject was off-limits.

"If you ask, I'll tell you... if I can. But I have something else in mind. We both know that Luke and I can't be here every minute, so I need someone I trust to be my eyes when I'm not around, someone who'll know what to do in an emergency."

"Oh, now I understand. The man downstairs is my bodyguard. I'm warning you right now, Bill, I won't let anyone treat me like a prisoner."

"It won't be like that, Chére. Zach Johnson is a good man. I think you'll like him."

"And if I don't?"

"Then I'll find someone you do like. Please, Chére, do this for me."

"Alright. I'll meet him. Now, if you don't mind," I said, ushering him out of my room.

I needed time alone to sort and file away the day's events and clear my mind before adding another twist. This was turning out to be the strangest day I had in a long time, and it wasn't over yet.

Before I went back downstairs, I needed to talk with Mama. Without some verification that what Miss LouAnn said was true, I wasn't sure what to do about that vial waiting in my purse.

"Hello Mama. How are you?" I tried to sound cheerful.

"Oh, hello, darling. I'm fine. How is everything going out there? Are you alright?" She must have heard something in my voice.

"I had a fight with Bill. He was mad because I wasn't here when he got home today."

"Where were you?" she asked, more concern seeping through the phone line.

"Mama, do you recognize the name Louisa Ann Whitlock?"

She paused, as if weighing her response. "Where did you hear that name, darling?"

"That's who I went to see today. Did you know her?"

"I didn't know her well. She was older than me, but I knew her younger sister. No one has seen or heard from Louisa in decades. How did you meet her? What did you talk about?" I could hear the caution in her voice, a hesitation that worried me.

"She's the grandmother of the young man who brought me across the lake. She wanted to talk to me... to make sure the Bentley curse had ended. Did you know about that, Mama, about the curse on the Bentley wives? Did you know?"

"There have always been stories like that about the old families of New Orleans, darling. It's a way for people to make sense of unexplained tragedy. I never paid much attention to them."

"But you knew about the Bentleys, didn't you? You never liked them."

"I remember the day Louisa disappeared, leaving Clayton practically standing at the altar without a bride. It devastated Elizabeth, losing her sister that way. The year that Bill and I married, Elizabeth married Clayton. He was twenty-three years older than her—a scandalous age difference even by my standards—but her father forced her to marry him, to fulfill the contract Louisa had broken. Theirs was a loveless marriage, just a business arrangement between men. Poor Elizabeth was never happy with Clayton, but she kept a brave face in public. Things got a little better for her after Carson was born. She seemed happier for a while. Then Charlotte came along, and Elizabeth fell into a depression she never fully recovered from. Carson and Beau were about twelve when she died."

"Mama, Miss LouAnn believes Clayton Bentley and the curse on his name killed her sister. She said there has been a curse on every woman who married the Bentley heir since the slave times. They all died young after the next heir was born. Have you ever heard that story?"

"I don't believe in curses, darling. I disliked Clayton because he was thoughtless and cruel to Elizabeth, which contributed to her unhappiness and ultimate death. If there was a curse, it ended with Carson. He was the last Bentley male."

"Not if Evie is carrying his child." My statement fell like a bomb on an unsuspecting population.

"Oh, dear God! Let's pray she isn't."

"Where are they?" I asked Jolie as I came into the kitchen after talking to Mama and decluttering my brain. I expected to find Bill and company in the living room, but they were nowhere in sight.

"They went into Bill's office when he came down after your argument. How'd that go?" she asked, looking up from the pot she was stirring on the stove.

"We reached a temporary compromise. I'm sorry if I got you in trouble with Bill."

"It wasn't that bad. They'd only been here for twenty minutes before you got home. Not enough time for Bill to really explode. Luke tried calming him down, saying you'd be back just like you promised. What did that old woman want, anyway?"

"It's a long story. I'll tell you later. Can I help with supper?" I reached into the refrigerator for the open bottle of white wine and poured myself a glass.

"It's all done. Just needs serving and people sittin' at the table. Do you want to go get them, or should I?"

"I'll go. I just need a minute with this wine. You want to join me?" I sat down at the kitchen table and lit a cigarette.

"Nah. I'll set the table. By the way, don't go out the back door. There's a big dog out there. That black fellow brought it with him."

"A dog? That's interesting. Set the table for five, Jolie. We'll see how progressive Mr. Johnson is."

Once I'd taken a few sips of wine, I went to Bill's office to call them all to supper.

"Good evening, gentlemen," I said, opening the door after knocking to announce my arrival. "Supper is ready."

Bill was sitting behind his desk smoking a cigarette, with Luke and Mr. Johnson sitting across from him. By the looks on their faces, they'd been deep in conversation.

I wondered if Mr. Johnson would accept an invitation to dine with us. That would tell me a lot about his character. They all stood up and followed me into the dining room.

"Mr. Johnson, please sit here." I directed him to a place across the table from me.

"Thank you, Miss Désirée, but I'll eat in the kitchen with Miss Jolie," he said, hesitating to assume what he obviously viewed as a privileged seat at the table.

"Jolie dines with us, Mr. Johnson, and if you choose to be a part of this household, you will too."

He looked to Bill and Luke for confirmation, who both shrugged their approval. They both knew my views on racial discrimination.

"Her house, her rules, Zach. You might as well get used to them now. Have a seat," Bill said, sitting down at the head of the table.

"Thank you kindly, Miss Désirée," Zach replied with a respectful nod, but he stole another look around the room to make sure before he sat down.

"May I offer you some wine, Mr. Johnson?" I held the bottle of burgundy over his empty wineglass.

"Don't mind if I do. Thank you, ma'am."

I poured his wine, then went around the table filling glasses as Jolie came in with the meal. The scent of tender braised beef with potatoes, carrots and a savory gravy filled the air, and I was suddenly famished. I took the platter from Jolie, directing her to take her seat while I served.

"Mr. Johnson, guests have first choice at this table. Please, help yourself," I said, holding the platter close so he could take what he wanted.

Even though I could see trepidation in his eyes, he nodded and served himself a healthy portion, then waited while I served the rest of the table.

When the food was served, I offered a prayer to the universe, not to God, because so far, there wasn't any evidence that he ever listened. "Bless this food and the hands that prepared it. Thank you, Jolie. It smells delicious."

The meal was delicious, but I'm sure it felt more like a job interview for Zach Johnson than a dinner party. Throughout the evening, I bombarded him with questions to assess his compatibility and gather information directly from him, without Bill's bias: his background, family ties, military service, post-war activities, and his relationship with Bill and Luke. I even asked about the dog.

"Gus? Oh, he's a good old dog, Miss Désirée. He's smart as a whip and loyal as the day is long. You'll never hear a peep out of him, less he don't like something. I'll introduce you to him after supper."

"Does he bite?" Jolie asked, clearly uneasy about the dog. Her mother died after being bitten by a rabid dog, and ever since, Jolie kept her distance from them.

"Only people I tell him to, and if he thinks someone is a threat, but I'm sure he's gonna like you just fine, Miss Jolie." A broad smile lit his face when he looked at her, bringing a rare blush to her cheeks.

Luke pushed himself away from the table with a satisfied grin. "Well, y'all. I need to take my leave and go see if my wife needs any help at the restaurant. Miss Désirée, have you heard enough from Zach? Is he staying or going?" he asked, though with a look that said he already knew my answer.

I took my time scanning their faces; Bill sitting back with a hopeful look, Luke, confident in the outcome, Zach, looking unsure and maybe a little hesitant, and then Jolie, whose eyes I held the longest. The addition of Zach to our band would affect Jolie the most, and I wasn't about to add him without her agreement. She gave me a half smile and a shrug, endorsement enough to secure Zach's place in the house.

"Mr. Johnson, welcome to the lake house. I hope you'll be happy here," I said, reaching across the table to shake his hand.

"Thank you, Miss Désirée. I'm sure I will," he replied with a firm handshake.

"Alright then, now that we have that settled, I'll say goodnight," Luke said, rising from the table and patting Zach on the shoulder. "Thank you for another delicious meal, Jolie. I keep telling Shelby what she's missing. Goodnight, I'll see y'all in the morning."

"I'll help clear the table." Zach stood up and started scraping and stacking plates. "I'd like to give the scraps to Gus, if that would be alright."

"That's fine, Zach," Bill said. "Jolie, will you show Zach where to put his things in the back bedroom?"

"Sure thing, Mr. William. Is the dog gonna sleep in there too?"

"Don't worry, Miss Jolie," Zach assured her. "Gus is an outdoor dog. He'll be happy sleeping under the house. Do you want to meet him?" he asked as he collected the plates and silverware and headed for the kitchen.

"Alright, but you better be right about that dog, or you and I are gonna have a problem," Jolie warned, following Zach through the door.

"Are *we* alright now, Chére?" Bill asked, looking at me across the now empty dining table.

"If you mean, am I still upset, then no. Zach appears to be a decent man, and I can see how he might fit in. Jolie seems to like him well enough."

"Will you come to my office so we can talk privately?" When I nodded my agreement, he held my chair, grabbed an open bottle of wine from the bar cart, then led me down the hall.

Bill's office wasn't a room I often went into, not even when I would spend the summers at the lake. It was always the men's place; Uncle Henri's sanctuary, or Charlie's summer office when the family vacationed there. It smelled of men, with the lingering scent of cigar smoke and the heady tang of bourbon in the air, plus the musky aroma of testosterone.

When I walked in, I was even less inclined to enter that male dominion than I had ever been, not because I felt out of place—which I did—but because I sensed something else coming. With a nervous bite to my lip, I sat in one of the leather chairs next to the window and reached into my pocket for a cigarette. Before I could retrieve my lighter, Bill flicked a match to light it, then sat down across from me with a pleased but nervous look in his eyes.

I figured there wasn't any reason to wait for the bad news. The day couldn't get much worse. So far, the best thing all day was the addition of Zach to the house. It felt like he might even be a blessing in disguise.

"Will you please tell me why I need someone with military training to protect me? What else is going on? Has Carson's threat to expose me materialized?" That thought was enough to send me running for cover.

Bill uncrossed his legs and leaned forward with a worried frown. He poured us each some wine, took a quick mouthful, then leaned back with a tired sigh. "I'm never sure how much I should tell you."

"The truth is always a good place to start, Bill. I'm not as fragile as you think I am." I took a sip of my wine and a drag from the cigarette to brace myself.

"I know you're not, Chére. If I could spare you any distress, I would, but it's better if you're aware of the potential danger."

"Is it Carson's threat?" My heart began beating faster.

"If Carson had arranged for something to be released upon his death, it wasn't with his attorney or any of his staff. We would have known by now. I've searched every place I can think of and have come up empty-handed. If he had any documents as evidence against you, he kept them well hidden."

That didn't relieve my mind at all. Loose ends, Uncle Henri called them.

"But there's something else troubling you. What is it?" I might as well hear it all at once.

"I already mentioned that we haven't located the man Carson was working with. His name is Anthony Gatti, and he has a couple of reasons to hide. The first is his employer, the Genovese family, who are trying to keep Frank Costello's business interests out of New Orleans. Gatti's bosses sent him down here to secure that goal by making a substantial investment with Carson. That investment is now worthless, and they are looking to recoup their loss."

"The other reason Gatti is hiding is because on the ninth of January, one of Steiglers operatives in Mexico gave him a down payment of $25,000 for a package that was supposed to be delivered to Merida on the eleventh. An additional $25,000 was to be paid upon receipt of the merchandise. On the tenth, a deposit of $20,000 showed up in Carson's personal bank account. I'm sure Steigler will want his money back or the merchandise he paid for."

"That's a lot of money, Bill. Is $50,000 the going price for a young woman these days?"

"No, I don't think so. According to Eduardo Reyes, Steigler's business is drugs, gambling, and prostitution, but I doubt he pays that much for any of his acquisitions. This transaction feels personal, which is why I'm not taking any chances with your safety. Steigler won't risk coming here, but he has a long reach and a lot of connections."

"It's hard to believe I'm worth that much to him. He must really hate me. Do you know if Katarina is alright?" If Anton Steigler hated me enough to pay that much money to get me, then he would undoubtedly be after his ex-wife, Katarina, too, because she was the one who saved me from him.

"I have people in Havana watching her. Eduardo Reyes gets regular reports from one of his people who works in her household. So far, Steigler is a ghost, but he'll surface again. He almost had you, Chére."

"It might be easier if you use me as bait. That would solve a lot of problems." I don't know why I said it, maybe because I was tired of being on guard all the time.

"I won't do that, Désirée. You're too important to me."

"Why? Why have you sacrificed so much for me?" I really wanted to know, to make sense of all this somehow.

"Because I can't imagine my life without you in it." He kept his eyes riveted to mine, speaking through them the words he was reticent to speak out loud.

I shouldn't have asked. The girl I used to be to him was gone, and I could never be that girl again.

I set my glass on the table and stubbed out the cigarette. My head was pounding, blood pumping through it in rhythmic pulses. I rubbed my temples and rolled my neck to ease the discomfort.

"Do you have a headache?" he asked. "Mother says it helps when I massage her head and neck. Can I... will you let me try? It might help."

Unsure of how I would react to his touch, I hesitated, even though I longed for his comfort. But after everything that happened, I couldn't give in to him. I was too afraid to let him close enough to see what I had become.

"No... I'm fine. It's just been a long day and I'm tired. Thanks for keeping me informed, Bill." I quickly stood to leave before I lost whatever self-control I had.

"Do I frighten you, Désirée?" His tormented expression said my rejection hurt him.

I shook my head. "No. It's not you... it's me. I'm sorry." I fled as quickly as I could, never daring to look back.

Chapter 14

Confessions

I sat by my bedroom window, watching the candle on the windowsill burn down, its flame dancing and twisting against the backdrop of the night sky. My nightly ritual of focusing, sorting, and storing away the events of the day wasn't completely successful. Miss LouAnn's story of the Bentley demon refused to be stored away. I tried to find a happy memory that could ease me to sleep, but it was hopeless. There would be no peaceful rest, not for my tormented mind.

It was after ten when Jolie came upstairs to get ready for bed, her eyes filled with questions. I could tell by her arching brow she wouldn't let the night end without getting some answers.

"What do you think of Zach?" I asked, hoping to distract her.

She shrugged and shook her head, tossing her apron in the wash basket in the corner. "He's alright, I guess. He's not bad to look at, but he's no domestic worker, that's for sure."

She stood in the middle of the room with her arms crossed, her brow pinched in a deep v above her nose and her lips tight, looking as if she would not put up with any of my distractions.

"I think it's about time you told me what's really going on, Désirée. Why does Bill think you need a bodyguard? And while you're at it, what did that old woman say that got you so upset?" She sat down on her bed, kicked off her shoes, then laid back with her head propped on her crossed arms, waiting for my response.

She deserved to know what she was getting into, and I hated lying to her. "If you really want to know, Jolie, then we're going to need a bottle of wine. It's a long story." I wasn't sure I could tell it without additional fortification.

"You drink too much, Désirée." Her bold, wide-eyed stare stifled any denial I could have offered.

She was right; I drank more than I should, probably a lot more than other girls my age, but then they hadn't experienced the life I had.

"Are you going to mother me now, Jolie?"

"No. I'm just pointing out the obvious, in case you missed it."

"Alright, no wine. Go get ready for bed and then I'll tell you a bedtime story, but don't expect a happy ending."

It was well after midnight when I finished telling Jolie my history, including the night I killed Carson. But I didn't tell her about the brand he left on me during his first attack. That wasn't something I could share with anyone.

Of the few times I'd told my story, this was the least traumatizing, mostly because Jolie kept interrupting me with questions, keeping me rooted in the present instead of fully immersed in the past. When I was done, she leaned back against her headboard, pulled her legs up, wrapping her arms around her knees, and just stared at me for the longest time.

"Damn, girl. It's hard to believe you kept all that bottled up inside you all this time, never telling no one. I guess I can't really blame you for wanting to drown it in a few shots of whiskey."

"Sometimes it helps to quiet the ghosts, but not always... not lately."

"What happened with that old lady today?"

I blew out the candle and climbed into bed. "That's a ghost story best left for the daylight. I'll tell you tomorrow." I didn't want to chance speaking about the curse or the spirit, fearing doing so would call it to me. My memories of Carson were torment enough.

Jolie lay down on her bed, pulling the blanket over her shoulder, but then she propped herself up onto her elbow and looked over at me. "Do you really remember everything like it just happened? I mean, everything?"

I nodded and sighed, wishing with all my heart that it wasn't so. "Yes."

"Damn. It's got to be hard living like that, never forgettin' nothin'."

"You can't tell anyone about this, Jolie, none of it, not to anyone. Okay? It would cause a lot of trouble for Bill and the family. Promise me."

"Of course, I promise. I'll even cross my heart and hope to die, if that will make you feel better."

"I'd rather you not die, Jolie, if you don't mind."

Miraculously, I slept through the night without waking Jolie with my usual nocturnal ravings and ramblings. Even more surprising, I was up before her for the first time since she'd been there. I left her snoring softly into her pillow and hoped my bedtime story hadn't given her nightmares.

When I went downstairs to get the coffee started, I found Zach in the kitchen, looking through the pantry cupboard.

"Good morning, Zach. Can I help you find something?" His wide-eyed expression said I'd caught him off guard.

"Oh, morning, Miss Désirée," he said, lifting his head out of the pantry. "I was hoping to get the coffee on, but I can't seem to find the essential ingredient. Do you know where Miss Jolie keeps the coffee?"

"Let me make it, Zach." I pulled out one of the kitchen chairs for him. "You sit down and tell me about yourself, something I don't know yet."

"You sure, Miss Désirée? It ain't no trouble, soon as I learn where things are."

"Sit, Zach. I'll make the coffee." I opened the freezer to retrieve the tin of coffee beans that lived in there. There was nothing like fresh coffee in the morning, and keeping the whole beans chilled helped them stay fresher longer, especially in the Louisiana weather.

Zach watched in silence as I performed my coffee-making ritual: grinding the beans to the perfect texture, filling the basket and inserting it into the coffee pot, and setting it on the stove to heat over a medium flame. I put a small pitcher of cream next to the stove to warm as the coffee was brewing, then I took a seat across from Zach.

"Did you sleep well? Were you comfortable in your new surroundings?" I asked, opening the window and lighting a cigarette as I waited for my morning coffee to brew.

"Very comfortable, miss. I slept like a baby. How about you? Was it hard having someone new in your home?" His look was deferential but curious, like he was trying to figure me out and place me into a recognizable category.

"Not at all. In fact, I slept better than I have in a while. Perhaps I have you and Gus to thank for that."

"I'm glad we can oblige, miss. Would you like to meet him? You didn't get a chance last night."

"I'd love to as soon as I have my coffee. I haven't had a dog since I was a little girl."

Just then, Jolie walked in, tying her robe and shaking her head at me. "Why didn't you wake me up, Désirée? Morning, Zach."

"Morning, Miss Jolie."

"I didn't want to wake you, Jolie. You were sleeping so soundly, and you needed the rest. The coffee is almost ready. Is Bill up?"

"He'll be down any time now. I'll get breakfast started," she said, turning on the oven, then pulling coffee cups from the cupboard and setting them on the counter as the coffee finished perking, filling the room with my favorite morning aroma. On the opposite counter, she gathered the eggs and ham from the refrigerator, then pulled out a large bowl from the cupboard and started mixing the ingredients for biscuits.

"I'll help," I said, rising to join her.

"No. I've got this, Désirée. You come get your coffee, then go out and meet that dog. You're the one he needs to get to know. Help yourself to coffee, Zach." she said, taking the now fully perked coffeepot from the burner and filling two cups full of the brew. She set the cream next to the sugar bowl with a couple of teaspoons, then went back to making the biscuits.

After doctoring my coffee, I headed out the back door to enjoy it on the porch in the morning sunshine. Zach followed me out and let out a whistle, which brought the dog up to join us.

According to Zach, he raised Gus from a pup, a mix of hound and chocolate lab. Gus was a big dog—his head reached almost as high as my waist—with golden eyes as sharp as an eagle's, long floppy ears, and a soft, short-haired coat of cocoa brown. He sat on his haunches next to Zach, waiting for instructions.

"Gus, this is Miss Désirée. She's your number one job now," Zach told the dog verbally as he made a series of hand gestures that Gus followed with rapt attention.

"Does he understand what you're saying?" I asked.

"He knows what he's supposed to do, Miss Désirée. Let him get your scent, maybe lick your hand so you'll imprint on him." He gave Gus another hand signal.

I stayed as still as I could, though I couldn't help being nervous as Gus approached my outstretched hand with a mouthful of sharp teeth. He looked straight at me for a few seconds, lifted his nose to sniff my hand, then circled me twice, sniffing as he went. When he was done, he stood in front of Zach, let out a little yipping sound, then he came back to stand next to me, licking my hand and snuggling his head beneath it. I stroked his head and rubbed his ears between my fingers.

Zach took a drink of his coffee, watching for a reaction from me or the dog—I couldn't tell which.

"I guess this means he likes me."

"Yes, miss, he likes you just fine," Zach said, shaking his head like he couldn't quite believe it. "It's just I've never seen him do that, nuzzle up like that to someone new. Gus is usually all business, so this must mean he's adopted you into his pack."

"Morning, Zach," Bill said, coming out onto the porch with his coffee cup in hand. "Good morning, Chére. I see you've met Gus. Does he meet with your approval?"

"I think he approves of me," I said, petting my new companion, who nuzzled my hand again.

"That's good. Zach, you and I are heading out after breakfast. I want to get you familiar with Mandeville and the surrounding area, introduce you to a few people. Will Gus be alright here on his own?"

"Sure thing, Mr. William. He'll patrol the property and watch over Miss Désirée. Gus knows what to do."

Upon hearing his name, Gus stood upright and let out a couple of yips. I wondered if he really understood what Zach expected of him, or if his reaction meant something else, like maybe he was asking when he was going to be fed. Not having had a pet since I was eight, I couldn't read his posture or expressions, which felt like a handicap to our relationship.

"Zach, will you teach me the signals? I want to learn how to talk to him."

"Course, Miss Désirée, I'll teach you, but you can tell him just about anything, and he'll understand. Gus is the smartest dog I've ever known."

"Yip, yip!" Gus agreed.

"I've been thinking about what you told me last night," Jolie said as we finished cleaning up the kitchen after breakfast. "About that German officer who was there when they arrested you and your friend. Why didn't he identify you to the French police? Seems to me he knew you would be there, so someone had to tell him. Any idea who? Maybe that driver told him. Maybe he had something to gain by betraying you. Did you ever find out what happened to him or to that German officer?"

I sat down at the kitchen table and lit a cigarette to consider her question. I'd always thought it had been bad luck that Alex and I were so quickly arrested the night I ran away from the Steiglers. Maybe it was Annalise who wrote those names then forgot about them, but I couldn't believe she would do anything to harm Alex, not purposely. The girl I knew at La Maison loved Alex, but she was forgetful, and she hated me.

"I don't know what happened to anyone. They could all be dead now and I'll never know. The Germans were still in control of France when that happened. It was six months before the liberation, and I went into hiding. It doesn't matter who betrayed me, Jolie, because I'm the one they arrested. The police found those Resistance names with me, and the Nazis killed them all. After the liberation, when the police discovered who I was, who I'd been during the war, I was automatically guilty in their eyes. They labeled me a collaborator, a traitor to my country."

"You were just a kid, Désirée. You didn't have a choice."

"Ask any French girl who lived through those years and she would say different. She would tell you I had a choice, and I took the cowards' route, the one that kept me warm and well fed, while the rest of the country starved under the boot heels of the Nazis. Ask the people who got arrested and executed because of me. Ask their families if I deserve forgiveness. I think they all would agree I don't."

Chaz Maret's face loomed in my mind, filled with hatred and anger toward the girl who caused his parents' execution. *"I'd like to strangle the life out of her, just like the Nazis strangled my parents."* Chaz didn't know that I was the girl he hated.

"Seems to me what you gotta do is forgive yourself, Désirée. You're not responsible for what other people did. Not the Nazis and not Carson Bentley. None of it was your fault."

"That's not entirely true, Jolie. What happened to Evie *is* my fault. It wouldn't have happened if I told Mama after the first time Carson hurt me. If I had, Evie never would have met him, and at least three other women would still be alive. It's hard to forgive myself for that."

"Maybe once all this is over, it will get easier."

"Thanks, Jolie. That psychiatrist wants me to talk about my past and I can't, for obvious reasons, so it feels good to talk about this to someone."

"Can't you talk to Bill? He knows about you."

"It's hard with Bill. It's different now... after Carson. Some things I just can't tell him."

"I guess not. Well, maybe that will get easier too. Now, what about that old woman yesterday? You said you'd tell me what she wanted."

"Do you believe in curses and spirits?"

"Course I do. A person would have to be a fool to live in New Orleans and not believe in such things."

"Miss LouAnn told me there was a curse on the Bentleys, like the curse on the Mayfairs. A demon cursed the wives of every Bentley heir for generations. After they produce the next living heir, they die before they turn thirty-five. Miss LouAnn is Carson's aunt, his mother's older sister. She wanted to know if I was pregnant with Carson's child."

A look of horror filled Jolie's face, though not about the curse. "Are you?" she asked.

"No, but Evie might be."

"Damn. I can't imagine having to carry that man's child inside me for nine months. What else did that woman say?"

"She wants me to end the Bentley curse. Carson was the last male heir, and the curse would end with him, but I don't think it's over yet. Evie keeps falling back into the nightmare. Something is keeping her there. Every time I think I've reached her; she fades away again."

"What did that woman ask you to do?"

"She gave me something to give to Evie. A tincture, women's medicine, she called it. She said it will kill whatever is growing inside, but it won't hurt Evie. I'm supposed to make sure she drinks it soon. If I wait too long, it might not work, and it could hurt Evie."

"You know what that means, don't you? If you give it to her and she really is pregnant?" Jolie looked at me for a long time, trying to put herself in my shoes. "Damn. What are you going to do?"

"I don't know. I hate making this decision for Evie, but she's not conscious enough to make it herself, and I can't talk to her mother or

Doctor Neville about it. They wouldn't let me see her again. You're the only one I've told. What should I do, Jolie?"

"I guess you got to ask yourself, would you drink that medicine if you were pregnant, and you knew drinking it would end it?" She gave me a look that demanded honesty.

"Yes."

"Then there's your answer, Désirée. If you're really her friend, you'll help her get her life back."

The following morning in the pre-dawn hours, I woke up in a cold sweat, jolting up in bed, my heart racing, my breath ragged and panting, as if I'd run from a predator. The sound of his whispers still echoed in my ears.

"Damn you, Lottie. Damn you to hell."

His face loomed over me in the shadows, taunting me, tormenting me.

"Go to hell," I whispered back.

Rather than risk waking Jolie, I escaped to the cool comfort of the upper terrace to find sanctuary under the early morning stars, but I wasn't alone for long.

His footsteps were silent as he climbed the stairs from the patio below. He made his presence known by gently touching my hand with his wet nose, then laying his head on my lap as I lounged on the chaise. With a low whine, he nuzzled my hand, sensing my distress.

"Hello, Gus. Did I wake you?"

He licked my hand in response. His soft fur and the warmth of his head in my lap felt better than anything. He was a quiet, steadfast, comforting presence who demanded nothing of me except perhaps some food and kindness.

We comforted each other for the rest of the night, watching the stars traverse the night sky and twinkle out as a new dawn arrived.

A sharp whistle brought us out of our dreamy state a little after dawn.

"Gus. Where you at, boy?" Zack called from the porch outside the kitchen.

Gus looked up at me and whined, as if to ask if he could go.

"Go on. We both need to get our day started. No use putting it off," I said, rising from the chaise. I stroked his head and rubbed his ears one last time before releasing him. "Thanks, Gus."

Chapter 15

Vial Choices

By Thursday, the bruises on my face were gone, but my neck still had dark marks along the sides. I refused Jolie's offer of a scarf to hide them, instead laying the collar of my blouse open over my lightweight jacket. I checked my pocket to make sure the vial was secure.

"Are you gonna give it to her?" Jolie asked as she leaned against the bathroom doorway with her arms crossed, giving me a look filled with compassion.

I caught her reflection in the mirror and shook my head. "I don't know. Maybe, if she's responsive today and if there's an opportunity. Everything depends on Evie."

"Yeah, I guess, but whatever happens, you watch out for yourself. Ya hear?" Her deep brown eyes stared at me in the mirror with her mouth turned down in a frown she rarely wore.

"I don't know how I can ever repay you, Jolie?"

"I've got a few ideas when you're ready. You still haven't taught me how to make croissants." She raised her eyebrows, which eased the worry lines from her forehead, as a sly grin curled up the corners of her mouth.

"Really? After all this time? I guess that's because it takes time to make them, and we only had a few hours together each week."

"Well, we've got plenty of time now. I'll see you when you get home."

"Right. I better go before this stuff burns a hole in my pocket. See you later."

"Now, Miss Désirée, you just sit back there and let me do the driving," Zach said, holding the front seat forward so I could climb into the back seat of my Ford Coupe.

"This is my car, Zach," I said, stubbornly refusing to get in. "Bill gave it to me for graduation and I want to drive today." I thought driving might help distract me from the nerves doing flips in my stomach.

"Mr. William hired me to be your driver, Miss Désirée. I'm just trying to do my job. Besides, how would it look if people were to see you driving with a black man sitting next to you?"

"It shouldn't make any difference to anyone."

"It shouldn't, but it does, Miss Désirée, and I don't want to make no trouble for you or for me. So please, let me do the driving."

He was right, of course. The level of prejudice hadn't lessened in the five years I'd been in the States. It might even have increased, especially in the deep south, and I was sitting nearly as far south as one could get. I blew out my frustration and climbed into the back seat.

By the time we got to Glen Oaks, my palms were sweating and the vial in my pocket felt like a lead weight tugging on my conscience. All the way there, I imagined different scenarios. In one, I would get Evie alone and make her believe it's a magic potion that would end her nightmares. In another, I just threw the damn thing out the car window before we got to Glen Oaks. Neither gave me a good feeling about myself. There were no good options available.

I never knew what I would find when I visited Evie after my sessions with Doctor Neville. The last time I'd seen her, she sat slumped in her chair, staring at the wall, unresponsive except to the invisible spirit tormenting her. Whatever was keeping her in the delusion had a powerful hold on her mind. But I was determined to reach her, free her from her nightmare, even if it meant risking my immortal soul.

"Good morning, Miss Désirée," Nurse Johanna said as I approached the nurse's station next to Evie's room. "Miss Evelyn is waiting for you. I'll bring in her lunch after you visit for a while. We have Miss Evelyn on a special diet now."

"*Bonjour*, Johanna. Thank you, but why the special diet?" I couldn't imagine why... unless Evie really was pregnant.

"Oh, uh. I'm sorry, Miss Désirée, I can't say anything about... well, I hope you understand. Patient privacy, and all that."

"Of course. How is she today?"

"She asks for you often. I'm sure she'll be glad to see you."

"It's so nice outside today, Johanna. May I take her to the garden for a stroll before lunch?" I quickly formed a plan to take Evie far enough out of sight for me to give her the vial of medicine without being seen... if I could even convince her to take it.

"Yes, of course. She's still unsteady on her feet, so I'll bring you a wheelchair. You can go in now, Miss Désirée."

For a moment, it felt as if time hadn't touched Evie since Monday. She was sitting in the same chair I'd left her in, dressed in the same hospital gown and robe, her hair brushed, but lifeless. Her face had the same tormented expression, her eyes riveted to the corner of the small room as if someone were there. She closed them and looked away, glancing toward the door, toward me.

"*Bonjour, Evie.*" I kissed her cheeks in our familiar greeting. "*Comment ça va, mon amie*?"

"You're here. You came." A shudder rolled through her frail body, releasing a mournful sigh, as if she had feared I wouldn't come back... or maybe that I would.

"Of course, I did, Evie. We're friends, and I won't stop coming unless you don't want me to."

She glanced toward the corner, then shook her head several times as if she heard something. "No. I won't. No," she said to the apparition that I couldn't see but could feel in the depth of my stomach.

"Who are you talking to, Evie? Is it Carson who haunts you?" I took her hand to give her a physical presence to hold on to.

She looked up at me, shaking her head. "No, not Carson. The other one, the dark one. Doctor Neville and Johanna don't believe me. They think I'm crazy, but he's there, always there in the corner watching me, whispering to me. You believe me, don't you, Désirée?"

"Yes, Evie. I believe you. I can't see him, but I feel his presence."

"He doesn't want you here. He wants me to send you away." She gripped my hands as if afraid I would leave.

"What do *you* want, Evie?" I hoped this moment of fragile lucidity wasn't temporary.

"I want *him* to leave." Her voice was barely a whisper as her eyes pleaded for my help.

"Let's go outside for a while. Maybe he'll be gone when we come back," I said as the door swung open and Johanna brought in the wheelchair.

"Here you go, Miss Evelyn," Johanna said, wheeling the chair over to us. "Let me help you get settled in so you can go enjoy a little sunshine before lunch."

Johanna fussed over her until satisfied Evie was comfortable and wouldn't tumble out while I pushed her through the garden.

Once we were outside and safely out of range of any prying eyes or ears, I guided the chair along the garden path to a bench beneath a large oak. I sat on the bench, positioning Evie in front of me, with her back to the building.

"Did he follow us?" I asked.

She looked around the garden, then focused on the tree trunk to my left, her eyes widening with renewed fear.

"Yes, he's there," she said, throwing her hands over her face. "He won't leave me alone, Désirée. He says I belong to him now."

"You don't, Evie. Here, I want to give you something that may help," I said, slipping the crystal heart from around my neck and placing it around hers. "Hold this close to your heart. It will ward off evil and keep you safe."

The instant she placed the stone next to her heart, the heady scent of bergamot orange filled the surrounding air, but there were no citrus trees at Glen Oaks.

A chill ran down my spine. "Is he still there?" I asked.

"Yes," she said, her voice soft and trembling.

"Evie, if you really want him gone forever, *you* must decide. You must choose to send him away. I have something else for you, a woman's potion that will destroy him and send him back to hell where he belongs. Do you want it?"

"Please, Désirée. Please help me. I can't go on like this or I really will go mad."

I put the vial of medicine in her right hand and uncorked it for her. "This won't taste good, but you must drink it all and keep it down. Do it quickly before anyone sees. They don't understand how evil he is, how dangerous, but I do. Drink it, Evie. Send him back to hell."

Her hand shook as she lifted the vial to her mouth, tipping out the contents in a desperate gulp, then gagging at the taste of it. "Ugh. It's horrible."

"Keep it down, Evie. Don't let him win," I said, just as a torrent of wind roared through the oak branches above us, encircling us with his rage while Evie doubled over in misery.

I looked toward the tree trunk and saw him clearly for the first time. He was tall, dressed in dark clothing from a bygone era, riding boots up to his knees, a dagger in his belt, and a look of pure hatred in his golden eyes. I'd seen those eyes before, on the face of Carson Bentley the night I killed him.

"Do you still see him, Evie?" I hoped she didn't. I hoped this gamble was worth the risk, but I knew I may have doomed myself.

She lifted her head and opened her eyes to scan the area, then shook her head. "No, and I can't hear him anymore, either. Is he really gone, Désirée?"

"Yes. I don't think he'll bother you again. Let's go back inside so you can get something to wash the taste out of your mouth." I pushed the chair quickly up the path toward her room.

There was a real possibility the potion might not work, but I wanted her to believe it would. I wanted to believe it, for my sake as well as hers. Only time would tell, and I hated waiting.

By the time Zach got me home that afternoon, I was a wreck. Every bit of mental energy I possessed went into trying to rid myself of the memory of that spirit, demon, whatever it was, but it was an exercise in futility. The vision of him standing under that tree with the scent of bergamot swirling through the air was a memory that resisted filing away. It was the stuff of nightmares... as if I needed more of them.

Jolie met me at the back door, with dark eyes filled with worry once she got a good look at me. "How'd it go with your friend? Is she any better?"

She was eager to hear what happened, but right then, I couldn't talk about it, couldn't admit to the mortal sin I'd just committed.

"I'll tell you later. Right now, I need a shower." I rushed upstairs to wash the orange smell off my skin as quickly as I could. I hated ignoring her, but I didn't want her to know the curse was real... that I'd seen the demon and was afraid I'd brought him home.

Gus was waiting for me on the upper terrace when I came out after my prolonged shower. As I opened the door, he nuzzled my leg and licked my hand, then stood in front of me as if he didn't want me to go outside.

"What is it, Gus? Is something wrong?" I asked, taking my cues from this dog who'd become my guardian.

He yipped, then turned toward the lakeside corner of the terrace, growling low and menacing as if he saw something in the treetops.

A faint scent of bergamot drifted through the branches, sending me into a near state of panic as Gus charged toward its source. He stood tense in the corner, growling and snapping at something I couldn't see but knew was there.

Old wives' tales warned against inviting a spirit into your home. If I didn't speak directly to it, he couldn't enter, so I felt safe, even though I'd left the crystal talisman with Evie.

With a courage I didn't recognize in myself, I walked toward it, unwilling to give in to fear. I bent down to hold Gus around his neck, then whispered in his ear. "He's not welcome here, Gus. He cannot come in unless I invite him, and I don't want him here."

A deep growl rumbled in Gus's chest, then he barked menacingly toward the treetop, making his dominance known to whatever was there.

"Good dog, Gus. Stay by me and don't let him near." I turned my back on the spirit and took a seat on the chaise.

"Is everything alright, Miss Désirée? I heard Gus barking at something," Zach asked, coming out onto the terrace with concern in his eyes.

"We're fine, Zach. Must have been a squirrel up in the tree. Will you tell Jolie that I'll be out here for a while and that I'm fine? I just need some quiet time to myself."

"Sure thing, Miss Désirée. Let me just raise up this canopy so the afternoon sun don't burn you. You want me to bring you out something to drink?" he asked as he sheltered me from the damning rays of the sun.

"No thanks, Zach. I'll be fine." *Eventually,* I hoped as I eased back on the chaise, intending to sort and file away every detail of this day's events.

Chapter 16

Dining out

It was just before sunset when Bill came out onto the terrace to join me. As he did, Gus quietly slipped away down the back steps, leaving us alone.

"You look like a woodland fairy, with the last rays of the sun kissing your cheeks," Bill said as he pushed back the canopy, which had lost its contest with the setting sun.

I looked up into his eyes, the same eyes I'd seen one afternoon five years earlier in a country field outside Versailles. "You called me that once before, as I recall."

"I remember, but your hair was a different color then." He reached over to touch a lock of my hair, rubbing it between his fingers. "I like this better. In this light, it looks like cascading waves of spun gold. So beautiful."

I struggled with the need to lean into him, seek his comfort, and the opposing need to pull away for fear of being burned... or burning him. I reverted to old habits, hiding my true feelings behind a mask. Not that it did much good. Bill could always see through them.

"You're home early. How was your day?" I tried to sound normal.

"Better, now that I'm here. All the way home, I was hoping I'd be able to catch the sunset out here... with you. Seems I made it just in time."

He sat down in the chair next to me, leaning back with his legs crossed and a relaxed smile on his handsome face. He didn't press me for details of my day, nor even ask how my session with Doctor Neville was, a courtesy I was grateful for. I wasn't sure what I could say without lying to him, and I didn't want to do that.

Through the scattered clouds, the sun was setting in a blaze of crimson and gold, filling the sky with the special light only available at sunset.

As the sky began darkening, Bill looked over at me with an irresistible smile on his face. "This is my favorite time of day. I'm glad I could be here to share it with you. Would you go out for supper with me tonight? There's a little Italian place in Lacombe I've been meaning to take you to."

I used to love going out for dinner, but since the newspaper printed my photo, identifying me as the Phantom Slayer, it felt too difficult. Unsure if I could face being in public, I hesitated.

"I'm not sure." I hated being cowardly about it, but knew I'd eventually need to go out. It seemed to mean something to him, like he was trying to bridge the gap between us and create a sense of normalcy in our life. The look in his eyes held such hope, a plea that was hard to resist.

"Alright Bill. Do I need to dress up?"

"No. Emiliano's is a casual place, though not as informal as the Abita Springs Café. Wear whatever you're comfortable in. I need to make a few calls first. Can you be ready around seven? Will that give you enough time?"

"I'll be ready, but can *I* drive?"

A smile beamed across his face as he helped me to my feet. "Your car? Or mine?"

"Mine," I said as I headed inside to change.

Emiliano's sat on a quiet street off Highway 190 in central Lacombe. Originally one of the older homes of the town, it became a restaurant and bar, offering the community a taste of Italy with its authentic menu. A polished wood bar with several stools and a mirrored wall shelved with various liquors hugged the left side of the main dining room. The linen-covered tables beneath soft lighting and the Italian music helped to create an intimate atmosphere.

I wasn't sure what Bill's intentions were, nor what to think or feel as we sat at a corner table, so I let Bill take the lead.

"Mind if I order for us, Chére?" he asked when the waiter came to take our order.

This is becoming a habit.

I nodded my agreement.

In what sounded like perfect Italian, Bill ordered us both the dinner special: an Antipasto salad and Veal Scallopini, with a bottle of their best Chianti.

"I didn't know you could speak Italian," I said, realizing there was a lot I didn't know about him.

"One of a few languages I've picked up along the way. In my line of work, a fellow can't have too many," he said with a wink and a smile.

I might have pressed him on what exactly he did for a living, but his unwavering look made me decide against it.

It's better if you don't know, Désirée.

Bill's world and his social circle felt light years away from mine. He was fourteen years older, and it baffled me why he would choose to spend his time with me instead of doing whatever it was he usually did.

I sipped the wine and watched him over the rim of my glass as I formed my question.

"It's Mardi Gras season, Bill. Don't you usually attend lots of parties during Mardi Gras?"

His brow furrowed slightly. "I do, and there were a few I planned to take you to. I planned to spend as much time with you as you'd let me. But this feels... more natural. Just you and me, and I don't have to share you with anyone." His brow smoothed and the light in his eyes sparked a sensation I hadn't felt in a long time, a tingling feeling that permeated through my body all the way down to my toes.

I tried to hide the blush filling my cheeks with my napkin, but he saw it, capturing my eyes with his.

"Is this alright, Chére? Or have I presumed too much?" He sounded as unsure as I felt.

"No, you haven't, Bill. It's just a little... I don't know. I just feel unsettled, and that's not very comfortable."

"You don't need to be, not with me." His eyes reflected his sincerity. I had nothing to fear from him, of all people.

We knew each other, but not well. Our paths had separated years ago by design and necessity. Merging them felt awkward now, especially after what happened with Carson. I knew the closer I got to Bill, the harder it would be to leave him... but I didn't have to think about that yet, so I let myself experience the moment. I had a special box for my memories of Bill.

We spent the evening enjoying a delicious meal and getting to know one another, sharing stories of places he'd been and places I wanted to see. Talking with him was easier than I expected; his voice was soothing, and his smile familiar, just like when we first met, and I slowly relaxed in his company.

"If you'd like, we can go visit some of those places," he suggested. "We could do a grand tour of the states."

"I promised Bobby that I would visit him in California this summer," I said, trying to imagine if I could even do that, let alone a long trip with Bill.

He smiled, raising one eyebrow. "Isn't the Golden Gate Bridge on your list of places you'd like to visit? That bridge is in Bobby's neighborhood. We could kill two birds with one stone."

"That's a horrible expression, Bill, but I understand what you mean."

I leaned back and sipped my wine, pondering the idea of traveling with him. Right then, it felt impossible to even consider. A dinner out for a couple of hours was one thing, but a long journey across the country was another entirely.

"*Mi scusi signore*," the waiter said, coming up to our table and bending down to speak softly to Bill.

I only understood a word or two, but not nearly enough to guess the subject.

Bill nodded. "*Grazie, Gino. Digli che arrivo subito.*"

The waiter retreated, then Bill turned to me. "Will you excuse me for a moment, Chére? I need to speak with someone. I'll be right back." When I nodded, he rose and headed toward the front desk.

I wondered what that was all about, but before I could delve too deeply into assumptions, a woman sat down across from me in Bill's chair.

"Hello. You're Désirée Gautier, aren't you? I recognized you from the papers. The pictures don't do you justice at all. You're a lot prettier in person," she said, her eyes full of curiosity and speculation.

"I'm sorry. Have we met?" I asked, attempting to point out her rudeness at not introducing herself. She looked to be in her late twenties, pretty, with a touch too much makeup, but nicely dressed and sure of herself.

"I'm Regina Larson, an old friend of Bill's... and Carson's." She waited to see if I would take the bait. When I didn't and instead met her inquisitive stare with my own, she carried on with her agenda.

"You know, you're all anyone is talking about this season. No one seems to know much about you. The people who knew Carson find it hard to believe he could do such horrible things. We're all terribly shocked."

Her shameless ploy to dig for information was the shocking thing, but I met it with stoic calm.

"Apparently, none of you knew Carson as well as you thought you did. Only a handful of people really knew him, and most of them are dead." I hoped that would shut her up, but luck wasn't on my side. Regina was relentless in her pursuit of information.

"How is that other girl? It's Evelyn Duret, right? I hear they committed her to Glen Oaks Sanitorium."

"She's recovering." At least, I hoped she was.

"That's good, I suppose... I heard Charlotte is in town to bury her brother. The poor thing. I can't imagine how awful it must have been for her to lose her husband *and* her brother on the same night."

She was still trying to get a reaction from me, but all I gave her was a raised eyebrow.

"It's funny that I ran into you, here at Emiliano's, of all places, but I guess you're staying with Bill at his house in Mandeville. That must be nice for you," she said with a snooty air of privileged superiority.

Her presumptuous attitude was maddening and horribly rude. I wanted to set the record straight, though I didn't know why I felt the need to explain myself to her.

"The Marchand Lake House has been my summer home for the past four years. I've always been comfortable there," I replied, staring back at her.

"Hello, Regina," Bill said, finally coming to my rescue. There was an unmistakable coolness to his tone, but I doubted Regina was intuitive enough to detect it.

"Hello, Bill. Nice running into you. Will we be seeing you tomorrow night at the Comus ball?" she asked, giving him a dazzling smile as she rose from his chair.

"I'll be there." His tone turned from chilly to annoyed, but Regina remained oblivious.

"That's splendid, Bill. I'll see you tomorrow night then," she said, stroking his arm with a familiar touch. "It was a pleasure speaking with you, Miss Gautier. Enjoy your stay in Mandeville."

Once she was gone, Bill resumed his seat, lines creasing the corners of his eyes.

"What did Regina want?"

"She was seeking information about me; gossip fodder she can use at the Comus ball. She said I'm the talk of the town, but no one knows anything about me."

"I'm sorry if she upset you."

I shook my head and finished my wine. "Don't be. You didn't invite her over; she invited herself. It doesn't matter, Bill. This was bound to happen eventually. Can we go? I'm tired and it's been a long day."

"Of course, Chére. Let's get out of here," he said, throwing some money on the table as he rose to take my hand.

Too distracted to concentrate, I let Bill drive us home. We spent the twenty-minute trip in silence, neither wanting to test the fragile bond we'd forged during supper. Reality had already entered our lives in the guise of

Regina Larson, and I knew she wouldn't be the last to test the strength of that bond.

"Thank you for tonight, Bill. It was nice... except the last part," I said as he pulled into the driveway and parked the car.

"I'm sorry, Chére. Regina has never been the most tactful of women."

"It wasn't your fault. Besides, you're the one who must face your friends at the Comus Ball." I got out of the car and headed to the house.

He stopped me at the bottom of the stairs with a light touch on my arm. "I wouldn't go if I could opt out, but I made an obligation to the Comus Krewe months ago. I'll stay tomorrow night with Mother, then bring her over on Saturday. Luke will be here."

He seemed to think Luke's protection would reassure me, but there was no protection from gossip.

I started up the back stairs, frustrated by my current circumstances. "Zach, Jolie, and Gus will also be here. Thanks, Bill, for keeping me well protected." That sounded sarcastic even to me.

He tried to change the subject as we entered the kitchen. "Could we have another supper date next week? Maybe try again, somewhere less populated?"

"I'll check my social calendar," I said, trying to lighten the mood.

Bill and I would share the house for the next four months, and I needed to make that time as painless as possible for both of us. The obvious problem was getting too close, too attached to him. I wouldn't let that happen if I could help it.

Chapter 17

Charlottes' gift

The following Monday morning, Doctor Neville ushered me into his office for our fourth session. "Good morning, Désirée. Please make yourself comfortable. How are you feeling today?"

"I'm fine, doctor. And you?" I took my usual seat on the couch and waited for the hour of lies to start.

We always began with the pleasantries, slowly merging into territory I'd rather avoid, but he persisted in his inquiries into my past. Lying to him felt terrible, but I had no choice if I intended to protect the Marchands. So, I spent another hour feeding him believable half-truths while dodging his deeper inquiries.

"Before we end our session today, there's one more question I need to ask," Doctor Neville said as I rose to leave at the end of our prescribed hour. "Did you give Miss Duret something when you were with her last Thursday?"

My heart skipped a few beats as he waited for my response. *Does he know what I did? Did Evie tell him?*

"Yes, I did," I confessed as calmly as I could. "I gave her an amulet to guard against evil. A crystal heart. It seemed to comfort her when she held it."

"I thought as much," he said, relaxing back in his chair. "Nurse Johanna tried to take it from her, but Miss Duret begged to keep it, saying it kept away the spirit that was haunting her. Normally, I wouldn't indulge a patient's delusion with something like that, but you're right, it seemed to keep her calmer. In the future, Désirée, please check with me or Nurse Johanna before giving Evelyn any more gifts. We have strict policies about such things for our patients' protection."

"Of course, doctor. May I see her now?"

When I went into Evie's room, I was relieved to see her up and dressed as if she was expecting visitors. With her hair brushed and styled, a rosy glow touching her cheeks, and her eyes clear and alert, she looked like the Evie I knew before.

She smiled and lifted her hand toward me. "*Bonjour*, Désirée. I'm so glad you've come."

"*Bonjour*, Evie. You look well today." I bent to kiss her cheeks.

"Thanks for noticing. I feel much better, though I had a terrible night last night."

"What happened?" I asked as I took a seat across from her.

"It was just awful, Désirée. I had another nightmare, but it wasn't like the others. In this one, I was running from something, trying desperately to get away. Then it felt like I was being stabbed... here in my stomach," she explained, touching her lower abdomen. "This morning, I woke up in a pool of blood. I cried and cried, but Johanna told me not to fret about it. She said it was just my monthly starting early. I feel much better now, except somehow it feels like I lost something."

"I'm glad it's over, Evie. The nightmares, I mean."

"Do you have them, Désirée? Mother said that Carson hurt you, too."

"Yes, Evie, he did, but I try not to think about it. I'm focusing on putting all that behind me now."

"I wish I could. Mother said the police want to question me about Carson, that I have to tell them what happened. I don't know if I can bear to re-live that horrible memory."

"I know it will be hard to speak about it, Evie, but you must tell them. Once you do, it will be over, and the healing will begin. I had to tell them what happened to me, too."

"You did? It must have been horrible telling strangers what Carson did to you. I'm not sure I can do it."

"It wasn't easy, but I got through it. So will you, and when you do, everything will get better. You'll see."

"Nothing is ever going to be like it was before, Désirée. I'm not the same girl I used to be."

I reached across the table, took her hands in mine, and squeezed them. "Neither am I, Evie, but we're both still alive and healing. That's all that matters right now. Whatever happens next, we'll get through it together."

Bill called Monday night to let me know he and Luke would be in DC an extra day and wouldn't be home until late Wednesday night. He said he'd be in meetings with Charlie early Thursday morning, but asked if I would go to supper with him on Thursday night.

"Is everything alright, Bill? Are you okay?"

"I'm fine, Chére. There's nothing for you to worry about. I'll see you Thursday."

Despite his assurances, Bill's delay in Washington, DC, left me feeling anxious. Did they know about me and the recent notoriety around the Phantom murders? Did someone find out about me? Anything was possible. I worried about the consequences to Bill, should his superiors in the government learn who I'd been in France and how I came here.

Not everything is about you, Désirée. Bill has his own life, or at least he used to until you messed it up.

On Tuesday, I spent the afternoon digging my hands deep into the rich soil of my new garden beds, setting in young starts of useful herbs and greens. Basil, cilantro, parsley, kale, and lettuce were things I could use in the kitchen as they grew and then not worry about once their season was over. I didn't plan on staying past June, so it made no sense to invest time and money in perennial plants that would go untended after I left.

Around two o'clock, Gus heard something that caught his attention. He barked once, then took off toward the front of the house.

A few minutes later, Zach came out to get me. "Miss Désirée, there's a Mrs. Barone here to see you. She says it's important she speaks with you. Do you want me to send her away?" Zach's dark eyes held concern. We rarely had unexpected guests and usually sent away any who arrived unannounced.

I knew Charlotte Bentley Barone was in New Orleans, but I didn't expect her to come out to Mandeville. Her sudden arrival took me by surprise, especially considering Bill was out of town.

"I'll see her, Zach. Have her wait on the veranda downstairs and offer her something to drink. She likes sweet tea with a little bourbon in it. I'll clean up and be right up," I said, brushing the dirt from my hands.

"Yes, Miss Désirée." He signaled Gus to stay with me as he returned to the house.

While I put away my gardening tools and cleaned up with the hose, I considered Charlotte's purpose for coming. What could she possibly say that would change anything for her or me? What could I say? *'Sorry I killed your brother.'* Not likely. More like, *'I'm not sorry he's dead.'*

I didn't know why, but my normal anxiety wasn't present the way it usually was just before something awful would happen. No stomach acrobatics signaled caution or impending doom. I felt calm, ready to hear whatever Charlotte needed to say.

"Hello, Charlotte," I said as I joined her on the veranda.

"Hello, Désirée. It's been a long time," she said, casting a critical eye over me.

"Four and a half years, to be exact," I said. She looked ten years older than the last time I saw her. I supposed two back-to-back funerals would do that to anyone.

"Hmm. As I recall, you were working in the garden the last time we met, and there was dirt under your fingernails. Doesn't look like much has changed... except perhaps your location."

I looked down at my hands, noticing the telltale lines of dirt embedded beneath my nails, and quickly covered them.

"Is there a reason for your visit, Charlotte? Bill won't be back until tomorrow night."

"I didn't come to see Bill. I came to speak with you. There are a few things I need to say, things I can only say to you."

"I'm sorry... about your husband."

"But you're not sorry about my brother." She shook her head, as if she expected as much. "Never mind, Désirée. I appreciate your condolences for Joe, but I don't need your apology. You didn't kill my husband. My brother did." She took a deep breath, then a sip of her sweet tea before continuing. "When I buried Carson last Saturday, I hoped to put this nightmare to rest. However, it's apparent my brothers' notorious activities make that impossible. So, I've instructed my attorney to liquidate the entire Bentley estate: the business, stocks, furnishings, the house, everything. I want my family name and everything associated with it to disappear from memory. When I leave New Orleans, I have no intention of returning."

"If only it were that easy, Charlotte. His victims and their families will never forget."

"I suppose not, but I've asked my attorney to offer them a generous cash settlement for pain and suffering in lieu of any lawsuits. One hundred thousand dollars each, for you and the Duret girl, and fifty thousand to each of the families of the other confirmed victims. I'm told this is a generous offer that will probably consume the balance of the estate after I pay off Carson's debts. I've spoken with Charles Marchand and Jonathan Duret about this. Jonathan has agreed to settle on behalf of his daughter. Charles said he would consult with you and Bill."

"I'm not interested in your money, Charlotte, nor will I seek any lawsuit against your estate. I just want this whole thing to be finished, so I can leave here and start over somewhere else." I'm not sure why I told her that. Maybe because now that Evie was recovering, I could start making plans to leave.

"You'll need money to do that, Désirée. Take the money. You've earned it. Which leads me to the other reason I came today. I need to thank you for doing what I couldn't, for ending the hold my brother had over me, and freeing me from a life of torment." Her brow arched high as she offered this confession.

"It's funny, you know. I was right about you. You looked like trouble from the start; this strange young girl Bill found so fascinating. All of Carson's carefully laid plans thwarted by a little French girl who came out of nowhere. I would have laughed about it even then, but my brother made my life miserable because of it."

"There was a time when I thought Bill Marchand would be my savior, but it turned out to be Joe Barone, and that was only possible because of you. Joe and I loved each other, and we had a few good years, thanks to you. But my brother refused to lose what he thought belonged to him. An unfortunate Bentley trait."

I wondered if Charlotte knew about the curse.

"Did you know about Carson? What he really was?" I didn't expect an answer to such a pointed question but asked it anyway to gauge her body language and facial expressions.

She smirked and huffed out a few breaths, then sipped on her sweet tea, assessing me over the rim of her glass.

"I was born a Bentley, Désirée. Did you ever wonder who his first victim was?"

Duly humbled by her revelation, I lowered my gaze. "Sorry. I didn't realize... Why did you tell me this?"

"I've told no one until now, but I needed to say it out loud and leave it all here before I left New Orleans for good. Turns out, you're the only person I know who can keep a secret." She handed me an envelope stuffed with papers, then sat back to watch my reaction.

"What's this?" I asked, reluctant to touch it, let alone open it.

"Something Carson sent me a few months ago. He told me to safeguard it for him. Said it would ensure the Bentley fortune, and my future."

"Do you know what's in here?" I asked, suspecting what the envelope contained, and sensing she knew too.

"Nothing in there has any value to me, Désirée. I thought you should have it. Perhaps it will ease your mind a bit."

"Thank you, Charlotte," I said as I put the envelope in my pocket. "If I may, I'd like to ask that you make sure whatever funds you set aside for Evelyn Duret go directly to her and not to her father."

She gave me a long, hard look before responding. "Of course... I understand. Jonathan Duret is a greedy man and apparently an unsympathetic father, not unlike my own. Perhaps you can reciprocate the favor. Her parents informed me that Evelyn is carrying my brother's child. I offered to take the child off their hands once it's born and agreed to pay an additional fifty thousand dollars in compensation for their trouble. Jonathan was all too eager to accept that offer. Will you help convince Miss Duret this is in her best interests?"

"Why would you want a child conceived by rape?"

"Children are not responsible for the sins of their fathers. That child will be the last of the Bentleys, and the only child I will ever have."

"I'm sorry, Charlotte, but there is no baby. Evie's monthly cycle began yesterday. She's not pregnant."

"Hmm. That's it then. I suppose it's for the best that it all ends here." She stood to take her leave. "Thank you for seeing me, Désirée. I've kept you from your gardening long enough."

I walked her to the front door and shook her hand. "Goodbye, Charlotte."

"Goodbye, Désirée. I hope you have a good life. Give my best to Bill."

I watched her drive away and was grateful for her visit. She had eliminated the threat Carson held against me, and that was no small thing.

Chapter 18

Outside Challenges

The next morning, while Jolie and I were finishing up the breakfast dishes, I noticed she had something on her mind. Each time Zach came through the kitchen, her body would tense a little, she'd stand taller, her head tilting with confidence.

I nudged her shoulder as I passed her on my way to the sink. "You like him, don't you?" It only mattered if I thought she didn't like Zach, because then I'd have to reconsider his employment. But so far, it seemed the two of them were getting along just fine.

Jolie shrugged, trying to hide the blush blooming on her cheeks. "I like him fine," she said, shaking off her embarrassment. "Zach's taking me to the beauty shop in town so I can get my hair done this morning, then he's going to the barbershop while I'm there. Is there anything you want us to bring you from town?"

"Are you two going to some special occasion I don't know about?" She would usually ignore me when I teased her, but not this time.

"No, nothing special. Zach asked me to go to the picture show tomorrow night while you and Bill go out for supper. That's all. You don't need to make a big thing out of it."

"Hmm. I think I'll go into town with you. It's been weeks since I've had my hair trimmed."

"Mabel doesn't do white people's hair, Désirée, only nappy hair like mine."

"That's alright. There's another salon in town across from the drugstore. I'll stop in there while you're having yours done."

"Alright, if you're sure. We'll be leaving in a few minutes."

After taking Jolie to her hair appointment, Zach dropped me off in front of the Beaux Cheveux Beauty Parlor on Main Street. "I'll be back to get you in about an hour, Miss Désirée. You go on and take Gus with you. He can wait outside while you're having your hair done. Don't you worry, he'll stay put till you come out."

"Thanks, Zach. We'll be fine."

I wasn't as confident as I sounded. This was my first solo venture out in public, and I wasn't sure what to expect. My hope was, no one would recognize me, or if they did, they'd have the grace to ignore me. Invisibility would be nice, or better yet, total anonymity. I wanted to be just an ordinary girl out having her hair done.

Gus and I stood outside the beauty shop, watching my car disappear around the corner. When it was gone, I bent down to pet him. "Well, Gus, here goes. Wish me luck. You stay here till I come back." I gave him the hand signal for 'Stay' as I opened the door, ringing the overhead bell.

Beaux Cheveux Beauty Parlor was colorful, noisy, smelly, and a lot busier than I expected for a Wednesday morning. The two front windows, draped in rose floral chintz and a sheer fabric, only allowed filtered light to penetrate the interior. Several overhead light fixtures cast a warm glow throughout the salon. On the right sat a small reception desk holding a vase of gardenias and an open appointment book. Flanking the desk stood two tall glass display cases filled with beauty products. Merle Norman cosmetics, a brand Mama used religiously, commanded a middle shelf.

Two uniformed women were working on clients occupying the swivel chairs that faced the mirrored wall above a long hairdresser station. Another woman was hands deep in the central washing station, scrubbing a client's hair in one of the two available sinks. On the left wall sat a curved bench, upholstered in a dark mauve color to match the chintz roses and topped with four hair dryers. Two older women, their hair in rollers and hairnets, sat under the dryers closest to the front. The whole place smelled of hair dye and peroxide, with an overlay of gardenia, a combination that was giving me a headache.

"Be right with you," the young woman at the wash station called out over the hum of the hair dryers and chattering women.

I stood by the reception desk, patiently waiting as she wrapped her client's head in a towel and shifted her to the empty swivel chair in front of the hairdresser's mirror.

"Now, what can we do for you? Do you have an appointment?" she asked, looking down at the appointment book, then up at me.

"I'm sorry, I should have call ahead. I just need my hair trimmed. Do you have time?"

"A wash, cut and set? I think we can fit you in. Mind waiting for a few minutes? What's your name?"

"My name is Désirée, and I don't need it set, just a couple of inches trimmed off the ends. I usually let it air dry."

"No problem, honey," she said. "Have a seat and I'll be with you in a minute."

I sat in a chair next to the hair dryers and as far from the chemical fumes as I could get. While I waited my turn, I couldn't help but overhear the two women talking under the hairdryers, their voices raised to be heard over the hum.

"Look, Lorraine. Isn't that the girl we've been reading about in the paper? The one they say killed that Phantom killer after he... you know? I'm sure it's her."

The other woman turned her head, catching my eye as she did. I met her stare without blinking. She turned back to her companion with a scornful look on her face.

"You're right, Dora. I'm appalled she'd have the nerve to go out in public. Any decent young woman would be ashamed to be seen, after what she did."

I should have expected this, but it still stung to hear it. There was no escaping the notoriety or the gossip.

I stood up as the stylist came over to check the dryness of Lorraine's hair, turning off the dryer. "Won't be but a couple more minutes, Miss Désirée," she said with a friendly smile in my direction.

"I'm sorry, but I've changed my mind." As I headed for the door, I hesitated, then turned back to confront the old gossip.

"Pardon me, madame, but I could not help but overhear your conversation. My parents taught me it was rude to gossip about someone, especially in their presence. And for your information, I have done nothing I need to be ashamed of, but I would not wish this experience on any woman... including you, madame." I turned and left the salon as quickly as I could, unwilling to engage the hateful woman any further. What would be the point?

The stylist followed me out the door. "Excuse me, Miss Désirée. I'm real sorry about that. Those two are notorious gossips with nothing better to do with their time. I can come to your house to do your hair, if you'd like.

Won't be any trouble. Here's my card. You just call and I'll come over, ya hear?"

"That's very kind, thank you. I'll consider it," I said, stashing the card in my purse.

With more than half an hour to kill before Zach came to pick me up, I crossed the street and went to the drugstore. "Come on, Gus. Let's get something cool to drink while we're waiting. I'll see if I can get you some water."

Inside Walburn's drugstore, a pleasant young man in a white coat greeted me. "Morning, miss. What can I get you?"

"A Coca-Cola on ice, please, and some water for my dog, if that's not too much trouble. We'll be sitting out front."

"No trouble at all, miss. I'll bring it right out."

While Gus slurped up his water, I sat under the striped drugstore canopy at a small table, sipping on my soda and ruminating about the old gossip. Why I even confronted the old bat was a mystery. People like that didn't deserve attention, but she made me angry enough to shame her back, as much good as that did.

"This isn't going away soon, Gus," I told my companion. "I guess I'd better get used to it."

"Excuse me. Do you mind if I join you?" a young woman asked, taking the seat across the table before I could respond. She was in her early twenties, dressed nicely in a stylish blouse and suit, the jacket opened to allow in the breeze. After deciding there wasn't anything threatening about her, Gus settled down next to me, keeping his eye on the newcomer.

"My name is Meghan O'Connell. And you are..."

"I know who I am, Miss O'Connell."

"Of course. May I ask you a few questions, Miss Gautier?"

"That depends on what they are." I really wasn't interested in repeating the scene from the beauty shop.

"The District Attorney just issued a press release stating that the Phantom murder case is closed. The police have established that Carson Bentley was indeed the killer of all those women. How do you feel about this? Do you have a statement?" She looked hopeful, like she was eager for a scoop.

"Are you a reporter, Miss O'Connell? If so, I don't give interviews. I have no comment."

"I'm a freelance reporter. The Mandeville Gazette sometimes publishes my work. The Times-Picayune is doing an exposé on Mr. Bentley, and I thought you could correct some rumors going around about you."

"Why would I want to do that? Nothing I say will change anyone's mind."

"Don't you want to tell your side of the story?"

"It won't make any difference, Miss O'Connell. People gossip about these things to make themselves feel better about their miserable lives. Nothing I say will change anything."

"It might help some other young woman who finds herself in a similar situation," she offered.

"Hmm. You're obviously looking to break into the news business, and you're finding it difficult because they think it's a man's profession. I understand your frustration, Miss O'Connell, but you'll have to do it at someone else's expense. Sorry, I can't help you. Besides, my story isn't that interesting."

She wasn't happy with this response, apparently disappointed that I wouldn't want to correct all the misperceptions about me. Maybe I would have if I didn't have a history that required concealment.

"If you really want to make a name for yourself, Miss O'Connell, why not write something that will make a difference? Something that wakes people up and impacts their lives. Something meaningful."

"What do you suggest, Miss Gautier?"

"Perhaps you can research what happens to the other women who find themselves in my situation, but who don't have the family connections or resources I have. Find out what happens to them, then expose that information. That would be something worth reading. But I must warn you, don't use my name or any mention of me in what you write, or you'll hear from my attorney and never get the job you hope for."

Just then, Zach pulled up to the curb in front of me and came around to open the door. "You ready to go, Miss Désirée?"

"Yes, Zach, we're ready. Come Gus. It's time to go home. Nice meeting you, Miss O'Connell. Good luck," I said as I climbed into the back seat with Gus.

When we got home, Jolie went upstairs to change while Zach and Gus walked around the property to make sure everything was as it should be. I went into the living room to collect the mail from the slot by the front door, hoping for a letter from Bobby. What I found, nestled among Bills' mail, was a plain white envelope without a stamp or complete address. Written in block printing, it simply said, *Désirée.* Its presence inside the house with the usual mail meant someone came to the door and slipped it through the mail slot. That gave me an uneasy feeling.

I was afraid to open it, but I had to know what it said. Knowing was always better than wondering.

Inside, one sheet of plain white paper held a simple message written by the same hand as the envelope:

Hello Kätzchen,

I will see you soon.

There was only one person who ever called me *Kätzchen,* Anton Steigler, the Kommandant. My heart nearly stopped as I struggled to take a breath.

Chapter 19

Bill

I didn't tell Jolie or Zach about the note. It would only worry her, and I wasn't sure how much of my history Bill had explained to Zach. I needed to talk with Bill first.

That afternoon, Elijah Tillman called to inquire if I would come to his bayou party on Saturday. I accepted, even though I knew Bill would object, especially considering recent events.

"Great! I'll pick you up around six," Elijah said, obviously pleased.

"No, don't bother, Elijah. I'll drive out with Jolie. I remember the way."

"You sure? It's no bother, and Gran says I should introduce myself to your guardian."

"I'm sure. It's better this way... for now. We'll see you on Saturday night. Give my best to your grandmother." I wasn't sure how I'd convince Bill to let me go, but I was determined to try.

After Jolie was sound asleep, her new coiffure wrapped tightly in a kerchief, I slipped downstairs to await Bill's return. He usually went to his office to sort through the mail when he got home, so that's where I waited with the desk lamp on.

While I waited, I tested Miss LouAnn's dried flower buds in one of Uncle Henri's' old pipes that lived in a rack on the bookshelf. First, I crushed the buds into the texture of tobacco, then filled the pipe. With a glass of Bill's whiskey on the table next to me, I sat on the couch to try this new remedy.

Miss LouAnn said it would help me relax, and God knew I needed to, so I lit the pipe and took a drag. At first, all I could taste was the residual tobacco from the well-used pipe, but suddenly, the heady taste of the flower hit the back of my throat and sent me into a coughing fit.

Take it easy, Désirée. You don't know what this is yet.

Cautiously, I took another drag, though not as deep as the first, letting the effect wash over me like a gentle wave. It had a slightly sweet flavor, berries maybe, coupled with an earthy taste. It wasn't long before I noticed a mellow feeling permeating through my body, relaxing the tension in my shoulders and filling me with a sense of peace. I liked it, so I leaned back, took another cautious drag, followed by a sip of whiskey, and then waited for Bill.

"Désirée?" Bill's gentle touch on my shoulder pulled me from a restful sleep. "What are you doing down here?"

My eyes blinked open as I sat up and stretched to push the sleep away. "I was waiting for you, but I guess I fell asleep."

"Enough whiskey and this stuff will do that," he said, arching his brow as he lifted the pipe to smell its contents. "This is cannabis, Chére. It's illegal. Where'd you get it?"

I sat up straighter, tucking my legs under me and rubbing the sleep from my eyes. His look triggered protective feelings for Miss LouAnn, so

I dodged the question. "It was a gift. And I don't know why it should be. It helped me relax a lot better than drinking does."

"I can see that." His eyebrows remained arched as he gazed down at me. He picked up my glass, still holding a finger's worth of whiskey, then tossed it down his throat. Rather than pursue the cannabis question, he changed the subject. "Did you wait up to talk to me?"

"I need to tell you a couple of things that can't wait till tomorrow."

"Alright, I'm all ears." He sat down at the end of the couch and lit a cigarette.

"Charlotte Barone came to see me yesterday." I wondered if he knew about Charlotte, about her relationship with her brother.

"I heard about her meeting with Charlie, but not that she was coming here. What did she say?" He looked guarded, as if Charlotte's unexpected visit was a problem to address.

"She wanted to thank me... for killing her brother. And she gave me this. She said I should have it." I tossed him the envelope Charlotte had given me.

He opened it, quickly scanned its contents, then blew out a heavy sigh. "It figures. Of all people, Carson never really understood Charlotte. Does she know what this is?"

"She said it had no value to her, so I suppose this cancels Carson's threat, for now."

We both knew it could happen again. Someone else could dig into my past just as easily as Carson had. I'd been living in a house of cards for five years, longer even. It was just a matter of time before it would all come crumbling down on top of me and anyone close enough to be buried with me.

"Was there something else?" He still seemed on high alert, his posture straightening to meet a potential threat.

I retrieved the letter from my robe pocket and handed it to him. "This was with the mail today. Someone put it in the mail slot while we were in town. It's from the Kommandant."

As he stared down at the paper, frown lines deepened around his mouth. "How do you know it's from Steigler? Do you recognize the handwriting?"

"He was the only person who ever called me *Kätzchen.* It's from him, Bill, but it's not his handwriting." At that moment, I didn't feel fear, only a firm resolve to not let fear rule me.

"Shit... Did you show this to Zach? Where was the dog? He's supposed to keep people off the property."

"Gus was with me in town. We were only gone for a couple of hours. I didn't tell Zach about it because I wasn't sure how much you told him about me."

"He knows, but not everything. I'll take care of this, Chére. Don't worry, but it would be better if the dog stayed on the property from now on. And I'd feel more comfortable if you do, too."

"I already told you, Bill, I will not be a prisoner here. I intend to live my life as normally as I can. Besides, it's not like people don't know I'm here, so what's the point of hiding?"

"You're not making this easy for me, Désirée."

"If you want it easy, Bill, then find the Kommandant and eliminate that threat for good, like you promised."

"I'm working on it, Chére, but please, don't take any chances until I do."

"Alright. I'll be careful. I'm sorry to add this to your burdens, but I thought you should know as soon as possible. Goodnight."

I left him sitting on the couch, assessing the immediate threat and planning defenses. There really wasn't anything he could do to end this for me, not even killing the Kommandant. My history was unchangeable.

The following morning at Glen Oaks, Doctor Neville sat across from me, his notepad on his lap, ready to receive my responses.

"Now that the Phantom case is closed, Désirée, I'd like to talk about what happened that night and how you feel about it."

"I'd rather not, doctor, if you don't mind." It was hard enough to relive the memory of it every single night.

"It's important for you to talk about this, Désirée. You're of an age when a young woman explores her sexual feelings, her relationship with men. The trauma you experienced can hamper your development, effecting your future relationship with a man. My goal is to help you come to terms with your experience."

"It happened, doctor. I can't change any of it. There's nothing more to say."

"Do you have nightmares about the attack?" He was persistent, clearly wanting me to look closely at my worst moment.

Waves of memories from the first rape washed over me, leaving me trembling in my seat.

"Yes," I admitted, unable to push the memories back into their boxes.

"Can you describe them? How do you feel when they happen?"

"Helpless, like I'm going to die, and then I wake up."

"Describe what's happening when you feel helpless."

"I can't. I don't want to. Please don't make me talk about this." I turned away, my hankie covering my mouth and catching my tears.

"Alright, Désirée," he said, concern in his voice, but he wouldn't let it go. "This is a safe place for you to look at those memories. I'm trying to help you move past them. Talking about what happened, the moments that frighten you can diminish their power over you."

"It's too hard, doctor. Talking about it makes me feel worse, makes it too real. I'd rather forget it ever happened." The idea of sharing those intimate nightmares, how they made me feel, was something I couldn't do with anyone, least of all him.

That night, while Jolie and Zach were at the movies, Bill and I had a quiet evening at home instead of venturing out in public. After my session with Doctor Neville and my visit with Evie—who was struggling with her own memories—I wasn't up for braving additional public scrutiny.

I made us a simple meal of grilled shrimp served over lemon-basil pasta. We shared a bottle of wine, keeping our conversation light-hearted and avoiding any difficult topics. After supper, we took a walk by the lake, letting the night sounds fill the silence between us.

Eventually, I broke the silence to inform him of my plan to go to Elijah's party on Saturday. Bill wasn't happy.

"I'd rather you stay home, Désirée. At least until I can get a handle on Steigler."

"I'm taking Jolie with me, so you don't need to worry," I said, offering a concession.

"Jolie isn't the protection I had in mind."

"In case you weren't aware, Jolie can be quite fierce when she gets riled, but if it will make you feel better, I will take Zach with me, too."

"Where's this party happening?" I could feel his radar antenna rising.

"At Elijah's grandmother's place, where I went before. It's her birthday, and I want to see her again. You've probably already investigated them... Am I right?"

"Yes. I know who they are. What I don't understand is why you want to see them again."

"I just do, that's all." I would not let him or anyone dictate my life.

"Alright, you can go as long as Zach goes with you." He always had to have the last word.

I grew quiet as we walked back to the house, lost in my thoughts about the day's events, especially my session with Doctor Neville.

Bill sensed my mood had changed as we climbed the stairs to the front porch. "Did something happen today at Glen Oaks? You seem... troubled about something."

"It's just these meetings with Doctor Neville. He wants me to talk about what happened... with Carson, and I can't. I don't want to remember those things, but he's insistent. He says it will help me get over it. Fat chance of that ever happening."

"You can talk to me about anything, Chére."

"Not about that." The feelings those memories gave me were hard to admit, even to myself.

"I know you still have nightmares. I hear you get up at night. Do you want to talk them through? Maybe I can help."

"I'm sorry, Bill, I can't, not to Doctor Neville or to you. Not to anyone. I just can't," I said, swallowing back tears as I went through the front door.

He caught up to me at the bottom of the stairs, taking my hand before I could escape up to my room.

"Wait, Chére. I need to say something."

"What is it, Bill?" I feared it might be something that would make this harder than it already was.

He stood close, holding onto my hand, and with his other, he lifted my chin to meet his gaze. "It's just this. I love you, Désirée. I have loved you from the moment we met, and I will always love you. Nothing will ever change how I feel. Not time nor circumstance... nothing. I love you, Chére."

My head dropped to his chest while tears streamed down my face. I had no words, couldn't say what was in my heart. All I could do was cry as he held me.

"You don't need to say anything, baby. I just wanted you to know."

Chapter 20

An Almost Perfect Party

At breakfast the next morning, Bill and I exchanged glances across the table. We held each other's eyes for a few seconds, then turned away. He looked tired, the dark crescents under his eyes matched mine. Apparently, I had caused him as many sleepless nights as he had me, especially the previous one.

We didn't speak beyond polite good mornings, though there were a thousand things I wanted to say. I wanted to tell him that loving me was a bad idea, that I wasn't good for him. Thinking it was difficult enough, vocalizing it felt impossible, but I knew I should, needed to, sometime soon.

May fifteenth, my eighteenth birthday, was only one hundred days away, and my plan was to leave as soon as I legally could. The idea of disappearing into the farthest reaches of America, where I could start over, felt like the best option for everyone. I just didn't know where to go yet.

Bill rose from the table with a parting look in my direction. "Thanks for breakfast, Jolie. I'll be home for supper tonight. Y'all have a good day. *À bientôt*, Chére."

"Thanks, Mr. William. You too," Jolie said, glancing from Bill to me and back again.

I simply nodded my goodbye behind my coffee cup, not yet ready to face that problem.

Once Bill was out the door, Jolie gave me a look that held a lot more questions than the one she asked. "You tell Bill about that party you wanna go to on Saturday night?"

"Yes, and he insists Zach go with us. That should make *all* of you happy." Jolies' movie date with Zach had obviously gone well, based on the glimmer in her eye.

"Sounds fine to me. Come to think of it, I wouldn't mind doing a little dancing with Zach Johnson. You said there'd be music, right?"

"So I was told, Jolie, plus lots of food and lots of people we don't know. It should be an interesting evening. Let's clean up in here, then plan what we're going to make as a gift for the hostess of this soiree." Jolie and I both knew that no self-respecting southern woman would dare arrive empty-handed to a birthday celebration.

Saturday evening, I went in search of a bottle of wine to add to the basket of fresh baguettes we made for Miss LouAnn.

"May I help you find something, Chére?" Bill asked, coming up behind me as I searched the cupboard under the stairs for the perfect wine.

"Do you have any French wines from '38 or earlier? No, I suppose not. The war got in the way." For over four years, the Nazis plundered every vineyard in the Champagne province of France, and I suspected the other wine-producing provinces had fared no better. It would take years for the devastated vineyards to recover and several more years to produce a decent vintage. It had only been five.

I dove back into the cupboard, feeling like a bundle of nerves around Bill. Facing him felt too confusing; feeling so much when I knew I shouldn't.

"This will do," I said, pulling out a bottle of California Pinot Noir '42. "If that's alright with you."

"Of course, but why wine? Mrs. Gatlin has lived out on the bayou most of her life, and I doubt wine is her drink of choice. Do you think it's going to impress her?"

"I'm *not* trying to impress anyone, Bill." That sounded defensive and harsh, so I softened my tone, unwilling to start a conflict with him before going to a party he didn't want me to attend.

"Offering bread and wine was a tradition in my family whenever we visited friends. Maman said there's no better gift from nature's bounty than bread and wine."

I wasn't sure why that memory came to mind—Mamans' wisdom—but the thought of her instantly calmed me, soothed my anxious mind, and gave me a boost of confidence.

"Are you going out tonight, Bill?" I wondered if he would go to another Mardi Gras party in town or if he planned to follow us to Elijah's place.

"I'm going to supper with Eduardo Reyes, but I'll be here when you get home."

I wondered if Bill would share the note from the Kommandant with Mr. Reyes, who had a network that kept tabs on the notorious South American criminal known as El Caco, formerly Nazi Kommandant Anton Steigler. If anyone had information about the Kommandant, Eduardo Reyes would. I didn't know whether to feel worried or relieved.

"Please give Mr. Reyes my regards."

"I will, Chére. Give mine to Mrs. Gatlin." He watched as I added the wine to the basket of long baguette loaves. "By the way, have I told you how beautiful you are? I wish I were going with you. Enjoy yourself... and please, be careful. Stay close to Zach."

My intention was to arrive before the sun went down, but we got a late start. Bill delayed our departure by giving Zach some last-minute instructions, and then Gus needed attention before we left for the evening. It would have been so much easier if I'd gone alone, but that wasn't an option.

The evening offered fair skies with scattered clouds, but a wind out of the northeast had brought down a cold snap the day before, dropping temperatures by almost twenty degrees. Even though the wind had died down by mid-day, I expected a cool evening on the bayou and added a warmer coat over my dress.

"You sure we're going the right way, Désirée? Looks to me like we're headed into the swamp," Jolie said from the front seat as Zach drove down the long stretch of empty country road toward the lake.

"It's not much farther. Turn left at the end of this road, Zach, then it's only a mile or so to the first road on the right. We're almost there."

When we arrived, there were already a dozen cars and trucks parked along the road leading to Miss LouAnn's place, confirming this was going to be a large gathering. My stomach flipped over a few times as Zach eased the car to a stop.

"The house is this way. Follow me," I said, leading Jolie and Zach along the path I'd taken with Elijah.

As we came through the opening in the trees, we ran into a woman hurrying up the path from the dock, carrying a bucket full of crabs.

"Oh, excuse me. You lost, honey? Need some help?" the woman asked. Her look said she suspected I'd lost my way and needed directions somewhere else, but when she turned her gaze to Jolie and Zach, her expression relaxed.

"We're here for Miss LouAnn's party. Do you know where we can find her?" I asked.

"I spect she's up at the house supervising the meal. Come on, I'll take you up there."

"May I carry that for you, ma'am?" Zach asked, reaching for the bucket as we followed her to the house.

"Thank ya kindly. I need to drop this off before they start the crab boil." She handed the bucket over to Zach as she led us up to the house.

"You'll find Miss LouAnn inside. My name's Ida Cormier, by the way."

"I'm Désirée, and this is Jolie Jefferies and Zach Johnson. It's nice to meet you, Mrs. Cormier."

"My pleasure, Miss Désirée. Thanks for your help, Mr. Johnson," she said, retrieving the crab bucket.

Mrs. Cormier left us at the steps to the porch, where the kitchen door stood open for frequent comings and goings. Jolie, Zach, and I walked inside and found ourselves amid controlled chaos: women mixing salads at the table, others tending big pots of something on the stove, or pulling trays of biscuits and corn muffins from the oven. Miss LouAnn was presiding over it all, looking much the same as the last time I'd seen her: a long silver and black braid down her back, wearing a man's shirt tucked into a full-length skirt that didn't quite hide her leather moccasins.

"Look who showed up," Miss LouAnn said as she glanced up to see us come in.

"*Joyeux anniversaire*, madame." As was my family's custom, I greeted her with a kiss on both cheeks and handed her the basket of bread and wine.

She returned the kiss and gave me a warm hug. "*Bienvenue*, Désirée. I'm glad you came, but no more mention of my birthday, if you don't mind. I'm feeling my years as it is. Who's this you brought with you?" she asked, stepping up to greet Jolie and Zach.

After welcoming them both, she turned to a young woman standing at the stove and lightly touched her back. "Sable, you take Miss Jolie and Mr. Johnson outside and get them something to drink, introduce them to the folks while Miss Désirée and I visit for a bit."

"Yes, ma'am. This pot of gumbo is ready to go out. The rice is about done, too."

"Here, let me carry that out for you," Zach offered, beaming a smile at the pretty young woman as he stepped over to the stove to lift the big pot brimming with stew.

I wasn't sure if it was the delicious smell wafting up from the pot or the dazzling smile that Sable gave him as he helped her, but Zach didn't look the least bit uncomfortable in this unfamiliar setting. Jolie, however, looked perplexed and maybe even a little put out by Zach's offer to help, based on the frown pulling down the corners of her mouth. As she followed him out, she gave me a backward glance full of questions and insecurities.

"I'll be out to join you in a few minutes, Jolie."

"Let's you and I go talk in the parlor, Miss Désirée," Miss LouAnn said once they'd gone. "Thank you for the thoughtful gift. It's been a long time since I've had a decent wine. We'll share a glass and toast the end of an era."

She found a corkscrew in a kitchen drawer, pulled two glasses from an overhead cupboard, then tore off a piece of baguette, and with a tilt of her head, motioned for me to follow her.

We settled ourselves in two old armchairs in front of a stone fireplace where a small fire burned cheerfully. She opened the wine with ease—as if she'd been doing it her entire life—poured us each a glass, then tore the bread in half, handing me a piece. I found it remarkable that a woman who'd spent the past forty-plus years living on the bayou hadn't lost her understanding of old-world customs.

"*Bonne santé,*" we said in unison, tipping our glasses together, then tasting the bread and wine.

"How did you know the era ended?" I asked.

She regarded me for a moment. "Hmm. I didn't know for sure, but last Monday night, a feeling of peace washed over me, like someone had lifted a burden from my shoulders. When you walked in tonight, I knew it was over. You wouldn't have come otherwise."

"You're right, I wouldn't have. Evie miscarried on Monday, so there won't be any more Bentleys troubling the world. She's free of that nightmare."

"And you? Are you free of it, Désirée?" she asked, examining my face with intense scrutiny.

"Not entirely. Memories of it still haunt me, especially late at night when I try to sleep."

"They say time heals all wounds, child. Even these."

"I wish you were right, Miss LouAnn. I'd really like to forget it ever happened." Along with a lot of other horrible memories that shaped my life, but that was impossible. Time can't give me that kind of peace.

"Your niece, Charlotte, came to see me the other day. She's liquidating the Bentley estate and moving away for good."

"That's for the best."

"Don't you want to see her before she leaves? She has no other family but you." I felt sorry for Charlotte, for all the things she must have endured, and wondered if Miss LouAnn would reach out to her, to let her know she wasn't totally without family.

"She probably doesn't know I exist, and my family here isn't aware of the Bentley connection. I'd like to keep it that way." She drained the last drop of wine from her glass, then set it on the table. "Where's Mr. Marchand this evening? Since your welfare appears to be important to him, I assumed he would accompany you if you came tonight."

"I didn't invite him. My apologies if his interest in you made you uncomfortable." Bill's protective inclinations felt too intrusive this time. Miss LouAnn wasn't a threat, nor was Elijah.

"I live in a tight-knit community, Désirée. When an outsider comes in asking questions, word gets around. Don't worry, he was discreet enough, but it left me wondering why." Her eyes held a lot of questions I wouldn't answer. "Perhaps we should leave that conversation for another time. What do you say we rejoin the party? Food should be ready about now, and your friends are probably wondering what's happened to you."

The party was unlike any I'd attended since living in Louisiana, free of all the trappings of high society, it was just regular people, bayou people, enjoying each other's company, sharing good food and an evening of music and celebration. It was nearly perfect.

"Have you ever seen anything like that before, Désirée?" Jolie asked as we stood facing one of two large barbecues.

It wasn't the barbecues that widened my eyes—though I was envious of the ingenious use of a steel barrel—it was the beast roasting inside.

"No," I said, savoring the delicious smell rising from the grill. "I've tasted alligator before, but I've never seen it prepared." A five-foot alligator, its tail curled round, its mouth stuffed with a chicken, and the whole the thing completely wrapped in thick slices of bacon, lay roasting on the grill over a low fire. And there were two of them.

"There's enough food here to feed a small army," I said to no one in particular.

"It's food that brings people together, Miss Désirée, and it keeps them together," Zach said, standing behind me. "Same is true where I grew up. We'd have parties like this all the time, sharing good food and dancing to good music. I met a few fellas here who are gonna play some tunes later. Do you like to dance, Miss Désirée?"

"I do," Jolie said, dropping a big hint that Zach immediately caught.

We joined the rest of the partygoers, helping them arrange the tables and chairs around the yard for the feast. Sable Honoré and her brother Dorien, who was Elijah's deckhand, invited us to share their family's table. Everyone there was directly or indirectly related to Miss LouAnn, either by blood or marriage. Sable and Dorien were her great-niece and nephew, the grandchildren of her sister-in-law, Miss Odette, who joined Miss LouAnn, her daughter Stella and her husband Tom, and Elijah at the table. They were a lively group.

"I'm surprised to see you again," Stella said in a low voice across the table to me. "Glad to see you're doing well. I knew Elijah would take care of you, but I didn't expect him to keep in touch."

"Elijah came by to see me and invited me to this celebration. He can be very persuasive."

Elijah smiled with a shy blush and a scolding look for his aunt.

No one asked me anything about the Phantom or what happened, not once. If they knew who I was, they didn't mention it, a courtesy I felt enormously grateful for. They all knew I was out of my element, clearly not from the bayou, but they treated me as a welcome addition.

After filling my belly with boiled crab, shrimp gumbo over rice, Cajun roasted alligator, and a variety of side dishes, not to mention the beer I consumed, I found it hard to move, let alone dance. But dance I did, to zydeco music that I hadn't known, but somehow seeped into my bones to take up residence. I danced with everyone who asked me, but mostly I danced with Elijah.

"Elijah, I'd like to take a breather. Can we take a walk down by the water?" I asked, catching my breath as I tumbled into the nearest chair.

"Sure. Come on," he said, taking my hand and grabbing a couple of beers as we left the dancing crowd.

The moon was in its waning, gibbous phase, just about half full and glowing above the scattered clouds. It was a beautiful night and so different from the last time I'd been there. All that luscious green vegetation bordering the water had darkened to black. It felt like a dream, with the moonlight guiding us to the water.

"I'm glad you came tonight," he said.

"So am I. Thanks for inviting me... us. Jolie and Zach seem to be enjoying themselves."

"It appears so," he said, looking back at Jolie and Zach still spinning around to the music. "This must be so different from what you're used to. I know we're not as fancy as all those Mardi Gras balls in the city, but we have a good time."

"You want to know a secret, Elijah? I'm not fond of those Mardi Gras parties, especially the ones with masks. People always try to be someone else at those parties, and even when there aren't any masks, they try to out-do each other with their social skills and positions. For me, tonight was real, free from all that pretense. Everyone I've met here is who they really are. This is what a party should be."

"You're sure not like any girl I've ever met before."

"Is that good or bad?"

"Good... I think. But I'd like to get to know you better. Maybe we can go out sometime... to a movie, supper, or something."

"Will you take me out on your boat again?" I asked, standing on the dock next to *La Belle*.

"Not unless you promise you won't try to jump off," he said with a grin. "Sure, I will, as long as your guardian approves."

I wanted to protest Bill's control of my life, but couldn't, at least not for another ninety-nine days, plus an hour, give or take. I survived the past ten years following the rules, and a change in strategy at this point felt defiant and self-destructive. *Wait a little longer, Désirée.*

"I'll ask him. He'll say yes, I'm sure." I hoped so, anyway.

"Y'all should head home soon. It's getting kinda late. He'll probably be worried."

Before saying my goodbyes to everyone, I went into the house to relieve my bladder and wash up. When I stepped out of the restroom, Silas Watson, Elijah's fishing friend, stood right outside the door, blocking my exit. He was a large man, over six feet tall and muscular. My body immediately tensed, sensing danger.

"Evening, Miss Désirée," he said in a slow drawl, smelling of too much beer. "I've been waitin' all night to get a little time with you, but Elijah's been keeping you all to hisself. How about you and me go somewhere quiet where we can get acquainted?"

"I'm leaving, Mr. Watson. It's late and I have to get home." I tried skirting around him, but he grabbed my arms, pulling me close to him.

"Ah, don't be like that. I'll show you a good time. A lot better than Elijah can."

"Silas Watson! Why the hell are you bothering this girl?" Miss LouAnn asked in a tone that demanded attention. She inserted herself between Silas and me, forcing him to release his hold on my arms.

"I ain't botherin' her, Miss LouAnn. We's just having a friendly conversation is all," he replied, feigning innocence.

"I heard your version of friendly and didn't much like it. Now get out of my house and don't come back till I invite you in. You heard me, git." He left in a hurry, unwilling to further risk her wrath.

"You alright, honey?"

"Yes, thank you. I'm fine," I said, trying to still my racing heart. "Why are men like that?" I didn't think it would be the last time I'd have to contend with that kind of unwanted attention, but I hadn't expected it here.

"Most men aren't, honey, just the ones who didn't have the benefit of a good mother to teach them how to treat a lady. Come on, I'll take you out to Elijah. It's time you got home."

Chapter 21

Kitchen adventures

It was nearly midnight when we arrived at the lake house. Bill was standing at the top of the back stairs when we pulled in.

"How was the party?" His tense posture and the tone in his voice told me something was wrong, but I wasn't sure if he was upset with me or something else. My sensitivity to his moods unsettled me.

"It was good, Major," Zach said, following me and Jolie up the stairs. "Everyone behaved themselves. The food was excellent, and the music was lively. It was a good old bayou party, just like I figured."

"Good to hear. Thanks, Zach. We'll talk in the morning. Did *you* have a good time, Désirée?" Bill asked as I went inside.

"Yes... What's wrong, Bill? Did something happen with Mr. Reyes tonight?"

"No, but we need to talk. Let's go to my office for a minute. Goodnight, Jolie. I'll see you in the morning."

"Night, Mr. William." Jolie scurried up the stairs to get ready for bed as I followed Bill to his office.

"Did Mrs. Gatlin like the wine?" Bill asked, pouring himself a glass of red from the bar. He held up a glass, silently offering me one.

I shook my head, took a seat by the window and lit a cigarette, blowing the smoke and my frustration out into the cool night air. "She did, but your investigation of her was unwelcome. Her family doesn't know about her connection to the Bentleys, and she would like to keep it that way."

He sat across from me, sipping his wine and dismissing my concerns with an arched brow. "I'm sorry, but I wasn't willing to take a chance with your safety. I had to know who she was, and her interest in you. There are only two things that matter to me, Désirée: your safety and your happiness."

"Hmm. I wonder what that would feel like: being safe and happy, free from my past. But you know something, Bill, even if I can't always control what happens to me, I can choose how I respond to it. How I feel and react is my choice. My happiness is up to me, so you don't need to worry... Is there something else you need to say?" I stubbed out the cigarette, positioning myself to leave. I wanted to be angry with him, though he really hadn't given me a valid reason.

"Yes, Chére, there is. Mr. Philgood had an accident at the restaurant tonight. He burned his hand badly. Shelby said he got dizzy and stumbled, and his hand fell into the fryer. He's in the hospital down in Slidell. She's going to come by in the morning to talk with you."

"Oh, my god! Will he be alright? Shelby must be frantic."

"I know little more than what I told you, but I believe she's going to ask you to help at the restaurant. Is that something you could do, help her out in the kitchen for a while?"

"Did Shelby ask for your permission?" It would have surprised me if she had, so I wondered if this was his idea to keep me home and occupied.

"No. It was Luke who mentioned it, but I told him it was up to you. It's like you said, Chére, what happens next is your choice, not mine."

"Of course, I'll help with whatever Shelby needs, and I'm sure Jolie will want to help, too." I stood to leave, feeling sad for Shelby and her father, and overwhelmed by the possibility of working in her restaurant. "If there's nothing else, I'll say goodnight. It's been a long day and I'm tired."

"Alright, goodnight, Chére. Sweet dreams."

Shelby and Luke Terrebonne came over early the next morning wearing exhausted faces. Luke filled us in on the details while Shelby sat at the table looking numb from the night's ordeal. Apparently, Mr. Philgood was in fair condition, having suffered a mild stroke, which caused him to stumble and severely burn his right hand. His burns were the worst of his injuries.

Shelby took over the conversation with an anxious look on her haggard face. "The doc says Pa will be in the hospital for a week or more and he said Pa may not regain the use of his hand... the burns caused permanent damage. I tried to get him to slow down, but the old fool wouldn't listen." She looked like a woman whose life had irreparably altered, and she was searching for a solution. "I need help at the restaurant, Désirée. Luke told me Parker Landry wanted you to work at his restaurant before... Do you think you could come help me out for a while? At least until I can figure things out?"

"Of course, Shelby, whatever you need," I said, imagining the possibilities working in a restaurant kitchen would offer. I'd dreamed of it a thousand times, but until that moment, that dream was beyond my reach.

"Are you sure about this, Désirée? I know things have been rough for you lately, but I really need your help till I can find someone to take over for Pa." Shelby clutched her coffee cup as if it offered salvation.

I glanced at Jolie, who nodded, confirming her willingness. "Yes, I'm sure. Jolie and I will both help. I've got a lot of free time on my hands,

Shelby, so I might as well keep them busy helping a friend. When do you want us to start?"

"I need to get some sleep, but can you both meet me down there around four? Glenna will be there cleaning the place with Terrance. We can show you what needs to be done to get ready to open on Tuesday. I really appreciate it, honey. This takes a big load off my mind, Désirée. I thought I might have to close the place until Luke mentioned you might help."

"Don't worry, Shelby. We'll keep the Lakeside going for you. I've spent plenty of time watching your father in that kitchen, so I know what to do. Everything's going to be fine. You'll see."

I had studied culinary techniques with Parker Landry at Gaston's throughout my high-school years and observed the food preparation in several New Orleans restaurants—the ones that let me into their kitchens. I'd lived for a year with one of the best chef/restauranteurs in Paris, and before that I'd spent countless hours watching the cooks in the kitchen at the George V hotel in Paris during the war, not to mention what Maman taught me when I was very young. It had all led to this singular moment. I would finally become what I'd always dreamed of: a real restaurant chef, and I would do it cooking with my closest friend. My future felt a lot brighter.

Jolie and I knew how to cook together, knew all the steps to creating a delicious meal, but it took time for our rhythm to sync with Mr. Terrance Harrison, who'd been cooking alongside Mr. Philgood for many years.

Mr. Terrance had his own way of doing things, and at first, he struggled with the adjustment of working alongside two young women, one of them black.

"That ain't the way Mr. P does it," he said for the millionth time. "You need to shake off them pieces better before you drop them in the fryer. Otherwise, the breading will fall off in the oil and I'll have to clean it out."

"I've been making fried chicken since I was old enough to stand," Jolie replied with an equal tone of impatience. "I know what to do."

"Why don't you handle the fryer, Mr. Terrance? Jolie and I will take care of the specials and the grill," I suggested, doing my best to keep the peace.

"Alright, Miss Désirée. I'm just trying to keep things going like Mr. P would. I meant no offense."

By the end of the first week, the three of us had found our rhythm, delivering plate after plate of sumptuous food to the hungry customers of the Lakeside Bar & Grill.

Initially, we stuck to the original menu, but the offerings weren't much of a challenge for Jolie and me. We longed to bring something unique to the menu; to give the customers a taste of New Orleans cuisine. After some discussion, Shelby agreed to let us add a couple of dishes to the menu to see how her clientele would respond. We added Veal Piccatta with Lemon Risotto and Roasted Beef Tenderloin with French Onion Au Jus served over Garlic Smashed Potatoes to the menu, the first of several changes.

"Looks like both your specials sold out, Désirée," Shelby said at the end of the second week. "The folks seem to like what you're cooking. Honestly, I wasn't sure if this would work out, but business seems to be picking up."

"They're coming to get a look at the Phantom Slayer," Jolie said, giving me a sidelong glance. "But they're coming back for the food."

"You might be right, Jolie, but whatever the reason, I'm grateful they're coming. It looks like this might be the best season we've had in a long time, thanks to you two."

I couldn't have been happier. My life, though busy, was heading in the right direction. Even the low moments during my sessions with Doctor Neville and visits with Evie couldn't mar the contentment I felt while working in that kitchen. I wouldn't let anything take that from me, not even the gawkers who came to see the Phantom Slayer.

They can look all they want, as long as they eat a meal while they're looking.

It took Evie time to recover from her initial shock at hearing I was working in a restaurant five nights a week, but she settled into the idea once I assured her that I would continue our regular visits. She feared I would abandon her, like her father and many of her so-called friends.

My sessions with Doctor Neville became routine and less stressful once he heard I was working and saw what he deemed a positive improvement in my state of mind. Whatever change he saw was unclear to me. From my perspective, I hadn't changed at all since meeting him. I was still hiding my true identity, still wanted for treasonous crimes in France, still raped and still a man killer. I was a few other things, too, but my situation remained unchanged. Therefore, I was stuck in the same place, the same situation, at least until Bill made good on his promise. Whatever future I would have wouldn't be secure until that happened.

On Fat Tuesday, Mardi Gras day, three weeks after Jolie and I started, the Lakeside was bustling with activity. The customers appeared eager to savor one last day of culinary delights before the start of Lent. Besides our regular menu, we offered Crawfish Beignets with Cajun dipping sauce, Cajun Pecan-crusted Catfish, Blackened Redfish with a bourbon sauce over greens, Shrimp Etouffee, Steamed Crab with garlic butter, and Andouille Sausage Soup. Plus, I made three King Cakes in honor of Mardi Gras and Cheesecake with strawberry sauce for those with a more discerning palette.

The service was non-stop from the moment we opened. Jolie, Terrance and I never took a break until we'd put out the last order before closing down the kitchen at around ten. By then, we were dog-tired and ready to clean up and go home.

When I went out to grab a cool drink from the bar and help clear away the dirty dishes, I found Silas Watson sitting at the bar with another man I didn't recognize.

"Hey sweet thing," Silas said with a dangerous glint in his eye. "I heard you were working here. How about you and I get together after you finish work? I can show you a *real* good time." His friend laughed at the bold proposal.

I ignored him and his vile suggestion, placing their empty plates and cutlery into the dish tray with my right hand as I wiped down the bar with my left.

Apparently, Silas couldn't take a silent no for an answer. He grabbed my left wrist with a firm grip as my hand wiped the bar in front of him. "Don't be like that, Désirée. I know you want to."

Without thinking what the consequences might be, and faster than the thought crossed my mind, my right hand grabbed the steak-knife from the dish tray under the bar. I swung the knife up then brought it down in a swift motion to within millimeters of his arm, pinning his jacket to the bar.

"Take your hand off me, sir," I snarled, staring daggers at him while my right hand still gripped the knife. "And I suggest you rethink that proposal. It didn't turn out too well for the last man who tried something like that with me."

He quickly released my hand, but his jacket remained pinned to the bar by the knife I still held in my right hand. "You crazy bitch! You nearly cut me! And look what you've done to my good jacket!"

Shelby came up next to me, placing her hand over mine, still clutching the knife. "Désirée, honey, let go of the knife."

I released my grip and stepped back, trembling with a surge of adrenaline.

Shelby pulled the knife from the bar, freeing his jacket. "You two, pay your bill and get out. Don't come back. You're not welcome here."

Silas Watson and his friend quickly got up and threw some money on the bar before heading to the door under Shelby's stoney glare.

"Are you alright, honey?" she asked.

The encounter left me shaken, but I pulled myself together before I spiraled out of control. "Yes. I'm fine."

"Okay. After you take a minute to calm down, there's a gentleman at the corner table who wants to have a word with you."

I looked over to see who she was referring to and immediately knew I couldn't avoid him. The distinguished gentleman sitting in the corner, wearing a very expensive suit, leaned over to the two rather large men at the next table and whispered something. They immediately got up and followed Silas and his friend out the door.

I watched them exit the restaurant, a little sorry that I'd made a scene, but not as sorry as I suspected Silas was going to be.

"Alright, Shelby, I'll go talk to him." I poured myself a shot of whiskey and took a drink before heading over to the table.

"That wasn't necessary, Mr. Costello," I said as I approached his table.

"I think it was, Miss Gautier. Offensive behavior toward women is intolerable. Some men need to be taught a lesson. Please, will you join me? Jim, do you mind leaving us alone for a moment?"

"Not at all, Frank. I'll go check on the boys, make sure they're handling things quietly. Pleasure to meet you, Miss Gautier," he said, getting up from the table. Diamond Jim Moran was a New Orleans nightclub owner who I'd read about in the newspaper. His club was only a couple blocks down from the Marchand Guesthouse in the Quarter.

With adrenaline still coursing through my veins, I sat down across from Frank Costello, one of the most notorious mob bosses in New York City. I sipped my whiskey and waited for him to make his purpose known.

"I wanted to meet you because I owe you a debt, Miss Gautier. You single-handedly solved two very serious problems for me by avenging the murders of my niece and a dear friend."

"I'm sorry about your niece. We only met once, but she seemed nice. She liked to sing, as I recall. I never met Mr. Barone. What I did wasn't for you or anyone else, Mr. Costello. It was simply an act of survival and nothing more. You don't owe me anything."

"I disagree, Miss Gautier, and I never forget a debt. So, if there is anything I can do for you, all you need to do is ask."

"I doubt my guardians would approve, Mr. Costello, but thank you for the offer. Sorry you had to come all this way to be disappointed. I hope you enjoyed the meal, at least."

"I hear I have you to thank for the delicious Veal Piccatta and Risotto. It was the best I've tasted outside of New York. Perhaps when you're ready to open your own place, you'll let me help. I've helped set up a few young restauranteurs in New York. I can do the same for you."

"Thank you for the offer, sir, but it will be a long time before I'm ready to do something so ambitious. Is there anything else I can get you? I really must get back to work."

"There's one more thing," he said, pulling a slip of paper from his inside breast pocket and handing it to me. "Give this to Mr. Marchand. Tell him the man he's looking for is at this address, under the watchful eye of my associates."

I wasn't sure if the man in question was the same one Bill told me about, the one who Carson made a deal with and then disappeared after Carson died. Frank Costello wasn't giving any clues as to his knowledge of those events, but I couldn't take any chances. I had to play it as cool as he was.

"I'll give Bill the message. Thank you, sir." I got up to leave, my mind filled with questions I couldn't ask.

"It's been a pleasure meeting you, Miss Gautier. I hope you'll consider me a friend."

Chapter 22

You have to break a few eggs

Bill wasn't happy about the incident at the restaurant, and the look he gave me once he heard Shelby's account of it made me think he might try to stop me from going back to work. I was determined to do whatever I could to prevent that from happening.

"You can't go around pulling a knife on people, Désirée. There are better ways to deal with those situations."

"I didn't cut him. I just got his attention and told him what's what. That's all."

Bill shook his head, unwilling to argue the point. "I hear someone gave him a beating he's not likely to forget."

"That was Frank Costello's doing, not mine. Anyway, I doubt Silas Watson will come around again, so you don't need to worry."

"But I do, Chére. Maybe Zach should stay down there while you're working."

"You can't keep me wrapped up in cotton, Bill. I can take care of myself. Oh, and Mr. Costello wanted me to give you this." I handed him the paper Frank Costello gave me. "He said you'll find the man you've been looking for at this address in Pensacola. He's being held by Costello's men."

Bill's expression changed from worry to acute interest. "Did Costello say anything else?"

"He thanked me for killing Carson. That seems to be a recurring theme, at least from the families of Carson's victims. Mr. Costello thinks he's indebted to me, but I told him he was mistaken."

"Alright, I'll handle this," Bill said, holding up the paper. "But if you don't mind, will you please watch your back? The Phantom murder publicity hasn't died down yet, and you're making more with your success at Shelby's."

"I'll be careful, Bill, if you will." There was no telling what he might walk into at that address.

"I always am, Chére."

Bill left with Luke on Wednesday after our talk, then he called late that night to tell me he would be out of town for a few days. It was late Saturday night before he came back. By then, I was sitting on pins and needles, worrying about him and what he may have discovered talking to that man. I hated being left in the dark about things that would affect my future.

On Sunday morning I went into his office and placed a tray with a pot of hot coffee and two cups on his desk, intending to end the waiting vigil. "What happened, Bill? Was he the man you were looking for?" I poured us each a cup, then took a seat across from him to await his response.

Bill blew softly across the cup to cool the coffee before taking a cautious sip. "He was. Poor guy thought I was there to rescue him from Costello's thugs. He was wrong."

"What did you do? You didn't kill him, did you?" More ghosts haunting me was the last thing I needed.

Bill's eyes briefly met mine as he sipped his coffee. "No, I didn't, but it took some convincing to get him to talk. In the end, Gatti told me what I wanted to know. He would have given up his mother by then. When we left, he was alive, but I can't guarantee he still is. Costello's men seemed eager to have their own conversation with him."

"Don't give him a second thought, Désirée. Anthony Gatti is one of the bad guys, an opportunist and a stone-cold killer. He doesn't deserve your pity."

This was a side of Bill I rarely saw. It was as chilling as the man he described.

"What did he tell you?" I asked. In for a penny, I wanted to hear all of it.

"He gave me some names and locations. The first was a stooge in the city. Gatti paid him to drop that note in our mailbox, but the guy sent someone local to do it. The second name was Raul Alonso Hernández, a businessman in Veracruz. I gave the name to Eduardo Reyes to check out. Hernandez is the man who paid Gatti. The last was the most troubling, a name and address in Havana. I went there to investigate. The house was closed but not abandoned. It felt like the owner would return. The thing is, Chére, that place is only half a mile from Katarina. Gatti said that's where he was supposed to take you."

My heart skipped a few beats after hearing that. *You really are a lucky girl, Désirée.*

"Did you see Katarina? Is she alright?"

"I spoke with her, but I didn't tell her I was in Cuba. She's fine and has heard nothing recently about Steigler. She sends her best."

"Is she in danger, Bill?"

The look he gave me was somewhere between tortured and angry. I felt horrible that I'd brought all this into his life.

"You both are, Chére, as long as Steigler is still out there. But he's somewhere close, I can feel it, and when he shows his face, I'll get him."

I wondered what Bill planned to do when he found him. The thought sent an icy chill down my spine.

Somehow, life returned to normal, or at least as normal as mine could be. Worrying about the what ifs was a waste of my time and energy, so I concentrated on making the most of the opportunity Shelby gave me by becoming the best cook I could be, filling my thoughts with food and very little else.

Sundays, Jolie and I would spend hours diving through my cookbooks and cooking journals, searching for new recipes to bring to the Lakeside customers. We tested each new recipe, seeking Shelby's approval before adding it to the menu.

Early on Monday mornings, before going to Glen Oaks, I would accompany Shelby to the local farm-stands to select the produce for the week, and then to the butcher to choose the meat. I suggested she buy her fish from Elijah Tillman, and after a trial run, Elijah was bringing us his fresh-caught fish three days a week: catfish, bass, redfish, crawfish, crab, and even gator when he had it. I suspected he was giving Shelby a discount to ensure she bought her seafood exclusively from him and maybe so he could spend a little time with me.

While working at the Lakeside, my cooking skills weren't the only things I sharpened. Shelby taught me everything she knew about running a successful restaurant; how to calculate food and liquor costs, the ins and outs of kitchen maintenance, employee relations and payroll, everything. I absorbed it all like a sponge, dreaming of the day when I would have a restaurant of my own.

Between working at the Lakeside and my sessions at Glen Oaks with Doctor Neville and visits with Evie, there was little time for a social life. It felt easier that way, staying isolated, insulated in Shelby's kitchen, where at least I could be productive while limiting my exposure. Being social still felt dangerous in several uncomfortable ways. Never letting my guard down was the worst. But I was a girl on a mission, determined to get to the finish-line fully prepared to venture out on my own. That was all that mattered.

By mid-March, I was twenty-nine days away from completing my mandatory psychiatric care with Doctor Neville, and sixty days from independence, my eighteenth birthday.

I needed to make a concrete plan, but every time I thought about leaving, the Kommandant's looming threat paralyzed me. Unless I could disappear without a trace—which felt impossible—I would drag that threat along with me wherever I went. I prayed Bill could somehow keep his promise in the next sixty days, and eliminate Anton Steigler once and for all, but that, too, felt unlikely. So far, there was no trace of him.

On a Friday morning, the seventeenth of March, Elijah Tillman stood at the back door of the restaurant kitchen after storing the fish order in the cooler. With his hands stuffed in his pockets, he shifted his weight from one foot to the other as if nervous to speak. "Uh... I was wondering, Désirée, would you go out with me on Sunday to a matinee and maybe for a bite to eat after?"

Ever since the Silas incident, Elijah seemed shy around me; polite, but shier than before. I didn't know if it was embarrassment at his friend's actions, or because he'd heard some twisted version of mine. His invitation surprised me.

Jolie gave me a look, complete with raised eyebrows, a crooked smile, and a shrug. Little slipped past Jolie's rapt attention.

I was in a mood that morning; anxious from waiting and bored with being couped up in my self-inflicted cage. I needed a change of scenery, and a date with Elijah Tillman sounded like it might fit the bill.

"That sounds wonderful, Elijah. What time should I be ready?" I asked, knowing I'd have to clear it with Mama and with Bill.

"Is two o'clock, okay? The movie starts at three and I'd like to visit with your folks... I mean, with Mr. Marchand before we leave."

"Two o'clock is perfect, Elijah. I'm looking forward to it."

"Great. I'll see you then, Désirée. So long, Jolie," he said, waving goodbye.

Jolie just looked at me and smiled. "It's like Mama always said, 'You can't make an omelet without breaking a few eggs. It sure is gonna be interesting seeing Elijah and Bill together."

"Jolie Jefferies, I don't know what you're talking about." I turned away to hide my blushing face.

"Right. And I'm the Queen of Sheba."

Sunday morning at breakfast was my first opportunity to speak with Bill. He'd been in Washington DC all day Friday, then he stayed in New Orleans till late Saturday night. Mama was out of town, visiting Julianna.

"Just so you know, Bill," I said, capturing his attention from the Sunday paper. "I'm going out this afternoon with Elijah Tillman to a matinee and then to supper, somewhere in Slidell, I think. He's coming by at two to pick me up… and to meet you." I wasn't asking for his permission; I was simply informing him of my plans. He looked surprised and disappointed.

"Hmm. I thought we could spend some time together today, take a drive in the country on your day off, but I guess you've made other plans. You say he's coming at two? I'll be here to meet him." The look in his eyes reminded me of the time he caught me kissing Jimmy Wilcox.

That should have been a warning.

"Désirée. Elijah is here," Jolie said, grinning as she watched me put the finishing touches on my hair and makeup. "He's downstairs talking with Bill. You better go rescue him before Bill scares him off."

She'd been teasing me about Elijah for two days, taunting me to reveal how I felt about him, and about Bill. I tried very hard not to feel anything, but with little success. No matter how much I told myself to remain aloof, to keep my feelings in check regarding Bill and Elijah, I couldn't help but feel a tingle of excitement at being the object of their interest. It gave me a sense of power I hadn't known before.

"I'm ready," I said, glancing in the mirror to make sure.

"I sure hope so," Jolie said as she followed me downstairs.

Bill was sitting in the living room, smoking and nursing a whiskey, looking like a protective guardian. Elijah sat across from him, perched on the edge of the sofa with his feet planted firmly in front of him, as if ready to jump into action at a moment's notice.

"Well, here she is," Bill said, raking his eyes over me and nodding his reluctant approval. "You look nice, Chére."

"Hello, Désirée," Elijah said, rising to greet me. "He's right, you look beautiful."

"Hello, Elijah. Thanks. I'm glad you think so. What have you two been talking about?" They looked like two dogs sizing each other up, trying to decide which was the alpha.

"Oh, just fishing. Mr. Marchand offered to get me a job with one of the big commercial fishing outfits that work out in the Gulf. I told him I preferred being the captain of my own boat, setting my own goals. But I appreciate the offer, sir," Elijah said, nodding to Bill.

"Fair enough, son. Maybe you could take me out fishing on that boat of yours one of these days and show me some of those honey holes you were talking about. It's been a while since I've fished the bayous."

"Be happy to, any time, sir. Well, we should probably get going, Désirée. I'll have her home by ten, Mr. Marchand."

"Alright. I'll be here. Y'all have a good time. I'll see you later, Chére."

Elijah climbed in behind the wheel of his truck, then turned to look at me. "He isn't what I expected. I thought he'd be old, like an uncle or a father or something, but he's younger than I thought."

I could see the wheels turning in his head, forming questions I couldn't answer honestly.

"He's thirty-two, and older than me, but then, so are you. What difference does it make?" I tried to sound indifferent, wanting to make him think Bill was nothing more than my caretaker.

"None, I guess. I was just saying. It surprised me, is all."

He shook off his doubts and started the ignition. "You ready? We should be there before the previews so we can get good seats."

"I'm ready if you are. Let's go."

Chapter 23

Bridges to cross

Early the following morning, Shelby and I were on our way to the farm stand to buy produce when she questioned me about my date with Elijah. She usually kept her questions to herself, unless it had to do with the restaurant, but this time her curiosity got the better of her.

"I heard you went out with Elijah Tillman yesterday. Where'd he take you?"

I wondered why she wanted to know, but made light of it, as if the date with Elijah was nothing out of the ordinary. "We went into Slidell to see a double feature. *Adam's Rib,* which was kinda funny and interesting. The second movie was *All the King's Men.* That was more serious. Then we had a bite to eat at a coffee shop, and he brought me home. Is there anything else you'd like to know?"

"I was just curious, is all," she said, shaking her head as she kept her eyes on the road. "Last night at supper, I noticed Bill didn't look happy, so it surprised me when I heard he let you go out with Elijah."

"Who I see or where I go isn't up to Bill, Shelby." It annoyed me how everyone thought Bill was the last word about how I should conduct my life.

"No, I guess not, but it's obvious he cares about you."

"He needn't concern himself with me because I'm fine. Bill has his own life to worry about, his work and the family. I'm just trying to rebuild *my* life the best way I know how. That's all."

"How do you feel about Elijah?" She sounded a little hopeful, but also cautious.

"He's nice, easy to be with, and he expects nothing from me. He's just a friend, nothing more."

"You sure friendship is all *he* wants? Seems to me Elijah spends a lot of time coming round to see you."

"We're just friends, and that's all it can be. I'm not ready for anything else with anyone. I'm not sure I ever will be." The thought of falling in love, being that close to a man, scared the hell out of me.

"I know it feels like that now, honey, but someday it will be different. You'll meet a man who'll change your mind about things, someone you'll feel right with."

"That's not likely to happen around here, Shelby. There probably isn't a man in the entire state of Louisiana who doesn't already know what happened to me and what I did, including Elijah. No man in his right mind would want a girl with my reputation, at least not for anything serious."

She shook her head as she kept her eyes on the road and the morning traffic. "I used to distrust men that way... until I met Luke. Then everything changed. That can happen for you too, honey. You'll see."

"Maybe, but not for a long time. And not here."

"It sounds like you're planning on leaving, Désirée. I hoped you and Jolie would stay on at the Lakeside. Pa ain't going back to work in the kitchen, and I sure would like you two to keep doing what you've been doing. The Lakeside is humming, thanks to you and Jolie."

"I haven't made any plans yet, Shelby, but I'll let you know when I do. Besides, I can't go anywhere before summer starts, but you should ask Jolie what her plans are."

"I will, and I hope by summer you'll change your mind."

Life became routine for me, Jolie, and the rest of the residents of the lake house. Bill and Luke were frequently out of town on business, which made things simpler for me, less explaining to do, though I was certain Zach kept Bill informed as to my comings and goings. Mama would come for the weekend a couple times a month, even though it took a toll on her. Neither Mama nor Bill ever mentioned her illness, so neither did I.

Occasionally, Jimmy and Olivia would come for supper, which was always a pleasant distraction, and I continued to see Elijah for casual dates, usually on Monday evenings. Nothing romantic, just friendly conversations over a meal in some quiet out of the way place.

While my life remained the same, Evie's changed dramatically. In all the time she'd been at Glen Oaks, her father had never visited nor called her. That abandonment more than the others devastated poor Evie. She found out why when she asked her mother in early April.

"Do you know what she told me, Désirée?" Evie asked, looking stronger than I'd seen her in months. "She told me Papa wasn't my real father. He married her to save her reputation because she was pregnant by another man and because her father guaranteed Papa a position at the bank if he married her. The man who was my real father died before she could tell him about me. Grandfather made her marry Papa, but she said she didn't want to. She said she was sorry she ever did."

"I'm so sorry, Evie. That must have been hard for you to hear. How do you feel about it?"

"Numb, I guess, but the funny thing is, it all makes sense now. How he treated me, sometimes like a princess and other times like I couldn't do anything right. I was a tool for him to get ahead, just like mother was. Now that my reputation is ruined, he doesn't need me, can't use me anymore. It all makes perfect sense now."

"What are you going to do when you leave here, Evie? You can always come live with me, at least until you decide what to do. There's plenty of room at my place."

"I can't. Mother said she's divorcing Papa, and we're moving to Aunt Martha's in St. Louis as soon as I can leave here. Doctor Neville gave her the name of a doctor there who can help me adjust. He said I could leave as soon as I feel ready."

"Do you think you're ready?"

"I don't know. Right now, I feel ignorant, foolish, gullible. Do you know why I really went with Carson that night? Papa encouraged me to pursue him. He said Carson Bentley was the type of husband I should have, and I believed him because I thought I belonged in that world, wanted to belong there. It was what I'd always dreamed of, but I didn't realize until it was too late what that dream really was. I don't know if I can ever trust a man again."

"I know how you feel, Evie, but the only way we'll ever find out is to cross that bridge... when we come to it."

A few days later, while Jolie and Zach were at church, I was reading the Sunday paper and came across an article about Jonathan Duret.

"Oh, dear god. As if Evie doesn't have enough to deal with. Now this," I said, shaking my head.

"What is it, Chére?" Lines creased Bill's brow as he looked over at me.

"It's Evie's father, Jonathan Duret. He was found dead in his car outside his office last night. The police are investigating."

"I heard about it," Bill said, laying down the book he'd been reading. "Jonathan has been in trouble with the bank since Carson's death, suspicion of embezzling funds, authorizing loans filtered through his personal accounts. They were about to file charges against him. I learned he was deeply involved with Carson and Tony Gatti on that hotel/casino project, so the Genovese family was probably interested in him, too. There's no telling who got to him first, or maybe he took the easy way out."

"This news is going to be hard on Evie. Just when she was getting better, something like this could set her back. But maybe it's for the best that he's dead. Evie said he never really loved her; he only used her. She and her mother are moving to St. Louis at the end of the week after her last session with Doctor Neville."

"Mother told me about that."

"You seem rather well informed, Bill. Did *you* have anything to do with Mr. Duret's death?" I wondered if he would be honest about it.

He gave me a hard look, as if hurt I would ask him such a question.

"No, Chére, but I'm not grieving him. He doesn't deserve our pity. He helped Carson try to destroy us, so I'm glad he's dead. Now there's one less problem for me to solve." The chill in his voice felt like an icy river flowing through my veins.

And now there's another ghost haunting me. When will it ever end? I tried to shake off the chill.

"Doctor Neville wants you to come to my last session on Thursday. Will you be around? If not, I can ask Mama or Charlie."

"I'll go with you, Chére. Maybe I can see Evelyn, to wish her well before she leaves town."

On the thirteenth of April, Bill walked me into Glen Oaks Sanitorium for the last time. Doctor Neville was waiting for us in the lobby, a friendly smile on his usually stoic face.

"Good morning, Désirée. Mr. Marchand, thank you for coming. If you don't mind, I'll meet with Désirée alone for a few moments, then we'll call you in to join us. Please make yourself comfortable."

"No problem, doc. I'll be here waiting."

I followed Doctor Neville to his office, eager to get this farce over with.

"How are you feeling today, Désirée? Do you feel prepared to face what comes next for you?" he asked after I'd taken my usual seat on the couch across from him.

"I'm fine, Doctor Neville, and you needn't worry. I'm prepared."

"Yes, I believe you are. You're a remarkable young woman. Resilient, intelligent and determined. I believe you can handle any problem that besets you. Do you have any concerns you'd like to share with me in this, our last session? Are there questions I can answer for you?"

"Yes, doctor, there are. In our first meeting, you said you hoped to get to know me by our last. Do you think you have?"

"An interesting question, one I've asked myself several times over the past three months. The answer is, I know the Désirée you've shown me, but I believe there is a lot more to know. You're a cautious young woman. Your history of abandonment and uncertainty makes you so, but you've used those experiences to strengthen your resolve to succeed in anything you pursue. I don't doubt you will."

"Do you think it will ever be different for women, doctor? I mean, the way this male-dominated society treats women who defend themselves?" I wondered if he would give me an honest answer or evade the question completely.

He dropped his chin and took a drag from his pipe, watching me over the burning bowl. "Perhaps it will be different one day, if there are women like you to take up that cause. Have you ever thought about pursuing a career in psychology? You're well suited to it, based on what I've observed during your time with Evelyn."

"I did what I had to for Evie because she's my friend and she needed me. Psychology doesn't interest me, doctor. I was just curious if you thought things could ever change for women."

"Eventually, time shifts all societal perspectives, Désirée. Think about how different it was for women during the Middle Ages or even as recently as the 1920's. Strong women lead the way to change, and there is very little that men can do to stop that change from happening."

An idea had been brewing in my mind about what to do with the money Charlotte gave me, and his response brought it clarity. At that moment, I knew what I needed to do.

"Shall we call Mr. Marchand in now, or is there something else you'd like to talk about?"

"No, doctor. I'm finished here. Let's get this over with."

A moment later, Bill was sitting next to me, cradling my hand in his. "Well doc, how's our girl doing?"

"Désirée is a unique young woman, one with many talents. She can be successful in anything she chooses. I've suggested she pursue a career in psychology, but it seems she has other interests. That's unfortunate because her IQ scores were the highest that I've seen in my years of practice. It's a shame to let such talent go to waste. Perhaps you can convince her to enroll in college, Mr. Marchand, where she can find a passion to direct her intellect."

"Désirée *is* very talented, doctor, as I'm sure the patrons of the Lakeside Bar & Grill can attest to. Her passion is for cooking fine food, and she's very good at it. As to pursuing a college career, well, that is her choice, not mine nor yours. Now, I assume there are some papers I need to sign releasing her from your care."

"Of course. I have them right here," Doctor Neville said, pulling two documents from a folder. "My final report to the court should free them of any doubt as to her ability to function normally in society."

"I never doubted it for a moment." Bill signed the papers and handed them back.

"Are we done, doctor? Can we see Evie now?"

"We are, but if you ever need to talk, Désirée, I am merely a phone call away. Thank you for coming in, Mr. Marchand. Good luck, Désirée."

Bill and I met Evie in the solarium, then we walked out to the garden to find a place to sit in the shade beneath the oak trees.

"I didn't know you were coming, Mr. Marchand, but I'm happy you did," Evie said shyly. "It gives me a chance to thank you for saving me. I don't know how I can ever repay you."

"There's no need, Evelyn. I'm happy I could be of service and that you're doing well. I came because I wanted to offer you my condolences about your father, and to let you know that if there's anything I can do for you, please don't hesitate to ask."

"Thanks. You don't know how much your offer means to me. Mother will be happy that we spoke. She's taking me to the funeral tomorrow, but I'm not looking forward to it."

Bill gave her an understanding smile, then skillfully changed the subject. "Désirée mentioned you're moving to St. Louis. I hope you and your mother will be happy there. It's a friendly town, a bit quieter than New Orleans, but I think you'll like it."

"I hope so, but I'll miss seeing Désirée."

"She'll be free to visit come summer. I'll leave you two alone to say your goodbyes. *Bonne chance*, Evelyn." He stood to leave, taking her hand in his and planting a tender kiss on her forehead. "I'll be waiting for you in the car, Chére."

Once Bill was gone, Evie gently squeezed my hand in a gesture that felt like appreciation. "He's so nice, Désirée. You're lucky to have someone like Bill to take care of you, but you've always been lucky."

"You're right, Evie. Lucky should be my middle name."

"You know, Désirée, I'm going to miss this place, especially spending time with you. I couldn't have gotten through all this without your help. Thanks for everything, for not abandoning me. Will you thank Bobby for me? Without his help, I don't know where I'd be."

"Of course, I'll tell him. He'll be glad to hear you're doing so well. We've both been through a lot, Evie, but we're on the other side of it now. You've helped me as much as I've helped you, and that makes us sisters with an unbreakable bond." I handed her a slip of paper from my pocket. "Here's my address and phone number. If you ever need to talk, well, you know what to do."

Nurse Johanna came over to tell us Mrs. Duret was there to take Evie to her last session with Doctor Neville. I didn't want to let her go, but knew I had to. We both had our bridges to cross, but I hoped someday our paths would converge again.

"*Au revoir, mon amie. Je t'aime,*" I said, pulling her into my arms for a last embrace.

"*Moi aussi. Au revoir*, Désirée."

Chapter 24

Making plans

"Now that ya got all this free time on your hands, what ya planning on doing with it?" Jolie asked as we stood side by side cleaning the bucket of shrimp Elijah delivered to the restaurant earlier that morning.

"I thought about making bread. What we get from the bakery is alright, but not as good as I can make. I want to try it out and see what Shelby thinks."

"Does that mean you plan on staying? Shelby told me she asked you to stay on here, but you didn't give her a straight answer. She asked me to stay, too."

"I don't know, but I can't make any plans yet anyway, so I might as well be useful while I'm waiting. What did you tell her?"

"Just that I enjoyed working here and appreciated the opportunity." She kept ducking her head, as if reluctant to share her thoughts, which was unusual for Jolie.

"It sounds like there was a BUT coming."

"Well, yeah. But I feel like I should stick with you, whatever you decide to do, only..."

"Only you like it here. You like cooking for Shelby, and you like how things are going between you and Zach. It's alright, Jolie. I understand and you're not obligated to me at all. You need to choose what's best for you and not worry about what I do."

"What about Elijah and Bill? They're gonna want you to stick around."

I stretched my shoulders, as if trying to shed a burden. "It's complicated with them, but for different reasons. Sometimes I feel like I'm standing on the edge of a cliff looking down into a pool of clear deep water, but there's a storm brewing offshore, ready to whip up the waves. I don't know whether to jump or run for cover."

"Well, we still got some time to decide, Désirée. The storm ain't hit yet."

"Does that mean you'll help me with the bread?" I asked as I counted the cleaned shrimp into portions and tossed them into a bowl.

"Course I will. Wouldn't be a very good *sous chef* if I didn't."

"Mind if I eat in here tonight?" Bill asked, coming into the restaurant through the back door just as dinner service began and taking a seat at the corner table usually reserved for staff.

When Bill was home on weeknights, he would have his supper at the restaurant, since Jolie and I weren't around to cook for him at home. He and Luke would sit at one of the small tables in the bar and have a drink while Shelby served them supper. Sometimes, Luke and Zach would eat at the staff table in the kitchen when Bill wasn't around, but Bill rarely came into the kitchen.

"Where's Luke tonight? Aren't you eating with him?" I asked.

"Luke and Zach are busy doing something for me, and I hate eating alone. Besides, this gives me a chance to spend some time with you. I should have thought of this before." He looked hopeful, which was hard to resist.

"I'm working, Bill. Fridays are busy, and I don't have any time to chat."

"That's alright, Chére. I'll try not to distract you. What's on the menu tonight?"

His unexpected presence brought on a familiar tingling sensation I tried to ignore, to hide from. But it was clear he was intent on staying, so I used a professional approach to ease my discomfort.

"Tonight's specials include Braised Short Ribs Bordelaise with Garlic Mashed Potatoes and Sauteed Haricots. Our seafood special is Grilled Cajun Shrimp over Roasted Garlic Risotto with Sauteed Asparagus. Classic French Onion is our soup this evening. If the specials don't appeal to you, you're familiar with our regular menu. I'll ask Irma to take your order."

"No need, Chére. I'll have the soup and ribs, but you can ask her to bring me a bottle of your best red wine, if you don't mind." He flashed that brilliant smile again.

"I'll have her bring it in. Your soup will be ready in a moment."

Most of the cooking that goes on in a restaurant is in preparing each recipe before service even begins and knowing how many servings you'll need. From order to table, each course shouldn't take over fifteen minutes, twenty tops, or you risk displeasing the patrons. Preparation is the key. Without it, everything can go terribly wrong.

Fortunately, being prepared is something I insist on, so Bill's menu choices were simple to put together.

The soup was ready and warming on the stove. All that needed doing was to make the cheese toast for the top. I placed a slice of crusty bread down on the hot grill for a moment, then flipped it over for another minute before placing it on top of the soup I'd scooped into a bowl. After covering the bread with shredded gruyere cheese, I stuck the bowl under the broiler for a couple of minutes to melt and toast the cheese. It took less than five minutes to serve Bill his first course. By then, Irma had already brought him the wine.

Earlier in the day, I had braised the marinated short ribs in the oven to just shy of their final cooking temp, then held them in a covered pan to keep warm. I then made the Bordelaise sauce from the drippings, adding a little Cajun spice for an extra kick of flavor and set it aside to keep warm. Jolie had cooked and mashed the potatoes, and they were ready for plating. The only thing left to do for this dish was to sauté the vegetables and the final preparation of the ribs… whenever Bill was ready for his entrée.

As I worked alongside Jolie and Terrance, preparing the orders that came in at a steady pace, I kept my eye on Bill, to gauge when to start his entrée. Occasionally, he caught me looking and smiled. It shouldn't have made me self-conscious, but it did.

When the time was right, I sauteed the haricots in butter with minced shallots, put a final sear on the ribs, tossing them with some Bordelaise sauce, then plated the meal, along with Jolie's garlic mashed potatoes. It only took fifteen minutes to complete.

"Here you are, Bill. Can we get you anything else?" I asked, setting the plate down in front of him, while butterflies flittered in my chest.

"It looks delicious, Chére."

"Thanks. Enjoy your meal."

Bill remained at the staff table after his meal, just watching us cook, and making me nervous. By the end of the night, I was exhausted from being watched while I worked and from trying to ignore the feeling his presence gave me.

"Are you staying to talk with Mr. Luke, Mr. William?" Jolie asked Bill after we'd finished cleaning the kitchen. "Zach is here to walk us home. You ready to go, Désirée?"

"You go on with Zach, Jolie. I'll walk Désirée home," Bill said.

"Yes, sir. I'll see you later, Désirée." Jolie gave me a look that brought an instant blush to my cheek. I tried to hide it with a swipe of a kitchen towel across my face.

"Will you sit and have a glass of wine with me, Chére?"

"Sure." I grabbed a clean glass from the drying rack and collapsed into the seat across from him.

"I'm sorry if I made you uncomfortable tonight. I just wanted to spend some time with you, and this seems like one of the few ways I can do it."

"It's alright, Bill. You didn't distract me... too much."

"I hadn't realized before tonight how difficult this job really is. It's hard work, but you make it look easy. It's obvious that this is what you love doing, this is who you are. Thank you for letting me witness it. I hope you'll let me come again."

"Thank you, Bill," I said, trying to shrug off my discomfort. "We did good tonight. Not too many mistakes, which is always a good sign. Of course, you can eat in here anytime." I thought it might get easier if he came more often, but then again, it might not.

"Was there something else you wanted to talk about, Bill? I'm a little tired. Maybe we could finish the wine, then talk on the way home," I said, lifting my glass to take a couple of sips.

"Alright. Let's finish with a toast. Here's to your continued success as one of the youngest and best new chefs in New Orleans." We tipped our glasses together and drained them.

Bill held my hand as we strolled up the dark street toward the house. It felt good, almost natural, like very few things in my life felt. His touch had that effect on me, something both soothing and exciting all at once.

"Shelby said she asked you to stay on at the restaurant, but you didn't give her a firm yes or no. She thinks you're planning to leave. And Mother has been asking when you're coming home, now that you're finished at Glen Oaks."

"It's hard to make plans, Bill, when things are still so uncertain." With my eyes straight ahead, I mentally counted the steps that took me home as I tried to still my pounding heart. "I won't go back to Mama's because I can't live in that house again. I don't belong in that world anymore, and it would be too hard trying to fit in. Staying here feels safer for now, but eventually, I'll need to decide what I'm going to do, where I'm going to be. I just don't know yet."

"Is it Elijah Tillman who keeps you here? You've been seeing a lot of him. Is he that special to you?"

"Elijah is special, but not like you think. He's just a friend. There's nothing to be jealous about, Bill."

"Well, I'm vain enough to want to be the center of your attention, so yes, I am jealous. I've told you I love you, Désirée, and that will never change, no matter what. If you choose to leave, I'll have to let you go, b ut *I* want you to stay." He gently stroked my hand, lifting it to his lips. "I want you to choose *me*, the man who has always loved you."

I couldn't take another step. My hand pulled away from his and covered my mouth. It took a minute to recover my composure. For months, no, years, I'd longed to hear him say what he really wanted, but now I had to be practical. Whatever was between us, was impossible now.

"Bill, I'm not the woman you should be with. I can never live in your world or be the type of woman you need. Too much has happened to me. Too much can still happen that could destroy you and hurt the family. I can't do that to you."

"Please, Chére, don't give up. Give this a chance, give *us* a chance. I don't want to lose you." He would not accept defeat so easily.

As we reached the front gate, I turned to him. "I'm not giving up. I'm just being realistic."

"So, Bobby, tell me about this house you're renting," I asked during our Sunday evening phone call.

"You're gonna like it, Dez. It's in a little town called Sausalito, just north of the city. A ferry goes back and forth across the bay every day. It's a fully furnished house with three bedrooms, two bathrooms, a living room, dining room, and a kitchen. There's also a studio apartment over the garage that I think would be perfect for you. It has a deck overlooking the bay. I took a lease on it for six months, starting the first of June and I've got a housekeeper ready to start as soon as we move in. She's a widow who used to run a boarding house in the city. You're still coming, aren't you?"

"When are you out of school?"

"June seventh is my last day. I'm moving in the next day with some friends; Owen, Brett, and Steven. They'll share it with me during the summer. After school starts in the fall, the place could be all yours. Tell me you haven't changed your mind, Dez. I've been bragging about you and your cooking, but the guys want to taste it, to believe it."

"I'm coming, Bobby, but I'm not sure exactly when. Things need to settle down here before I can make any solid plans."

"Why? What's going on?" Bobby didn't know the danger my presence in his life posed.

"Nothing. But a lot can happen in six weeks, and I need to talk with Mama and Charlie about it before I decide anything."

"What about Bill and that guy you've been seeing? What's his name again?"

"Elijah Tillman. I need to talk with them, too. And with Shelby and Jolie."

"Jolie can come, if she wants to."

"Thanks. I'll let her know, but I think she may decide to stay here and work for Shelby. Besides, I think she's falling in love with Zach Johnson."

"I guess that was bound to happen. Anyway, let me know when you're coming. I want to make sure I set everything up real nice for you: your room and the kitchen and everything."

"You'll do that anyway, Bobby. I know how meticulous you are about things."

"Yeah, you're right. I am, but that doesn't mean I wouldn't do it for you. I really want to see you, Dez. It's been hard being separated, especially while you've been going through so much."

"I'm fine, Bobby. Don't worry about me. I'll let you know as soon as I can about coming out there this summer. You just concentrate on studying for those finals, alright?"

"I will. I'll call you next week. Take care, Dez. Bye."

That night I thought long and hard about what my options were; go to Bobby, disappear, or stay with Bill. I decided going to Bobby, at least for a little while, was the best choice I could make. Better for Bill and the family, even better for Elijah. I could take some time to regroup with Bobby, then decide what to do and where to go next. Sausalito could be my haven for a while, a quiet place where no one knows anything about me.

My false identity—a consequence of Bill smuggling me into the country—and the looming danger of my French past being uncovered, pressed down on me like a physical burden, a constant, icy dread. If that happened, it could ruin everything. I wasn't sure I could take the risk of dragging my history to my best friend, unless by some miracle Bill could fix my immigration status and find Anton Steigler to put an end to that threat.

But even that wouldn't solve my problem, it would only postpone the inevitable. I feared there would come a day when my past would catch up to me, and I didn't want to be anywhere near the people I cared about when it happened.

Back and forth my tormented mind shifted, vacillating between my need to protect them and wanting the shelter they offered. It took hours, and a large shot of whiskey, to get to sleep, and even then, my mind was restless. My usual method of choosing a favorite memory to carry me into slumber was at first successful, but then my body betrayed me... again.

...Bill was carrying me up the stairs to my room. I felt safe with him, safe in his arms. I knew he would never hurt me. He laid me down on the bed, stroked my cheek with a feather touch, and whispered in my ear.

"Je suis là, ma chérie." I'm here, my darling.

I want to pull him to me, feel him next to me, but he's gone and only the effect of his touch remains.

My hand strokes my cheek with Bill's face behind my eyes, his words repeating in my mind, and I feel the petal soft skin his fingers touched. A tingle, and then a spark ignites and my hand travels down my throat, stroking gently as he might do, lingering for a moment, then continuing down to my breast, cupping it, caressing it, bringing it to attention. Gradually, my hand resumes its journey, traveling down my body, exploring the secret places as the sound of his voice caresses my mind.

Then suddenly, as my fingers find the place where ecstasy lies, the scene changes. It's no longer Bill's voice I hear, nor his face I imagine. It's Carson and the other one. My dream turned into a nightmare. They taunt me, torment me, torture me relentlessly with my memories, my perverse memories. The only way to make them stop is to give them what they want, to let my body find release, imprinted with their faces, the feel of their hands on me...

I woke from the nightmare, dripping with sweat, trembling, ashamed and disgusted by my weakness.

Chapter 25

New Information

The phone rang Monday evening, as Jolie and I were washing up after supper. With our hands wet and occupied, Zach answered it on the kitchen wall phone. Bill and Luke were out of town on business.

"Good evening. Marchand residence...Yes ma'am, she's right here. I'll get her for you." Zach held up the receiver to me. "It's Miss Bea calling, Miss Désirée."

"I'll take it in Bill's office, Zach," I said, grabbing a towel and hurrying through the house to Bill's office.

Mama and I hadn't spoken since the Sunday before my last appointment with Doctor Neville. She'd been out of town, supposedly visiting Julianna. Over the past four months Mama had taken three trips up to Boston, and I suspected it was for some kind of medical treatment, though I wasn't sure.

With a nervous stomach and a trembling hand, I picked up the receiver from Bill's desk phone and held it to my ear.

"I've got it now, Zach." I heard him hang up the kitchen phone. "Hello, Mama. I'm glad you called."

"Hello, darling. How are you?" she asked, sounding stronger than the last time we talked.

"I'm fine, Mama. How was your trip? Are you feeling alright?" I wondered if she would tell me the truth.

"Oh, I'm fine, sweetheart, better than ever. Julianna and Madalyn send their love. They're coming home at the end of the week. Julianna is insisting on having her baby in New Orleans. Her doctor says she's healthy enough to travel, and the baby is fine. She and Charles have scheduled her cesarean section for May third."

"Isn't that early, Mama? I thought Julianna wasn't due until the end of May."

"It may be a week or two early, but her doctor thinks she may have miscalculated her start date by a couple of weeks. She and the baby are both doing well, so Julianna wants to come home, and Charles has agreed. Anyway, we all will be happy to have them home again. Speaking of home, darling... have you given any thought to coming back to the city? I've missed you. We all have."

"And do what, Mama? Return to my old life? That's impossible now."

"This is your home, sweetheart. We can work through any difficulties together. You know that, don't you?"

"I can't go back, Mama. It's hard even thinking about it. I don't belong there anymore."

"Darling, I'm only thinking about what's best for you. Now that you're no longer under Doctor Neville's care, I think you should come home and live here with me. People will say it's unseemly for a young woman to live unsupervised with a single man."

"Oh Mama, that ship sailed a long time ago. People have been saying worse about me for months. It's better for the family if I stay here, away from all of you, until I can leave. I should be like Miss LouAnn and just disappear into the bayou, make a new life there... or somewhere else."

"Is it that young man, Elijah Tillman? Do you care about him that much? Enough to shut out your family like Louisa did?" She sounded shocked that I would consider such a step.

"No, it's not about him. All I'm saying is that I should go somewhere else. Far enough away from all of you that if something should happen, if someone uncovers my secret, maybe it won't affect the family as much as it would if I were here." She said nothing, but her breath sharpened, like the air was freezing.

"Actually Mama, I'm thinking about going to California to see Bobby in June. He rented a house in Sausalito for six months and wants me to go out there to see him. There'll be a housekeeper to chaperone, so you don't need to worry about how it looks. Everything will be very proper and above-board."

"Oh, I see. I hadn't realized you were already making plans. I hoped we could spend some time together as a family again." The disappointment in her voice reached through the line, tugging on my heart.

"I'm sorry Mama. You've all been so good to me, and I don't know how I can ever repay you."

"Darling, there's never a need for repayment between family. You're a part of us, and you have been since the day you arrived."

The following morning, Charlie called just as I was leaving for the restaurant.

"You go on ahead, Jolie, and get things started. I'll be there in a little while," I said, waving her out the back door.

"Hi Charlie. Thanks for calling. I hear you're going to be a daddy again soon."

"Yes, I am, and I'll be glad to have my girls home. Aunt Bea said you wanted to talk with me about something. What's on your mind, darlin'? Is everything going okay out there?"

"Everything is fine, and I know you're busy, but I have a question. You've been handling my bank account, so I was wondering how much money I have. I want to take a trip to California this summer and I'll need some money. Shelby has been paying me, but I'm not sure if what I've saved will be enough."

"Darlin' you've got plenty of money. The last time I looked, there was over three hundred thousand dollars in your account. Then there's a separate account with the hundred grand Charlotte Barone gave you. Let me know how much you need, and I'll get it for you."

"Over three hundred thousand?! I thought there might be a few hundred, maybe five, but not thousands. Where did all that money come from, Charlie?"

He hesitated before answering. "I assumed Bill would have told you by now, but it must have slipped his mind. He had me set up the trust account back in '45, the summer you came here, and he has been making regular deposits into it ever since. Then, about a year ago, large deposits began arriving every few months from an offshore account. Bill knows who they're from. There are also quarterly deposits from a leased property in France and the dividend earnings on the Marchand stock Bill gave you. You don't need to worry about money, darlin'. On your eighteenth birthday, you can do whatever you want with it... within reason. Your trustee, that would be me, approves all expenditures and investments until your twenty-first birthday. After that, it's all yours."

My breath caught in my throat. I didn't know what to think about that information. "Bill never told me, Charlie. Why wouldn't he tell me long before this?"

"You're forgetting how young you were back then, Désirée. He set up the trust for you as insurance in case something happened to him. Over the years, it's grown, and I suppose it's become a symbol of your independence... from him and from us. Bill always knew the day would come when you would decide to leave us, but it doesn't mean he has to like it. He's been waiting for you to decide what you're plans are."

"The only thing I've decided is to visit Bobby this summer."

"Maybe Bill hasn't said anything about this because he knows his long wait is nearly over, and he hasn't lost hope."

The news about the money certainly opened up a world of possibilities, but none where I end up happy.

"Alright, Charlie. I'll let you know how much I'll need for the trip to California. As for the money from Charlotte, I want to create a fund for women in need, women who can't afford legal or health services, who need family support, or job training. Can you help me start something like that? Is there enough to do that?"

"Well, a hundred thousand dollars is a hell of a start for a worthwhile, but very ambitious project. You're talking about something that takes months of planning and endless work to realize. Are you going to stick around to see it come to life?"

"I'm not sure yet. But I want Charlotte's money to do some good if possible."

"Alright, darlin'. I'll get one of my staff to do a little research; then we'll talk. I'll call you this weekend after the family gets home and settled."

"Thanks, Charlie. I'm late for work, so I've got to go. Give my love to everyone."

It felt like Bill was avoiding me. He was always gone before I got up in the morning and rarely home until I'd gone to bed, too exhausted from working long hours to stay up waiting for him. The only opportunity to talk with him was when he came into the restaurant with Luke for supper, and even then, it was difficult to get a moment alone with him until dinner service was over.

One night, when Luke got up to help Shelby close the restaurant, I sat down across from Bill in the chair Luke vacated. "You've been gone a lot lately," I said, trying to keep the hurt from my voice.

"Have you missed me?" he asked, giving me a look that held more questions than that one.

"It's just that... well, you've been out of town so much, I wondered if something had happened, something I should know about."

"I've been busy working, Désirée, tracking down Steigler. But you've been busy too, here and with Elijah."

I didn't want to talk about Elijah. "Have you discovered where Steigler is hiding? Did you get news from Mr. Reyes?" I was eager for any news that would end that chapter of my life.

"We have a few solid leads. I'll let you know when something comes up. Is that what you wanted to talk about, Chére?"

"Well, yes, and no. I want to know why..."

"Are you two going to be long?" Shelby asked, coming up to the table with her purse in hand. "It's dead in here tonight, and I'm ready to lock up. Jolie and Terrance have already gone home."

"No problem, Shelby. We'll get out of your hair," Bill said, rising from the table and taking my hand. "Let's go home, Chére. We can talk there."

"Thanks, Bill. Goodnight. I'll see you tomorrow, Désirée," Shelby said, holding the front door open for us.

Bill tucked my hand into his elbow as we walked back to the house, his body tense, as if on alert for any hidden danger. When we got in the house, he went straight to the bar cart to pour himself a drink.

"Will you join me for a nightcap?" he asked, holding up an empty glass in invitation.

"Sure."

He poured the drinks, then headed up the stairs. "Let's talk up on the terrace. The stars are out tonight." Funny how he knew the little things that pleased me.

The night was warm, with a steady breeze blowing from the south, and the moon was almost full, which made the stars fade behind its closer light. Gus came up the back stairs to investigate as I took a seat in one of the lounge chairs and kicked off my shoes. Bill and I both laughed when Gus stuck his nose into my shoes, then sneezed after getting a whiff of my stinky feet.

"Sorry, Gus. I've been working in those all day." Gus stepped away from my offensive footwear and laid his head on my lap for a consoling pet.

"What did you want to talk to me about, Chére?" Bill asked, handing me my drink. He sat in the chair next to me and lit us each a cigarette, handing one to me.

"I was wondering why you've been avoiding me. You're hardly ever here anymore." I hadn't planned on saying that, but it came out unexpectedly.

"It's not that I'm avoiding you, Désirée, it's just that we're both busy with work and there hasn't been much time to catch up." It sounded like a lame excuse to me and not completely honest.

"Is that all, Bill? It feels like there's more to it than that. Did Mama ask you to stay away?"

He looked away, unable to meet my eyes. "Mother is worried about how things look, and about your reputation. I think it's better for you if I limit our time together for now."

"My reputation is beyond repair already, and there's nothing you can do to change that. This is your home, Bill, and I don't want you to stay away because of me."

"I'm only thinking of you, Désirée, but... if you want me around more, I can certainly accommodate you. Was there anything else?"

"Yes, there is. Why didn't you tell me about the trust fund you set up for me? Why did I have to hear about it from Charlie?"

He hung his head as if embarrassed I'd caught him withholding information. "I'm sorry. I should have told you about it, but I never found the right moment. When I set up that account, I wanted to make sure you had something of your own in case something happened to me, and now you do. Keeping it from you wasn't intentional, Chére. I planned to tell you about it on your birthday."

"It's an awful lot of money, Bill. Charlie said someone is sending large deposits from an offshore account and that you know who it is."

He took a deep breath before answering, releasing it with a heavy sigh. "They're from Katarina Lang. She's been sending you the money to keep it out of Steigler's reach. Katarina said she wants you to have it because she has no one else to leave it to. She said Steigler never signed their divorce papers, and if something were to happen to her, he could gain access to her money. The deposits are her way of keeping that from happening. Her attorney makes the transfers every few months, per her instructions."

"Does the Kommandant know she's sending me the money?"

"I don't know. He could, I suppose, but there's nothing he can do about it."

"I'm not so sure about that, Bill. He's already sent me a note delivered to this very house. He knows where I am. What if he sends someone to get me?"

"I won't let that happen if I can prevent it. Don't worry, Chére. Even when I'm not here, someone is always watching over you."

"Do you really think you'll capture him, Bill?"

"I'll get him as soon as he crawls out of his hole."

"I wish you would do it soon. It feels like I have a target on my back. I can't go anywhere until this is over."

"Where do you want to go?"

"To California to visit Bobby for a while, but I won't go unless this trouble is finished. I don't want any of it spilling over onto him. He doesn't know about me."

"You never told him." It was an acknowledgement rather than a question.

"No. I tried to, but he didn't want to know. He said it doesn't matter to him. But it matters to me, and I won't go to him if Steigler is still out there looking for me. I shouldn't even be working for Shelby. If someone finds out about me, it could ruin her business."

"Shelby knows everything, Chére. Who you were and what happened to you doesn't matter to her, either."

That was new information and not as comforting as he seemed to think it should be. I hated being a liability, but I was, and there wasn't much I could do to change that. At least not yet.

"Find Anton Steigler, Bill. End this for me, please." I stood up and drained my glass. "I'm going to bed. Goodnight."

"I will. Goodnight, Chére."

Chapter 26

Crescent edge of madness

On the third of May at ten o'clock in the morning, Julianna Marchand gave birth to a baby girl weighing only six pounds, four ounces, but completely healthy, which was all that mattered.

"How are you feeling, Julianna?" I asked when I called from Shelby's small office at the restaurant before dinner service started.

"I'm doing fine, honey. A little sore and tired, but other than that, I'm over the moon that she is here at last. Did Charles tell you what we've named her?"

"No. What's her name?" I asked, expecting her to say Melissa or Angeline or something like that.

"Her name is... Marguerite Désirée Marchand. Isn't it lovely?"

My breath caught in my throat for a second. "Oh, Julianna, I'm honored. Of course, it's a beautiful name. I'm happy for you and Charlie. Madalyn and Henry must be so excited to meet their new baby sister. When do you go home from the hospital?"

"The doctor said we can go home on Sunday if Maggie and I are doing well. You're coming to see me, aren't you? Come on Mother's Day, sweetheart. That gives me more than a week to recover. I'll be up and about by then."

We'd spoken several times while she was in Boston, but I hadn't seen Julianna since the New Year, and dreaded the look of pity she would try to hide once we met again. I loved her, but she lived in a world I couldn't inhabit anymore. Julianna was an Uptown lady, and I wasn't.

"Sorry, Julianna, dinner service is starting. I need to go, but I'll call you again. Congratulations, and give the baby a kiss from her namesake."

After a busy Saturday night, Jolie and I stayed late to give the kitchen a good cleaning. Jolie liked her Sundays off, unlike Terrance, who came in after church services with his wife Glenna to clean the fryer and mop the entire restaurant. Either way was fine with me. I enjoyed being there, no matter what day it was.

"You sure you don't mind me leaving for a few days, Désirée? It'll be Thursday to Saturday. You think you'll be able to handle this on your own?" Jolie asked as we stood in front of the grill, scrubbing it down.

"She ain't gonna be on her own," Terrance said on his way out the back door, then he turned to share his final thought of the day. "I've been cooking in this kitchen longer than you two been alive, and I'm gonna be here to see she does alright. So, you go on ahead, Jolie. We'll be just fine. Night, y'all. See ya Tuesday."

"Goodnight, Terrance," I said, locking the back door after he'd gone. "He's right, Jolie. I'll be fine, and of course I don't mind. You haven't seen your family since January. Go, have a good time."

"Are you gonna go out to see the Marchands next Sunday? You got to go see Miss Bea and Miss Julianna on Mother's Day, at least."

"I don't know," I said, dismissing the idea as too difficult to consider. "I've got a late date with Elijah on Saturday night, so I might be too tired to drive out to see them on Sunday."

"Bill could drive you," Jolie suggested. "He said he was gonna be around while I was gone. I'm sure he'll want to see his mama on Mother's Day. You should go with him."

"What exactly are you trying to do, Jolie?" I bumped her shoulder with mine, trying to get her to change the subject. She knew I didn't want to go back to the city.

"Uh, nothing. It's just that you and Bill have been dancing around each other for months now, and I thought this would be a perfect opportunity for the two of you to learn how to dance in step for a change. What harm could it do? It's obvious he loves you, Désirée."

"When did you become an authority on love?"

"I got eyes, don't I? It ain't hard to see the sparks flying between you two. Why are you fighting so hard against it?"

"Because it's complicated." *And impossible.*

"That's what you always say when you don't want to give a straight answer." She returned the bump to my shoulder to get my undivided attention. "Love isn't that complicated, Désirée. Either you love him, or you don't. You should decide before it's too late."

"It was too late eight months ago. Let it go, Jolie." The memory of that night flashed through my mind, making me shudder and pull away from her. She didn't know about the brand Carson left on me. No one knew but Mama and Doctor Easton.

Jolie worked extra hard from Tuesday through Thursday morning, helping me prepare for the next three nights. Zach drove her home to New Orleans on Thursday afternoon.

That night, while I prepared meals for the residents of Mandeville, Bill consumed my thoughts. I imagined his face, his smile, his eyes, arms, hands, everything about him, and knew the next three nights were going to be difficult without Jolie to shield me from my baser instincts.

"It's obvious he loves you, Désirée." Jolie's voice reminded me.

He doesn't know what Carson did to me. How could he love me if he knew? How could any man? I can't even love myself.

"Order up," Terrance called out, dragging my attention back to the next task.

Saturday morning, I woke up in my usual state of anxiety and disgust after spending the night on the crescent edge of madness, falling into another landslide of guilt and shame. Neither a hot nor cold shower could wash away the feeling, the need for something I could never have.

Zach was standing by the stove, pouring me a cup as I entered the kitchen in search of my morning coffee. "Morning, Miss Désirée. Here you go," he said, placing the cup in my outstretched hand. "Didn't you sleep good? You're lookin' a bit tuckered out this morning. Mr. William said he'd be down after he dressed."

"Good morning, Zach. Morning, Gus." I scratched Gus's head as I sat down at the kitchen table with my coffee. "No, I didn't sleep well, but I'm fine. Bill said you were going to see your family today."

"Yes'm. My mother lives with my sister out in Houma. I'm going out to visit with them, but I'll be bringing Miss Jolie home on Sunday night, like we planned."

"Are you going to introduce Jolie to your family, Zach?" I knew the question might embarrass him, but I wanted to know.

"Well, Miss, I'd sure like to if I can get her to go, but she might be a bit too busy with her own family this time around. Can I get you some eggs and toast, Miss Désirée?"

"Just toast and jam. Thank you."

Zach put a plate of toasted bread in front of me and refreshed my cup, then went outside to feed Gus, who followed him out with his tail wagging eagerly.

As I sat there nursing my coffee, my mind replayed the nightmare until I couldn't stand it anymore. I hated myself for not being able to fight it off, to lock it away forever. The only thing that was going to save me from it was to distract myself with work... and the late date I would have with Elijah. I downed the coffee and went upstairs to dress.

When I went back down an hour later, I hoped Bill would be gone or in his office, but he was sitting at the kitchen table, dressed for the day and sipping on a cup of coffee, the morning paper spread out in front of him.

"Good morning, Chére. Are you going to work already? I thought you started at eleven," he said, glancing up with a surprised look in his eyes.

"I need to get an early start. Saturdays are always busy, and with Jolie gone, I..."

He interrupted my bumbling attempt at being casual. "What's that you've got there? Looks like you're taking some clothes with you. Are you going somewhere?" Suspicion and maybe a little fear crept into his voice and stayed behind his eyes.

"I'm going out with Elijah tonight. He's picking me up after work at nine-thirty. I thought changing there would save time." I shifted the garment bag containing my after-work clothes out of Bill's view.

"Oh. I didn't realize you had plans tonight. Where's he taking you?"

"I don't know. He says it's a surprise for my birthday. I'll be home by one." The last thing I wanted to do was stand there and discuss Elijah with Bill. I prayed he wouldn't want more details. I didn't have any.

"Hmm. I'll wait up for you, Chére... to make sure you're home safe. Are we still going out on Monday for your birthday? I've planned something special."

His face relaxed into a hopeful smile that was impossible to resist, but I knew I should. There'd always been a part of me that couldn't resist him, the part that held my memories of Bill and wanted more.

"Yes, of course, Bill. Sorry, but I've got to run. Lots to do today. I'll see you later." I rushed out the back door to avoid more talk of surprises, which were my least favorite things, but then Bill knew that about me, or at least I thought he did.

"Have a good time with your family, Zach. I'll see you tomorrow night," I said, hurrying past him down the driveway with the garment bag hanging over my shoulder.

"You look nervous, honey." Shelby said as she guarded the door while I changed my clothes in her office later that night. "Don't see why you should be. You've been out with Elijah half a dozen times."

I adjusted the fit of the navy button-down dress, trying to see myself in the small mirror she held up for me. "Yes, I guess I am. He didn't say where we're going, and I'm not fond of surprises."

"I wouldn't worry about it, honey. Elijah is a nice guy, one of the few still around. He'll take you somewhere special. He obviously likes you."

That was the last thing I wanted to hear, but it was true, and I needed to do something about it.

"Does this dress look alright, Shelby? I hate not knowing what to wear." My stomach was doing flip-flops.

"You look beautiful, Désirée. Are you ready? I think I heard him come in. Pinch those cheeks, honey, it's showtime," she said, opening the door for me after I took a deep breath and nodded.

"Well, lookie here. Ain't you a picture? You clean up nice Miss Désirée," Terrance said, leering at me as I stepped into the kitchen.

"Thank you, Mr. Terrance." I said, trying to conceal my blushing face with my hand. He rarely handed out compliments, and his attention embarrassed me.

"You look swell, Désirée, really pretty, but you always are," Elijah said, taking my hand. "Are you ready to go?"

"Have fun, you two," Shelby said as we headed out the back door.

Elijah squeezed my hand as we walked to his truck. "I wasn't just saying that back there. I meant it. You're the prettiest girl I know."

"Stop it, Elijah. I don't need compliments. Are you going to tell me where we're going?" I asked, trying to shift his focus off me. He didn't reply until we got in the truck.

"I wanted to do something special to celebrate your birthday, but all the fancy restaurants are already closed or will be by the time we get there, so I had to get creative."

"What, exactly, does that mean, Mr. Tillman?"

He started the truck and headed south, toward home. "Well, I usually spend Saturday nights with my friends, just sitting by the bayou talking, eating whatever we throw together, doing a little drinking, and having a good time. I thought we could do that, give you a little taste of bayou life. I don't have much else to give you for your birthday."

"It sounds wonderful, Elijah, and you don't need to give me anything. Your friendship is gift enough."

My comment had the intended effect. As we drove down the highway, he pulled away from me, but just slightly, taking his time to reassess his position, but I could see he wasn't giving up. Friendship wasn't his goal.

"Dorien and his girlfriend, Loraine, will be there with Sable and her fiancé, Peter. Gran wants to see you, too," he said as we turned down the road to his house, the sound of hope springing back into his voice.

"Good evening, Désirée," Miss LouAnn said, greeting us at her back door. "Please come in and talk for a minute, won't you? Elijah, your friends are out by the dock. I'll send Désirée down after we're done talking. Go on now and see to your friends."

His look seemed to ask if I was okay with that arrangement.

"I'll join you in a moment, Elijah."

When he was gone, Miss LouAnn took my hand and led me deeper into her home. "Let's talk in the parlor, where it's more comfortable. Can I offer you something to drink?" she asked, ever the southern lady despite her years on the bayou.

"A shot of whiskey would do well right now, but I'll take whatever is available." I needed something stronger than tea to help calm my nerves and strengthen my resolve to get me through the evening. It didn't hurt to ask.

She gave me an evaluating look, both her eyebrows raised above piercing green eyes, then she pulled a half-filled bottle of whiskey down from the shelf and poured two glasses, handing me one.

With a huff, she sat back and sniffed the rim of her glass. "This reminds me of when René and I would sit in here late at night, sharing a glass of whiskey, talking things through till we figured them out. Cheers, Désirée." We touched our glasses, then each took a drink, sitting back to assess one another.

"Elijah said you wanted to see me. Is there something on your mind, Miss LouAnn?" I figured there was no sense in making small talk. It wasn't my style and Elijah was waiting.

"Yes. It's my grandson," she said, watching me carefully as she lit her pipe. "He's in love with you and I'm afraid for him."

Clearly, she wasn't one to mince words. Her directness didn't surprise or offend me, but I wondered what she really knew about me.

"You needn't be, madame. I'm going away soon and planned to tell him tonight. Not very good timing, I know, but I like Elijah, and I don't want him to think this is more than friendship." I took a sip of whiskey, letting the liquid burn its way slowly down my throat, then I waited for her reaction, but she was better at the game of waiting than I was.

"However, I must confess I entertained the idea of living out here like you, abandoning my past life. Fortunately for all of us, I realized it could never work for me the way it has for you. We are not the same, madame."

"No, dear, we're not. *Your* path, Désirée, is one my grandson should not follow. He's not equipped for what he would encounter. It's best if you both understand this before it's too late."

"Yes, madame, *je comprends*, and I regret complicating your life... but I will never regret meeting you." I stood up to leave. "I should join Elijah and his friends. Thank you for the drink. *Bonne nuit*, madame."

I finished the whiskey, placed the empty glass on the table, and left her sitting in the parlor, her wise old woman's face lit by a single lamp.

The sound of music and laughter filtered up from the dock, mixing with the night sounds of nature; insects, owls, and small creatures bravely foraging under the cover of darkness. This place was a world apart from the way I'd lived for the past ten years, but it still felt familiar. A simple life to aspire to... but not with Elijah.

As I headed towards the laughter, I vowed to make the most of this moment, no matter how brief. I didn't normally socialize for a variety of reasons, but needed to know if I could let myself relax in an intimate group setting. The whiskey helped calm my nerves as I joined Elijah and his friends on the dock.

Elijah stood up when he saw me coming. "Here you are. I was getting worried Gran was gonna keep you talking all night. Do you remember Dorian and Sable Honoré? And this is Lorraine Hall, Dorian's girl, and Pete Sander, Sable's fiancé. It's alright if I say that, right Sable? They just got engaged," he said, slipping his arm around my waist and leading me to the vacant chair next to his.

"Happy eighteenth birthday, Désirée," Sable said, lifting her beer toward me.

"Yeah. Happy birthday, Désirée," the rest chimed in.

"It's not until Monday," I protested, feeling embarrassed by their attention.

"Close enough, darlin'. Elijah, get this woman a beer," Pete said, toasting me with his.

During the next couple of hours, I let myself be the girl I really was: young, healthy, and eager to enjoy myself with people my age, or at least close to it. After the first beer, my hair came down, literally. For most of the evening, the men talked about fishing, while Sable and Lorraine were more interested in asking me about my job at the Lakeside: how I got the job, where the recipes came from, what it was like cooking in a popular restaurant.

By the time they left after midnight, I was completely relaxed, even though I knew I still had a difficult task ahead of me. The whiskey and two beers had something to do with my physical and mental state, but relaxed didn't mean drunk. That condition would require a lot more alcohol.

"Will you take a ride with me?" Elijah asked as I stood at the end of the dock, looking up at the stars.

"Where to, Mr. Tillman?"

"Out there, on the lake under the stars."

It probably wasn't a good idea to go on a starlight cruise with him, but I didn't want the night to end, or the feeling of being a normal girl for a change.

"Alright, let's go, Elijah. I'm already going to be late getting home. An extra hour won't make much difference." I climbed aboard his boat, my heart beating furiously and stomach giving me warning signs I chose to ignore.

Elijah pulled *La Belle* away from the dock and headed toward the mouth of the bayou, then out on to the open water of Lake Pontchartrain until he found the spot to drop anchor. A wide expanse of open sky lay above us, filled with thousands of stars and the waning crescent moon. It was a perfect night for stargazing. Bobby would have loved it.

"Did you have a good time tonight? I know it wasn't what you're used to, but did you have fun?" He was trying to act casual but kept nervously pushing his hair off his forehead with his hands, then stuffing them into his trouser pockets only to pull them out and repeat the gesture.

"It was great, Elijah, and this is wonderful," I said, sweeping my hand across the sky. "Thank you for doing all this. Tonight was a birthday gift I'll always remember."

He stepped close to me, took my hands, and pulled me closer. "That makes me happy, Désirée, cuz I want to tell you something. I mean, ask you something."

I slipped my hands away, instinctively knowing what he was going to say. "Elijah, I must tell you..."

"No! Please wait, Désirée. Let me talk first, cuz if I hear what I think you're gonna say, I won't have the courage to tell you, and I'll always regret not giving myself a chance."

I had to give him that, at least. "Alright, Elijah, you go first."

"It's just... well, you know, at least I think you know, how much you mean to me. You're all I can think about. I know I'm not the type of guy you're used to being with, but we have a good time together, so I thought... Ah, hell. I love you, Désirée, and I think we could be happy together even though I don't make a lot of money, but I'm a hard worker and loyal. You'd have everything I could give you."

Moment of truth, Désirée. Tell him.

"Despite what you think, Elijah, I've never had a real boyfriend, so there's no need to compare yourself to anyone. You're a great guy, and some girl is going to be very lucky to have you, but that girl isn't me. You think you know me, but you don't. I'm broken, Elijah, too broken to fix, and even if you tried, I'd end up disappointing you."

"You could never do that, Désirée." He took me into his arms as if trying to convince me of his love.

"I'm disappointing you right now," I said, pushing away from him. "I'll be leaving in June, and I don't know when or if I'm coming back."

"But why leave? You've got a job here that you love, you live in a nice place, and you have people who care about you. Why run away from all that?" He didn't want to give up.

"It's complicated, and I can't explain why. I'm sorry this didn't turn out the way you hoped. I really am. You should probably take me home now. It's getting late."

"Yeah, I guess we should go." The defeat in his voice was palpable, his body rigid as he pulled up the anchor and started the engine.

Our ride back to Mandeville was quiet, with barely a word passing between us the entire way. During the long miles of silence, my mind filled with shame and regret for hurting him. It wasn't intentional. I could easily love him if I were a different person, if my past didn't always get in the way.

When Elijah pulled the truck up in front of the house, he shut off the engine, got out, and came around to open my door, taking my hand to help me out, but he didn't let go. "I just have to say this last thing. Nothing that happened to you before we met makes any difference to me. The girl I met at Stella's five months ago is the girl I fell in love with. That was day one for me. Nothing before matters."

"It matters to me, Elijah. I'm sorry, but I can't do this. It's late, I have to go in." My self-control was rapidly slipping away. If I didn't get inside the house soon, it felt like I'd throw myself into his arms and beg to stay there forever.

"If you need time to... heal, then I'll wait for as long as it takes. I can't just give up, Désirée."

"No, please, Elijah, don't wait for me. Goodnight."

Chapter 27

How to end a nightmare

Once I got inside, Gus began barking at Elijah, warning him to leave. I leaned against the door in the empty living room, my body shaking with stifled emotions, riddled with guilt for hurting him and feeling undeserving of his love or anyone's. Useless tears fell down my cheeks, making me feel even more pathetic.

"*Merde.*" I wiped the tears away with my fingers and headed to the bar cart, intending to test my earlier theory about drunkenness.

"Désirée? What's wrong, Chére?" Bill asked from the hall outside his office. He came closer cautiously, unsure of my response. His instincts were good.

I turned my back to him, intent on filling the tumbler with whiskey without spilling it.

"Tell me what's wrong, baby. Did something happen tonight? Talk to me, Désirée." He turned me around to face him. Fortunately for him, I didn't spill a drop. Had that occurred, I might have gotten angry.

I looked up into his tormented face and shook my head, unable to confess my feelings to him. "I'm what's wrong, Bill, and no one can fix me. But maybe this will make it easier to bear." I held up the glass.

"Please, Chére. I'll do anything. Tell me what you need."

"I need to be alone with my misery, and this glass of whiskey. Goodnight, Bill." He didn't stop me as I headed upstairs, he just stood there in the wretchedness I inflicted on him.

By three o'clock in the morning, my glass was empty, and the ashtray was half full of cigarette butts and the butt from a cigarette I made with Miss LouAnn's cannabis flower buds, which helped, but not enough. I was officially drunk, but sleep was out of the question.

My mind wouldn't stop racing. Memories kept swirling through my head, feelings of bitter loss followed by tormenting moments I wanted desperately to forget, but they wouldn't relinquish their hold on me. I was afraid to lie down and close my eyes, afraid of seeing Carson's face looming over me, feeling his hands on me, hurting me again.

"*Peut-être qu'un autre whisky aidera*," I said, wrapping myself in my robe and stumbling to the door in search of another glass of whiskey to aid my quest for sleep.

As I stood at the top of the stairs looking down into the darkened house, I heard no sounds except the soft snores coming from Bill's room. Instinctually, I went towards them.

"*Peut-être autre chose.*" I thought maybe something else might help, so I reached for the doorknob and quietly slipped inside his room.

"*Tu as dit que tu ferais n'importe quoi pour moi*," I whispered to the sleeping form laying on the bed. He said he'd do anything for me, but this was a big ask and I couldn't help feeling frightened as I approached his bed.

I let my robe fall to the floor and climbed in next to him with only my night slip between us. The intrusion immediately pulled him from sleep.

"Désirée? What are you doing here?" He sat up onto his elbow, staring at me as if I were an apparition.

"*J'ai besoin que tu me fasses l'amour.* Make love to me, Bill." I buried my face in my hands at the brazenness of my request, but knew he was the only man I could ever ask. If he refused me, it felt like I would spend the rest of my life pining for that kind of love and never getting it. If I could have just one night, one memory to cling to, maybe I could live with that. Maybe it would be enough to erase the nightmares.

"Oh, baby. Have you any idea what you're asking?" He stroked my head and held my cheek in his hand.

"*Oui. Je sais, mais j'ai besoin de votre aide.* I need your help, Bill. You're the only one who can help me. Please. Please make him go away, make him stop haunting me. I don't want this memory. I never wanted it. Please, Bill, please erase it, give me something better to remember. I can't live with this anymore." I was lying next to him but not touching him. As I made my plea, my entire body shook uncontrollably, and I struggled to cover my quivering mouth with my hands.

What are you doing, Désirée? You shouldn't have come.

"Oh, my love, my sweet Désirée. Come here, baby, let me hold you." He pulled me into his arms, and I went willingly, grateful for his comfort.

"*Je suis désolé.* I'm sorry, Bill. I couldn't stop him. I didn't stop him. He hurt me, and I let him. Now, he won't leave me alone. Please forgive me... help me. Make it stop, Bill, please." My tears soaked his nightshirt as he held me close, merging my trembling body with his.

"I'm sorry too, my love," he said, his voice cracking with emotion, his tears falling on my upturned face and mixing with mine as he bent to kiss me tenderly. "*Je suis là, Désirée. Je t'aime.*"

I cried myself to sleep in his arms, his words of love softly whispered in my ear.

As the sun was coming up, I felt him slip out of bed and watched him go into the bathroom. Embarrassed by my drunken state the night before, I left his bed and scurried back to my room before he returned.

He hadn't done what I asked, and I felt rejected and ashamed of my brazenness. I wondered how I would feel if he had done it. I needed a shower.

Unfortunately, it didn't help.

An hour later, I was sitting at the kitchen table nursing a cup of coffee and smoking, blowing smoke out the open window with frustrated breaths.

"Can we talk about last night, Chére?" Bill asked, taking the seat across the table after pouring himself a cup of coffee.

"I'm sorry about that, about drinking too much and bothering you."

"Don't be sorry, baby. I'm not."

"But... you didn't..."

"No, Chére. Sex wasn't what we needed last night. We needed to reconnect and find forgiveness, and we both needed a good night's sleep, which I think we got. Did you have any more nightmares?"

"Well, no. but... you didn't do what I asked."

"Baby, it's not because I didn't want you. I have ached to hold you, touch you for months, but..."

"But what, Bill?"

His eyes held mine with a look of tender sincerity. "When you came to me last night, I thought all my hopes and dreams were finally coming true. I thought you were choosing me, but then I realized you only wanted one night. That's all you were asking for, and I want so much more than that. I couldn't take one stolen night's pleasure when what I want is a lifetime with you. Baby, it's all or nothing for me. Marry me, Désirée. Be my wife, my partner, my lover. Stay with me forever."

"But I'm not the right girl for you, Bill. I'm not the wife you need. It's impossible now."

"Nothing is impossible, Chére, and I think I'm a better judge of the kind of wife I need. I want you, baby. The question is, do you want me? You don't need to answer right now. Take some time to think about it. Come with me today to see Mama. She misses you."

If it hadn't been Mother's Day, I might have refused, but I missed Mama, too. It was going to take a lot of thinking to make an informed decision about Bill's proposal, and perhaps Mama could give me some perspective.

"Alright, Bill. I'll go see her, but only for a few hours. Bobby is calling at nine, so I want to be home by then."

"I promise, Chére, I'll bring you home whenever you want."

It was noon when we crossed the bridge into the city, and my nerves took over as soon as we started down St. Charles Avenue. I hadn't been back to Marchand House in months and dreaded walking into it again, feared all the feelings that being there would dredge up.

"Everything will be fine, Chére. I'll be with you the whole time," Bill said, pulling the car into the driveway.

I almost turned around and ran as we walked up to the front door. The thought of entering that house sent chills down my spine. The last thing I wanted to do was revisit those memories.

Mr. Jefferies greeted us at the front door. "Hello, Mr. William. Miss Dezrae, it's good to have you home again."

As I walked in, it felt like I was walking through the pages of a magazine. Everything had changed, completely transformed into a modern version of affluent design. New furniture and accessories filled every room, fresh paint on every wall, new rugs on every floor, old trinkets replaced by new designer choices. It felt like a completely different house.

"Hello, darling," Mama said, wrapping her arms around me to welcome me home.

"Oh, Mama. You didn't do all this because of me, did you?" I asked, sweeping my hand around to encompass the changes to her home.

"Well, darling, the old place needed updating. Do you like it? Julianna sent me her favorite decorator to help put it all together."

"But your things, Mama. All your memories." A bitter sense of responsibility washed over me; I had taken something precious and irreplaceable from her.

"I still have everything that's important to me, darling. You, my son, my memories. Come in and see the family. Julianna and Charles are here with the children. You need to meet our newest addition."

Bill kissed his mother and led me into the redecorated living room, where we found Julianna seated on the sofa with a tiny bundle in her arms.

"Hello, Julianna. Happy Mother's Day," I said, leaning down to give her a kiss on the cheek. "Hello, Charlie, Uncle Henri."

"Désirée, we're so happy to see you," Julianna said, patting the place next to her on the sofa. "Come and meet your namesake. Maggie, this is your cousin, Désirée," she said to the sleeping bundle, placing it in my a rms.

I adjusted my seat, holding the tiny infant lightly so not to disturb her. " *Bonjour ma petite. Je suis Désirée.*" She squirmed and opened her eyes, looking up at me with the most engaging stare. My heart sank to new depths, knowing that I'd never have this joy, never have a baby of my own.

I kissed Maggie's tiny forehead and passed her back to her mother. When I looked up into Bill's eyes, my heart sank even further.

"She's beautiful, Julianna. Thank you. Where are the twins?"

"They're outside playing in the gazebo," Charlie said, giving me a warm embrace. "They'll be excited to see you. We're all happy to have you home, darlin'."

"Thanks. I'll go find them to say hello. Please, excuse me for a moment."

This meeting was far more than I expected, more than I was prepared to deal with. I hurried away from them, stifling the tears that threatened to fall. I didn't deserve their love after everything I'd put them through.

The garden, it was flourishing, almost as if I'd never been gone. The herb garden was well tended, and the wisteria was beginning to bloom. I had missed my garden so much, missed the feeling of permanence it gave. The planters Bobby and Bill built for me at the lake house felt more temporary than the two large beds they created for me at Mama's during the first summer I came to America.

"Look, Henry. She's here," Madalyn said, jumping up to greet me.

"I told you she'd come. Bill promised he'd bring her today." Henry said, cuffing his sister lightly on her shoulder as I came up to join them in the gazebo.

"Hello, Madalyn. Hello Henry. I'm happy to see you both. Congratulations on your new baby sister. She's beautiful." I gave them each a hug.

"She is, isn't she? Mama says she's a miracle," Maddie said, sitting down on the bench next to me. "We're so happy to see you, Désirée. I was afraid you wouldn't come because of everything that happened."

"I'm sorry, Maddie. The past few months must have been hard on the two of you."

"We're alright, Désirée. I didn't let anyone say anything bad about you in front of me," Henry said, puffing up his chest.

"Henry got in trouble at school a few times while me and Mama were away. He was fighting with some mean boys who said bad things about you."

"Oh Henry. You didn't need to do that." I felt terrible that I had put him in that position.

"Course I did. You're my family, and I wasn't gonna let anyone call you names."

"Thank you, Henry."

"Are you gonna marry Bill? I heard Mama and Papa talking about it," he asked with a hopeful look.

"Henry! Mama said we weren't supposed to talk about that." Maddie gave her brother a glaring stare.

"I don't know yet, Henry." My feelings about it were still unclear.

"Well, I sure wish you would. Mama said maybe I could carry the ring down the aisle and Maddie could carry the flowers for you... maybe."

I gazed into their hopeful faces, wondering how much all the scandal I'd caused had cost them. "What do you two think I should do? Should I marry Bill?"

"Yes!" they both said in unison.

"It would be perfectly wonderful if you did, Désirée," Maddie said, throwing her arms around me to make sure I believed her.

A moment later, Jolie came strolling out to the garden, giving me a sheepish glance. "Maddie, Henry, your mama is asking for you two," she said as she walked up to the gazebo. "You'd best go see what she wants."

When they'd gone into the house, I gave Jolie a hard stare. "Were you in on this secret, Jolie?"

"Yes," she confessed. "They've been trying to get you to come out here, and Gran asked me to help, so..."

"So, you decided I needed to be surprised. Thanks a lot, friend."

"This family cares about you, Désirée. They just wanted to do something nice for you, for your birthday, and I figured I could help."

"I'm not mad, Jolie, just overwhelmed, that's all. Did you see your father?"

"No. I tried talking to him on the phone, but he wasn't interested in mending fences. It's alright. Don't worry about it. So, what happened last night with Elijah?"

"I had a nice time, but his grandmother doesn't want me to see him again, so I told him I wasn't the girl for him. It didn't go well. We might have to find another fish vendor."

"That ain't gonna be a problem. Do you think you'll marry Bill? Has he asked you yet?" she asked, giving me a look that demanded a straight answer.

"Yes, this morning, but I'm not sure how I feel about it. It's so sudden and not at all what I planned."

"It ain't that sudden, Désirée. Bill has been waiting for you. If a man loved me the way he loves you, I wouldn't hesitate to jump the broom. True love doesn't come around all that often."

"Gee, thanks for the advice, pal. What would I do without you?" I asked just as Bill came looking for me.

"Flounder," she replied, bumping my shoulder. She stood up as Bill entered the gazebo.

"Laila said she needs your help, Jolie."

"Alright then, duty calls. We'll talk later, Désirée."

After she walked away, I looked up at him and sighed, "*You* planned this family surprise, didn't you, Bill?" I asked, as he sat down next to me and took my hand.

"Yes, I planned it. I wanted you to see how much the family all loves you and misses being with you. Are you disappointed?"

"No, how could I be, but did you have to enlist the twins in your marriage scheme? Now they're eager to be a part of a wedding."

"Ah, Chére, I needed all the help I could get convincing you. Did it work?" His fingers gently stroked my cheek, sending tingles through me from head to toe.

"Maybe, a little. You could have warned me, though."

"I was afraid you wouldn't come, and Mama really wanted to see you today. Are you okay, Chére?" His attention to my comfort felt good, felt right, like this was the way love should always feel.

"I'm fine, Bill. Just surprised, that's all."

"I hope it was a pleasant surprise, baby. Let's go in. Laila has made us lunch."

As we walked across the lawn, I glanced up to the gallery where I'd spent countless hours sitting outside my bedroom talking to Bobby, planning my future. It was my favorite place to be in the house.

"Is the upstairs the same or did Mama change that too?"

"It's all different except the guest bedroom and Mama's room. Do you want to go up and see it?"

"I think I should, just to reassure myself and maybe purge a few ghosts."

We went up the stairs from the garden, then through the gallery door into my old bedroom, which now looked like it belonged to someone else. Everything was different: new wallpaper and rugs, the furniture sleek and modern. Mama even had the bathroom updated. Nothing remained of my old life in that room, and oddly enough, I felt a twinge of sadness and loss as I looked around.

Bill's room, where Carson forged my worst nightmares, was the hardest to enter, but it, too, had undergone a transformation. The heavy mahogany four-poster bed was gone, replaced by a sleek platform bed with an upholstered headboard, the thick mattress was covered in a beige chenille bedspread topped with fluffy satin pillows. All that remained of his childhood room were a few select items: books, some trophies, a few photos, and the chessboard, all strategically placed in their new environment. A piece of framed modern art replaced the clipper ship painting that covered the wall safe.

"What did she do with all the old furniture?"

"Donated it. She kept a few pieces that were important to her, like Pop's chair, the old clock that was her grandfather's, and a few bookshelves, but the rest went to charity. Mama said she wanted a fresh start for all of us, free from the bad memories. We should go down to the family, Chére. They're going to wonder what we're doing up here."

I headed for the door then turned to look at him. "We're not doing anything, Bill... because you won't."

He reached for my hand. "I will if you marry me, baby. Will you?"

"I'm not sure yet. I need to talk to Mama before I decide."

"Well then, let's go see her and get this settled."

Lunch was a family affair, all of us seated around the new teak dining table, with both extension leaves pulled out to accommodate everyone. The conversation was light, focused on the twins and their antics and on me and my cooking adventures at the Lakeside Bar & Grill.

"I hear you're doing good out there helping Mr. Philgood at his restaurant," Uncle Henri said after the birthday cake was served. "So, I'm going to eat my words about women cooking in those places. Daniel tells me if it weren't for you and Jolie Jefferies coming to help out, his place might have gone to ruin after his stroke. You did a good thing, girl. Thank you. But... I wish you'd come around here occasionally. I haven't had a decent croissant since Christmas."

"I promise to make some for you, Uncle."

"See that you do, and for the record, since no one else here wants to offer their opinion, I think Bill Marchand is a good man and he'd make you a decent husband. Just food for thought, Désirée." The looks I was getting from everyone at the table seemed to confirm his sentiments.

"Yes, Uncle, he is a good man and I'm thinking about it."

"Well, get a move on and decide, girl. I ain't getting any younger."

"I believe it's time for us to leave, Father Henri. The children are getting restless, and I need to get Maggie home," Julianna said, curbing any further discussion of future nuptials.

During the lengthy farewells filled with hugs and kisses and lots of I'll see you soon's, I realized Bill accomplished his goal of showing me how much his family really cared about me. They were secure in who they were and untroubled by outside rumors and gossip. My problems didn't amount to a hill of beans, as Uncle Henri would say. But there was a lot more to consider than their approval.

Chapter 28

Mama and Decisions

"Now that the house is quiet, darling, perhaps we can sit and talk," Mama said after Charles and Julianna left with the children and Uncle Henri.

"I should help Jolie clean up first," I said, stacking the dirty plates on the dining table and suddenly nervous to speak with her.

"You go on and talk with Miss Bea, Désirée. Me and Gran got this," Jolie said, shooing me away from the table.

"Let's go up onto the gallery, darling. It's cooler up there this time of day. Beau, will you excuse us?"

"Certainly, Mama. I'll be here... waiting." Bill gave me a look that held one big question, which I had no answer to... yet.

I followed her up the stairs, admiring the bold, modern décor she'd chosen. It was a complete departure from the mix of traditional and art déco styles I'd grown accustomed to, but when we entered her room, I felt transported back to all the times I'd spent in there, talking, reading, sleeping in her arms after a nightmare. Everything was the same, plus a few additions. It felt like home and completely safe.

"Let's sit outside, sweetheart," she said, going out the gallery door.

We sat in the old wicker chairs outside her bedroom, gazing down into the yard, letting the peacefulness of the setting envelop us. I was grateful that part of the house hadn't changed.

"Beau told me he asked you to marry him," she began, taking my hand in hers. "I can't remember ever seeing my son so nervous or determined. But I'm concerned about you, darling. These past months haven't been easy for you, though you've managed them gracefully. I believe working at Shelby's restaurant has helped you gain back some of what you lost. At least, I hope it has."

"It has, Mama. Cooking for Shelby has been good for me. It's given me something to focus on other than my problems. But..."

"What is it, darling? What's troubling you? We've weathered the whole Phantom business. That's over and done with. Why do you want to leave now?"

"Because it's too hard being here, Mama, being with Bill when I know how he feels. I can never be the type of wife that Julianna is, or you. I have too many problems that won't ever go away. There's too much that still could hurt him, and you."

"Don't you think Beau is aware of these things, darling?"

"Probably, but he's letting his feelings blind his better judgement. He should be with someone like Julianna or Alina Reyes."

"Beau has had many opportunities to choose a mate over the past five years, Désirée, and has entertained a few candidates, but all of them were merely placeholders for you. You're the one he has been waiting for, darling. You're the woman he wants. The question is, do you want him?"

"What do *you* want, Mama?"

"What I've always wanted, Beau's happiness with someone he loves and can finally settle down with. And I'd like a grandchild or two, in time. But your happiness is equally important to me."

"I can't give him what you want, Mama. I can never have children. Doctor Easton told me I scarred my womb after the first time that Carson... Bill doesn't know."

The memory seared through my brain like the boiling wine vinegar had seared my womb. A desperate act I could never take back.

"I'm sorry that happened, but if I know my son, this will not matter to him. You must tell him, Désirée. Let Beau decide if this is an insurmountable hurdle. But you haven't answered my earlier question. Do you want him?"

"I've always loved him, Mama, even when I shouldn't have. Bill is a part of me, but I'm afraid of hurting him, and of losing him. I just think it would be better for everyone if I left now and never came back."

"Darling, running away doesn't solve this, but trusting in love might."

"Do you think I should marry him?"

"That decision is yours alone to make, Désirée, but I will love you, whatever you decide."

After talking with Mama, I was still undecided and knew I needed to have a serious talk with Bill, needed to tell him some things, explain why staying here, marrying him is impossible. But that conversation had to wait because when I went downstairs to find him, he was deep in conversation with Zach, sitting with their heads together in the room that used to be Mama's office but was now a cozy reading room. When they saw me walk in, their heads popped up with wide-eyed innocence, both looking like little boys caught scheming something.

"How'd it go with Mama?" Bill asked, trying to cover up his discomfort by turning the focus on me.

"She wants to speak with you. Laila is bringing her some tea. Hello Zach. How was your time with your family?"

"I better go see what she wants," Bill said, popping out of his seat and hurrying upstairs.

"It was good seeing them, Miss Désirée. Thank you for asking. Did you have a nice time at the party? Jolie seems to have her doubts."

I wondered what Jolie said to him. "No… I mean, yes, I had a pleasant time. Like you, it was good to see them all again, but it was also difficult. Are you here to take Jolie home?" Bill wasn't the only one who knew how to change the subject.

"Yes, miss. That was the plan, but Mr. Jefferies asked if I would go with Jolie and them to see her father. I'm not sure what I'm getting myself into, but Jolie said she wouldn't go unless I went with her. So, I guess we're gonna be a little late getting back tonight."

"Maybe you can help Jolie mend a few fences with her father."

"I hope so, Miss Désirée."

Jolie and I went outside to sit on the back steps to talk and share a cigarette while Bill was upstairs talking with Mama.

"Why did you insist Zach go with you to see your father? Won't that be awkward?" I passed the cigarette to her.

She took a drag, then passed it back. "Probably, but I figured Pa would let me in the door if I brought Zach with me. Zach Johnson is exactly the type of man Pa admires: a decorated veteran, an educated black man who is more than the white man's tool."

"I hope it works out the way you planned. All my plans have flown out the window." I flicked the ash into the flowerpot next to the steps, took a drag and passed her the cigarette.

She stared at me for a moment with a worried look. "Have you decided what you're going to do?"

"Not yet. Bill and I have a lot of talking to do before I can decide."

"Seems to me you're just wasting time, Désirée, when you could have what you want and enjoy it right now."

"Seems to me you're awfully sure that he's what I want."

"As sure as I am that you're white and I'm black."

"Mr. William, you be sure to lock the doors if you leave before we get back," Miss Laila said as she stood at the back door, her hat perched on her head and purse clutched in her hand. "Miss Bea's gonna wanna lay down right after you leave, and she don't hear nothin' whiles she's sleepin."

"We'll lock up, Laila. Don't worry," Bill said, leaning against the kitchen counter. "Y'all go have a good time. Give my best to Marcus. I'll see you later at the house, Zach."

Before leaving for home, Bill and I joined Mama in the living room for a few moments.

"I wanted to tell you both that I've decided to retire at the end of this school year. I will continue to tutor and mentor students, but I want more time to enjoy my family," Mama said, sitting back and trying to get comfortable on the new sofa.

"That's wonderful, Mama. We'll get to spend more time together now," Bill replied.

Mama looked tired, like the day had sapped her reserve of energy. No one had mentioned anything about her illness all afternoon, so I suspected she was still keeping it a secret. Laila and Jacob knew, of course, but Bill didn't.

"We should probably go, Mama, and let you get some rest. Bill and I have a lot of talking to do tonight."

"Alright, darling," she said. "You let me know what you decide. We'll talk tomorrow. Thank you both for giving me a wonderful Mother's Day."

We kissed goodbye and Bill walked her up to her room, then we left after making sure all the doors were locked.

"Did you have a good time? You seem quiet, Chére. Are you alright?" he asked as we exited the city and headed across the bridge.

I was about as far from alright as I could be. My heart felt torn between loving him and feeling like I would be the instrument of his destruction. I didn't know what to do. All I could say was, "Let's talk about it when we get home."

When we got there, I immediately kept myself busy: feeding Gus, opening the windows to freshen the house, anything to avoid the inevitable moment I would have to tell him what Carson did, what I let him do. Eventually, there wasn't anything left to do but tell him. But I needed a drink to do it.

"Can I get you anything?" I stood at the bar pouring myself a healthy shot of whiskey.

"Whatever you're having," he replied from the sofa in the living room, music playing softly in the background.

When I brought him his drink, I wasn't sure where to sit. I chose the opposite end of the sofa. It seemed the safer choice.

He could see I was nervous and shifted his posture to appear more open and welcoming. "What's on your mind, Chére?"

I took a healthy swig of the whiskey, sat back amongst the cushions with a deep sigh, then told him what he needed to know.

"Before anything else, I must tell you I can't have children. I can never give you what Charlie has."

The news surprised him, and it broke my heart. "How do you know? You can't be certain of that."

I had to tell him everything, even though it was the last thing I wanted to do.

"Uh... I know because after the first time Carson raped me, I did something that damaged me permanently. I burned him from my womb with boiling vinegar and wine. Doctor Easton said I won't ever be able to carry a child."

"Oh baby, I'm so sorry." He reached for me, but I pulled away from his comfort.

He nodded, wanting to be supportive, but also needing to be honest he said, "I confess, I've dreamed of being a father someday, but baby, I've dreamed of you more. It doesn't matter, Chére. You are all that matters."

"There's more, Bill." My hand shook so much I had to put the glass down on the table, else risk spilling it down the front of my dress.

"I told you last night that Carson hurt me, but you didn't see what he did. He... branded me Bill, left a mark on me for you to find... so it would always remind you that... oh god, I'm so sorry. I couldn't stop him."

"Désirée, my love." He moved closer, reaching for me, but I pulled farther away. "Nothing that happened before makes a damn bit of difference to me. I saw what Carson did to Evelyn, saw the mark he left on her, and I knew he had probably done the same to you."

"But... every time we... seeing it will always remind you of what he did. We won't be able to forget. It will always be there." Tears fell down my cheeks like a waterfall. I couldn't stop them.

"Désirée, nothing can come between us. I love you, all of you, and that will never change."

"But... but what about Anton Steigler, and the French warrant for my arrest, and my illegal immigration?" I asked, trying to dry my tears with my hankie, trying to be sensible. "Someone else could find out and turn me in. It would ruin you, Bill, destroy the family's reputation. I can't let that happen. It would be better for all of you if I just disappeared."

"Those are all solvable problems, my love, as long as we're together. The only valid reason for you to leave is if you don't love me. Do you love me, Désirée?" He tried again for my hand, and I gave it to him, needing desperately to touch him.

"Yes, but Bill..."

"There are no more buts, baby. If we love each other, we can solve any problem. Stay with me, Chére, marry me, give us a chance. I know we can be happy." He lifted my hand to his lips, kissed my palm along the love line, looking at me with such longing. My whole body tingled with his t ouch.

"You're making this very hard for me, Bill."

He kissed my hand again, lingering there a moment longer. "Walking away from this kind of love should never be easy, Chére."

The sound of Gus barking alerted us to Zach and Jolie's arrival. I stood up, embarrassed by my feelings, unsure of myself and the whole situation.

Bill got up from the sofa and took my hand. "You haven't answered my proposal."

"I need some time to think about it." I heard the car pull down the driveway and stop.

"Well, then let me give you something else to ponder." He pulled me into his arms and kissed me the way I had dreamed of being kissed: tenderly, passionately, lovingly.

I could have stayed in his arms forever, but the sound of the back door opening broke the spell. When he released me, my legs felt like Jello, all wobbly. I had to sit down for a minute to regain my composure.

"How was your visit with your father, Jolie? Any progress?" Bill asked as Zach and Jolie came into the living room.

"Some, thanks to Zach." Jolie looked as if there was a lot more to say, but she was holding back, which was unusual.

"Did Marcus give you a hard time, Zach?" Bill asked.

"No sir. Mr. Jefferies was very gracious. He welcomed me right into his home. We had a pleasant visit and before we left, I asked him if he'd give me his permission to marry his daughter. I wanted to assure him that my intentions were honorable, the two of us living out here and all."

"Did he give it to you?"

"Why, yes sir, he did. Now I'm just waiting on Miss Jolie to give me hers," Zach said as Jolie retreated up the stairs.

"I know exactly how you feel, brother."

Chapter 29

Vanquishing Doubts

"Why didn't you tell me?" I asked Jolie as soon as I stepped through the bedroom door.

"I didn't know Zach was gonna spring it on you like that. It just happened a couple of days ago. Then he goes and asks Pa for permission and now I got to decide."

"I know how you feel," I said as I fell face first onto my bed, completely overwhelmed by the day's events.

"Oh, I'm gonna say yes. I'm just letting Zach simmer for a while. What about you, Désirée? Who's simmering in your pot? You or Bill?"

I lifted my head to look at her. "Both, I think."

Then the phone rang, and Bill came upstairs to get me. "Bobby is on the phone, Chére."

I took the upstairs phone out onto the terrace so I could talk to Bobby under the night sky, where the sliver of a moon barely blocked the starlight. After our usual catching up on school talk, I needed Bobby's advice about Bill.

"Bobby, something came up that might change my plans this summer. Bill asked me to marry him." Bobby's sharp intake of breath seeped through the phone line.

"Marry him, Dez. Let yourself be happy for a change. You deserve it. To hell with the rest of us."

"What does that mean?"

"Ah, don't mind me. It just means I'm jealous and disappointed you won't be here this summer, but I'm happy for you. I've always known Bill was the guy you wanted. It just took a few years for you to figure it out."

"Bobby, I can't do this without my best friend's support. Will you be here with me and hold my hand if I do this?"

"Have you set a date?"

"No! I haven't even accepted. This just happened this morning."

"Dez, you tell me where and when, and I'll be there to hold your hand, looking as dapper as ever. But can you wait till after finals? Dang, I'm gonna need to tell the guys that my girl threw me over for a Major. It'll make a good story, though. Maybe you can come to Sausalito for your honeymoon."

Bobby approved and forgave me and that's all I needed from him.

For some silly reason, I thought being eighteen would feel different. It didn't. When I woke up, everything was just as confusing as it had been the night before, except I'd slept really well the entire night, dreaming of Bill. That was different, and I took it as a good sign.

"Good morning, Chére. Happy birthday. Are we still on for later?" Bill asked, touching my hand as I passed him on my way down the stairs to meet Shelby for our Monday morning farm shopping.

Bill had something planned for my birthday, but it couldn't be more surprising than what I planned to say to him.

"Yes. You said five o'clock, right? I'll be ready. *Bonne journée.*"

I was as nervous as a kitten as I dressed for my birthday date with Bill. A million questions needing answers floated through my mind, and I had rehearsed them all day, but when the clock struck five, they completely vanished. All I could think about was seeing him.

He was waiting for me at the bottom of the stairs, dressed in a dark suit and tie, looking every bit the vision of Rhett Butler. I wore a slim fitting black skirt with a white silk sleeveless blouse tucked in, topped by a light-weight red bolero jacket with three-quarter length cuffed sleeves and closed under the bosom with a single white button. Black heels, a matching clutch bag, and the essential short white gloves completed my ensemble. I was nervous, but also excited.

"*Joyeux anniversaire ma chère*. You look beautiful," he said, reaching for my hand and devouring me with his eyes.

"*Merci monsieur*. Shall we go?" I took his hand, letting him lead me to the door.

"Have fun, Désirée," Jolie said, waving goodbye with a big smile on her face. She had a pretty good idea how my birthday celebration was going to end.

"Where are we going?" I asked as he pulled the car out of the driveway and headed east. It didn't really matter as long as I was with him.

Bill brought my hand to his lips for a tender kiss. "There's a little place over in Gulfport I've been wanting to take you to. It has views of the Gulf and fine dining. I hope you'll like it. We should be there in about an hour."

Simone's was a beautiful old white house with traditional Southern charm nestled amongst lush greenery and majestic oaks on the Gulfport waterfront. Inside, clean white walls and polished dark wood floors created a welcoming environment with tables covered in white linen and elegant place settings.

"We have a reservation for two. Marchand is the name," Bill informed the hostess as we entered the restaurant.

"Welcome to Simone's, Mr. Marchand. Your table is ready. Right this way."

She led us to an intimate table by the window, where we had a view of the water.

"May I bring you something to drink?" she asked.

Bill glanced across the table at me with a hopeful look. "Is it too early to order champagne, Chére?"

"Perhaps later, Bill. I'd like white wine to start," I said, lowering my gaze to explore the dinner menu.

"Bring us a bottle of the Mayhill Viognier. Thank you," he told the hostess after looking over the wine menu.

"Excellent choice, sir. I'll bring it right over. Your waiter will come by to tell you about tonight's specials and take your order. Enjoy your evening."

Once the waiter poured the wine and took our orders, Bill put his elbows on the table, clasped his hands together and leaned forward, giving me that hopeful look again. "Are you going to keep me in suspense, Chére, or have you decided?"

"I've decided I won't run away, but I have questions, doubts about how this marriage could work for us." There were so many ways it could end in disaster before it even got started.

He reached for my hand, squeezing it gently, relief sweeping over his face. "Tell me what they are, baby, so I can ease your mind."

"Well, where would we live?" I didn't think I could live in the city again, not after the scandal I'd caused.

"Anywhere you want, babe. I'll go wherever you want to go. It doesn't matter as long as we're together."

"Bill, I won't take you away from Mama again. She needs you."

"She needs us, Chére. We don't have to live in the city. We could live at the lake house."

"Would it bother you if I wanted to keep working? According to Uncle Henri and Julianna, a proper southern wife is supposed to make her home the priority, not a job."

He smiled and shook his head. "It's 1950, Chére, and times have changed. I don't share their outdated ideas about what a wife should be. I know who you are, Désirée, what you love, and there's nothing I want to change."

"Won't your wife need to entertain your friends and business partners? Won't it cause another scandal if you married me? I'm not exactly a suitable match for you."

"I admit you're a handful and not exactly the bride people expect me to choose. You're willful and defiant, outspoken and unconventional, but you're also brave, beautiful and disarming like no other woman I've ever known. I have no doubts about your ability to entertain even the most challenging of crowds. Whether or not you do will be your choice, Chére."

"But what about children? You'd make such a wonderful father, and I can't give you that."

"There are other ways to build a family. You were an orphan yourself. I'm sure there are countless children out there needing a home like the one we could give them. We could adopt... when you're ready."

He was vanquishing every doubt in my mind, leaving me out of ammunition to protest this crazy idea.

He got up and came to kneel next to my chair, taking my hand in his. "You still haven't said if you'll marry me. Will you?" He looked so hopeful, so sure that he could make me happy. I couldn't resist him any longer.

"Yes, Bill. I'll marry you on one condition: you must never leave me." The thought of losing him terrified me more than anything else.

He lifted me to my feet, slipped a gold band embedded with diamonds on my left ring finger, and pulled me into his arms, kissing me with a fierce passion in front of the entire restaurant, which erupted in applause.

He gently stroked my face. "My love, I guarantee I'll love you forever. How much time we get isn't up to either of us, but I'll never leave you willingly."

Bill ordered champagne for the entire restaurant to celebrate his victory over my trepidations. Everyone toasted our happiness with raised glasses as Bill kissed me again.

After things settled down and my blushing face resumed its normal color, Bill and I sat down to share a delicious meal. First came an appetizer of Sweet Chili Shrimp, then Simone's Seafood Salad arrived tossed in a Creole mustard vinaigrette. After that, we shared a Whole Flounder stuffed with crabmeat dressing and topped with Mornay. It was a perfect meal.

"Do you want to see the kitchen?" Bill asked after the waiter cleared our dinner plates away. "I'm sure I can arrange it."

"No, thanks for thinking of it. This has been wonderful. Thank you, Bill."

"Alright, then let's get out of here, baby. There's a place close by where we can catch the sunset by the water."

Less than ten minutes later, Bill parked the car next to an old oak tree living by a white sandy beach with an unobstructed view of the gulf. The sun was just beginning to dip into the western horizon, coloring the sky in infinite shades of gold and red and indigo blue.

We leaned against the car, just holding each other and watching the sky paint itself in a dazzling array of color and light. There was no other place I wanted to be.

He pulled me closer, nuzzling my neck. "This sunset is one I will cherish for the rest of my life. Thank you, Chére, for trusting me."

"I love you, Bill. I always have."

"That's the first time you've told me you love me. It feels good to hear you say it, baby." He bent down to kiss me, gently at first, then deeper, more passionately until he forced himself to stop and pull away. "We'd better get on the road. There's a long drive ahead and we both have work tomorrow."

"I don't want this night to end, Bill," I said, refusing to let him go.

"Oh babe, we'll have a lot more of these in our future, and even better than this one. An entire lifetime full of them."

On the way back to Mandeville, all the questions I'd forgotten to ask came flooding back; when, where, and how. We talked about it and agreed that the last Sunday in June was the earliest likely date for the wedding. By then, Bobby would be in his new place in Sausalito and could fly out for the weekend. The location had to be Mama's garden, under the wisteria arbor, officiated by a priest or a judge. It didn't matter to me either way. Something private and intimate, with only family and close friends attending. I wanted nothing fancy or flamboyant, just a simple exchanging of promises. Bill agreed to it all.

"And I don't want our engagement announced in the papers. No one needs to know in advance unless we invite them." I was adamant about that.

Bill smiled, stroking my cheek. "Alright, Chére. We won't post our bands in the Sunday Times. Anything else?" he asked as he pulled into our driveway and parked.

"No, but I reserve the right to add to this list."

"Add anything you want, baby, and it's yours," he said, leaning over for a kiss.

Chapter 30

Wedding plans and other calamities

"Well? Did the pot boil over or did you take it off the heat?" Jolie asked as soon as we were alone upstairs.

"I could ask you the same question, Jolie," I said, keeping her in suspense.

"Mine's still simmering, but I gave Zach a little hope while you were out with Bill. Now, are you gonna tell me what happened or what?"

I waved the hand wearing the engagement ring in front of her in answer to her question.

"Oh lordy, look at that. I knew you'd come around, Désirée. You and Bill belong together. We'll need to be planning the weddings now, I guess."

"Weddings?"

"Sure. You didn't think I would marry Zach unless you were here with me, did you? If you were leaving, then I was going with you. We're connected, Désirée. We always have been."

I threw my arms around her, hugging her tightly, overcome by emotion. "You're right, Jolie, I would flounder without you."

Tuesday was the start of our work week and the one thing I wasn't looking forward to was seeing Elijah and telling him I was going to marry Bill. I wasn't sure he would even deliver the fish order after what happened on Saturday night, but his truck pulled in behind the restaurant at the usual time, only this time Dorien climbed out. Elijah didn't come.

"Eli asked me to deliver your orders from now on, Désirée. He said it would be easier that way."

"Thank you, Dorien. I suppose that's for the best. Jolie will show you where to put them." I held the door open for him.

When he came out of the cooler, I handed him the payment and the order for the next delivery, then walked him to the truck.

"Will you tell Elijah I said thank you for not dropping us as a client? I really appreciate it. And I'm sorry I hurt him. It wasn't intentional."

"Eli knows that, but don't you worry, he's a tough guy. He'll get over this, but it might take him some time. He really likes you."

"I like him too, just not in the same way. Thank you, Dorien. Give my best to Sable, and Elijah."

I walked back inside, glad to have resolved the problem of our fish orders, though I didn't feel good about how it worked out for Elijah.

"Now that the hard part of the day is over, let's get to work, Jolie."

Later that evening, after we shut down the kitchen, Jolie and I walked home with Gus as our guardian. Zach had trained him to come to the back door of the restaurant at closing time and wait for us to come out. We always knew Gus was there because he'd scratch the frame of the screen door and bark twice. Terrance would toss him a bone or some other treat as a reward for being an obedient dog.

"So, when are you going to tell Zach?" I asked, as Gus made wide circles around us, surveying the area as we walked up the dark street toward home.

"I already did, early this morning, while you and Bill were making eyes at each other across the breakfast table."

"We weren't making eyes."

"Yes, you were, Désirée. Lord, it's gonna get steamy in that house real quick."

"Well, maybe I was making eyes at him, but ever since I gave in to loving him and felt what it's like to kiss him, I want to do it again. Is that the way you feel about Zach?"

"Yeah. That's exactly how I feel. Like I said, it's gonna get steamy in that house. That's why Zach and I are going to the courthouse next Monday to get hitched. He says he doesn't want to wait. Says he wants to... well, anyway, next Monday is the day at the courthouse in New Orleans. Will you be there with me?"

"Of course, I will. I need to catch the bouquet, don't I?"

"I let Mama and Charlie know about our plans, Chére," Bill said later that night as he attempted to disable my hands, which seemed to have a mind of their own.

All I wanted to do was touch him, kiss him, feel his arms around me, that's all.

"And I explained your list of... Désirée, stop. You're making this terribly difficult for me, baby."

"Then stop fighting and kiss me, Bill," I said, pulling his head down toward my lips.

He kissed me, but held back his passion, then he pulled my hands down and held them tight.

"Baby, listen. It's going to be difficult enough for the next six weeks. Let's not make this harder than it has to be."

"I thought it was supposed to be hard, Bill." I knew it was a wicked thing to say, but it just slipped out.

The look in his eyes told me I might have overstepped.

"Mother has suggested I move back to town until the wedding," he said, stepping away from me. "She said it would look better if I did, or if you went back to live with her until after the wedding."

That cooled me off. I needed a breath before responding, and a moment to gather my thoughts, otherwise I might have said something regrettable. I took a sip of my drink, then lit a cigarette.

"I have a job here and can't miss work, so I'm not moving back there, even for six weeks. As for how things look..." I huffed out a frustrated breath. "You and I have been living together for nearly five months, Bill. Whatever people will say or think about us, they already have. You moving back to the city won't change what they think. Besides, you promised you'd never leave me."

"I'm not leaving you, baby, but I might have to be away from time to time. It's just that I want us to start out right. I want to wait for our wedding night to make love to you. It's not that long, Chére, only six weeks. We've waited this long, baby. A little longer won't hurt us."

"Does that mean you won't even kiss me?"

"It's going to be extraordinarily difficult keeping my hands off you, but you need to help me resist."

"Alright, Bill. I'll be good, if you promise to kiss me like you mean it, at least once a day... whenever you're home."

He pulled me into a fierce embrace, devoured my lips, kissed my cheek, my neck, then back to my lips. I was breathless when it was over.

"Bonne nuit ma chérie."

On the following Monday afternoon, Jolie and Zach, with me in the back seat, drove into the city to meet her family at the courthouse to witness their marriage. Bill met us on the steps outside the building. Jacob and Laila Jefferies were there with Marcus, Jolie's father, standing next to Bill, which I took as a good sign.

The courthouse ceremony was short and sweet. Just the way I wanted mine. I squeezed Bill's hand and leaned against him as Jolie and Zach made their promises, and I hoped with all my heart that Bill and I could find the happiness Jolie and Zach would surely find.

For the next month, Bill, me, Jolie and Zach lived in much the same way we'd been living since February, with a few adjustments and added benefits.

Jolie moved her things into Zach's room after their wedding, which I thought made it crowded for them, but she rejected his idea of moving into the studio apartment over the garage.

"It's better for you if we live in the house, at least till you're married," Jolie told me a few days after they wed.

We adjusted, compromised, gave each other the privacy and space needed. The hardest part was watching them love each other, openly, without hesitation. I couldn't help but long for the same, but Bill held himself back and all I could do was dream of the day my wait would be over.

Chapter 31

The Kommandant

Ten days before our wedding, Bill went on a mission that threatened to shatter my world.

"Luke and I will be gone for a few days, Chére. I received a tip that Steigler is in Havanna. This is my chance to get him."

Bill was heading on a quest to end my past, but one that could also end my future. My heart sank to the floor. A million what ifs marched across my mind, but I showed him a brave face.

"Be careful, Bill. Please come back to me."

He pulled me into his arms and kissed me, and a moment later, he was gone. There was nothing for me to do but wait to hear from him and hope that he was safe.

For the next two days, I heard nothing. Bill didn't call or send a message, but that wasn't unusual. The wait was agonizing.

By Wednesday, I needed to talk to someone who was familiar with this waiting game.

That morning, I took Shelby aside in the empty dining area. "Shelby, can I ask you something?"

"Sure, honey."

"Do you worry about Luke when he's gone?"

The look on her face said she understood what I was going through and sympathized.

"Of course, honey, but I know Luke will come back to me. Don't worry, Désirée. They always come back."

"How do you... I mean, it's so hard not knowing if they're alright."

In a gesture of camaraderie, she patted my back. "You just gotta have faith in your man, honey. That's all."

A little before four o'clock that afternoon, the phone rang in Shelby's office while I was sitting at the desk calculating food costs for the prior week's receipts.

"Lakeside Bar & Grill," I greeted the caller.

"*Hallo Kätzchen,*" a familiar voice said in German.

My heart stopped beating, then began racing as the old terror coursed through me.

"Have you nothing to say to your papa?" he continued in German.

"Why can't you leave me alone?" I asked in his language, trying to still my heart. Panic welled up inside me, sending bolts of fear down my spine.

"Because you are one of my biggest mistakes, and I won't let it go uncorrected. I have my other mistake sitting here next to me. Would you like to say goodbye to your Mama Kat?"

"Désirée! Run!" Katarina screamed and then I heard a slap and another scream.

"Your soldier will be here soon, *Kätzchen,* so we haven't much time, but I wanted you to know that you're next. Once I eliminate the American and this bitch, I'm coming for you. You can't hide from me, Désirée. *Auf Wiedersehen, Kätzchen.*" The phone line went dead.

"NO!" I screamed, then quickly covered my mouth with my hands to prevent another from escaping. My breath came in gasps, my body was paralyzed with fear. I couldn't think, couldn't move, but I had to. I had to warn Bill.

Jolie rushed into the office and when she saw me, she knew something bad had happened.

"Désirée, what is it? What's wrong? Did something happen to Miss Bea? To Bill?"

I shook my head, unable to speak. My breathing felt like panting, like I'd just run a marathon.

Désirée! Run!

"No, it's not Mama! I have to help him, Jolie!" I jumped out of the chair and tore past her on a dead run out the kitchen door, racing for home.

"Oh god. Please. Not now, not again. Please!" I cried, running at full speed until I pushed through the front door.

"Help, Zach! Help!" I screamed, running through the house, searching, then finding him rushing into the kitchen from the back.

"Miss Désirée? What's wrong?"

"Zach... it's a trap! Bill and Luke are walking into a trap!" I could hardly get the words out.

"Come into the Major's office and tell me what happened. Looks like someone scared the daylights out of you," he said, leading me into Bill's office.

"He did. He said I'm next. Oh god. Zach, we have to do something!"

"You just sit there and calm yourself, then tell me what this is all about. I'll get you something to drink to help settle you." He went to the cabinet and poured me a club soda.

"Now, who scared you, Miss Désirée?" he asked, placing the glass in my shaking hands.

"Steigler. He called the restaurant and said he was waiting for Bill. He said he's going to kill him and Katarina, then come for me. We must warn them, but how? Oh god, please. What can we do? Help me, please!"

"Don't panic, Miss Désirée. I'll call Mr. Reyes and see if he can help. You just sip on that drink and calm yourself. Worrying won't do no good."

While Zach made the call on Bill's private line, I sat on the small sofa, clutching the glass of untouched soda. Every horrible scenario flashed across my mind, sending shockwaves of panic and grief racing through me, followed by a weight of unbearable guilt. This was all my fault. Mine alone. Bill and Luke wouldn't be hunting the Kommandant if they didn't know me. Anton Steigler was a minor Nazi war criminal, albeit a dangerous one, and not high on the U.S. list of escaped Nazi officers. But he was also the notorious South American gangster, El Caco, with connections throughout the continent and beyond. In the years I'd lived with Anton Steigler, I never doubted that he meant what he said.

Oh god, please. I can't lose Bill, not now. Please don't take him from me. Please.

My tears were unstoppable.

"Mr. Reyes would like to speak with you, Miss Désirée," Zach said, handing me the phone.

"Eduardo, you must warn Bill... Yes, I'm sure it was him... Alright, but please let me know as soon as you hear anything. I'll wait by the phone... *Si señor, gracias. Adiós.*"

"You alright, Miss Désirée?" Zach asked. His eyes, filled with worry, and a slight frown tugging on the corners of his mouth, clearly expressed his concern for my emotional state.

"I feel so helpless, Zach. If I lose him, it will be the end of me," I said, collapsing on the sofa in a flood of tears.

Zach sat down beside me, putting his arm around my shoulder. "Now, Miss Désirée, you listen to someone who knows something about what those men do. The Major and Mr. Luke know their business and they don't take any chances. They'll be watching from all angles before they make their move. You wait and see, they'll be alright."

With as much courage as I could muster, I dried my tears and tried to still my racing heart. "Thanks, Zach. I'll just wait in here for Eduardo's call."

"Alright, I'll send Gus in to be with you if that's okay."

"Yes, thanks, and would you call Jolie, to let her know I'm alright?" Jolie would worry no matter what I told her.

"I'll take care of it, Miss Désirée. Don't you worry."

I lay on the sofa for hours staring at the phone, praying it would ring and bring me news of Bill. During my long vigil, Zach had draped a blanket over me as I lay dozing, with Gus curled up against my legs. It was midnight before the phone rang. Gus jumped off the sofa then outside as I raced to answer the phone.

Please let this be good news. My heart lodged in my throat.

"Hello? Bill, is that you?"

"It's Eduardo, Désirée. I heard from my contact in Havana. There was a clash at Katarina's home this evening. The police found several people dead at the scene, including a CIA agent. Mr. Marchand and Mr. Terrebonne were not there, nor was there any trace of El Caco."

"That means Bill is still alive. Is Katarina..."

"She was among the casualties, along with her housekeeper and guard. The Cuban police believe it was a robbery but are looking into the CIA's connection to Miss Lang. You must be vigilant, Désirée, until Mr. Marchand returns. El Caco remains at large. I will call if I hear anything more."

"Thank you, Eduardo. Thank you." There was no other way to express how I felt.

"Get some rest, niña. Mr. Marchand should be home soon. Goodnight."

I collapsed into Bill's desk chair, feeling as if someone had sucked all the air out of me, anxious relief swept over me like a tidal surge. I didn't lose him. He was coming home.

Sometimes, prayers work.

In the middle of the night, I heard Gus bark once, waking me from my restless sleep, but then there was silence. I rushed to the window, hoping to locate him in the yard, but the moonless night cast an impenetrable cloak of darkness over the yard.

Suddenly, someone forced a gag into my mouth and covered it with tape, then placed a sack over my head, plunging me further into darkness. I tried to spin around to fight him off, but he twisted my arms unmercifully and tied them behind my back.

"We're going for a ride, Désirée. There's someone who wants to meet you," the voice of Silas Watson said with his face next to my ear as his hand brutally squeezed my breast.

I delivered a swift knee to his groin, desperately attempting to break free, but his grip tightened on my shoulder, and he retaliated with a blow to the side of my head, sending me crashing onto the sofa in a daze. He quickly tied my ankles together with a cord, then threw me over his shoulder and left the house.

He flung me into the trunk of a car, quickly secured my wrists and ankles in a tight hogtie, leaving me unable to move and completely helpless.

"Get comfortable, Désirée. We've got a long drive."

The trunk lid slammed shut, and a moment later I felt the car race down the highway toward a destination I knew would likely lead to my death.

Silas was taking me... and no one knew I was gone.

It felt like hours, or even days, passed before the car finally stopped. I had no sense of time by then. The constant jostling, lack of sufficient air, and being deprived of sight had left me bruised and barely conscious.

"Looks like we're the first to arrive," Silas said as he raised the trunk lid, exposing me to the sun's heat and providing a much-needed breath of fresh air, albeit through the sack covering my head.

"We'll have a little time to ourselves before the party gets started." He released the hog-tie binding my ankles and wrists, then pulled me from the trunk to stand by the car.

Incapable of remaining upright, much less walking, any thought of fighting him was out of the question. I collapsed to the ground in a heap, panting like a captured animal.

With an exasperated breath, he yanked me to my feet, threw me over his shoulder again, then pushed his way through a creaking door.

"Oh," Silas said, sounding surprised and disappointed. "I didn't think anyone was here yet."

"Is that the girl?" a deep voice asked from somewhere in the room.

"Yeah, it's her. Is the boss here?"

"He should be here in after dark. Tie the girl in that chair and take the bag off her head."

"Isn't it better if it stays on, so she can't identify us?" Silas asked, suddenly sounding unsure of himself.

"That won't matter in the end. Take it off. I need to make sure you brought us the right girl."

Silas roughly dumped me into a cushioned chair, securing my arms and legs to prevent my escape. "This is the girl Gatti asked for. Désirée Gautier, also known as the Phantom Slayer." He laughed as he pulled the bag from my head with a flourish, as if presenting a prize catch.

I blinked a few times, adjusting my eyes to the dust-filled light streaming in through the window opposite the chair. Silas stood on my right, with his hand pressing down on my shoulder. Two men stood in the dark corner, behind the light, their faces recognizable, even in shadow. I should have been terrified, and I was, but not by those men.

Beto Moretti and Giancarlo Labazzo worked for Frank Costello. They had come to the restaurant back in April with a note from their boss explaining that his men would be around to watch out for me.

As soon as Giancarlo knew I recognized them, he shot me a glance, silently urging me to remain calm. He walked toward me as if to inspect the prize, then swiftly removed Silas's hand from my shoulder with a vicious grip, twisting it behind Silas' back, then slammed him against the wall.

"That is no way to treat a lady, you swine." He plunged a dagger into Silas where his liver should be, then stepped back.

A second later, Silas was staggering, clutching his side, barely able to stand, shock filling his eyes.

"Take him outside, Beto. Feed him to the gators. I'll take care of Miss Désirée," Giancarlo said as he gently removed the tape from my mouth. "Are you alright?"

"How did you know where to find me?" I asked, shocked but grateful for the rescue.

"It's a long story, one I think the boss should tell, not me. We still need to deal with that German and Tony Gatti when they get here, but reinforcements are on the way. Do you want to freshen up? When they get here, you'll need to pretend you're still a captive, at least until we can take them down. Can you do that?"

"Yes, but first I really need to use a bathroom and then get something to drink." First things first.

He led me to a small privy closet in the far corner. The tiny, windowless room held a cracked basin without water and a toilet that opened to a hole in the ground below the structure. I finished my business as quickly as possible, fretting over the creatures that could easily climb up out of that hole.

"Where am I, Giancarlo?" I asked when I returned to the main room, looking around to better understand my surroundings.

"This is an abandoned lighthouse just south of Tallahassee on the Gulf coast. Here's some water." He handed me an open canteen.

As I sat down on the cushioned chair, I noticed the stains and rips in the upholstery, and a series of disturbing images popped into my mind. A cool sip of water soothed my parched throat and gratefully washed away the images. I had more pressing problems to contend with.

"Must you tie me up again?" I asked. Being vulnerable in the face of the Kommandant wasn't something I looked forward to.

"Yes, but I won't make it tight. They'll expect you to be tied and guarded, but Beto and I are ready to take them out when they come in. It shouldn't be much longer. The boss said to expect them at sundown."

"You said reinforcements are on the way. Who is coming?" I prayed it would be Bill and Luke, though I couldn't imagine how they could know where I was.

"My guys, and maybe yours. I just hope they get here before the bad guys do."

By the time Beto came back in, the sun had set. Giancarlo lit an oil lantern, filling the space with a ghostly light.

"I heard the plane land as I was getting rid of that piece of shit in the swamp. The calvary just arrived too. They're outside setting up. Better get things ready in here in case that German comes with something we didn't expect." Beto looked at me with the face of a soldier, stern and confident, ready to face the enemy. "Sit tight, Miss Désirée. We're gonna get you out of this." Then he went back outside.

The hardest part of any situation for me was waiting for it to happen. Normally, I hated that part, but at that moment, when I was about to face my worst nightmare, the waiting wasn't so bad. I was unusually calm while Giancarlo tied me loosely to the chair, and grateful he didn't replace the gag across my mouth.

"It's alright. I'm fine," I told him.

Giancarlo stood in front of me, facing the only entry point, and then he waited with me.

There were only two possible outcomes to this situation: I die, and it's over, or the Kommandant dies and it's over. Either way was fine with me, though I wanted to see Bill at least once more.

Roughly fifteen minutes had passed when we heard muffled voices outside the door, then someone—probably the Kommandant—gave a sharp order.

When the door swung open, Giancarlo stood his ground in front of me, with his hand on his gun.

"Stand aside, you fool, so I can see her," Anton Steigler ordered, walking slowly toward me. He looked the same as the last time I'd seen him, only dressed in an expensive suit instead of a Nazi uniform.

Several things happened in rapid succession. Giancarlo took a step to the left, giving the Kommandant his first glimpse of me in over six years. A man, I assumed to be Anthony Gatti, followed the Kommandant through the door, but Beto quickly grabbed him from behind, covering his mouth and lifting the smaller man off his feet, then quickly backed out into the darkness before the Kommandant noticed. Then Bill instantly replaced Gatti's expected presence and stood silently behind the Kommandant.

"*Scheisse*," Steigler said, speaking in German and staring at me the way he used to when I was a child. "You look more like her than ever. That was my mistake. I couldn't resist her... or you. But the two of you cost me my son and for that, you both must pay."

"We didn't kill Karl. He killed himself because he couldn't live with what you and Hitler made him into," I snarled defiantly back at him in German, knowing full well I was provoking him, but that's what I wanted to do. Bill stood poised for action behind him.

"You little bitch. I should have killed you long ago," Steigler said, pulling out his revolver and aiming it at me.

Giancarlo quickly fired his gun, shooting the gun out of the Kommandant's hand, then Bill knocked the Kommandant to his knees, secured his wrists behind his back, hog-tied him, then gagged him. It all happened in a flash.

The shock and anger stretching across the Kommandant's face as he kneeled at my feet on the filthy floor was more gratifying than I expected.

Bill stood over him for a moment, then he came to me. "Are you hurt, Chére?" he asked, cutting my bonds with a knife he pulled from his pocket.

"No, I'm not hurt."

He stroked my cheek, then turned back to the Kommandant, grabbing his hair and tilting back his head.

"You killed the wrong American in Havana, Steigler," Bill said calmly as he sliced a line across the Kommandant's throat with the knife; not deep enough to sever an artery, just enough to bleed profusely. A survivable wound. I wondered why Bill didn't kill him.

I stood over the Kommandant, staring down at the monster who had taken my identity and almost destroyed my life. He'd threatened to dispose of me many times while I was under his control, but Katarina saved me, and he killed her for it. The look of hatred in his eyes hadn't changed over the years, may even have deepened, but it didn't matter. I would live and he would die, and then that chapter would be over for both of us.

"You're right," I said, locking eyes with him. "You should have killed me. It would have saved a lot of lives if you had. I was never what you thought I was. *That* was your mistake, and now you're going to get what you deserve, a just reward for all your crimes. *Auf Wiedersehen, herr Steigler.*"

The door opened cautiously, and Luke looked in, checking if it was safe before stepping inside. "The boys have everything secured outside, Major. All good in here?"

"It's all good, Luke. Take Steigler out and give him to Beto. Feed Gatti to the swamp. Tie him tight, and make sure he's conscious, so he knows what's coming for him," Bill said with an icy calm that sent ripples of dread down my spine.

"My pleasure," Luke replied, giving me a nod, then he grabbed the Kommandant by the collar and drug him out, ignoring his futile attempts to evade his inevitable fate.

"My men and I will help with the cleanup, Mr. Marchand, then we'll get going," Giancarlo said as he moved to follow Luke out. "The boss will want a report on this as soon as possible."

"Thanks for your help." Bill reached out his hand to shake Giancarlo's, gripping it firmly. "Tell Mr. Costello that we're very grateful for what he's done for us."

"I will. It worked out exactly like the boss planned. He'll be pleased, especially when he sees the seaplane we're bringing him. We'll see you outside." Giancarlo nodded in my direction, then left.

Bill pulled me into his arms, holding on like I might disappear if he let go. "Oh babe, I'm so sorry you got dragged into this and had to witness it. Come on, let me get you out of here," he whispered, his voice trembling with emotion.

I leaned back so I could see his face. "Did you plan this, Bill? Did you use me as bait to catch him?" It didn't really matter. The result was what we both wanted, and I'd even suggested as much to him, but now that it was over, I wanted his honesty.

"No, baby," he said, shaking his head and stroking my cheek. "I didn't know about this until Costello contacted me in Havana. I would never have agreed to put you in danger, but by the time I learned what Steigler was planning, you were gone, and we only had hours to get here in time to intercept him."

"Thanks for coming to save me. Can we go home now?"

"Yes, my love."

Chapter 32

The end and beginning

The flight back to Mandeville in the Kommandant's seaplane took over four hours. Beto, who had flown supply planes during the war, served as pilot, assuring us of our safe arrival. Luke sat next to him in the co-pilot seat, and I sat behind them snuggling close to Bill.

For the entire trip, I tried to silence the memory of the sounds I heard as we were getting on the plane at the old pier near the lighthouse. Low guttural growls and thrashing sounds coming from the lake on the opposite side of the causeway kept replaying in my mind, evoking images I didn't want or need.

I had a general understanding of alligator hunting from the descriptions Elijah had given me. Gators were opportunists, always seeking an easy meal. Hang some rotten bait from a sturdy hook and the gators will come for it.

Silas Watson and Anthony Gatti undoubtedly met a gruesome fate, the stuff of nightmares. The Kommandant was still alive when Luke dragged him out of the lighthouse, but I didn't think he would be for long. His fate was in the hands of Costello's men, and there was no telling what his end would be.

Banishing those haunting sounds and images into the deepest recesses of my mind would be a challenge. Finding peace with my new first-hand knowledge of Bill's other life would be even harder.

We arrived home after three in the morning on Friday, and the first thing I did was search for Gus. When he didn't come to the gate as we walked up the driveway, I knew something was wrong.

I went around back and peeked underneath the stairs where he usually slept. He wasn't there and my breath caught in my throat. *Did Silas kill him?*

"Bill, Gus isn't here! I know Silas hurt him. I heard him cry out the night Silas took me. Oh god, where is he? We have to find him!" Panic gripped my heart, as an accumulation of all the feelings I had held in check during the long ordeal poured out of me.

"I'll find him, babe. Let's get you inside and up to bed before you collapse."

"Major?" Zach said from the top of the stairs. "It sure is good to see you both home, safe and sound. I got a call last night, sir, letting me know you were on your way back." He held the back door open for us as Bill led me up the stairs. "I'm so sorry, Miss Désirée. I didn't hear the shot that got Gus, didn't hear that man take you. God, I'm so sorry," he said, concern and guilt behind his bloodshot eyes.

"Where is Gus? Is he alright?" I asked as I stumbled into the kitchen past Jolie, who looked relieved to see me.

"He'll be home from the vet tomorrow, Miss Désirée. Don't you worry, Gus is doing fine."

"We'll talk in the morning, Zach," Bill said as he led me to the stairs.

"Get some sleep, Chére," Bill said, his voice tight with concern as we reached my bedroom door.

I laid my head on his chest, trying to pull what comfort I could from his presence. "I don't know if I can. So much has happened, it's going to take time for me to sort it all; to understand why it happened and what to think about it."

"Would you like me to come in and sit with you, help you talk it through?" He rubbed my back and drew me closer.

"Thanks, but I need to get out of these clothes I've been wearing since Wednesday and take a shower. Don't worry. I'll be fine. Goodnight." I kissed him lightly and retreated to the privacy of my room to sort through the nightmare on my own.

I wasn't able to close all the boxes nor shut my eyes until the sun had come up and I could hear Jolie and Zach downstairs in the kitchen. The delicious smell of fresh coffee almost tempted me to join them, but my body craved rest, so I curled up on my bed and drifted off to sleep with the comforting aroma easing my rest.

By the time I woke up, the sun had traversed the sky and was dropping into the western end of the lake in a blaze of crimson, and I realized I was late for work. I jumped out of bed, washed the sleep from my eyes, threw on some work clothes, and headed downstairs.

Bill was at the kitchen table reading the newspaper when I came in. "How are you feeling, babe? Any better?" Deep furrows creased his brow as he looked for signs of distress.

"I'm late for work, Bill. Why didn't anyone wake me?" I asked, pouring myself a glass of juice from the fridge.

"I told Shelby you wouldn't be back at work until Tuesday, Chére. You need time to process what's happened. I thought we could spend some time together this weekend." He reached for my hand, drawing me to him. "And we have a dinner engagement tomorrow night... with Frank Costello. He called this morning to set it up. He wants to see you."

"Where? He's not coming here, is he?"

"No. We're meeting him at La Louisiane, in one of Jim Moran's private rooms. Are you okay with this?"

"I owe him my thanks for sending the calvary in to rescue me. And I'd like to know how he knew where to send them. Is Jolie alright? She must have been frantic when they discovered I was gone."

"Jolie is fine, babe. She said you shouldn't worry about work. She and Terrance can handle it. Mama and Charlie were very concerned when they heard you were missing. I've talked to them both and given them a briefing. Mama wants to talk with you when you're ready."

Just then, Zach came in through the back door, with Gus limping in behind him with a bandage around his head. "Here he is, Miss Désirée, almost as good as new. The doc said there's no permanent damage. the bullet grazed his skull and knocked him out."

I dropped to my knees and threw my arms around Gus, burying my face in his fur. "I'm so sorry he hurt you, buddy."

Gus licked my face repeatedly and nuzzled my neck, making sure I was alright and back where I belonged.

On Saturday evening, Bill drove us into New Orleans for our dinner engagement at La Louisiane. He turned the car into the Guesthouse drive, unlocked the gate, and pulled into the parking area behind the building.

I was nervous. My stomach started doing flips the moment we crossed the bridge into the city. Taking deep breaths as we traveled the streets of New Orleans did nothing to relieve my anxiety.

"We don't need to stay long, Chére," Bill said, taking my hand to help me from the car. "If you're uncomfortable and want to leave, give me a sign, and I'll make excuses."

Diamond Jim Moran's restaurant, La Louisiane, was only down the street from the Guesthouse, and we were walking through the side door a few minutes later, which was not nearly enough time for my stomach to settle.

"Marchand is the name," Bill told the host stationed at the door. "We're expected upstairs."

The man led us up a long straight flight of stairs to the second floor, then into a private dining room where Frank Costello was sitting at a table set for three. He looked much the same as the last time we met, still elegantly dressed and carrying himself with an air of self-assured royalty.

"Welcome," he said, rising from his chair to take my hand. "I'm pleased you both came tonight. Miss Gautier, it's good to see you again, and Mr. Marchand, it's a pleasure to meet you. Please, join me."

He held my chair, then waited until Bill sat down next to me before resuming his seat.

"Thank you, Mr. Costello, and thank you for... saving my life. Giancarlo said you planned my rescue," I said in an accusing tone, suddenly feeling the need to confront him.

He didn't respond. He just looked at me as if reassessing his opinion.

"How did you know where Silas would take me?" I figured direct questions were best, under the circumstances. Bill sat silent, understanding my need to lead the conversation.

"May I offer you some wine?" Costello held up a bottle of chilled Pinot Grigio for my inspection.

I nodded, and he poured the wine for me and Bill, then began his tale, speaking to me rather than to Bill.

"Since our first meeting, Miss Gautier, I have felt protective of you. Call it fatherly instinct. I had my people watch over you and keep track of the man who accosted you the night we met. Silas Watson was his name, I believe. Earlier this month, I learned that Mr. Watson had a meeting with Anthony Gatti in Biloxi, then drove to an abandoned lighthouse on the Gulf Coast, just south of Tallahassee. My people followed him there. The significance of the event became clear when I learned of Gatti's connection to a South American boss called El Caco, who was attempting to intrude on my business interests in Cuba and Florida, using Gatti's connection to the Genovese family."

Bill interrupted, obviously disturbed by what he heard. "You had Gatti months ago. Why didn't you eliminate him when your men had him in Pensacola?"

"It wasn't in my interests, Mr. Marchand. I had a bigger snake to snare and knew Gatti would lead me to him."

"You used me as bait," I said, holding the older man's gaze.

"Unfortunately, Miss Gautier, you were the price El Caco wanted from Gatti. Until Gatti delivered you, he refused to negotiate with Genovese. His singular focus on you became his downfall."

"How did you know *when* I would be there? Did your people see Silas kidnap me? And if they did, why didn't they stop him?" Had they done that, it would have saved me hours of tortuous trauma tied up in the trunk of a car.

"My people in Cuba informed me on Wednesday evening of El Caco's arrival in Havana and of the assassinations of his ex-wife, her staff, and a CIA agent. They discovered his location in an isolated bay on the north shore of Cuba, where his seaplane was waiting. We contacted you, Mr. Marchand, as soon as we knew his plan was to fly to Florida before returning to Colombia. By then, Mr. Watson had already taken you, Miss Gautier, and the plan was in motion. We had mere hours to get the stage set for his arrival at the lighthouse. My deepest apologies for putting you through such a traumatic experience. I hope you can forgive me."

"What did you do to Anton Steigler? Is he dead?" I asked.

"Yes he is. The Miami police found his body outside a nightclub owned by the Genovese family. They're calling it a mob hit, and the Feds are taking over the investigation. They'll discover his true identity and link him to what happened in Havana. Then the CIA will get involved." He glanced at Bill, who gave a nod of affirmation.

"I guess this makes us even, Mr. Costello," I said, letting the residual trembles roll off my back.

"By my tally, Miss Gautier, I am still in your debt. You helped me eliminate El Caco and dismantle a coup by a rival family."

"We're very grateful for your help, Mr. Costello," Bill said, reaching for my hand, "but I would appreciate it if you would let me handle Désirée's protection in the future. Given the recent events with the

Senate's Kefauver Committee, any continued association with you could be problematic."

The two men stared at each other across the table, assessing their risks, evaluating their options.

"I understand, Mr. Marchand, however, I believe a little extra insurance never hurts." The tension between them built as they locked eyes.

It felt like the perfect time to leave before these two powerful men tested the others' will any further. I was ready to end this nightmare for good.

"Thank you again, Mr. Costello, for all your help. Unfortunately, we won't be staying for supper." I held out my hand to Bill and stood to leave. "We should go, darling."

Mr. Costello walked us to the door and shook my hand with a fatherly squeeze. "Of course, Miss Gautier. Thank you for seeing me and please allow me to congratulate the two of you on your upcoming nuptials. I wish you both much happiness and a long and prosperous life together."

Bill shook Costello's outstretched hand. "Thank you, Mr. Costello. Good luck to you."

"And to you, Mr. Marchand. *Buona notte.*"

After our meeting with Mr. Costello, I felt numb, not weak, just stunned that this particular threat was finally over. I would never again fear the Kommandant. That burden was finally lifted from my shoulders. But the imprint he made on my life would remain indelible, forever written in my memories. The years I spent as Steigler's Girl shaped who I became every bit as much as the five years I spent with Mama Bea. I was a culmination of all my experiences and the choices I had made.

The version of Désirée that emerged from the latest test Fate sent my way felt more authentic than all the others. I felt courageous yet vulnerable, determined to live my life on my terms. More than any other lesson, I learned the value of giving love and being loved.

In eight days, June 25, 1950, Bill and I would start our life together, facing whatever challenges Fate chooses to throw at us. Our future wasn't guaranteed, but we had a good shot at happiness, if Fate would stand back and let us.

End Part Four of Désirée's Story

Acknowledgements

As anyone who has ever attempted to write a novel will tell you, despite the long, lonely hours it takes to put the words on the page, it doesn't happen in a vacuum. There are many people to thank for their wisdom and support in getting this story out to the world.

Thank you, Shari Evans, who led the Kingston Writers Group for many years. Your steadfast support through the years has been invaluable. And thanks to all the KWG members I've connected with over the years, for your insights and critiques. My deepest thanks are due my wonderful beta readers who braved my early drafts and offered their keen insight to help me improve this story; Deb Smith, Gale Smart, Janice Cespedes, Jessica Kirchhofer, Lindy Bryson, and Vicki Schiller, who encouraged me to pursue this quest. I couldn't have done it without your support, dear fr iends.

Deepest gratitude goes to Trent and Anna Shadburne of Shadburne Creative for this beautiful original cover art and design. Thank you both so much for your creative skill in making this cover come to life.

To my sister, Waaknee Lerner, who brings joy to my life every day and to my children, Bliss Ogilvie and family, and my son, Diego Moreno for your continued support.

Also, a heartfelt thank you goes to my husband, Robert, who gives me all I could ever need or hope for after forty-plus years of marriage. Thank you, my love.

Finally, I owe so much to Desi, the woman who gave me the inspiration for this story. Her willingness to share her long-held secret prompted my unquenchable thirst to find the answers. Desi never shared more than a few remarks about her early life, but what she shared made me want to dig deeper into the realm of possibilities. I like to think that the story I've written would please her. Thanks, Desi. You will live forever in my heart, *Belle-mère*.

Denise

About the author

I'm an avid reader and have kept a daily journal my whole life. When I retired in 2015, a dear friend encouraged me to lean into my passion for words. It was the best advice I've ever received. Thus began my writing journey in earnest.

A story had been burning in my mind for nearly twenty years, and I now had the time to write it. After dedicating months researching the historical context of this story, learning more about WWII than I ever expected, I spent years honing my skill to tell it.

Desiree's Story is inspired by a secret my stepmother revealed one Sunday afternoon in 1997.

On a more personal note, I live with my husband and sister in our humble forever home, nestled in the woods along a quiet little bay in the Pacific Northwest. I'm still a reader, still a student of something (science, French, cooking, among other pursuits), and I channel my passions by writing stories of resilience, courage, and hope.

Connect with me on:
Facebook: @DeniseMoreno
Instagram: @driesaumoreno
Threads: @driesaumoreno
Bluesky: @denzstuf.bsky.social

Made in the USA
Monee, IL
14 May 2025

17371254R10187